AN EYE FOR AN EYE

By the same author

Harry's Game
The Glory Boys
Kingfisher
The Harrison Affair
The Contract
Archangel
In Honor Bound
Field of Blood
A Song in the Morning

AN EYE FOR AN EYE

GERALD SEYMOUR

WILLIAM MORROW AND COMPANY, INC.
NEW YORK

Originally published in 1987 in Great Britain by Collins Harvill Ltd.
under the title *At Close Quarters*.

Library of Congress Cataloging-in-Publication Data

Seymour, Gerald.
An eye for an eye / Gerald Seymour.
p. cm.
ISBN 0-688-07914-8
I. Title.
PR6069.E734E9 1988
823'.914—dc19 87-36075
CIP

Printed in the United States of America

First U.S. Edition

1 2 3 4 5 6 7 8 9 10

BOOK DESIGN BY CAROL BARR

AN EYE FOR AN EYE

1

He turned sharply. He disliked to be touched. He shook the sallow hand from his sleeve. Around him the reception was warming. He was, for a moment, alone. Alone except for the man whose hand had tugged at his jacket for attention.

Seconds ago he had been disposing of a small but tiresome problem with his Australian counterpart, minutes earlier he had been deep in conversation with his French colleague. He heard around him English and French and Spanish and Arabic, and European Russian. His glass was empty; the Australian had left in search of a waiter. His host, the host of all of them gathered in the gold and white, tapestry-hung, chandelier-lit salon, was stationed beside the high double doors for the entry of the General Secretary. The tides of many languages flooded his mind, and the hand rested once more on his sleeve.

The Australian was lost in the throng. Cosse-Brissac had insinuated his way close to the door, no doubt to be among the first to shake the General Secretary's hand. His private secretary was out of reach and engrossed with an angular blonde from the Finnish contingent. He lifted the hand from his sleeve and dropped it as if he were in the street and the hand were the wrapping of a sticky sweet that had attached itself to his jacket.

The man was short, dumpy at the waistline. He thought

the man's suit certainly cost more than all of those in his own wardrobe. The man wore a vivid orange silk tie, knotted wide in contrast to his own slim knot that carried the faded emblem of the All England Lawn Tennis and Croquet Club. The man seemed scented by a cocktail of lotions, and his thick dark hair was heavily oiled.

"If I might have the privilege of a moment of Your Excellency's time . . ."

"I would be so grateful if you would kindly remove your hand," he said.

"Sir Sylvester Armitage?"

"I am."

"The ambassador of England?"

"Of the United Kingdom," he corrected.

For a fleeting second the Foreign Minister himself caught his gaze over the shined head of this creature, but then the Foreign Minister raised his two hands, fingers and thumbs extended, indicating another two minutes before the General Secretary arrived, then turned his back. His sleeve was tugged.

"Please don't do that again," he said.

"I have the honor to be, Excellency, the Political Counselor of the Embassy of the Syrian Arab Republic."

"Do you indeed?" Extraordinary that the Australian had not cornered the wine waiter by now. And he'd have a sharp word for his private secretary for leaving him exposed to the Syrian.

"It is difficult at this time for there to be effective contact between our two governments. You would agree, Excellency?"

He could clearly see an airliner in flight. He could see rows of passengers. He could see the cabin crew moving along the aisles of the huge airliner.

"It is intended to be difficult, otherwise my government would not have severed diplomatic relations with the Syrian Arab Republic."

The political counselor had edged closer. In a rhythm his hands clasped and unclasped. There were two heavy gold rings on his right-hand fingers, one on his left.

"There were misunderstandings, Excellency. Through a

restoration of normal relations between our two governments such misunderstandings can be erased."

He could see a young woman passenger. He could see her nervousness. It was the first time she had made a long-distance air journey. He could see the bag that had been given to her by her fiancé, nestled between her legs and close to the brightly decorated shell of the aircraft. He could see the restless movement of the digital clock face of the pocket calculator resting at the base of the bag.

"My government does not accept that there were misunderstandings," he said.

The political counselor's voice was a whisper. "My government can see no benefit to either of our countries by continuance of a situation of misunderstanding. Please to listen carefully to me, Excellency. I have the full authority of our Head of State to say . . ."

He saw a flash of light. He saw the rupturing of the outer wall of the aircraft. He saw the disintegration of the young woman, the passenger.

"How interesting."

The Syrian looked up, surprised, but he resumed, "Our Head of State wishes it to be known to the government in London that privately it is accepted in Damascus that junior functionaries in a division of the military planned and attempted to execute an attack on an El Al jet while en route between London and Tel Aviv. I am further instructed to inform you, Excellency, that our Head of State sincerely regrets the actions of these junior functionaries who have now been severely punished."

He saw the snow topping the steep peaks of the mountains of Austria. He saw the spiraling fall of the airliner down toward the nail bed of the rock crags.

"Have they really?"

He did not notice that the Australian ambassador stood a pace behind him holding two glasses of brandy. He did not register that his private secretary was at his shoulder.

"I can tell you that these junior functionaries have been purged from the armed forces. I am instructed to tell you that my country is totally and without equivocation opposed to international terrorism, and we are thankful that the attack on the airliner was thwarted in London. Without reservation we condemn such attacks. What we seek, Excellency, is the speedy restoration of diplomatic links and the ending of this most unfortunate period of misunderstanding."

He said, "I will of course pass on your remarks to London."

"I am most grateful, Excellency."

"For nothing."

"We look forward to the quick return of your ambassador to Damascus, and ours to London."

"My opinion, personal, is that we'll want deeds, not words."

A frown formed on the forehead of the political counselor. "What deeds?"

"Off the top of my head . . . the expulsion from Syria of all terrorist groups, Abu Nidal and all the other abattoir gangs. An end to the financing of such groups . . ."

Color lit the cheeks of the political counselor's face. "We are innocent of all such involvement."

Because he was angered, because he was tired, because he wished to be among his friends, his voice rose. He sought to be rid of the creature.

"And you might just use your *influence* in Lebanon to win the freedom of the foreign national hostages."

"We are innocent of hostage taking."

He was not aware of the turned heads, of the talk congealing around him.

"So innocent that evidence of Syrian involvement in terrorism just about keeps one of our computers turning full time. My dear sir, we have found your country's finger on the trigger, on the grenade pin, too often."

The political counselor said, "I insist on our innocence."

He was not aware of the audience gathering about them. "Bloody nonsense."

"We deplore terrorism."

"Bloody nonsense."

"I am instructed . . ."

"Then your instructions are bloody nonsense."

Half the salon was hushed, following the sport. The Australian laughed out loud.

"Innocent."

"In a brothel, sir, you would not be believed. Senior officers in your armed forces planned, and did their damnedest to achieve, the destruction in midflight of a fully loaded civilian aircraft. You and your clan, you disgust me."

The laughter ran. The tittering amusement spread over the end of the salon.

The political counselor seemed to rise on his toes.

"You insult my government."

He boomed, "The man's not born who could do that."

The political counselor swung on his heel, thrust his way through the diplomats. The laughter would have been a tide in his ears. His back vanished.

The Australian handed the British ambassador the glass. "Bit strong, Sylvester, but you gave us a good laugh."

He looked keenly at his friend. "My elder daughter, Aggie, she's doing a year's voluntary work on a kibbutz in southern Israel. If those bastards had had their way she'd have been obliterated along with 300 others. She happened to be on that flight."

After two more drinks and a full minute's conversation with the General Secretary, he left the reception, down the steps to his waiting car. He shuddered. The dark depression of autumn was settling on Moscow.

2

Just before midnight the British Airways Boeing 737 touched down at Sheremetyevo, modern and miserable and the gateway to Moscow.

An hour later, Customs and Immigration on high-quality go-slow, young Holt met his girl.

"Pretty damn late, young man."

"They had to hold the flight so I could say goodbye to my lady."

"Pig," Jane pouted.

And she came to him and grabbed him and hugged him and kissed him.

The Second Secretary stood back and looked at his watch and coughed and shuffled, and wondered whether the Foreign and Commonwealth Office had got itself into the business of love brokering, for crying out loud. He had to cough twice more, and there was a ring of petal-pink smudges around young Holt's mouth.

"Fifteen pairs, right . . . Just the same as usual. Fifteen at Extra Large, *with* gussets . . . Just as long as you don't forget . . . and give my love to Hermione . . . Bye, darling, keep safe."

The ambassador put down the telephone, and looked up.

God, and the boy seemed young. Not tall and not short, but with an impact because of the set of his shoulders and the sturdiness of his hips. The sort of boy who would have captained the Fifteen at Marlborough, an adult's body and a youngster's face. He had been in the room through the latter part of the ambassador's call and had stood midway between the door and the desk as if on a parade ground and at ease, relaxed and yet formal.

"So, you're young Holt. Welcome to Moscow, Mr. Holt."

"Thank you, sir."

"None of that formality. I'm not 'sir.' We're a family here. I may be the patriarch, but not a frightening one, I hope. What's your first name, Mr. Holt?"

"It's Peter, sir, but I'm generally just Holt."

"Then we have a bargain. I'll call you Holt, and you don't call me 'sir.' Done?"

"Thank you, Ambassador."

"You're a stickler for etiquette, young man . . ." Did he not look young? The smile was that of a teenager, bright and open. He liked his naturalness. He reckoned a man who could smile well was an honest man. ". . . What do you think of the job they've given you?"

"It seemed to me that private secretary to the ambassador was about the best first posting that a Soviet specialist could expect."

"I was where you are three weeks before the Cuban missile crisis broke. I loved every day of my year here—and I hope you will . . . No, I wasn't talking in code on the phone. My wife's had to go back to London, mother not well, and she may be stuck there for a couple of weeks. We have a tradition of always bringing back some presents for our staff, the Soviet staff. Money doesn't matter to them, so we try to get them merchandise that's hard to come by here. You won't have seen the ladies who clean our apartment, cook for us, but they're all former Olympic shot putters, so it's Marks & Spencer's tights that keep the cobwebs out of the corners and the pots scoured. We're a small compact unit here. We all have to pull our weight. It is as interesting and fascinating a posting for me as it is for you, but it's only by damned hard work that we stay afloat. There are no passengers in this embassy. Now I have to move on to the facts of life for you in the Soviet Union. Everything you have been told in London about the hazards of illicit contacts with the local population is true. We call it the honey trap. If the KGB can compromise you, then they will. If you don't believe me then go and talk to the Marines, the American Marines, at their embassy, they'll tell you how sticky a honey trap can be. Our security officer will brief you at much greater length, but my advice is always, always, always be on your guard."

"Understood."

The ambassador liked the reply, couldn't abide waffle.

"Miss Davenport showed you in, she's my personal assistant, but you as my private secretary will be responsible for keeping my schedule workable. You're my troubleshooter if things need sorting out, and you'll find I have a very short fuse when the planning goes awry."

"I hope it won't come to that."

"In twelve days we're heading for the Crimea, that's something of a bonus for you, getting out of the rat cage so quickly. We're away for five days, based on Yalta. You'll find it all in the file that Miss Davenport will give you—pity there couldn't have been a hand-over from your predecessor."

"I understood he has pneumonia."

"We flew him out. Always get a man out if he's sick, standard procedure . . . I'd like you to go through the file and check each last detail of the program. I don't want to be pitching up at a hotel where the booking isn't confirmed, and I don't want to be in a black tie when our hosts are in pullovers."

"I'll get on with it."

The ambassador's head ducked, but his eyes were still on Holt. There was a glimmer of a smile at his mouth. "I hear you're engaged to be married."

Holt couldn't help himself, blushed. "Not officially, it'll happen sometime."

"She's a lovely girl, our Miss Canning, broken all the bachelors' hearts here, a touch of romance will lift our spirits.

You'll both be in demand. But I expect it to be a circumspect romance."

"Yes, Ambassador."

"Nose to the grindstone, Holt."

Holt took his cue, left the room.

The ambassador was Sir Sylvester Armitage. When he had been young he had cursed his parents for the name they had christened him with, but as he had risen through the ranks of the Diplomatic Corps, as the honors and medals had gathered in his pouch, so the given name had achieved a certain distinction. A tall, bluff man, working crouched over his desk with his suit jacket hooked to the back of his chair, and his braces bright scarlet. He had warmed to young Holt, and if young Holt had won the heart of Jane Canning then there had to be something rather exceptional to be said for him. He had a silly idea, but enough to make him laugh out loud. He loved the hill stream freshness of youth. He loved romance, which was why he spent all he could afford on scholarly works on the Elizabethan poets. He had meant it; he generally said what he meant. A youthful romance inside the embassy that looked across the river to the towers of the citadel of the Kremlin would hurry them all toward the Moscow spring, and young Holt had seemed to him the sort of man who could keep it circumspect.

He gave a belly laugh as he jotted the note on his memory pad.

He had always been young Holt.

The name had stuck to him from the time he was first sent from his Devon home near Dulverton to the south of the county and boarding school. Something about his face, his appearance, had always been younger than his age. He'd lost his first name at school, and there were always enough of his school contemporaries staying during the holidays to call him by his surname. His parents had picked the name up from the boys who came to stay. At home he was just Holt.

At University College, London, three years and an upper second in Modern History, he was just Holt. Nine months in the School of East European and Slavonic Studies, language learning, he was just Holt. Two years in the Soviet department of the FCO and still just Holt. He didn't discourage it. He rather liked the name, and he thought it set him apart.

For the whole of the first morning in the outer office attached to the ambassador's, Miss Davenport watched him. Large owl eyes, and her attention distracted sufficiently for her to make more typing errors in 140 minutes than she would normally have managed in a month. Holt had looked once at her, wondered if she was in the running for a set of Lady Armitage's tights, and discarded the thought as cheap.

She brought him three cups of coffee as he unraveled the file for the visit to Yalta. If his predecessor had stayed the course then Holt would have been glad of a gentle run-in to his duties. But it was a mess, had only been taken so far, had missed two necessary weeks of knocking into shape. Holt reckoned the file could have been part of the aptitude test they'd given him at FCO after the entrance exam. He attacked the problem, and wished Miss Davenport didn't smoke. Holt was a smoker and trying to kick it and the Camel fumes were rich temptation.

He wrestled the Crimea program into shape, so that he could dominate it. First flight to Simferopol. Helicopter transfer to Yalta, check in at the hotel, hire car booked with Intourist. Lunch at the City Authority with the chairman and the deputy chairman, and then back to the hotel for an hour's break before meeting the local newspaper editors. Dinner at the hotel, the British hosting, and the guest list including the same chairman and deputy chairman and the legion of freebooters they would have in tow. That was day one . . . day two in Sevastopol, day three in Feodosiya, and the ambassador had said that if he was coming all that way he was damned if he was going to be prevented from walking the length of the Light Brigade's charge—his predecessor's note on that was underlined twice.

Another note in the handwritten scrawl of his predecessor. The ambassador intended to lay a wreath at any British military cemetery that was still fit to visit. "Stormed at with shot and shell, / While horse and hero fell, / They that had fought so well / Came thro' the jaws of Death, / Back from the mouth of Hell." Good for Sir Sylvester if he was going to remember Cardigan's heroes with a poppy wreath, but there was no sign of the cemetery yet. That he would have to do himself.

Holt worked late that first day, and he didn't see Jane. Only a cryptic message on his internal phone to state that she was going straight from the office to the *Oklahoma!* rehearsal, that he should get his beauty sleep.

For young Holt the first week flew. He would have sworn he had learned more from life in the capital of the Soviet Union in that one week than he had gathered together in two years shuffling paper, and calling it analysis, on the Soviet Desk at FCO.

He went with the ambassador to the Foreign Ministry and was present at a preliminary planning meeting with the Secretariat of the Deputy Foreign Minister for the arrival in Moscow the following month of the Inter-Parliamentary Union from London. He attended a reception thrown by the Foreign Trade crowd for a Scots firm working on the natural gas pipeline across Siberia. He explored the Metro. He was taken out to dinner, with Jane, by the Second Secretary Commercial and his wife. He was invited to supper, with Jane, by the First Secretary Political and his wife. He went to the disco, with Jane, at the British Club. He drove out of the city, with Jane, in the British Leyland Maestro that he had been allocated, to the embassy's dacha for a weekend picnic with her boss, the military attaché, and his wife. That he was determined to be circumspect, and that Jane had the curse, were the only drawbacks.

At the end of that first week he had the program for Yalta beaten, also the draft of the program for the Members of

Parliament when they flew out, and he had persuaded Miss Davenport to restrict his coffee ration to two per day, and he had seen the wisdom of the ambassador.

Because of his girl, he was the center of attraction in the confined oasis that was the embassy community. Of course he didn't touch her, not in public, not where anyone could see. But they were light in the darkness. Their laughter and their fun and their togetherness were a lift to the embassy personnel who had endured the short-day, long-night misery of the Moscow winter.

At his morning meeting with the ambassador, Holt presented the program for Yalta.

"There's one problem. Lady Armitage isn't back so her aircraft seats are extra; should we cancel them?"

"Wouldn't have thought so."

"Whom would you like to take, Ambassador?"

"I'd like to have a hostess for our receptions, and I would like to take the most competent Russian linguist on my staff. To you she may, among other things, just be personal assistant to the military attaché, to me she is a very highly regarded member of the team . . ."

"Jane?" A flood of pleasure.

The ambassador's voice dropped. "Miss Davenport has hearing that puts to shame the most sophisticated state security audio systems . . . I fancy that a few days out of the clutches of our colleagues' wives would not distress you."

"That's very good of you."

"She's coming to work, and don't forget to make double sure that you've booked an extra single room for every hotel we're staying in."

"Will be done."

"Holt, it's a good program, well presented. I learn more about the life blood of the Soviet Union from these visits than from anything else I do. And, most important, we are on show. We are the representatives of our country. You'll give Miss Canning my respects and request her to accompany us, having first checked with the military attaché that he can spare her. You will fix the hotel accommodation, you will sort out the necessary travel permission for her from the Foreign Ministry . . . Get on with it, Holt."

"Darling, nothing's what it seems . . . Ben's not an agony aunt . . ."

"He talked about us getting out of the clutches of the embassy wives."

They were in the bar of the British Club, not up on the stools where the noise was, where the newspaper men and the business community gathered, but against the far wall. She was on her second campari and soda, and there was a strain about her that was new to him. He drank only tonic water with ice and lemon because besides cutting out cigarettes he had forsworn alcohol from Monday to Friday and he was suffering.

"Don't be silly, Holt, don't think he's taking me to Yalta just so that we can have a cuddle in the corner without anyone knowing."

"Why is he taking you, then?"

"Put your thinking cap on, Holt. I'm a hell of a good linguist. At East European and Slavonic I actually had a better mark in the oral than you did. Had you forgotten that? I'm in Moscow. I'm personal assistant to the brigadier who is the military attaché. An excuse has been found to take me down to the Crimea."

He stared at her. She was taller than he was. She had fair hair to her shoulders. She had gunmetal-gray eyes that he worshiped. She wore a powder-blue blouse and a severe navy-blue suit.

"As I said, Ben's not thinking of you and me, Ben's thinking of the job."

"And at Sevastopol there is . . ."

"I don't want to talk about Sevastopol, nor do I want to talk about what's at Simferopol—I want to have a drink at the end of a vile day."

He was bemused. "I honestly didn't know that that was your line."

"When do you tell a bloke? First date? First time in bed? First night after you're married? Bit late then. Leave it . . . Raise your glass to Ben—curse is over tomorrow, poor darling . . ."

His elbows were on the table, his chin rested on his knuckles. He didn't know whether to be shocked or proud. He'd always thought of Jane as a souped-up secretary, and now he had lit upon the truth that there was enough to her line for her to be required in the Crimea. Bloody hell. She was probably on a higher grade than he was.

"To Ben," she said. Holt raised his glass, clinked hers. "To adjoining rooms in Yalta." Under the table she squeezed his knee.

"Why do you call the ambassador Ben?"

Her voice sunk, and he had to crane to listen, and from the bar it would have seemed like sweet nothings from the love birds.

"Remember the guy who tried to plummet the El Al, spring of '86? He was organized by Syrian Air Force Intelligence. Name of Nezar Hindawi. Nasty man, put his lady on a plane with three pounds of Czech-made explosive in the bottom of her hand baggage, timed to detonate over Austria. The Syrians didn't just burn their fingers, they were scorched right up to their armpits. Shouted like hell, but they were caught still smoking when Hindawi rattled off his confession. So we broke off diplomatic relations, big deal, told the Syrians that if they didn't behave like gentlemen then they were going to get booted out of the club. They were pretty upset, big loss of face, and they started doing their damnedest to get our ambassador back. They made their first overtures right here at a reception in the Kremlin. One of their diplomats sidled up to Sylvester and gave him the glad news that the El Al had all been a dreadful mistake, the wild fantasies of a couple of bottle washers, that Syria was dead against terrorism. What their little man didn't know was that Sylvester's beloved daughter was booked on that very same flight. He's got a big voice, right? Well, half the Kremlin heard him dismiss these fervent Syrian protestations of innocence with repeated and thunderclap replies of 'Bloody

Nonsense.' You'd have thought he was a Guards sergeant at drill. Stopped the show, he did, they heard him all over the room. 'Bloody Nonsense . . . Bloody Nonsense . . . Then your instructions are Bloody Nonsense.' Just like that."

"Spirited stuff."

"Everyone heard him. First World chaps and Second, and Third World, they all heard him. Within days he was known all over the place as Bloody Nonsense Armitage. It came down to B. N. Armitage, and from that to Ben. In this little-minded town he's Ben, half the time to his face."

"So our man in Moscow won't be taking his summer holidays in Damascus."

"You're very clever tonight, my darling."

"I wish I'd known how clever you were," Holt said.

"Cleverer even than you think. Clever enough to get Rose and Penny tickets for the ballet tomorrow. Will you by any chance be free for dinner?"

He would like to have kissed her, but circumspection ruled and he simply smiled and gazed at her lovely gray and laughing eyes, and their wretched bloody secrets.

"So you're young Holt. I was going to look you up, but you've beaten me to it. What can I do for you?"

It was his first visit to the secure section of the embassy. Next to the diplomatic section the largest in the building was that of the security officers. The former policemen and army officers were a group apart, he had already recognized that. They had staked out their own corner in the British Club, and they had the ingrained habit of closing down their conversations when anyone came within earshot.

Jane had pointed that out to him and said they were probably talking about the price their wives had paid for potatoes on the market stalls, or why the Whitbread draft had gone cloudy, but they still went silent.

The security officer's face was florid, a jungle of blood vessels, and his head was lowered as he sat at his desk so that he could see over tiny half-moon spectacles. He wore a thick wool shirt, loud checks, with twisted collars, and a tie that was stained between the shield motifs. Holt took him for a regular army half colonel on secondment to the security services in London, and on double secondment to FCO.

"I was letting you settle in for a bit. So much to learn, eh? I find if I rush in with the heavy security lecture the new chaps tend to get a bit frightened, best wait, eh? Sit down."

They were in the heart of the building. Holt thought that further down the basement corridor would be the Safe Room. He had heard about the Safe Room in London, the underground steel-walled room where the most sensitive conversations could be conducted without fear of electronic eavesdropping. He was disappointed that he had not yet been invited to attend a meeting in the Safe Room.

"My wife was saying only last night that you must come round to supper, you and Miss Canning—super girl, that. My wife'll be in touch with Miss Canning, that's the way things get done here."

Holt reckoned that he had spotted the security officer, allocated him his responsibility, by the second day he had been in Moscow. It was his little game, but he was still searching through the faces for the top spook, the guy from the Secret Intelligence Service who was Jane's real boss—might be the one in Trade with the Titian beard who looked like a naval officer, could be the one in Consular who always kissed Miss Davenport's hand when he came to see the ambassador.

"I'm a busy man, youngster, so what's troubling you?"

"No crisis."

"Be a bit soon for a crisis."

"It's only that I'm going with the ambassador and Miss Canning to the Crimea on Saturday, and I wondered if there was anything I should know."

"About what?"

"Well, about security, that sort of thing . . ." He felt absurdly pompous. He should have stayed at his desk.

The security officer looked sternly at him. "Just the obvious. What you'd naturally assume. You don't discuss anything of a confidential nature in your hotels, nor in any vehicle. You don't accept invitations late at night to a Soviet household—what they'd have told you in London. Your rooms might be bugged. There will probably be a KGB operative with you as chauffeur or interpreter, a natural assumption. But His Excellency and Miss Canning know the form. Should be rather a nice trip. Good idea of H.E. to take in the battlefield, wish I was with him; if you could walk down that field with a metal detector, God, you'd make a fortune . . ."

"There's nothing else I should know?"

"Like what?"

"Well, I just wondered . . ." Holt stopped, making a fool of himself.

"Ah, I get you." The security officer beamed, all avuncular. "You wondered about security, your own security, eh?"

"Just that."

"This is not Beirut, young man. H.E. does not have minders in Russia. This is a very peaceable country. Hurts me to say it, but H.E. can walk the streets of any city in the Soviet Union, any time of day or night, and have less prospect of getting mugged, assaulted, stuck up than in a good many cities at home. This is a highly policed country. The Moscow posting is categorized as Low Risk. I'm not a bodyguard, the personal security of the staff here is about bottom of my agenda, and that's the same with every western embassy in town. My job, young Holt, is to protect the confidentiality of this establishment, to block KGB attempts to compromise and recruit our staff, and that takes the bulk of my time. Right?"

"That's all I wanted to know."

"Good—well, as I say, my wife will be in touch with Miss Canning."

"You're very kind."

Holt left. He dreaded being summoned for the full security briefing. He thought it would be as hideous as the promise of dinner with the man and his woman.

"A penny for them, lover."

She lay on her side, and her clothes were on the floor, and the streetlights gleamed through the thin curtain, and her fingers played with the hairs on Holt's chest.

What to tell her? To tell her that he had been rotten in bed, again, because he couldn't get it out of his reinforced concrete skull that this lovely girl of his worked with the embassy spook? To tell her that he thought spooking was a shoddy, grubby way of life? To tell her that he had thought Bloody Nonsense Armitage was doing them a favor, when in reality he had contrived an opportunity for a well-qualified operative to run a trained eye over the port facilities of the Soviet Navy at Sevastopol, and over the cap badge insignia of the troops in the garrison town of Simferopol?

He turned to face his Jane. He took his stranger in his arms. Over her shoulder he could see the traveling clock—and no bloody time, because in half an hour the other girls would be back from the Bolshoi. No time to tell her. Body to body, and his head was buried in the softness of her breasts, and he ached with his love for her. He could think it out, he could work it through but it would take him an age. He had thought he knew everything about her, every mark of her mind and her body, and he knew nothing. What he thought he owned was not his. Clinging to her, holding her for the comfort.

He fell away. Her head and the silk of her hair were on his arm.

"Just a bit tired, that's all . . ."

She kissed him, wet and sweet and belonging.

"Stay safe, darling."

"What else?" She laughed at him, head back, hair falling.

3

By rights they should have traveled in the embassy Range Rover out to Vnukovo Airport from which the internal Aeroflot flights left. The Range Rover was supposed to be used for all the ambassador's journeys that were not official. But Holt had decided they would go in style, and so Valeri had been roused early, and the Silver Cloud Rolls-Royce was at its polished best.

The ambassador and Jane sat far back in the rear seat upholstery, while Holt shared the front with Valeri. Holt reckoned that the chauffeur was about his own age. He had expected an old retainer, had not anticipated that His Excellency's driver would be a smartly turned out young man with the sort of haircut that any limousine man in Mayfair would boast. It was still dark when they pulled away from the embassy courtyard onto the riverside across from the Kremlin. There was no traffic. He had learned that at the best of times cars were in high demand and short supply, even at rush hour the streets were good for a pretty fast run, but at this time they were empty. The pavements showed life. The dribble of a night shift heading for the Metro tunnels, and street cleaners and the office advance guard appearing at street level, making darting runs across the wide streets.

He had barely spoken to Jane when they had met, while they waited for the ambassador. Mercifully the man had been punctual, striding down the steps from the main door with that unnecessary glance at his watch to demonstrate that he was on time. He hadn't known how to communicate or what to say. So there was a problem, last night's problem, and he didn't want to talk about it, not in whispers.

He had known Jane for two weeks under three years. Met at the School. Met in the way that most young men meet the girl who will one day become their wife—one seat free at a canteen table, and a curled gammon steak that needed disguising, and a request for the tomato ketchup, please. Two young people, both older than the average students around them, the one shuffling the tomato ketchup and the other pushing the salt and pepper. What a meeting—the young man thinking that the girl was quite beautiful, and the young girl thinking that he looked interesting. The young man able to say, quietly and without conceit, that he had done well in the Civil Service entrance examinations, and then well in the Diplomatic Corps entrance aptitude tests. She had said, looking straight at him, that she was just a secretary in Whitehall, nothing specific, and that she was damn lucky to have been plucked out of the pool and given the opportunity to learn Russian. More time together, and he'd thought she was struggling sometimes in the tutorials, and the relationship started when he made a habit of calling round at her Earls Court bed-sit to give her a hand with the essay that was the fortnightly chore. Fingers touching, mouths meeting, the unhurried building of something lovely. Weeks and months of learning to share lives, work and fun. A young man who was determined to be something special at his chosen career, and a young girl who was just a secretary in Whitehall. Right, no messing, he'd been pretty shattered by the marks she had won at the end of the course—not quite at his overall level, though pretty close—but young Holt had never questioned how it was that a girl who was just a secretary won marks that were pretty damned close to his own . . .

"How do you like Moscow, Mr. Holt?"

"Very well indeed, thank you, Valeri."

His thoughts drifted away from Jane, away from him being hopeless in bed with her, away from the deception. His thoughts were on the ambassador's driver. Be a chosen man, wouldn't he? Not chosen by the British, chosen by the Organ of State Security. Nice-looking fellow, but he'd large ears, and they'd be well rinsed. They would hear everything said in the car. Holt wondered how it was done. Did the men from KGB call by on a Friday evening after Valeri's shift finished for a quick résumé on what he'd learned that week while piloting the Rolls? Did he write out a little report every Saturday morning before he took his small kids to dancing class or the ice rink? He was far gone, concerned now with whether Valeri had a large wife, or an extra large wife, whether he was on Lady Armitage's list for tights with gusset.

They traveled in the fast lane, where the government officials were driven. Big blasts on the power horn to keep clear the path of Her Britannic Majesty's ambassador. There were men with brushes, there were old women with bundles of sticks; the street and pavement cleaning had started.

Holt could have cried, he felt so bloody miserable.

But how could she have told him? Of course she couldn't have bloody told him.

At the airport there was already a slow-moving confusion of queues. Valeri deposited their luggage at the rear of a queue and checked with Holt when they would be back, and the time and number of the return flight. He wished them well, and said the Crimea would be beautiful after the Moscow winter. He had good cause to be pleased. With the big man away he'd have time on his hands, the chance to burnish the bonnet of the Roller with a leather. Holt carried the ambassador's briefcase, and Jane carried her own, and Holt hoped to hell that there wouldn't be a foul-up with the tickets.

There wasn't.

Nor were there special facilities for the ambassador and his party. It was the way he liked things done. Didn't want a brace of officials there to shake his hand and wish him well. That's what he'd said to Holt. On such a trip he could sense the mood of the nation, and the temperature could not be taken in a VIP lounge. They took their place in the queue. The ambassador lit his pipe and unfolded yesterday's *Times* from London. Holt craved a cigarette, the prohibition could not last. And Jane touched his arm. They had been in the queue for five minutes and not moved an inch.

"Do you know the hoary old one about queuing here? If you do you're still going to hear it again. Ivan was in a queue for two hours trying to buy a pair of winter boots, and he snorts to the people around him that he's had enough, and he's going down to the Kremlin, and he's going to shoot old Gorbachev, and that's going to be his protest about the inefficiency of the Soviet Union. Off Ivan goes, and three hours later he's back. He's asked if he's indeed shot Comrade Gorbachev. 'No,' Ivan says, 'I couldn't be bothered to wait, the queue was too long.' Like it?"

Holt managed a small smile. Jane squeezed his arm, as if to tell him to calm down, as if to say that a queue at Vnukovo wasn't his fault.

"Certainly hoary, Miss Canning," the ambassador intoned. "I have heard that anecdote told in turn of Messrs. Brezhnev, Chernenko, Andropov and now Gorbachev. But I think that I am safe in stating that it was never said out loud during the revered leadership of Uncle Joe Stalin . . . Don't fret, Holt, it won't go without us."

The blockage at the head of the queue was removed. A man was shoved aside, hoarse with complaint and waving a ticket. Jane said it meant the flight was overbooked, and they were shedding the least important. A sour-faced woman behind the counter examined their tickets, looking at them as if to ascertain whether they could possibly be forgeries. They were checked once more by a bored militiaman at the gate, who then took an age studying Holt's and Jane's Foreign Ministry permission to leave the Moscow environs zone. They went on to the security barrier. Two more militiamen, an X-ray machine, and a metal detector arch to pass under. Jane had a camera, a palm-of-the-hand-sized Olympus that she took out of her handbag before it went on the belt. The ambassador's spectacle case attracted the flashing red light and earned him a cursory body patting.

They were in the departure lounge. Holt and Jane went off in search of coffee for themselves and an orange juice, diluted, for the ambassador.

"Bit heavy, wasn't it, the security?"

"They've their quota of nasties just like the rest of us."

He'd noticed, since reaching Moscow, how much she enjoyed filling him in on insider detail. Couldn't have happened in London, when he was doing his initial FCO time and she was just a secretary in Whitehall. "Georgians and Jews and Estonians and Ukrainians, they've all got grievances, they all foster little cells that want to get out. Not easy. They've sent up fighters to shoot down aircraft that have been hijacked in the past. And if there's half a chance of settling the problem on the ground then they go in firing. Happened last year. They don't play about here, none of your patient negotiation. Storm and shoot is their answer. Not that they admit there's a political problem. It's always drug addicts and delinquents. I laugh like a drain each time I hear of a hijack. It's the biter bit, isn't it? That little shit Carlos was trained at the Patrice Lumumba University right here in downtown Moscow. And he's only the tip of the iceberg. They train them to do horrible things to us, and we broadcast on BBC World Service and the Voice of America what they've done, and the folks back home pretty soon get into the same act."

"Is that what you specialize in?" Holt asked.

She smiled at him, a big and open smile. She said, "God knows why Ben wants orange juice, it's quite foul here . . . There's a fancy dress party at the dacha next Saturday, what'll we go as?"

"I'll go as a boar with a ring in my nose, and you can go as a farmer and lead me round, and show everyone who's boss."

They both laughed. She thought it was funny and he thought it was sad, and the ambassador's orange juice looked as awful as their coffee tasted.

They boarded, and takeoff was only 25 minutes late. The ambassador was behind them, in the aisle seat, and next to a man in a dark suit with a bulging briefcase. Before the belt sign was off the ambassador was booming out his conversational Russian, angling for a rapport. A one-class aircraft, a Tupolev 134, rear engines and 72 passengers. He had hardly slept, not after she'd run him back to the embassy, and he'd been plagued with the niggling worries about getting the trip moving well—he started to doze. There was the drone of the voice behind him, and he was wondering how the ambassador managed to test the waters of Soviet opinion when he talked so much that the fellow next to him barely had the chance to get three consecutive words up his gullet. He'd sort it all out. He'd sort it all out with Jane in time, because he had to, because he loved her. Up to cruising altitude, and he was nodding, eyes opened then collapsing shut, so damned tired. He was a wild pig, and she was pulling him round, and they were all laughing, all the Second and Third Secretaries and their wives, and all the personal assistants, all laughing their heads off because his girl had him on a leash.

Flying due south. A journey of 750 miles. A route over Tula, Kursk and Charkov. Cruising at 29,000 feet, ground speed 510 miles per hour.

He felt her pull him forward, and then to her. And his eyes were closed, and he waited for the soft brush of her kiss behind his ear, where she always kissed, and he waited. He opened his eyes. She was looking down at her watch, concentrating. His head was forward, as if guarding her, hiding her breasts and her hands and her lap. Away from her watch, looking through the porthole window, the visibility was stunning and the daylight spreading, the fields sharp and the roads clear and a city laid out as a model. She took three photographs quickly, and the camera slipped back into her bag, and she grinned at him and eased him back so that he was fully into his seat. Then she kissed him, behind the ear, a fast peck.

He was a pig on a lead, and he didn't have the strength to argue.

The vapor trails of the airliner were brilliantly clear five and a half miles above the ground surface. The first airliner of the day, and a lorry driver leaned from his cab to watch the slow progress of the puffy white scars in the blue skies. The lorry driver was delivering prefabricated walls for a factory development on the east side of Charkov. The factory development was an extension of 260,000 square feet, and when in production would manufacture one-piece cast turrets for the T-72 tank.

It was the evaluation of the experts in British and American Intelligence who concerned themselves in such studies that the T-72 main battle tank was technically superior to those of the NATO forces. The factory, when enlarged, could greatly increase its output of the low-silhouette turret, so low that the crews fighting in them could be no taller than five feet four inches. To have a photograph of the tank turret factory extension would not be an Intelligence coup, but it would be useful. There were few coups in that painstaking world, but much that was useful. The size of the extension would enable the analysts to calculate the increased output of new T-72s.

The vapor trails bowled on. The lorry driver reached the building site gate.

At a military airfield west of Moscow, an Antonov transporter bearing the insignia of the Air Force of the Syrian Arab Republic was in the final stages of loading. The manifest listed a cargo of MiG interceptor spares, a sizable cargo, but not enough to fill the aircraft because space had been set aside for basic seating forward in the hold. The pilot was engaged in his final checks before takeoff clearance and the start of a filed flight plan that listed a brief stop at Simferopol to take on personnel and then a direct onward flight to the El Masr base close to Damascus.

On that Saturday morning in the Yalta spring, a major had command of the city's militia force. His superiors were at home in their gardens, or in the shops with their wives, or in the mountains with their children. This particular militia major, 49 years old and twice passed over for promotion, sipped a poor imitation of gritty Turkish coffee and cast his eyes wearily over the backlog of reports on his desk. He was responsible for the Department for Combating Theft of Socialist Property and Speculation, for the Department of Criminal Investigation, for the Internal Passport Service, for the State Automobile

Inspectorate, for the Patrol Service and the Preserving of Public Order in Public Places, and for the Department of Visas and Registration of Foreigners. His in-tray contained the overnight reports of apartment block caretakers, reports on the hunting of draft dodgers, an essay on the failure of the traffic lights on Botkin Street, a surveillance report on two Latvians who would be arrested in the following week to face charges of leading an Antisocial and Parasitic mode of life.

The radio in the control room spluttered occasionally to life to disturb his halfhearted concentration. He had to last until six o'clock in the late afternoon, and then he could take off his uniform tunic, put on a sweater and go home to his family.

Deep in his in-tray was a memorandum stating that the British ambassador was arriving in Yalta in company with his private secretary and an interpreter for a semi-official visit, and would stay at the Oreanda Hotel. He was not required to furnish the delegation with a militia car escort.

It was the militia major's belief, for what little that was worth, that unless the traffic lights on Botkin Street were repaired their failure would lead to an accident, but there was nothing he could do. A waste of his time to try to dig out an engineer from Roads and Transport at a weekend.

In his briefcase was a book that would help him through the afternoon.

He was held up at the lights at the junction on Botkin. A main intersection and all the lights showing red, and the dumb fools waiting as if they had a day to kill.

Could not have happened in Moscow. Could only happen in this second-class junkyard to which he had been consigned. After eleven months in the backwater of Yalta it still burned in him that he had been dismissed from the capital and posted to oblivion.

He had been a captain in the Organ of State Security. He had had a promising future in the KGB. By hard work, by passing his exams, he had entered the favored Guards Directorate. He had served in the personal protection squad of the Politburo member who was First Deputy Prime Minister. He had been tipped for membership of the guard assigned to the General Secretary of the Party. And he had drunk too much, been smashed out of his skull. He had been reduced to corporal and transferred.

He was no longer the high flier. He no longer possessed the plastic card that gave him access to the luxury goods at the State Security Commissariat. He no longer lived in a three-bedroomed flat with a view over the park. One bottle of vodka, after a stint of 41 hours' continuous duty, had greased him down the pole. Caught drunk in uniform on the street, on his back in the gutter, and dumped with his wife and two toddler children onto a 23-hour train journey to nowhere, Yalta. Of course it still burned. From the personal protection squad of a Politburo member, with the magic card and the right to carry a Makarov PM 9mm automatic pistol, down the chute to KGB corporal. He was unarmed. He was at the wheel of a sluggish Chaika car which needed a new gear box. He was a chauffeur, and held up at the lights on Botkin Street, and his job was to drive the ambassador from Great Britain.

The KGB corporal hit the horn to clear the dumb fools out of his way.

Holt didn't wait for the lift. There was too much of a queue. He went up the two flights of stairs, and down the corridor to the ambassador's room, knocked, went in.

"The car's here, finally."

"Relax, Holt. You are in one of the most unpunctual regions of a country noted for its tardiness. If we're there on time we'll be standing around on our own, scratching our backsides—not Miss Canning, of course, but you and me certainly."

"I've checked the room for this evening, and the menu . . ."

"Don't try too hard, Holt, for heaven's sake. Foul-ups make life so much more entertaining . . . I feel a younger man already, damn nice air down here."

The ambassador slipped on his jacket, straightened his tie, knocked his pipe out into an ashtray.

"I'll go and rout Jane out."

The ambassador frowned sharply at his private secretary. "Damn it, Holt, haven't you been listening? I am not in a hurry. I want to make an entrance. I will not make much of an entrance if I am the first to arrive. You may put it down, if you wish, to old imperial grandeur. But I do mean to make an *entrance* when I visit the worthies of the Yalta municipality. Got me?"

"Got you."

"You've the Bridport stuff?"

"In my briefcase." Holt wondered how on earth Bridport on the English south coast had made the decision to twin itself with Yalta, must cost the sad ratepayers a fortune in exchange visits.

"Then best foot forward, Holt."

He snapped the door open. He went out into the corridor and rapped gently on Jane's door. The ambassador led the way down the corridor, no glance backward, the Viceroy's procession, and Jane exploded out through her door, thrusting her small Olympus into her handbag. Down the staircase, the ambassador leading, and Jane happily in pursuit.

"Thanks be to God that we didn't forget our camera," Holt said. He was always useless at sarcasm.

"Don't be childish, Holt," she said coolly, quietly so that His Excellency would not hear.

Down the stairs, across the foyer. The ambassador smiled warmly at a group of exhausted tourists speaking German and attempting to check in, and none of them had the least idea who it was that smiled at them.

Holt reached the door first, pulled it open and stood back. He saw the driver moving to open the rear door of the vehicle. He saw a young man, dark-skinned, long hair, ambling across the road toward the hotel and holding a windcheater across his stomach. Distraction, because the ambassador had passed, playing the old-world gentleman, ushering Jane through first. Jane was out onto the steps, and hesitating, as if the light of the Crimea's lunchtime sunshine were too bright for her, as if she needed to adjust. Slow, stilted moments, and each slower than the last. Jane going forward and giving her winning grin to the driver, and the driver bobbing his head in acknowledgment, and the ambassador beaming, and Holt coming through the door. Each movement, each moment, slower. And the man who was dark-skinned, with long hair, coming off the road and onto the pavement, and the windcheater falling past his knees and past his shins and past his ankles. And something black and stubbed and squat in his hands, something that he was lifting to his shoulder, something that was a protuberance from his head and mouth and nose, *something* that was a gun, for Christ's sake.

He stared at the man. He stared at the barrel of the rifle. No longer slow movement, the moment the world stopped.

Jane in front of the ambassador, Holt in the doorway, the driver with his back to them all, bent inside the car to smooth down the rug that covered the leather upholstery.

Everything frozen. No voice in Holt's throat. The warning scream locked in his mind.

Gazing into the face of the man, and then the flash, and the flash repeated, and the smoke. Then Jane spinning away, beaten and kicked and punched backward. Jane falling against Ben, and Ben not there to hold her upright. Ben fading from his feet, sliding down. The glass shattering to his right and to his left, caving in. Holt shaking his head, because he couldn't understand . . . looking at the face that was topped by a wig that had inched over the right ear, looking at the scar on the man's left cheek, puzzling how a face came by a scar that looked like a crow's foot.

The rifle dropped to the man's side. He peered forward as if to be certain of his work.

All movement now, speed returning to the world.

The man ran.

In that moment Holt found in his ears the crash of the gunfire, and the cordite in his nostrils, and the scream from his throat.

He was on his knees. His body covered their bodies, to protect them.

So bloody late.

4

He lay across them, sheltering them, as if they were still in danger. Blood was on his hands and on the cuffs of his shirt, red on white. He had taken Jane's hand in his, an unresisting hand, as it was when she was exhausted or sleeping.

The scream in his throat had died with them.

He was aware of men and women, fearful, around him. They formed a circle at the level of the door, and on the steps, and on the pavement. The shoes of one of them crunched the glass fragments, and the shoes of another nudged the spent cartridge cases.

"Ambulance," Holt said, in English. "Get us an ambulance."

The duty day manager called that the ambulance was sent for. Holt saw his face, quivering and streaming with tears. He saw that the driver was talking urgently into a personal radio, couldn't hear the words, could see the white-faced shock of the man. The street was blocked from Holt's view, only the line of knees and skirts and trousers and shoes for him to focus on. Empty ground between the legs and the feet and where Holt lay covering the bodies of Jane and Ben, empty ground laced with blood trickles and with shards of glass. He held tightly onto Jane's hand as the misery welled in him. He had seen the face of the man. He had seen the smooth pine-varnish skin, and the eyes that were burnished mahogany, and the thin chisel of the nose, and the clip of the moustache. He had seen the scar hole on the man's cheek and had followed the lines that ran from it, four lines, into the shape of a crow's foot.

There was the faraway sound of a siren.

He had been behind Ben and behind Jane. He had been behind them and safe. He had seen the man with the aimed gun, and he had done nothing. Could not explain to himself how he had watched the slow ballet movements of the man raising the weapon and aiming, and done nothing. Desperate misery, and it had all been so slowly drawn out in front of his eyes. He squeezed Jane's hand, her fingers, hard enough for it to have hurt her, and she did not flinch.

The driver broke the circle. He jostled the people back, and was shouting to them to retreat, pushing a corridor clear through them. Holt could see down the corridor, down the steps, across the pavement, into the street. He could see where the man had stood and taken his time to aim. He was aware of the closing bleat of the siren.

His view of the street was cut by the white bulk of the ambulance.

The driver was tugging at his shoulders, trying to pull him upright, trying and failing to break his hold on Jane's hand. He still held her while the ambulance men swiftly heaved Ben onto a stretcher, carried him away down the corridor to the open rear doors. They came back for her, for his Jane. He saw the shrug in their shoulders. The shoulders and the faces told him that they knew this was not work for ambulancemen. They lifted her more gently than they had lifted Ben, and more awkwardly because his hand never unclasped hers.

The doors closed behind him. Ben's litter lay on one side of the ambulance's opaque interior, Jane's on the other. Holt crouched in the space between. One ambulanceman was with them, going perfunctorily through pulse checks, and bending to listen first at Ben's chest and then at Jane's breast. The ambulance was going fast, siren loud.

Her last words were clear in his memory. Scathing words.

"Don't be childish, Holt."

Young Holt had loved Jane Canning and the last time he had seen her face it had been puckered, screwed up in annoyance. He bit at his lip. He looked down at the fright that was set like wax on her face. That was the obscenity of it, that all the good times, wonderful times, were blasted out.

"Don't be childish, Holt."

He had a bowl of beetroot soup in front of him and a tub of sour cream and two slices of black bread. He had a quarter bottle of vodka in the desk drawer beside his knee. The militia major was tucking a napkin into his collar when the news broke out of the control room.

Garbled, staccato chaos. A shooting on Lenin Street. He was gulping a spoonful of soup. A killing at the Oreanda Hotel. His napkin sliding into his soup. Foreign visitors attacked with rifle fire. He was careering from his desk, the sour cream slurping over his papers. A call for all assistance . . . It was Saturday lunchtime. It was the time that Yalta closed itself down and the militia headquarters was at one-third strength. He felt sick. The tang of the beetroot and the chopped onion was choking in his throat.

Into the control room. A relay coming through on the loudspeaker from Ambulance Control. The young sergeant at the console listening at the telephone and writing urgently. The telephone slapped down.

"Major, the management at the Oreanda Hotel on Lenin Street reports that the British ambassador and his interpreter were shot outside the hotel . . ."

"Dead?"

"They did not know . . . Ambulance Control reports that they are carrying two cadavers and one survivor to the clinic on Naberezhnaya . . ."

A foreign diplomat, possibly dead . . . Everything he did now was going to be examined under a microscope at the investigation in a week, in a month.

"Inform the KGB Control, exactly as it comes in."

The sergeant was reaching for his telephone. To go to the clinic, to go to the Oreanda, to stay in headquarters? Which?

He picked up a telephone himself. He rang the number of Criminal Investigation two floors above, and the telephone rang and his fingers drummed on the console surface and his feet shuffled. Bastards gone to their lunch. The sergeant came off the telephone and the major told him to send all militia cars to the Oreanda.

The major ran out of the building, howled in the yard for a driver, had himself taken to the Oreanda.

The KGB had beaten him. Half a dozen of them there. Crowds gathering but back on the far side of the street. He shouldered his way forward to the knot of men all with radios, all either talking into them or listening to the return messages. In front of the broken plate-glass front door he saw the bloodstains. Perhaps, in the car, he had half hoped the radio at headquarters had carried an aberration . . . well, that some hysterical idiot had . . . The bloodstains and the KGB swarming over the steps of the hotel wiped that out.

They treated the militia major as dirt. They were the Organ of State Security, he was a common policeman. Brusquely he was told what had happened.

"You had a very fast call," the militia major said.

For answer there was a cursory gesture, down the steps toward a black Chaika car. A man was sitting haggard over the wheel of the car, a radio in his hand, shaking his head in response to the questions of two others. The driver, the militia major understood; a KGB driver had been assigned to the British ambassador's party.

"So you have a description, something I can broadcast?"

The man he spoke to looked away.

"If I am to seal the city, put in roadblocks, I have to have a description."

"He saw nothing."

"What? A close quarters shooting, right under your own man's nose, and he saw nothing? How could he see nothing?"

"There is no description."

"There has to be," the militia major shouted.

"He did not see the killer approach. He took cover when the shooting started. He did not see the killer leave. There is no description."

"Shit," spat the militia major. "You pick your men."

The KGB officer walked away. The militia major sighed his relief. The fear of failure was shed. A KGB matter, a KGB failure. Best news he could possibly have been given.

He followed the KGB officer.

"What do you want of me?" the militia major said flatly.

"We have closed the airport, we have suspended all telephonic communication from the city, we have referred all details to Moscow. You should put blocks on all routes out of the city."

"For what are they looking?"

No response.

He sat on a long wooden bench in a corridor of white walls and polished linoleum flooring. Two old ladies had at first shared the bench with him, but they had long since been ordered away by the militiaman who stood with arms folded and watched over him. Through the flapping rubber doors on the other side of the corridor the trailing white coats of the doctors and surgeons and the white skirts of the nurses came and went. He waited. Another militiaman stood on guard by the rubber doors. He hadn't fought it, he hadn't wanted to be inside the Emergency Room. He was alert now, conscious of everything around him, aware enough to know that he did not want to see the last medical rites performed on the girl he loved and the man he admired. Each man and woman who went into the Emergency Room, or came from it, gave him a glance and then looked away when he met their eyes.

It was an older man who came to him. White haired and lean, and with his smock coat bloodstained. He spoke with his hands: his hands said that hope had gone. In Russian, Holt was told that the man was the senior surgeon on duty at the hospital. He was told that the injuries had been too severe for treatment. He shook the hand of the surgeon, and thanked him.

Holt said that he needed a telephone. Again the hands of the surgeon were in motion: it was outside his province. The surgeon backed away. Two trolleys, sheet shrouded, were wheeled through the rubber doors and down the corridor. He sat numbed, watched them go.

His attention was to his right. The man wore perfect creased slacks and a well-cut wool jacket. The man flashed an identity card, didn't linger with it but it was there long enough for Holt to recognize the Komitet Gosudarstvennoy Bezopasnosti. Holt read the name of the KGB officer.

"I want a telephone," Holt said, speaking in Russian.

The KGB officer was fishing a notebook from his pocket, and a ballpoint pen.

"I said that I wanted a telephone."

"There will be a telephone, Mr. Holt. But my first priority is to apprehend the despicable culprits responsible for this crime."

"Just a telephone—the street was packed solid. You don't need me to tell you."

"Mr. Holt, we need to have a description from you."

He was in a police state, a state controlled by the leviathan apparatus of the Organ of State Security. A state where the KGB crushed all dissent, kept the gulags filled. He was in a country that boasted no terrorism, no law and order problem, no incidence of armed crime. He believed, as never before, that in this country nothing moved, nothing happened, without KGB authority. Now a charade about the need for a description.

"Ask someone else what the bastard looked like," Holt yelled at him.

The militiaman close to him had clenched his fist, ready to intervene, and the militiaman beside the rubber doors had his hand wavering close to the wood truncheon fastened to his belt.

The KGB officer strode away.

All so clear now to Holt. The State had butchered them.

The authorities had killed them . . . He went off down the corridor, he shrugged away a feeble attempt by his militiaman minder to stop him. He went into an office that was empty because of the weekend. He picked up the telephone, he dialed a zero and then seven for long distance, he waited for the clicks, he dialed the Moscow code and the embassy number. The "unobtainable" whine sang back at him. He tried twice more. Twice more the same blank whine.

Out of the clinic. The short walk along the sea front, the two militiamen trailing him, a distance away as if he might turn on them, savage them.

He reached the Oreanda Hotel. The street and the half steps picketed off, brown paper stuck where the glass panels had been, the glisten of soap and water on the steps. In past the militia and more KGB, up to the reception desk. He wanted a telephone call to Moscow. It was regretted there was no telephonic communication with Moscow. Then he wanted a telex connection with Moscow and he wanted it now, right now. It was regretted that there was also no telex communication with Moscow. By whose authority? By the authority of State Security.

So tired, so bloody exhausted. Slowly, deliberately, "I have to speak to Moscow."

"I am so sorry, Mr. Holt, but it is not possible for anyone to speak to Moscow. All the lines are closed."

"Is there a post office?"

"It is Saturday afternoon, the post office is closed, Mr. Holt."

"I *have* to speak to my embassy."

"I am sure that later, Mr. Holt, the lines will be restored."

The reception manager gave him his room key and then reached below the counter and shuffled to him Jane's handbag. Dropped it when she was hit. It was a small, kind gesture by the reception staff, to have retrieved the handbag, kept it for him. He offered his thanks. He went slowly up the flights of stairs to his room. He locked the door behind him. He tipped her bag out onto the coverlet of his bed. Her purse, her passport, her notepad, her pen, her embassy ID, her lipstick, her mirror, her hairbrush, her letter from home, her photograph of Holt in Whitehall held in a small silver frame, her camera . . .

He was shipwrecked. His landfall was a room on the second floor of the Oreanda Hotel in Yalta. His sea was a closed-down telephone and telex system to Moscow and a wall of silence. He had gone through shock and misery and fury, now his reserve failed. Alone, where no one saw him, Holt knelt beside his bed and wept, and his face covered her possessions, and he said over and over again the words she had spoken to him.

"Don't be childish, Holt."

The ciphered message whispered onto a teleprinter at main headquarters in Dzerzhinsky Square. A report from KGB Yalta to KGB Moscow, giving information, requiring guidance. Saturday afternoon in the capital city. The message, still in cipher, passed to Second Directorate, domestic counter-subversion, and to Fifth Chief Directorate, suppression of dissent. Rows of weekend empty desks in Second and Fifth Chief, dust covers over the computer consoles, skeleton staffing. The minutes sliding away. Second Directorate duty officer going in search of his senior, his senior telephoning home to the man commanding the Second Department of the Directorate, the man commanding Second Department waiting for a call back from the Directorate chief out walking his dog. Fifth Chief Directorate on hold and looking for a lead from Second Directorate. Foreign Ministry embassy liaison stating he would take no action until briefed by Second Directorate, and until consultation with Fifth Chief Directorate. The dog was a young German shepherd and needed a good long walk on a Saturday afternoon.

The duty officer at the British embassy whiled away his afternoon in the near-deserted building, and watched the ripple of the Moskva River from his upper room.

He had run down Lenin Street. He had turned away from the shore front into a small alleyway. No more running then. He had walked as he had shrugged into his windcheater. One bad moment, when the windcheater had been on the ground and he had had to scoop it up. The gun under the shoulder of the windcheater. Another right turn, and another left turn, and the Volga car in front of him, and the man starting the engine.

The rifle—magazine detached and metal stock folded down—wrapped in sacking on the floor of the car. Going fast out of the city and toward the Alushta road.

"Did you succeed?"

He punched the air in front of his face, and turned to the wide billowing smile of his commander.

There was no obstacle to their flight. They had beaten the roadblocks.

He was Abu Hamid. Abu Hamid was the name he had taken when he had joined the Popular Front for the Liberation of Palestine. He was 28 years old. His body was bone thin, spare, as if he ate little, as if he enjoyed no luxuries. The complexion of his face was smooth with the exception of the scar under his left eye. He wore no moustache and his matted dark hair was cut close to his scalp. Beyond the scar he was unrecognizable, unremarkable.

He was a chosen man.

He sucked hard, like he was panting, on his cigarette. He exploded the smoke from his mouth. He had stripped off the civilian clothes in which he had appeared on the front pavement of the Oreanda Hotel. He was now in military fatigues. They had stopped by the roadside at the city's limits and behind the cover of flourishing saplings Abu Hamid had swiftly dug a deep hole in the ditch and crammed in it the windcheater, the trousers, the shirt, the moustache, and the wig.

The city of Yalta was behind them. The high slopes of oak and beech forest that dominated the city were lost to them. In a corner of the car park of the Sechonov Climatic and Physiotherapeutic Institute, shielded by small recently planted acacia and laurel and magnolia trees, they had transferred from the Volga car to a military jeep. The car could not be linked to them. The car had been hired from Intourist. The car had been fitted with false plates. Later, the plates exchanged, the car would be returned, the bill paid. None of that was the business of Abu Hamid.

The commander knew that the journey from Yalta to Simferopol would take, given a few minutes either way, one hour and three quarters. They hammered through Gurzuf, past the signed turnings to the Defense Ministry sanatorium and the "Sputnik" Youth Camp. The commander's eyes flickered to the side mirrors of the jeep. They had no tail. Through Alushta, as if it did not exist, as if the narrowing streets in the town were merely an inconvenience on their journey. The commander pricked his ears to listen for a trailing siren. He heard nothing. The jeep straining when they climbed toward the lower reaches of the Chatir Dag that rose higher than any mountain in Lebanon, higher than the mystic Hermon of Syria, higher than any mountain of Palestine that was the homeland of Abu Hamid.

The aircraft should now be leaving Moscow. There was a schedule to be met. At the road's summit, under Chatir Dag, they did not pause to look back and down toward Yalta and the hazed seascape.

Abu Hamid leaned forward. He unwrapped the AK-47 assault rifle from the sacking on the floor space between his feet. He emptied the magazine. On semiautomatic, at a range of five or six paces, he had fired eleven bullets. He knew the weapon as he knew himself. Now he put the remaining rounds with the magazine and the rifle carefully into the mouth of the sack, wrapped it tight into a bundle and tucked it under his feet. A tradesman's tool, and he had finished with it.

Holt lay on his bed.

He had heard the whispered talk in the corridor outside his room. He had already been into Ben's room and into Jane's room and he had packed their belongings. Ben's case and Jane's were at the foot of his bed. He presumed the low voices outside were of a guard posted there. For his protection? To keep him inside the room?

Each half hour he rang reception to see if the line to Moscow was open, and each half hour he was told that it was not. Each half hour he requested a call to KGB headquarters in the city, and each time he was told that all KGB numbers were engaged.

There was no other explanation. Of course they had killed Ben and Jane. He lay on the bed, her blood still on his hands and on his shirt.

Simferopol is in the center of the Crimean Peninsula. The city, with a population of close to 300,000, is the hub of the Crimea and from this regional capital the roads snake out to Yevpatoriya and Sevastopol and Yalta and Feodosiya and Dzhankoi. It is an old city, dominated now by industrial estates, its university, several research institutes. At Simferopol is also a military academy.

For the colonel commandant (foreign cadre training) that Saturday was a hell of a good day at the military academy. His best day in six months, in fact. The colonel commandant would this day wave goodbye, without a shade of regret, to the delegation of Palestinians. For the Ethiopians, the Cubans, the Angolans, even for the North Vietnamese, he could find some words of praise. Nothing good could be said for the animal Palestinians, not even as a courtesy at the farewell airport parade before the animals filed onto their aircraft. When the doors closed on the fuselage they would get the sharp index finger. . . . Nightly in the mess, to his brother officers, he catalogued their abuses. Three of the animals caught trying to climb over the walls after curfew hour to hitch into the city. One with the insolence to complain that a prostitute in Simferopol had stolen his wallet. One returned to the academy by the militia after being arrested when trying to sell counterfeit American dollars. One brought back to the academy by the militia dead drunk and violent. Four who would be in solitary confinement right up to the last minute for attacking a senior instructor. One accused by a fine Party man of getting pregnant his fine daughter. Not much sympathy from his colleagues in the mess, and rudeness to his face from the odious commander of the animals. One rifle lost, damage done all over the camp, and throughout the course an atmosphere of indiscipline that was insufferable to the colonel commandant. He would cheer their going, every last one of them from their ridiculously named groups. Popular Front, Sai'iqa, Democratic Front, Liberation Front, General Command, Struggle Command—idiot titles. He was a career soldier. He despised these animals.

Through the colonel commandant's office window came the blast of Western music, loud and decadent, cassette players turned to full volume. The animals taunting their instructors, because the animals were going home.

His telephone rang.

The animals were in the gymnasium with their baggage waiting for transport to the airport. A fighter from Sai'iqa had argued with a fighter from the Struggle Command, and knifed him. The fighter from Sai'iqa was in the academy military police cells, the fighter from Struggle Command was in the academy sick bay.

"Where is their commander?"

Their commander was off base.

Too much. He slammed his fist onto his desk in fury. This was too fucking much.

The teleprinters linking Moscow and Yalta murmured through the afternoon, on into the early evening. Questions and demands for more information from Moscow. Scant detail relayed from Yalta.

A crisis committee sat at Dzerzhinsky Square feeding from the teleprinter material, and going hungry. No workable description of a gunman, no getaway car identified. Cartridge cases that were from the Kalashnikov family, and there were more than two million weapons in the country that could fire such bullets. The files on dissident elements in the Crimea were being studied.

In his office, the Foreign Ministry embassy liaison was left to clean his nails and watch his silent telephone.

The commander drove his jeep through the main gates of the military academy at Simferopol.

He waved cheerfully to the guard. He braked to allow a squad of Soviet conscripts to march across his path. All the conscripts were marched wherever they went in the camp, a difference in attitudes, he reflected, between the training demanded by the Red Army and the training required for the fighting in Lebanon. He checked his watch. He thought they had made good time, he thought the Antonov transporter would now be approaching Simferopol Airport. He stopped by the gymnasium, punched the shoulder of Abu Hamid. He was too concerned with the tightness of his schedule to take note of the three military policemen standing outside the main doors of the building.

The commander did not have to tell the young man to hold silence, to play a part of relaxed indifference when he was inside the gymnasium. His Abu Hamid would know. He drove away, drove to the office of the colonel commandant.

He breezed into the inner office. On any other day he would have waited more respectfully at the door, but it was the last day, and it was the day that was the brilliant culmination of a difficult and dangerous mission.

"Later than I thought, Colonel. Profuse apologies . . ."

He laid the jeep's keys on the desk of the colonel commandant.

". . . One last expedition for shopping in the city, an opportunity to purchase merchandise that will remind me for the rest of my days in the service of the Palestine revolution of the warmth shown to us by the Soviet people . . ."

He saw at once the barely controlled fury of the commandant.

". . . I trust my lateness has not inconvenienced you, Colonel. Shopping in the city is not always as fast as one would wish."

"You have been gone seven hours."

"Some shopping, a good lunch, time drifts . . ." He saw the clenched fist, the white knuckles. "There has been a problem?"

"A problem! . . ." the colonel commandant snorted. "While you took lunch and wine and shopped, your hooligans have been brawling. I have one in the sick bay, I have one locked in the guardhouse." The colonel commandant slapped a small double-bladed knife down onto his desk. "A knife fight while you were lunching and wining and shopping. I will tell you the military crime code for such an offense. Assault by one service person on another in the absence of any subordinate relations between them, that carries a minimum of two years' confinement and a maximum of twelve years . . ."

"My abject apologies, Colonel. I will deal with the offender at once . . ."

The colonel commandant stood. "You will do nothing of the sort. You will get it into your head that I have the authority to detain the entire cadre until a full investigation has been carried out."

The commander thought of Abu Hamid coming panting to the Volga car. He thought of the Kalashnikov in the sacking, hidden in the large shopping bag of the Simferopol *beryozka* souvenir store, and, hanging from his hand, the rifle listed as "lost on maneuvers."

"But our aircraft . . ."

"Fuck the aircraft. A serious breach of discipline has taken place among unsupervised personnel."

"We have to take the aircraft." The bombast gone from the commander. Nervous and wheedling now. "It is of critical importance that we take the aircraft."

"A fortnight's delay, a thorough investigation, will teach these hooligans the authority of discipline."

"It cannot happen."

"Don't tell me what can or cannot happen. It should happen and it will happen."

Out of the confusion in Yalta would soon come order. The commander shivered. The trap would close.

"I make a deal with you."

"You are in no position to offer me a deal, military regulations are not subject to negotiation."

"Give me a pistol . . ."

"For what?"

"And a mop and bucket . . ."

"For what?"

"And access to the guard room."

"For what?"

"So that I can shoot your hooligan and clear up the mess and remove your problem."

The colonel commandant blanched, sat down. "You would do that?"

"With my own hand. Give me the pistol."

The knife was returned to the drawer. "Take him with you, then. Take both of them and punish them at home."

"An admirable solution. The injured man is fit to travel?" He was told that the injured man could certainly fly.

The commandant regarded the Palestinian with disgust—and with awe.

He told his duty officer to send the bus to the gymnasium.

Even in the crowded interior of the bus, 58 seats for 61 personnel, and the luggage filling the rear compartment and the aisle between the seats, the commander thought that Abu Hamid was a man apart, dreaming his own dreams in his own privacy. The man from Struggle Command sat pale at the back of the bus with his left arm in a sling. The man from Sai'iqa stood in the aisle at the front, beside the commander, in handcuffs. They drove out of the gates. Only the commander and Abu Hamid and the man from Struggle Command and the man from Sai'iqa refrained from cheering as the barrier was lowered behind them. Through the drab city where a grayness hung that even the sunlight could not lift, past the Ukraina Hotel, and over the wide bridge spanning the Salgir River, and past the museum and the terraced parkland and the railway station, through the industrial estates, out toward the airport.

Around the perimeter of the airport fence. Waved through the gates into the military section. Past the buildings and the control tower, out along the edge of the tarmac.

The sun was low in the west, and it hit the silver lower belly of the Antonov transporter. The Antonov was decorated with the green and white and black roundels of the Syrian Air Force. The commander's breath squeezed between his teeth. Military bandsmen were grouped around a rostrum. There were steps in position at the forward door. A fueling tanker was driving away.

From his hip pocket the commander took a folded *kaffiyeh* scarf, shook it open and wound it round his head and his face, as if he were a revolutionary fighter for Palestine, not an embarking passenger at the military section of Simferopol Airport in the Crimea. As he descended from the bus the commandant's transport drew up. The camp instructors, impeccably turned out, jumped down from their truck.

The 61 men were lined up in two platoon-sized squads. The anthem of the Soviet Union was played by the Red Army band, interminable, and they were a single phone call from disaster. A phone call from Yalta to Simferopol. The band struck havoc with a fighting march of the Palestine revolution. In his ears the bell of a telephone screamed.

The colonel commandant, cold and contemptuous, scarcely pausing for the interpreter, addressed the men. If they had been seen transferring from the Volga to the jeep in the car park . . . In the mind of the commander the bell of a telephone clamored.

"Our Party supports and will continue to support peoples fighting for their freedom. We will never agree to the unacceptable American demands that the Soviet nation should cease to support its friends."

The commander stood at attention in front of his men. Only the major who was his friend, only Major Said Hazan, would have dared to launch the plan. Such daring, such brilliance. He pleaded for the speech to end.

"I wish you good fortune in your war for the regaining of your homeland. Long live Free Palestine. Long live the Soviet Union. Long live our friendship of iron . . ." The final words were drowned by the starting of the engines.

A ripple of applause from the two ranks of instructors behind the colonel commandant was lost in the aircraft's engine roar. The colonel commandant and the commander exchanged salutes, shook hands without warmth. The Palestinians gathered their luggage, and then scrambled to get aboard.

The commander came last, gesturing that Abu Hamid should be ahead of him. They threaded their way around the wooden crates that filled the center of the hold and looked for the canvas seats, their backs to the fuselage. The light from the doorway was blotted out, a member of the aircrew turned the locking handle. A terrible tension in the commander as the Antonov inched forward and started to swivel. He seemed to hear in his mind the ring of a telephone in the colonel commandant's office, and the squawk of a radio in the control tower. His stomach was knotted—they could still be brought back. The aircrew member was yelling at him above the drive of the engines for his belt to be fastened.

Four hours and three minutes after an incident in Yalta, the Antonov transporter lifted off the long Simferopol runway. It took a course, as it climbed, to the southwest and crossed the shoreline of the Crimea close to the old battlefields of Sevastopol and Balaklava, then swung south over the darkening Black Sea. The aircraft had prior permission to overfly Turkish airspace, a standard arrangement. Ahead of it was a flight of 2 hours and 20 minutes, cruising speed 450 miles an hour, altitude 25,000 feet. Within 18 minutes the four giant Kuznetsov NK-12MV turboprop engines had carried the Antonov beyond Soviet jurisdiction.

The captain made the announcement. The excited yelling rang inside the aircraft. The commander sat slumped, drained of the energy to celebrate. Beside him he saw that Abu Hamid sat back in his seat, swaying with the motion of the aircraft. The commander thought the killer was at peace, and marveled. Moving down the aisle toward them, steadying himself against the lashed-down crates, came Major Said Hazan.

The question was in the smooth child's stomach skin around the major's eyes.

"It was successful," the commander said. "The target was destroyed."

Abu Hamid saw that the major wore a smart Syrian Air Force uniform, but his face was hidden by a wrapped wool scarf and his head was hidden by his wide peaked cap. Only the eyes were for him to see. Abu Hamid leaned forward. There was pride in his voice. "There was a girl, with the ambassador, she too died."

Major Said Hazan ducked his head in acknowledgment, clasped the shoulders of the two men each in turn, with a leather-gloved hand. He made his way back to the cockpit.

The landfall would be high over the Turkish town of Samsun, the flight path would be above the central Anatolian mountains, the Syrian frontier would be overflown east of Aleppo, and then the long descent to Damascus.

The words as taught him in the camps of Damascus before the journey to Simferopol were soundless in the throat of Abu Hamid.

The thoughts echoed in his mind. The thoughts were of the Old Man of the Mountains who had built his fortress a thousand years ago in the valley of Alamut and gathered his followers, who were the Assassins. Enclosed in the valley that was paradise were palaces and pavilions, channels flowing with wine and honey, and young girls who danced and sang. Every pleasure was found here for the Assassins until the Old Man of the Mountains called one forward.

"Go from here and kill the man whose name I give you . . . When you return you will enter again into paradise . . . should you not return then my angels will seek you out and carry you back to our paradise."

A thousand years ago word of the skill and dedication of the Assassins of Syria, traveling from the valley of Alamut, had spread across the known world. Brilliant in disguise, unrivaled in their dedication and fanaticism, ruthless in murder, the Assassins were feared by kings and princes and military commanders and civil governors and the priests of Sunni Islam. Abu Hamid saw himself as the descendant of the old Assassins of ten centuries before.

The words, soundless in the throat of Abu Hamid, were those of the Old Man of the Mountains, handed down over a millennium.

"To kill these people is more lawful than rainwater."

There was no advance warning. The car drove unannounced into the forecourt of the embassy. Three men in the car, all pressed into service and summoned from their weekend break. A First Deputy Foreign Minister, a protocol official, a full colonel of the Second Directorate. They were shown into an anteroom on the ground floor where they were watched by a security man.

The duty officer for that weekend was a Second Secretary Trade. He was still buttoning his collar when he came into the room. Grim faces staring back at him, all three men standing. They introduced themselves, even the one from State Security. Not the moment to offer them tea, nor the moment to ask them to sit. Their seniority meant urgent business to be conducted without delay.

"I am the duty officer," he said. He produced a pencil and notepad and waited.

The First Deputy Foreign Minister seemed for a moment to examine the close patternwork of the carpet, from Bokhara, then he straightened.

"It is with the utmost regret that as the representative of my government I have the sad duty to inform you that His Excellency, Sir Sylvester Armitage, and Miss Jane Canning were today the victims of a cruel and cowardly attack in the city of Yalta. As a result of this attack His Excellency and Miss Canning have died. The third member of the delegation, Mr. Holt, is unhurt. I am instructed to inform you that the Soviet government has made available a military aircraft to take to Yalta any members of your staff who would wish to go. The aircraft is ready to leave at your convenience. I am able to tell you that a comprehensive criminal investigation has been launched in Yalta, and it is our earnest hope that the investigation will bear fruit soon."

The duty officer was scribbling his note, in longhand. Incredulity on his face. Lips moving, but they could not formulate the barrage of questions.

"The deaths were caused by shooting. His Excellency and Miss Canning were hit many times as they were leaving the hotel for lunch with the city authorities; they were dead on arrival at hospital. The initial indication is that the culprit was involved in an attempt to enter the hotel for the purpose of robbing the cash desk, but panicked as he was confronted by the British delegation leaving."

"Where's Holt?" The first stuttered question.

"He is in the hotel. He is quite safe."

"But this happened, you say, before lunch. Why hasn't he telephoned?"

"Mr. Holt is in shock."

The mind of the duty officer was racing, incoherent. "Didn't they have any protection?"

"Later there will be an opportunity for such detail."

The KGB colonel added, "There was a representative of state security at the hotel. He performed his duties with great bravery, but sadly was not able to prevent the attack."

"God Almighty . . ."

The First Deputy Foreign Minister said, "We shall be at the Foreign Ministry. We are at the disposal of the British people in this moment of anguish."

"It wasn't terrorism?"

"It was the act of a common criminal in pursuance of theft," the KGB colonel said decisively.

In darkness and among a sea of pimple landing-navigation lights the Antonov put down at El Masr military airbase. They were checked with military thoroughness for contraband goods. They were home, in that home for these refugee strays of the Middle East was to be found in the Syrian Arab Republic. They had been together six months, now they were to disperse. A minibus each for the Struggle Command, and for Sai'iqa, and for the Popular Front, and for the Democratic Front, and for the General Command, and for the Liberation Front. The culprit from Sai'iqa had lost his handcuffs five minutes after takeoff, the victim from Struggle Command embraced his attacker when they parted. The commander reflected that the Russians could never understand his children.

All went their separate ways, except that Abu Hamid with his commander traveled from the base in the Mercedes car that had been sent to collect Major Said Hazan. Abu Hamid, unshaven and with the sweat smell on his body from his sprint away from the Oreanda Hotel, rode out of the base cushioned in the backseat between the officer of Syrian Air Force Intelligence and the officer of the Popular Front for the Liberation of Palestine.

When the car had gathered speed along the wide highway from the airport, the commander said softly to Major Said Hazan, "It was magnificent, Said. It was just as you had said it would be."

The voice was muffled through the scarf. "You played your part, friend."

Two quiet men talking casually across Abu Hamid, as if he were not there.

"But you took a great risk."

"Risk nothing, and it is not possible to achieve victory."

"When will the claim be made?"

"Claim?"

"What has happened has been a triumph for the Popular Front. The Popular Front should be, must be, credited . . ."

"There will be no claim. There will only be silence."

Abu Hamid heard the ice chill in the voice. He felt the major shift his body further into his seat.

He was in the darkness, on the bed, when he heard the light knock on his door. He thought he might have been to sleep. He felt the wet of his tears on his face when he rubbed his eyes. He heard his name called. He slid off the bed, opened the door, let in the flood of light.

The security officer said, "Thank God we've reached you, young man."

Holt blinked at him, turned away from the door.

"They gave us an executive jet . . ."

"Bloody decent of them."

"I came down with the counselor. He's at the hospital, I've been at militia HQ."

"Super, first class."

"It's all right, Holt, you've had a bloody rough time, eh?"

Holt gazed into the security officer's face. "Rubbish. It's not bloody rough when you're *watching* a shooting . . ."

"Easy, young man."

Holt flared. "Easy . . . it's to be easy, is it? We come down here, Low bloody Risk bloody posting, we're set up for a shooting gallery. We're chopped down like Boxing Day pheasants . . ."

"I understand you were not exactly cooperative."

"Would you have been? What do they want cooperation for? They've just wiped out my boss and my girl, and they want me to help their bloody inquiry, put a gloss on their bloody lies. 'Course I didn't bloody cooperate."

A sharpness in the security officer's voice. "I have to tell you that the Soviet authorities could not have been more sympathetic and eager to help me. I have been given a very full briefing on their investigation and its conclusion . . ."

"So they soaped you up."

"A full briefing on their investigation and its conclusion."

Holt's voice dropped. "What conclusion?"

"They have told me that they identified an army deserter as the criminal responsible. It was his intention to rob the hotel at gunpoint. He panicked as the ambassador and Miss Canning and yourself were coming out of the hotel, and opened fire. They had good eyewitness descriptions of him, and this evening a vehicle in which he was traveling was waved down on the outskirts of the city. In attempting to evade arrest he was shot dead . . ."

"What else did they tell you about this 'deserter'?"

"That he was a 22-year-old Byelorussian."

"That's Minsk, he'd be a European."

"Did you see him, Holt, did you get a look at him?"

"At 15 feet. I saw his face."

The security officer lit a cigarette. The smoke spiraled in the quiet dark room.

"The man you saw, Holt, could he have been from Byelorussia?"

"They soaped and flanneled you."

"Give it to me straight, eh?"

"If he's from Minsk they'd had to have had a heatwave there through this winter."

"Soaped and flanneled, as you say. I'm very sorry, very sorry about your girl."

Holt went to the window, showed his back to the security officer.

On Sunday morning a Royal Air Force VC-10 was diverted from its Cyprus-to-Brize Norton flight run to drop down at Simferopol.

The coffins containing the bodies of Sir Sylvester Armitage and Jane Canning were carried to the cargo doors by a bearer party of Soviet Marines. The coffins were taken past an honor guard of officer cadets from the military academy who stood sternly to attention, heads down and rifles in reverse.

The sight of the coffins, and the presence among them of young Holt and the counselor and the security officer, was sufficient to subdue a company of paratroopers returning to the United Kingdom from a month's exercises.

5

"It was good of you to come. We appreciate it."

She was a small woman, brightly dressed, and with heavy makeup that he presumed was to hide the ravage of her bereavement. She stood in the front doorway and the rain lashed down onto the head and shoulders of young Holt. Strange, really, that in all the time he had known Jane he had never been asked to her parents' home in South London. He saw the water dribbling down from the black mock-Tudor beams and down the whitewashed stucco. He hadn't a hat and so his head was soaked.

Gently he said, "Do you think I could come in, Mrs. Canning?"

Her hand jerked to her mouth, and she was all movement, embarrassment.

"Whatever'll you be thinking of me? Of course come in . . . Father, it's Mr. Holt here."

Jane's father took his coat off to the kitchen, and Jane's mother led him into the front room. A friendly room full of the furniture that dated back to the beginning of a marriage. Worn armrests on the sofa and the chairs, a burn mark in the carpet by the fire, plants that needed cutting back. On the mantelpiece was a photograph of his girl, a posed portrait that was all shoulder and profile. He stood with his back to the fire, with his back to the photograph of Jane, and his damp trouser legs steamed. He wondered what it was like for them to meet the man who loved their daughter and who had slept with their daughter. Around the room he counted four more photographs of her, of his girl. Jane's mother had sat down in *her* chair, the most used chair, and she had her knitting bag on her lap and was rooting for needles and wool. She could see each one of the five photographs from her chair. She asked him to sit, and he said that he had been in the train a long time and that he preferred to stand. He reckoned that her clothes were a brave gesture, a Post Office–red skirt and a white blouse and a vivid scarf knotted at her throat. He admired a woman who would dress like that for her daughter's funeral. Jane's father came into the room wiping the raincoat's damp off his hands onto a handkerchief. He wore his best suit and a starched white shirt and a tie that was either dark navy or black. Jane's father seemed exhausted, as if the strain of the past ten days had sapped him.

"Nice of you to come, young man—she never told us your proper name, you were always just called Holt by her," Jane's father said.

"That's what I am, really, what everyone calls me. Please just call me that . . . It means a lot to me that I can be with you today."

He meant it sincerely. He had been two days in London, telling his story. He had spent a long weekend at his parents' home, walking alone on the soaked wilderness of Exmoor. He wanted to be with Jane's mother and father on the day of the funeral. Jane's father asked him if he would like coffee and he said no, he was fine, and he asked him if he wanted to sit, and again he declined, and Mrs. Canning knitted and Mr. Canning searched for flaws on his fingernails.

"I wanted to be with you today because quite soon, I think Jane and I would have told you that we were going to become engaged to be married . . ."

She didn't look up. Her husband still explored the tips of his fingers.

"I loved her, and I like to think that she loved me."

"You've got to put it all behind you," Jane's mother said.

"When I arrived in Moscow and found her waiting for me at the airport I don't think that I've ever felt such happiness."

"Jane's gone, Mr. Holt, and you're a young man and you've a life ahead of you."

"Right now I don't see it that way."

"You will, and the sooner the better. Life's for living."

Holt saw her bite at her lower lip.

Jane's father's head rose. His mouth was moving as if he were rehearsing a question, unsure of the form of words. The question when it came was little more than a whisper. "Was she hurt?"

Eight high-velocity shots fired at a range of less than ten paces, that's what the postmortem had said. He could feel the lifeless hand, he could see the table-tennis-ball-sized exit wounds.

"She wasn't hurt, there was no pain. What did they tell you, Foreign and Commonwealth?"

"Just that it was a grubby little business. This man was a heroin addict and an army deserter—they told us what was in the newspapers—that he had gone to the hotel to rob it. They said it was just a one in a million chance that he should have chosen that particular moment for his robbery, when our Jane and the ambassador and yourself were coming out of the hotel. They said the Soviet authorities were very sympathetic. They told us that the man was shot dead while trying to escape."

He saw the sallow face of the man with the windcheater and the rifle and the crow's foot scar on his cheek.

Holt said, "There's probably not much more that anyone can tell you."

Jane's mother stared at her knitting, her face puckered in concentration. "We were so proud, both of us, when Jane joined the Service, began to work for her country. It isn't easy for a girl to get a good position in it, and I think they thought she was outstanding. I'm not saying she told us much about it, a very discreet little soul, but we knew she was working in Intelligence. She probably told you more."

He remembered the photography over Charkov. He remembered his remark about the camera. He remembered the last words he had heard her speak. "Don't be childish, Holt."

"She was very much admired by all her colleagues."

Jane's father pushed himself up from the chair. "Like Mother said, you've your life ahead of you. It was good of you to come today, but we shan't expect to see you again."

Holt saw the black car outside. He saw Jane's mother putting her knitting and her needles back into the embroidered bag. He saw Jane's father straighten his tie.

"I loved her, Mr. Canning. We were going to be married."

He saw the trace of impatience.

"Get on with your career, get on with the living of your life . . . Pity it's raining, Mother."

Holt followed Jane's mother fast down the short path and through the front gate to the car. Jane's father carefully locked the door behind him. He sat with them in the back as they were driven to the crematorium that was away to the west, close to the river. They didn't talk on the journey, and Holt wondered whether they held their peace because of him or because of the driver. As soon as they had arrived at the crematorium, Holt removed himself from their side. There were cameras there, television and press photographers, and he felt that by hanging back he drew away from them the attention of lenses and the clicking shutters. Holt was good raw meat for the cameras. It had been leaked that they were close, that he had seen the killings. He tried to keep his head up, his chin jutting. He walked past the sprays of flowers and the wreaths. He saw the signature of the Foreign Secretary, and of the head of the Soviet Desk at FCO and there were four bundles of flowers which were simply signed with Christian names. Inside the porch of the chapel Holt saw a tall, austere man shaking the hands of Jane's mother and father. There had been FCO people outside, but Holt understood. The Director General of the Secret Intelligence Service could not stand in front of the cameramen, nor could his people sign their names on the wreaths. He wondered what had become of Jane's camera, what had happened to her photographs from the plane. He felt a surge of anger, as if these nameless men and the Director General of the Service were responsible for her death.

It was a short service. He sat alone behind her parents. He couldn't find his voice when they sang the Twenty-third Psalm. He watched the coffin roll away from him, he watched the curtains close. He was crying in his heart. He remembered her voice, her gray eyes, her soft hair, and her lifeless hand. He remembered the man with the rifle. He saw her parents walk back up the chapel aisle and they didn't turn to him. He sat in his seat and stared at the closed curtain.

"You're young Holt, yes?"

He turned. The chapel had emptied fast. The man was thickset with a fine head of gray hair and the brush of a military moustache was squashed between nose and mouth.

"I am."

"We have to be moving. They'll be queuing up outside for the next one, damn conveyor-belt operation. Do you have wheels?"

He had steeled himself to spend the day with Jane's mother and father. He had made no arrangements to get himself away, and now it had been made plain to him that he was not expected back to the semidetached home in Motspur Park.

"I don't."

"Have you the afternoon to spare?"

His studio flat in London was rented out. The tenant had signed for a year. Ahead of him was only a train journey back to Devon, plenty of trains, they ran all afternoon and evening. His father would come down to Exeter to collect him. An usher appeared beside the man, trying to hurry them.

"For what?"

"My name's Martins, Percy Martins, I'm from the Service. Your initial debrief by the FCO people landed on my desk."

He looked up at Percy Martins. He saw clear pale-blue eyes that never wavered from his glance. "What is there to talk about?"

"What you saw, what happened."

Holt felt the control going, voice rising. "I thought everyone knew what bloody happened. I thought they all swallowed the Soviet crap."

"Not swallowed by everyone—come on."

Holt followed obediently. He noticed that Martins walked out of the chapel well ahead of him, so that he would not be included when Holt was again the cameramen's target. Holt reached a small station wagon. Martins was already behind the wheel, engine started, pushing the door open for Holt.

"My son is at university in York. He's playing a match in London today, that's where we're going. My wife'll kill me if I get home tonight and haven't seen him. We can talk when we're there."

He drove fast and in total silence, occasionally peering down at the dashboard clock. On the M25 nothing passed them. Holt thought it must be a hell of an important game, a league decider or a cup final. He felt no urge to speak, was relieved to be left to his own company. He had had enough talking. Two whole days in London going through the program that he had confirmed for the ambassador, and working over and over his description of the shooting, and each time he had questioned what appeared to be the general acceptance of the Soviet version of the killings he had just been shushed and assured that all was being put into place.

They came to the playing fields. During the drive it had stopped raining, but now it had started again. Percy Martins flung himself out of the car and scampered round to the tailgate to fetch a pair of rubber boots. Holt saw that the back of the car was filled with fishing gear. An outsize rod bag, a cavernous landing net, a solid tackle box. He had to run to catch the man.

It was the farthest soccer pitch.

"Who's playing?" Holt said, when they reached the muddied touchline.

"York chemists against a gang of lawyers from University College, London."

"Is your boy good?"

"Bloody awful."

"Which one is he?"

"The one who can't kick with his left foot and hardly with his right."

"So what the hell are we doing here?"

They were the only spectators. There was no protection from the weather. Holt thought it was the worst game of soccer he had ever watched.

"As I told you, the report on your debrief landed on my desk."

Holt turned into the rain. He had to shout over the wind. "Why are you buying all this bullshit about a criminal robbery?"

"It suits us."

"Who can it suit?"

"Everybody—nearly everybody, anyway."

"Who is everybody?"

"Good question. Look at it, young Holt. There is a shooting in the Soviet Union, a highly embarrassing shooting, and they haven't a clue who is responsible. Best way to calm the matter down is to come up with a plausible story that cannot be disproved, that has the culprit removed and that does not show the Ivans in a particularly poor light. Just a bit of bad luck, wasn't it? Wrong place at the wrong time. They might just as easily have been walking along the pavement and a car had blown a tire and swerved into them. Professionally speaking one has to see it as a successful exercise in damage limitation . . ."

"And everyone's so supine that they accept this convenient lie."

"I'm not everybody."

"Why aren't we saying out loud that this killing was the work of an Arab—that our ambassador and Miss Canning were set up by the Soviets to be murdered?"

"I think you've jumped too far. I believe you are right in thinking the killer was Arab, but not that the Soviets set it up. Highly embarrassing, as I said. In my opinion, this was an act of terrorism in Soviet territory. They can't admit that, can they? Oh Christ Almighty . . ."

One of the players had tried to kick the ball that wallowed

in ankle-deep mud, missed and fell on his back, and left the ball to be slotted into the net.

"That's my son and heir. God, he's pathetic, his mother's boy . . . FCO wouldn't see they've much choice but to go along with Ivan's version."

"So I've been brought to this absurd game to be given a lecture in Anglo-Soviet relations."

"You're being asked to help. Jane Canning was a member of the Service, and we will not take her death lying down."

Holt saw that the player who had given away the goal had been dismissed to the wing. The young man was pencil-thin and pale. He was beginning to feel sympathy for the kid, particularly if his father was a pompous ass called Percy Martins.

"What does that mean in practice—not taking it lying down?"

"What it says. Holt, you were in the Crimea, in the center of the Crimea is Simferopol. In Simferopol is a military academy which takes groups of foreign cadets for periods of up to . . ."

"Where is this getting us?"

"Listen, will you? . . . Among the foreign cadets are always Syrian-sponsored Palestinians. The shooting was at lunchtime; that same Saturday evening a Syrian Air Force transporter put down at Simferopol and then flew on to Damascus . . ."

"How do you know that?"

"*Listen* . . . and that's none of your business. It is quite credible that a Palestinian, at least an Arab, shot the ambassador and Miss Canning and was flown back to the Middle East the same evening. It is even credible that the Soviets knew nothing of the plan."

"Why are you telling me this?"

"We need your help in identifying the man who killed Armitage and a member of our Service, your girl."

"And then?"

"That's none of your business either."

"I'd want him killed."

"So tell me what he looked like, everything."

Desultory cheers, H'ray, H'ray, H'ray; the game was finished. Martins's son tramped off the field. He didn't so much as look at his father. Martins made an attempt to greet him, but the young man kept walking. Holt thought Martins too proud to chase after him. And then it was too late. The two teams disappeared into the pavilion. Martins and young Holt paced the touchline. They were still there after the groundsman had come out to unhook the goal netting and to gather up the flag posts. They were still there when the two buses with the chemists from York and the lawyers from London drove away from the pavilion. Holt poured out every detail from his memory on the man who had held the Kalashnikov assault rifle. The way he moved, height, weight, age, the clothes, the wig, the shape of the eyes, movement, features. Again and again, the crow's foot scar. Still talking when it was too dark for Holt to see Martins's face beside him.

Finally they walked back to the car.

"You never even spoke to your son."

"Watched him play, didn't I? That's what I promised his mother . . . How close would you have to be to him to see the scar?"

"Well, I was ten paces and could see it as clearly as I described it to you. I mean, you wouldn't miss it if you met him. You'll go after him?"

"She was one of ours."

Martins dropped Holt off at Paddington Station, thanked him again and said he'd be in touch in a day or so. Then he crossed London and the Thames and parked his car in the basement at Century House. It was not unusual for him to be returning to his office as the commuters were heading for home. Martins lived in a torpid cul-de-sac in Putney, but his home was the seventh floor of Century. No need for him to ring his wife and tell her that he would be back late. She took it for granted that he would work eleven or twelve hours six days a week and that he would fish on the seventh. He had been 27 years in the Service. He had served in Amman and Cyprus and Tel Aviv. He was a graduate, years before the fighting ripped the city apart, of the American University of Beirut.

The debrief had taken days to reach him. It bore a string of FCO staff's initials and in Century it had come by way of the Soviet Desk. The seventh floor was Middle East. Martins was the Middle East Desk's third in the chain. The head of the Desk was 12 years his junior, his immediate superior was 14 years younger. Martins would climb no higher. Sometimes it rankled, most times in fact. His solace was his work.

On his desk was the debrief and transcripts of messages sent from an Antonov en route to Damascus. These had been intercepted by the Dhekelia listening post in Cyprus and deciphered at the Government Communications HQ in Cheltenham. It was indeed none of young Holt's business that the messages sent from the Antonov within minutes of its leaving Soviet airspace were in the code systems of Syrian Air Force Intelligence and not those of the regular Air Force.

For the next two hours he wrote down in neat longhand everything that Holt had told him. By the time he had completed seven foolscap sheets he believed he could build a picture of a face, a working likeness of a man. He was satisfied that he knew exactly where the crow's foot scar should be placed.

Later, at a time when the train carrying Holt was west of Taunton, Inter City 125 and hammering, Percy Martins took the lift two floors up the 19-story building to a small cubbyhole of a room where a technician had been whiling away the hours making a balsa wood 1:50-scale replica of a vintage Churchill tank. It would be a late night. The technician would work with Martins to make a likeness of the face of an assassin.

The following evening the actual size portrait and the four typed sheets of briefing were carried in a large buff envelope in the nearly empty briefcase of a government messenger en route to Tel Aviv. For the duration of the flight, a little over four hours, the briefcase was attached to the wrist of the messenger by a length of fine steel chain. It would have been impossible for the messenger to eat the airline meal without his chain being noticed so he went without food.

At Tel Aviv the messenger was met by the Service's station officer. A docket was signed. The papers were exchanged. The messenger flew back on the return flight after killing four hours in the transit lounge, and twenty minutes in the restaurant.

Before dawn a light burned in the upper room at the rear of the British embassy on Hayarkon. This upper room had no view of the stretching Mediterranean Sea. The walls of the room were of reinforced concrete, the windows were of strengthened glass. The room was reached by an outer corridor in which had been placed a gate of heavy steel vertical bars. Behind the locked door of the room, the station officer examined the face that had been built for him, and read Martins's brief.

The killer of Sir Sylvester Armitage and of Jane Canning was believed to be Arab, most probably Palestinian. The distinguishing feature of the Arab was a crow's foot scar of approximately one inch in diameter on the upper left cheek. The station officer smiled at what he called Martins's fingerprints all over the brief, his unlovely grammar, but the substance of it was good. Near the bottom of the third page was the text of the message—underlined in red, typical Martins touch—from the Antonov transporter after it had entered Turkish airspace.

"The target is taken."

It was left to the discretion of the station officer as to whether he went for help to the Mossad, Israel's external intelligence-gathering organization, or the Shin Bet, the state's internal countersubversion and counterterrorism apparatus, or to Military Intelligence. Since the trial of Nezar Hindawi and the severing by Britain of diplomatic relations with Syria, cooperation between London and Tel Aviv was unprecedentedly close. He had no doubt that he would get the help Martins requested.

As the low-level sunbeams rose above the squat, dun-colored apartment blocks of Tel Aviv, the station officer dialed the private telephone line of the man whose friendship he valued most in Military Intelligence. He liked the hours they worked. He locked his room behind him, and with the photo-fit in his bag he drove to the Ministry of Defense on Kaplan.

As the crow flies, and nothing larger than a crow can make the flight without plucking up a barrage of ground-to-air missiles, it is 125 miles from Tel Aviv to Damascus. The principal cities of the old enemies are adjacent in the currency of modern warfare. Behind the frontier that divides them, Syria and Israel have massed divisions of armor and mechanized infantry, regiments of artillery, squadrons of interceptor aircraft. The two client states scowl at each other from the cover of curtains of state-of-the-art United States and Soviet equipment. Two great coiled armies awaiting the order to commence the bloodletting, poised to exploit the moment of maximum advantage.

In the waiting time, as the troops idle away the hours in their foxholes and base camps, the tanks are kept armed and fueled, stacks of ammunition lie beside the heavy howitzers, the aircraft are loaded with their missiles and cannon shells and cluster bombs.

They wait, two nations obsessed with the need for one gigantic heave to ultimate victory.

For the Israelis the waiting is harder. They are the smaller nation and they are crippled by the cost of the feud.

For the Syrians the waiting is easier. They have a surrogate force obedient to their discipline. They have the Palestinians of the Salvation Front. The Palestinians from their bases in Lebanon or from the camps around Damascus can be organized to strike at Israel, to harass Israel, to wound Israel. And the Palestinians are expendable.

It was a dry, dust-laden morning. It was a morning when the flies with persistence crawled at the eyes and into the nostrils of the men who paraded in the dirt yard of the Yarmuk camp. The sun climbed and shortened the shadows, and the stink of the shallow latrine pits lay across the camp.

The recruits had been standing on parade in the growing heat for a little more than an hour because the guests from Damascus were late and there was no explanation for the delay, and no one dared to stand the men down. They had come from the refugee centers in West Beirut, from Sidon and Tyre, and from camps in Jordan and South Yemen. They were aged between 17 and 19. They had joined the Popular Front for the Liberation of Palestine, because they believed that that organization would give them the greatest chance to hurt the Zionist state. Some wore uniforms and boots that were Syrian Army surplus, some wore jeans and T-shirts and pullovers. Some had already shaved their heads, some wore their hair to their shoulders. All held their unloaded rifles as if it were second nature to them. They were children suckled on conflict.

The commander was at the gate, fretting with his watch.

Abu Hamid stood in front of the squad of eighty recruits. His uniform fitted him well. He wore the tunic and top, camouflaged in pink and green and yellow, of a Syrian commando. He carried, loosely over the crook of his arm, a Kalashnikov assault rifle. Occasionally he barked an order at the recruits, ordered them to straighten up. He felt a new degree of authority. No one at the camp other than the commander knew his part in what had happened in Yalta, but there were other signs of the favor that had fallen into the path of Abu Hamid. Two days later than the others who had flown back from the Soviet Union, Abu Hamid had reached Yarmuk and when he had rejoined his colleagues he had been driven to the camp in a Mercedes-Benz car by a chauffeur who wore air force uniform. Three times since then he had been off camp, and back late in the evening with the smell of imported whiskey on his breath, and his girl had been allowed to the camp, and he had been promoted, which was why he now stood in front of the recruits.

The cars, when they arrived, billowed a dust storm. Abu Hamid yelled for his men to stand still, he aped the instructors at Simferopol. He saw the commander fawning a greeting to an officer who wore the insignia of a brigadier general.

The breath came in a sharp gasp from Abu Hamid's throat. He thought that every recruit behind him gawped at the officer who now climbed from the official car that had followed that of the brigadier general into the camp. The officer strode forward. He carried his cap in his left hand.

The officer's walk was normal. His torso was ordinary. He had no fingers on his right hand, a stump at the knuckle. It was his head that captured attention. There was nothing sharp in the definition of his features. The skin across his cheeks and his nose and his upper lip and his chin seemed fragile and tightly drawn, the opaque skin of a butterfly's or a moth's wings. The skin had a lifeless quality, dead skin that had somehow been reprocessed for further use, and stretched over the bones of the face and the muscles by a human hand and not by nature. The nose of the officer seemed a squashed bauble, and his mouth was a parched slit. The earlobes were gone. The eyebrows were gone. What hair there was seemed to have been planted behind a line drawn vertically from the scalp's crown to the deformed ears. The hair was bleached pale.

A soft, small voice. A voice that he recognized. A voice with the lilt of a persuasive song.

"Good morning to you, Hamid."

He swallowed hard. "Good morning, Major Said Hazan."

He stared blatantly into the broken face. He saw the cracked, amused smile that rose in the expanse of skin. He saw the medal ribbons on the chest of the uniform tunic.

Major Said Hazan waved Abu Hamid forward. The commander was ignored as the major introduced Abu Hamid to the brigadier general. The ranking officer knew what Abu Hamid had achieved, it was there in his eyes for Abu Hamid to see, a shared secret.

Abu Hamid escorted the brigadier general and Major Said Hazan along the four rows of recruits. Only one cloud in Abu Hamid's mind that morning. Of course, he had expected that military security would check all the weapons issued to the recruits to ascertain that no live rounds would be carried on parade. He had not expected that his own AK-47 would be scrutinized, that he would have to clear the breach and show that his magazine was empty. One small cloud . . .

After the inspection the brigadier general called for the recruits to come close to him.

". . . In today's world no man can be neutral. A man is either with the oppressed or he is with the oppressors. We have to fight to our last breath. It is better to die with honor than to live with humiliation . . ."

When he was cheered, when the fists of the recruits were aloft, the brigadier general smiled his satisfaction. Abu Hamid clapped his hands, waved three of the recruits toward the administration building.

His remaining recruits formed a circle, facing inward. A photographer edged forward, stretching on tiptoe to see into the circle. A European photographer. Abu Hamid saw the brigadier general gesture to the photographer to push harder. A dozen live chickens were brought to the circle, thrust into the ring. Abu Hamid shouted, "Death to all enemies of the Palestine Revolution."

The circle closed. The chickens were caught, torn apart, wing from breast, leg from body, head from neck. Hands groping into a bedlam of movement. The raw meat of the chickens, the warm flesh of the chickens was eaten, the blood drunk. Young faces frothing pink meat, spewing red blood.

It was a tradition of the Popular Front, designed as the first measure in the breaking down of the human inhibition against killing. For the first ritual a live chicken sufficed to play the part of an enemy of the revolution.

The photographer was on assignment from a newsmagazine in the German Democratic Republic. He took a roll of film on each of two cameras. Among his images was the man who wore a *kaffiyeh* headdress across his face, and who chewed at a chicken wing.

The brigadier general congratulated Abu Hamid on the dedication of his recruits, and Major Said Hazan clasped his shoulder in farewell. Abu Hamid was bathed in pleasure.

The Prime Minister's cars swept into Downing Street.

There were a few older men and women on the head of government's staff who could remember when a prime minister traveled with only a single detective and the chauffeur for company.

But over the wreckage of a seaside hotel from which a Cabinet had been pulled by firemen or dragged by police minders, a spokesman of Irish liberation had declaimed, "You have to be lucky every time, we have to be lucky once."

The Prime Minister detested the paraphernalia of the bodyguards, and the closed-circuit cameras, and the alarm systems in Downing Street.

The Director General, who waited in the outer office, knew well the Prime Minister's impatience with security.

He saw the Prime Minister, hemmed in by Branch men, in the brief moment between the car and the doorway as he gazed down from the window above the street. The flash of the face that was reddened from the sunshine of the Asian tour and the jetlag. The Director General had the automatic right of access. He reported directly to the Prime Minister.

"It was a pretty dreadful funeral," the Prime Minister said, and shrugged off an overcoat. "Lady Armitage was first class, could have been welcoming us to a cocktail party, but there was a granddaughter there who cried her eyes out, noisily, rather spoiled things. What a thing to get back to, fourteen hours in the air and straight to church . . ."

The Director General knew the form. He allowed the talking to go on. Neither of the previous prime ministers he had served had exactly rushed to allow him to throw into the fray whatever hand grenade he was waiting to communicate.

". . . Do you know the Soviet ambassador read the second lesson, and read it pretty well. I thought that was a very spirited gesture . . ."

"He was badly overdue a spirited gesture, Prime Minister," the Director General murmured.

"I don't follow you."

"The deaths of Sylvester Armitage and Miss Canning are a considerable embarrassment to the Soviets. The killings were an act of political terrorism," the Director General said flatly.

"My brief from FCO said quite clearly that our diplomats were shot down by a common criminal."

"Which is regrettably untrue."

"Meaning what?"

"Meaning that the Soviet Union lied. Prime Minister, we are still looking for the last piece of evidence, but our belief is that the assassinations were the work of a Palestinian terrorist who was on a course in a military academy in the Crimea. We believe he flew out of the Soviet Union on the same day as the killings."

"Where does he lead us?"

The Director General said heavily, "The road goes directly to Damascus."

"Where he is beyond our reach."

The Director General produced a small leather notebook from his inside pocket. " 'They must never be beyond our reach,' Prime Minister. May I quote you your words? I keep this with me always. You said two years ago, when speaking of the threat of terrorism, 'We need action, so that the terrorist knows he has no safe haven, no escape.' Your very words, Prime Minister. As I remember, you were heavily applauded."

"What do you have?"

"A face; we hope soon to have a name."

The Prime Minister's head was shaking, the eyes ranged anywhere in the room but back to the Director General's face. "We cannot just storm into Damascus, of all places."

"Miss Canning was a member of my team. I have never taken anything you have said, Prime Minister, to be empty rhetoric."

"He'll be beyond reach," the Prime Minister said.

"He'll have to hide well."

"There is something I have to know."

"Yes, Prime Minister?"

"Were the deaths of the ambassador and your Miss Canning condoned by the government of the Soviet Union?"

"We think that they knew nothing of it—may not know it now. Hence the embarrassment, hence the deception."

"I find it beyond belief that Syria, a client state, for God's sake, would instigate a terrorist outrage inside the Soviet Union."

"They may be a client state, Prime Minister, but not subservient. Their missile systems, for instance, won't allow Soviet personnel near Soviet hardware. Most certainly they do not take orders. They had a target—a motive too if you accept their twisted logic—and they would have believed with some justification that they could get away with it."

"I repeat myself . . . We cannot just storm into Damascus."

"And I repeat myself . . . We need action, so that the terrorist knows he has no safe haven . . . I will keep you fully informed."

The flies surged in the room, careless of the swatting irritation of the commander.

He gestured that Abu Hamid should sit. He brought him a can of Pepsi from the fridge. The sounds of the camp drifted through the windows.

"What do you want of me?"

"Major Said Hazan," Abu Hamid said.

"You have pleased him."

"His face."

"What of his face?"

"What happened to his face, his hands?"

"You are not a child to be frightened, Hamid. You are a fighter."

"Tell me what happened."

"He was a pilot, MiG-21. In combat over the Golan Heights in 1973 he was shot down, hit by a Sidewinder air-to-air missile fired from an F-4 Phantom. There was fire in the cockpit. He had to level out before he could eject. He is not a man to panic, he waited. He would not know the meaning of panic. When it was safe to eject, then he did so. His parachute brought him down behind his own lines. His face was rebuilt in Leningrad. Perhaps in the hospitals there they are not experienced in such injuries."

Abu Hamid drained the Pepsi. "I just wanted to know."

The commander leaned forward, his face close to Abu Hamid's. "You should understand, Hamid, that a man, with his face and his hands on fire, who does not panic, does not eject until the right time, that man is to be treated with caution."

"What are you telling me?" Abu Hamid's finger flicked at the scar hole on his cheek.

"That Major Said Hazan works now for Air Force Intelligence, that he has great influence . . ."

"I have performed a service for him. I am his friend."

"Be careful, Hamid."

"He told me today that I would be rewarded for what I did. He himself signed the chit for my girl to come to the camp. On his orders cars have been sent for me, bills have been paid."

"Then you are indeed his friend," the commander said softly.

He was a clever young man, with a bachelor's degree in physics from the Hebrew University of Jerusalem. In the reserve of the Israeli Defense Forces he held the rank of sergeant, in civilian life he was a research scientist for a company specializing in the manufacture of military electro-optics. He was said to have the most complete knowledge among all the reservists of the labyrinthine computer files held by Military Intelligence on Palestinian personnel.

The computer failed to throw up any reference to the crow's foot scar. The failure told the sergeant that the man of the photofit likeness had not been in IDF custody since the scar was acquired. A disappointing start . . . He was left with the computer and with thousands of IDF and Mil Int photographs. There were few concrete items in the information he had that would help him to reject material unlooked at. A flight to Syria told him that his subject would not be a member of the Palestine Liberation Organization's Force 17. A man of Force 17 would never fly via Damascus. But the men had flaking allegiance. A fighter who was now in the Popular Front, or the Domestic Front or the Struggle Front, could have been in Force 17 a few years before . . . It would be a long slog with the green screen, and the photograph bank.

The sergeant reckoned from the age of the subject, and from the fact that he had been taken to Simferopol for a platoon leader's course, that it was possible he had been in Beirut when the Palestinians evacuated in the summer of 1982. There were 1,787 photographs available from the days when the Palestinians had trooped down to the docks and boarded the boats that would sail them to exile. The photos were blown up from American newsreel coverage that had been purchased unedited by the Israeli Broadcasting Corporation. The sergeant put up every print onto a screen for magnification. Each photograph was studied meticulously.

For five days the photographs flashed in front of him in his room, the blinds drawn over the windows, a cone of light from the projector to the screen.

He had a dogged persistence.

After 1,411 failures his squeal of triumph was heard in the adjacent rooms and corridors. He had found a thin young man riding on the top of the cab of an open lorry, a short-haired young man with a thinly grown moustache. A young man who had a rifle aloft in one hand, and whose secondhand was raised in the V-for-victory salute. He saw the wound on the upper left cheek. Standing close to the screen, a magnifying glass in his hand, he found the lines of what the report called the crow's foot . . . Back to the computer. The number of the photograph fed in. The search for cross-reference information. Long moments of stillness and then the rush began.

Popular Front for the Liberation of Palestine.

Of the six men shown in the photograph, two had subsequently been identified.

One man in the photograph named after his capture in the security zone . . . but later released when 1,190 Palestinians and Lebanese Shi'ites were freed in exchange for three IDF soldiers. The sergeant cursed.

The second man who had subsequently been named . . . captured, a dinghy chased to the shore by a patrol boat. A night gun battle on the beach close to Nahariya, lit by helicopter flares. Four infiltrators dead, one captured. Link with Popular Front.

Late in the night, while the prison slept, two army interrogators drove into the floodlit courtyard of the Ramla prison. A convicted prisoner was roused from his cot, taken to a room where no prison warder was permitted to be present.

The prisoner was shown the photograph. He knew the man. He remembered his name.

Four days later an East German newsmagazine appeared. The eighteenth page of the magazine showed a scrum of Palestinian recruits struggling for the privilege of ripping a chicken to pieces. One man in the photograph wore a *kaffiyeh* scarf around his throat, where it had slipped when he bit into the feathered wing of the chicken.

The face was in tight focus.

6

While his friend poured the coffee, the station officer peered down at the photograph.

His friend was Zvi Dan. The photograph from the magazine page had been enlarged and the scar was clear to the naked eye.

"You've done me damn well. A name for Chummy and a date and a place."

"But we have nothing much else with which to link him apart from the Beirut picture. Anything further can only be supposition."

Zvi Dan's career as an infantry officer had been cut short 15 years before when an exploding artillery shell on the Golan Heights had neatly severed his left leg immediately below the knee, and only two days before the cease-fire had wound up the battles of Yom Kippur. He had faced the prospect of civilian life or of finding military work that could be conducted away from the operational area. He had made major, Military Intelligence. He specialized in the study of Palestinian groups who were known to have firm links abroad, and whose operations against Israel were often far from his country's frontiers.

"I think that in London they are pretty concerned with this one. I think they'll take all the supposition they can get."

"Then we should begin to play the jigsaw."

Zvi Dan worked from an office in the Ministry of Defense.

His quarters were apart from the main complex of buildings that stretched the length of Kaplan. His base was surrounded by a coiled fence of barbed wire and with additional armed guards on the gate. He had access to Mossad files and to Shin Bet interrogations of captured Palestinians. He read voraciously. In the small circle where his name was known he was credited with supplying the information that had led to the arrest of a Jordanian who intended to carry on board a Swiss airliner two hand grenades for a hijacking attempt on the Cyprus-Jordan leg of the flight. He had supplied the lead that enabled the Belgian police to raid a video arcade in a small town in the north of the country and arrest two Palestinians and a Belgian couple, and uncover 40 pounds of plastic explosive. His warnings had led to the interception at sea of two yachts being used by Palestinian infiltrators, the *Casselardit* and the *Ganda*. If he regarded these as little victories, Major Zvi Dan could—and did—count as catastrophic defeats the assault on the synagogue in Istanbul, 22 Turkish Jews killed; the slaughter at Rome's Fiumicino airport, 86 killed and wounded; the massacre at Vienna's Schwechtat airport, 49 killed and wounded.

The station officer said, "I'll put my pieces on the board. The British ambassador in Moscow insults a Syrian diplomat, practically with a loud hailer, the entire diplomatic community looking on, right in the Syrian's master's sitting room. Claims of Syrian innocence in the El Al bomb laughed to scorn in public. Total humiliation of Syrians. Two: our man in Moscow is assassinated, oblique stroke mugged, in the Crimea, close to a military school where Palestinians are trained. Three: same evening a Syrian Air Force plane lands at the airport next door to the school and flies on to Damascus, en route sending a message saying in effect Mission Achieved. Four: our eyewitness at the shooting gets a clear view of Chummy and from that we follow through to the evacuation from Beirut in '82 and a member of the PFLP contingent. The last piece I can put on the board is what I'll call the Dresden photograph, that puts Chummy at a camp outside Damascus possibly seven, eight days ago. Those are my pieces."

"You want this Abu Hamid?"

"We want him, even if we have to go to Damascus to get him."

Zvi Dan laughed, a quiet croak in his throat, and the laugh brought on the hacking cough of the persistent smoker.

"Damascus would be easy. Damascus pretends it is an international city. There are businessmen traveling to Damascus, and there are academics, and there are archaeologists. It is a city of millions of people. In a city you can come shoulder to shoulder with a man. You can use the knife or the silenced pistol or the explosive under the car he drives. If it were Damascus then I would already offer you my felicitations, even my congratulations . . . The scar is only an inch across so you have to be close to identify the man you want."

"The girl who was killed, she was one of ours," the station officer said quietly. "Don't worry about getting close. We'll walk onto the bridge of his nose if we have to. That's the sense of the messages I am being sent from London."

The coughing was stifled. Zvi Dan beat his own chest. There was the rustle of the packet, the flash of the lighter, the curl of the smoke. The end of the nicotined finger stubbed at the Dresden photograph.

"Look at them. Other than the man you want they are all raw recruits. They are children who have joined the Popular Front and here they are participating in the first ceremony of induction. There will have been a parade, and there will have been a speech by a big man from the government. It is what always happens. . . . They will have been in Damascus for a few days only. They will be moved on. They will go to a field training camp where they will be taught, not well, the art of small-unit operations. Your man, the man you want, the older man among them, he will travel with the children as their instructor. Possibly it is a reward for what he achieved in Yalta. They will go to a training camp with their instructor for perhaps half a year."

"Where would the camp be?"

"Where it is impossible for you to be close, shoulder to

shoulder." For a moment the face of Zvi Dan was lost in a haze of smoke. "In the Bekaa Valley."

"Oh, that's grand," said the station officer. "The 19 bus goes right through the Bekaa Valley."

The valley is a fault, it is a legacy of rock strata turbulence of many millennia ago.

The valley floor is some 45 miles in length, and never more than ten miles in width. It is a slash between the mountains that dominate the Mediterranean city of Beirut, and the mountains that overlook the hinterland city of Damascus. It is bordered in the north by the ancient Roman and Phoenician city of Baalbek, and in the south by the dammed Lake Qaraaoun.

The sides of the valley, deep cut with winter water gullies, are bare and rock strewn, good only for goats and hardy sheep. The sides cannot be cultivated. But the valley floor has the richest crop-growing fields in all Lebanon. The Litani River, rising close to Baalbek, bisects the valley running south to Lake Qaraaoun. The valley floor is a trellis of irrigation canals, not modern, not efficient, but able to offer life blood to the fields. The best vines of Lebanon, the best fruit, the best vegetables, all come from the Bekaa, and the best hashish.

The history of the Bekaa is one of murder, conspiracy, feuding and smuggling. The people of the region whether they be Christian or Druze or Shi'ite Muslim, have a reputation for lawlessness and independence. Government authority has always taken second place in the minds of the feudal landlords and the peasant villagers.

Times, of course, have not stood still in the Bekaa. The villagers are better armed, each community now possesses RPG-7 grenade launchers, heavy DShKM machine guns, enough Kalashnikovs to dish them out to the kids.

The villagers are well off by the standards of torn, divided Lebanon, because when all else fails the hashish market bails them out. The trade is across the rifts of politics and religion. Druze sells to Shi'ite who sells to Christian who sells to Syrian.

The Bekaa now is a valley of pass papers and checkpoints. Shi'ite checkpoints on the approaches to their villages. Druze checkpoints, Syrian Army checkpoints on the main road from Damascus to Beirut, and more on the side roads that lead to their barracks, Palestinian checkpoints on the approaches to their training camps.

They had reached the high spot. Behind them were the customs buildings and the missile site. Ahead of them the ground, dun and gray, shelved away into the valley.

The recruits were in two military lorries, while Abu Hamid sat in the jeep driven by Fawzi, his liaison officer. Fawzi drove with enthusiasm, exhilarated in his role as middleman between the Popular Front training camp and the officers of Air Force Intelligence. Abu Hamid had thought that any man would be sick in his gut at such a job, but all the man cared for, all that he talked about on the climb to the mountain pass and the descent beyond, was the newfound opportunity for trade. "Trade" he called it. Televisions and videocassette players and electric refrigerators would come to the Bekaa from Beirut, freshly grown hashish would come from the valley, and Fawzi could take back to the old *suq* in Damascus as much as would cram into the covered back of his jeep. To Abu Hamid, the man was disgusting, the man was a criminal. He wondered how it was that Major Said Hazan would permit such a man to play a part in the Palestinian revolution.

But he had hardly listened to Fawzi. Yes, he had the babble from the man, from his thick spittle-lined lips, but after a while he had paid him no attention, thought only of Margarethe.

Abu Hamid did not know how long it would be until he next saw Margarethe. He had not been told. He fancied that if he put his hand under the vest below his tunic, and rubbed his hand hard against the skin, and that if he then put his hand against his nose, then he would smell the sweet scent of his Margarethe. With other women shyness made him brutal. It was so the first time with Margarethe, but she had slapped his face, right cheek and then left cheek . . . then come to him, rolled him onto his back, and loved him. He did not know where a woman had learned to love with such wild beauty. From that first time Margarethe made him love her with all the lights switched on; each time she stripped him, each time she straddled him. He could not comprehend why Margarethe Schultz worshiped the body of Abu Hamid, who did not have the money for shoes. He did not understand her dedication to the cause of a Palestinian homeland, did not understand the Red Army Faction of which she claimed to be a member. He had written to her on the last day of each month that he had been in Simferopol. And when she was naked she was beautiful to him . . .

What was wonderful was that she had waited for him, waited for six months for his return.

They were coming down into the valley.

He could hear the protests of the brakes of the lorries behind him.

"It is the hashish that gets the best price. I buy it here, I pay the major forty percent of what I have paid. I double the cost of my outgoings and that is the price I will get in Damascus. I don't know what charge is made by the man who sells it on from Damascus. When it gets to Europe the price is fantastic. It amazes me that people in Europe will pay . . ."

They passed through two checkpoints manned by Syrian commandos. They crossed the floor of the valley. The road took them alongside a small village, and there were women out in the fields hoeing the damp ground between the first early summer wheat crop. They bumped off the road and followed a stone track for four or five miles. Much for Abu Hamid to see. There were old bomb craters still with the scorched blackness that years of rain had not discolored. There was a tank regiment, hull down, in defensive position. There was a network of slit trenches, newly dug and lined with the brightness of corrugated iron. There were areas that were marked by a single strand of barbed wire and the skull and crossbones sign designating minefields. They crossed two army engineers' bridges over irrigation ducts, and then traversed a rolling plank bridge over the main flow of the Litani River. They skirted a formation of camouflage-painted pillboxes. They were close to the far wall of the Bekaa Valley.

He saw the small tent camp ahead. A dozen tents. The camp nestled under the rising ground beyond. He winced. There was nowhere else that they could be heading.

"Is that the camp?" The disgust was rich in Abu Hamid's voice.

"You want orange groves and villas? You should go and fight in the Zionist state. You will find all the orange groves and all the villas that you could wish for there."

When darkness had fallen over the Yarmuk camp, when the perimeter floodlights were reduced to small cones of light, a car drove through the gates and to the administration building. A runner was sent from the administration building to the hut where the commander had his quarters. The commander was seen by the runner to talk briefly to the men in the car, and then to get into the backseat. Two hours later the commander was dead, shot once in the head, and he was buried in a shallow grave beside the Quneitra road, beyond the airport, beyond the headquarters of Air Force Intelligence. When questioned by senior officials of the Popular Front investigating the commander's disappearance, the runner would be able to say in truth that the darkness prevented him from seeing the men inside the car, that they did not identify themselves.

For Major Said Hazan, the commander had outlived his usefulness. And he was a dangerous witness to a conspiracy, and he knew the author of that conspiracy. Of Abu Hamid, Major Said Hazan had no doubt.

Martins had come to the nineteenth floor.

He sat in an armchair with his papers on his lap. He sat uncomfortably upright. It was a strange habit of the Director General that he conducted his meetings from soft seating, never used the polished table and the straight chairs that were at the far end of the room. On the rare occasions that he was summoned to the Director General's office, Percy Martins was never at ease. The Director General seemed not to notice. Percy Martins read rapidly through the brief received from Graham Tork, station officer in Tel Aviv.

"So, it is his conclusion that Abu Hamid has by now either traveled to the Bekaa, or is about to."

"Which makes it awkward for us."

"In Tork's opinion—rather an eccentric one, in my view—Damascus would be tolerably straightforward, the Bekaa quite impossible."

"The Service doesn't believe in 'impossible,' Percy."

Martins sucked at his teeth. "With respect, sir, the Bekaa is virtually an armed camp. It is home for the Syrian Army, at least one division of armor, regiments of artillery, units of commando forces. It's also home for a violently anti-Western Shi'ite Muslim population in the villages. And for the Hezbollah Party of God fanatics, also for the units of Islamic Jihad who, although small, are strong enough to blast the Americans out of Beirut. And for half a dozen or more extreme Palestinian groupings . . ."

The Director General played with his pipe. "You're not addressing schoolchildren and you're missing the point, Percy. You're providing me only with problems, but let me quote Sir Winston Churchill to you: 'Grass never grows under a gallows tree.' Hit the terrorist in his safe haven and you destroy not only him, but you do a greater damage to the morale of his comrades. Have we the location of this training camp?"

"Not yet, sir. Tork reckons his locals should be able to give it to him within a couple of weeks."

"We need that location, we need a target area."

"Are you considering requesting the Israelis to mount an air strike?"

"Waste of time." The Director General waved his hand dismissively. He had that habit. He was only two years older than Martins. The habit had the effect of making the number three on the Middle East Desk seem half-witted. "An air strike tells the Syrians nothing. I want the man who tasked this Abu Hamid for his killing mission to know that we'll go to the ends of the earth to exact a specific revenge."

Martins read the familiar signs. The more he pointed out the objections the more annoyance he would cause. On the other hand, the less he objected the less cover he gave himself in the event of a foul-up.

"You'd actually consider sending a team into the Bekaa?" Martins sometimes wondered whether the Service activities were planned on a Christmas-present pencil-sharpener globe. "For all the reasons I have suggested, that Tork has set out, that is quite impossible . . ."

"Perhaps you didn't hear me the first time. That's not a word I care for. Get yourself down to Hereford, Percy."

Without invitation, Percy Martins heaved himself up from the low armchair. He strode round the room. Speak now, or forever hold thy peace. He heard his own voice, raised.

"So I go and talk to the Ministry and then to Special Air Service, and what's the first thing they'll say? They'll say the scar on Abu Hamid's face is an inch across, they'll say how close do they have to get to identify a man with a one-inch scar on his face?"

"We've a witness, and I daresay we've got a pair of binoculars."

Martins hesitated. "Our witness is a diplomat, not a soldier, sir."

"In the words of your report when you met this young man: 'I'd want him killed'—it seems to me that he would be prepared to learn to be a soldier. A further point. The witness not only saw the scar, the witness saw Abu Hamid, saw his stance, how he moved, saw him run."

"To take a young man, untrained, into the Bekaa, on a covert operation . . . Sir, are you quite serious?"

"When we had Leila Khaled, Popular Front hijacker, in Ealing Police Station I argued against swapping her for our airline passengers held hostage in Amman—I was overruled. When it was planned to fly a gang of Provisional IRA death merchants by Royal Air Force plane to London for a cozy chat with government, I argued against it—I was overruled. I was overruled then because I didn't have enough authority. Now I do, and the masters are going to learn how long and how ruthless our arm can be, and quite frankly, I hope they shit themselves in the knowledge."

Martins said, "I'll go and talk to Hereford."

"You'll do more than that. You'll get our witness down to Albury, dust the place out, get him up to the mark. No misunderstandings, Percy, this is going to happen."

They hadn't told her how long she had to make the rooms ready, nor how many people would be coming. She did not know whether they would be there in a day or a week.

She had her old vacuum cleaner, and a bucket of warm water with Jeyes fluid and a mop, and three ragged dusters, and a window cleaner aerosol spray. She had four sets of sheets ranged out in the frame in front of the Aga stove in the kitchen. It would be seven months since the house in the woods outside the Surrey village of Albury had been used. She had been afraid that if the house were not used then it would be sold off and she and George would be moved on.

There was no time for George's lunch that day. She had ordered him to fill each and every one of the coal hobs, light each and every fire on the ground floor, to split more logs, to find the fault in the hot water boiler, to go into Guildford with her shopping list, and to keep his brute of a dog off the floors she had washed.

Agnes Ferguson had seen it all. What a book she could have written. She had been housekeeper for the Service safe house at Albury for nineteen years. They had given it into her care in lieu of a widow's pension. She had kept the safe house for Eastern bloc defectors, for agents returning from imprisonment abroad while they were debriefed, for the preparation of men going into covert action overseas. It had been a long and anxious winter, and George not much company. The telephone call had seemed to breathe new life, new hope, into her that her future was assured.

"It's preposterous, no other word for it."

"It has the sanction of the Director General," Martins said grimly.

"It makes no difference whose sanction it has. It just isn't on," the brigadier said.

"Too dangerous, is that it?"

"It's not our way to duck a challenge, but nor is it our way to volunteer ourselves for a mission that has no chance of success. Understand me, no chance."

In the mist outside the brick bungalow, Percy Martins's car was parked beside the broad base of the clock tower. When he had locked the door he had noted the names inscribed on the stone plaque under the clock face, the fatal casualties among the men of the 22nd Regiment, Special Air Service. Had he not been under orders he would most probably have agreed with the brigadier.

"No chance of success, I'll report that back."

"Don't play clever games with me," the brigadier said. A hard man, piercing gray-blue eyes. "We have no experience of the Bekaa Valley. No man in the SAS has ever set foot in the Bekaa Valley. It is, and always has been, outside our theater of operation. We are not talking about the Radfan mountain ops of the sixties, nor about Oman in the seventies. For both of those we had firsthand experience to draw upon, and we had a wilderness area to work through. In the Bekaa we have no experience and we have no wilderness. It would take us months of reconnaissance and preparation before we could walk in there with any reasonable prospect of survival."

"I'll convey your message."

"They keep their hostages in the Bekaa. The reason they are there is that their captors believe it the most secure area in Lebanon. For strangers, the Bekaa is a dangerous, closed valley. The stranger won't last long enough to pick his nose.

To be frank, and it gives me no satisfaction to say so, we wouldn't stand a prayer."

"I'll report that you cannot be of help."

"But I can be of help," the brigadier said. "I can tell you who will get you into the Bekaa, who might quite possibly even get you out."

Percy Martins felt the surge of excitement. A name was given. He wrote the name in his notebook, and then he asked for permission to use a secure telephone.

The last light of the afternoon.

The sun was an orange orb away to his left and sliding.

It was a good time for him because the ground ahead was cooling, and the haze that had distorted his vision was gone, and his barrel was no longer warm.

His right eye, peering into the scope, ached. That pain behind his eye stabbed at him. The pain was nothing new to him, but it was more frequent and more acute, and that worried him.

The target was 600 meters away. Of course he had not measured the ground. In two days and one night he had not moved in his blind except to raise his hips the few inches that enabled him to urinate into a plastic bag. He was good at measuring distance. Without his expertise at gauging a distance ahead of him then all his work would be useless. The chart in his mind told him the rate of the drop in flight of a fired bullet. He knew the figures by heart. The difference in a drop between 500 meters and 600 meters was 1.53 meters. The difference in a drop between 500 meters and 600 meters was the height of a grown man. But he knew the distance to his target, his experience had made the calculation, and he had adjusted his scope sight for that distance. Beyond the target, away to the target's right, was a small fire that had been lit by a shepherd. He had watched the shepherd all day, hoping that the shepherd would keep his flock close to the stream and far from the rock slope on which he had made his blind. He was grateful to the shepherd for lighting the fire. The fire smoked right to left. The movement of the smoke enabled him to gauge the wind speed that would deflect his bullet. Another graph. His estimate of the wind speed was 5 miles per hour. His estimate of the deflection was 11 inches, for a target that was 600 meters away.

It amused him, the way that sometimes the figures in his head were metric, and sometimes they were yards and feet and inches, and sometimes the thoughts in his mind were Hebrew, and sometimes they were English. He reckoned that he was close now to the optimum moment, and so the throb of the pain behind his right eye was relegated in importance. He was old for work as a sniper. He was 48 years old, and the balance was delicately poised between his expertise at gauging the distance to the target and the wind speed, against the ache of a tired eye. On a range he could shoot well inside a melon-sized group at 600 meters. A man's head was wider than a melon. That he was not on a range made little difference to him. If he had been young, perhaps he would have been knotted in tension and he would have cramp in his leg muscles. He was not young, he was quite relaxed, and he had learned long ago to rotate his toes in his boots to beat the cramp. He was not looking for a head shot. His scope showed him, where the hairlines crossed, the upper arm of the target who was in profile to him. He waited for the target to turn, to face him, he waited for the hairlines to cross on the upper torso of the target.

Steady hands on the rifle. No shake in the elbow that supported the rifle. The target faced him, was gesturing. There was no caution from the target. The target had no need for caution. The target was standing on open ground that was four clear miles from the edge of the security zone, four clear miles beyond the stop point of Israeli patrols. He knew that the target, the man with the flowing beard and the old camouflage battledress, was a commander of a unit of the Hezbollah. He knew no more about him. He did not know why the man had been targeted. That concerned him not at all. He received his orders, he carried them out. He was only thankful that he still belonged, was still wanted, as a regular.

His finger slid slowly from against the trigger guard to

curl around the curve of the trigger. The hairlines were full on the chest of the target, they wavered around the flash of a small gold pendant. He knew the men of the Hezbollah talked at length of the glory of martyrdom. There was a wry, cold smile on his dirt-smeared face.

Crane fired.

The crack of a bullet. The collapse of a man. The scream of the crows taking flight. The bleat of stampeding sheep. The yelling of the men who had been with the target. . . . And the great silence.

The sun slipped. The dusk gathered. A gray blanket sliding over the valleys and watercourses and rock outcrops and *jebels* of south Lebanon. Shadows merging, features losing substance.

There would be no search, that was the advantage of firing in the late afternoon. There could be no search in darkness, and where to search? None of the men who had stood with the commander of a unit of the Hezbollah could have pointed out the source of the single shot.

In the black night, canopied by stars, Crane walked with his rifle and his backpack homeward toward the security zone. Each time he fired, each time he scored, he believed that he prolonged his life as a regular, he put off the day when life would mean little more than a seat at a pavement café on Dizengoff. In the darkness his strained right eye no longer throbbed, the stabbing pain was gone.

At the edge of the security zone an armored personnel carrier waited for him. From a distance he shouted a password, and when the response was yelled back at him, he came forward.

The crew of the carrier were all youngsters, all conscripts. They stared in awe as Crane slept in the back of the lurching, pitching vehicle. Each one of the conscripts knew his name, his reputation. They saw the worn filthy boots, and the torn trousers, and the muddied camouflage tunic, and the smeared face, and the woolen cap into which had been inserted sprigs of thorn bush. He was a legend to them.

At the camp, on high ground outside the town of Kiryat Shmona, two miles inside the border of the state of Israel,

Crane jumped easily from the tailboard of the carrier. No backward glance, no thanks, no small talk.

He was told that a helicopter was standing by to take him to Tel Aviv.

"You've done well."

"I'll confess, sir, I had doubts at first. I'm losing them."

"That's what I like to hear, Percy. I am tired of the rubbishing of the Service by every newspaper in London. I'm looking for a result we can be proud of." The Director General shrugged into his overcoat. His briefcase was on the desk, filled with the evening's reading. His bodyguard waited by the door.

"I'd like to be in charge, sir." Martins stuck his jaw forward.

"You'd *what*?"

"I'd like to run this show, sir—here and in Tel Aviv."

He saw the Director General pause, take stock, then jerk the coat into place.

"I was thinking of Fenner."

"Hasn't my experience, sir. I'd give it my best shot, sir. You could depend on me."

"Bit old, aren't you, for running in the field?"

"It's my show, sir, and I want it, I want it badly."

The Director General wrapped his scarf across his throat. He pulled on his gloves.

"What would I tell Fenner?"

"That life doesn't end at fifty, sir."

The Director General laughed. "Bloody good. . . . It's yours, Percy. Get it in place."

Young Holt had been all day on the moor.

He came down the long straight road toward the village. All the time he was coming down the hill he could see the front garden and the front door of the house that doubled as his parents' home and his father's surgery. There was a car parked outside by the front gate. It had been there for as long as he could see the house.

He had caught every shower of the day, and the winds from the west had spurred him along. He had seen deer and he had seen a dog fox, and he fancied that he might have found the holt of an otter. And he had decided that he would return to London, end his indefinite compassionate leave. The decision made the wet and the cold worthwhile. Impossible to have made the decision at home, under his mother's watching eye.

He was coming fast down the hill, looking for a bath, looking for a mug of hot sugared tea. He could see her face, he could feel her arms round his neck, he could hear her voice. In the rain on the moor he had cried to her, in the wind he had shouted to her.

He saw the front door open. He saw his father come out, and look up the road and discover him and wave to him.

The front garden was a picture. Daffodils and crocuses, and the leaves sprouting on the shrub bushes, and the path cleanly swept. He reached the gate. He saw his father's wheelbarrow piled with winter debris and the fork and the shears and the broom leaning against the wheelbarrow, as if the work had been disturbed.

"Been waiting ages for you, Holt. There's a chap here who's driven down from London to collect you. A Mr. Martins. Percy Martins, I think he said."

It was as if ropes tightened on his wrists.

He saw her face, felt her body, heard her voice.

"Don't be childish, Holt."

"Decent-seeming sort of chap," his father said. "Just a trifle impatient. Your mother's given him tea."

7

Holt walked gingerly down the staircase.

The carpet had had so much use that he thought his mother would not even have offered it to Oxfam. Most of the dull brass rods were loose. There were three oil paintings on the wall above the stairs just decipherable as Victorian military and all apparently smoked for years over a damp log fire. In the early morning light the house looked in even worse a state than it did by night. But he had had a good sleep, and at least the sheets had been aired.

Peeping through a door at the back of the hall was an elderly woman in a housecoat. She had a headscarf over her hair and the sharp angles told him that she had slept in her curlers and not yet removed them.

"Good morning," Holt said. He did his best to sound cheerful.

She told him that she was Mrs. Ferguson, that she kept house.

He hadn't seen her the night before. It had been a five-hour drive from Exmoor, and when they arrived there was hardly a light on in the place, and no food waiting, and no sign of a welcoming drink, even. Martins had been true to form, hadn't talked all the way, having muttered right at the start that he wasn't going to go off half cocked, that he would keep the mysteries until the morning. Better that way, that was Holt's opinion. He could be patient.

Away behind closed doors he could hear the muffle of Martins's voice, on the telephone.

"He'll be having his breakfast in fifteen minutes," Mrs. Ferguson said. She seemed to reproach him, as if by coming downstairs he had caught her unprepared, as if he should have stayed in his room until called.

Holt prised open the bolts on the front door and slipped the security chain. He could still hear Martins on the telephone. Thirteen minutes until breakfast. He had the impression that breakfast was like a parade. The lock on the door was a new expensive Chubb, and he had seen the fresh alarm wiring at the windows.

He stood on the front steps. He gazed around him. The house was a tower at his back, faded red Surrey brick, probably sixty or seventy years old with rounded corners topped by farcical battlements. In front of him were lawns, uncut since the previous autumn, and daffodil swards and beds of daisies and rosebushes that had escaped a winter pruning. There was a clatter of pigeons in flight from the oak and beech and sycamore trees that fringed the grass. He heard the stampede escape of a squirrel in the overgrown rhododendrons that hid the curve of a shingle drive. Holt thought the garden could have been a paradise. . . . A dog was charging toward him. Heavy shouldered, black and tan, ears swept back, a mouth of white teeth. Holt was good with dogs. There had always been dogs at home. He stood his ground, he slapped his hand against his thigh, welcoming. He heard a bellow, a yelling for the dog to stop, stand, stay, come to heel. The dog kept on coming, stripping the distance across the grass. Holt recognized the markings and weight of the German Rottweiler. Round the corner of the house came an elderly man, built like his dog, hobbling in pursuit, and shouting his command, and being ignored.

The dog reached Holt. The dog sat in front of him and licked Holt's hand. The dog had dreamy pleasure in the wide mahogany eyes.

The man reached them. He was panting.

"You shouldn't be walking outside, not when her's out. Damn bastard spiteful she can be . . ."

He wasn't looking at the dog. The wet of the dog's tongue lapped the back of Holt's hand.

". . . She's a trained guard dog."

"She's soft as a brush, a lovely dog. My name's Holt."

"I'm George, and you'd best not be taking liberties with her. Vicious, she can be."

Holt was scratching under the dog's chin. He could see the rank happiness in the eyes. Holt believed there must be method in the madness. A dog that was loving and called vicious, a garden that was beautiful and left to sink to ruin, a house that was magnificent and nearly splendid but was obviously not cared for. He could be patient, but, by God, he'd require some answers by the end.

"Breakfast, Holt." The shout from the doorway. He saw that Martins wore corduroy trousers and a Guernsey sweater. "And keep that beast under control, George."

Holt walked away. He turned once, briefly, to see the dog watching him going. As he went through the front door, Martins battered him across the shoulders with forced camaraderie.

"Sleep all right? Fine place. You shouldn't just take yourself outside, you were lucky that George was there to control that bloody animal. Word of warning about breakfast, eat everything, she takes it personally if you leave a crumb or a quarter of an inch of bacon rind. Straight after, we'll talk business."

They took breakfast in a dining room that could have, probably once had, housed a full-size billiard table, but the flooring was linoleum and there were five small square tables, each covered with a plastic cloth. Holt thought it was a civil service canteen, and the food was right for a canteen, and the coffee was worse. Martins said that the house had been bequeathed to the nation in 1947, and that since no one wanted it the Service had been burdened. He said that it cost a small fortune to run and to heat. He said that Mrs. Ferguson was the widow of a Special Operations Executive agent who had been parachuted into France just before the invasion, captured and shot. He said that George was a former serviceman, wounded by mine shrapnel in the Cyprus Emergency, and kept on by the Service as caretaker, gardener, driver, maintenance man. Holt wondered if Jane had ever been in a place like this.

Martins led the way across the hall and into a huge drawing room. The dustcovers were piled in the center of the carpet, and the fire had not been cleared or laid again. Martins cursed. He lifted the pile of dust sheets, took them to the door, flung them out. At the fireplace he emptied the hod into the grate and then buried a fire lighter under the fresh coal, and lit it. When the smoke billowed across the room he cursed again and went back to the door and left it ajar.

"Typical of houses like this. You have to leave a door open if you want a fire, otherwise you're smoke gassed. Why the Service has to put up with it defeats me. . . . I imagine you're pretty cut up about Miss Canning."

They were there, the patient waiting was over. Martins was bent over the fire, prodding with a grimed poker. Holt stood in the center of the room and stared through the windows. He could see the dog slouching disconsolately toward a rose bed, then squatting.

"I've done a fair amount of thinking while I've been at home."

"You must have been devastated, only natural."

"I was at first, but I've come to terms with it. I'm going back to FCO. Life is for living, that's what Jane's mother said to me."

"I don't quite follow you."

"I'm going back to work, I'm going to try to put Yalta out of my mind . . ."

Martins was up from the fire, and the poker was left across the grate. Shock in his eyes, the color flushing to his face.

"Your girl killed, shot down in cold blood, butchered in broad daylight, and you're talking about 'life is for living,' I don't believe my ears."

"Don't sermonize me, Mr. Martins. My feelings are in no way your business, not anyone's business but mine."

"Oh, very nice. Hardly dead, and you're talking about forgetting her, abandoning her memory . . ." There was a waft of contempt in Martins's voice, and a tinge that Holt saw of anxiety.

"She was my girl, I loved her and she is dead."

"And to be forgotten?"

"You're an arrogant bastard, *Mister* Martins. What I said is that I intend to go back to work, to go on with my life."

"Then, young Holt, you are a selfish little creep."

"If you brought me halfway across England to this slum to insult me . . ."

"I'm merely astonished to hear this gutless crap from a young man who said of his girl's killer, 'I'd want him killed.' "

"And what bloody option do I have?"

"That's more like it. That's the question I wanted to hear." Martins smiled quickly.

"What the hell can I do?"

"Much better." Martins heaved the air down into his chest, like a great weight had been lifted from him. "You had me rather worried for a minute, young Holt. You had me wondering whether there was an ounce of spunk left in your body."

"I don't see what more I can do for you," Holt said simply.

Martins spoke fast, as if unwilling to lose the moment. "You are, of course, a signatory to the Official Secrets Act, you are aware that such a signature places upon you an oath of silence on all matters concerned with the work of the Service. Everything that I am about to tell you is covered by the terms of that Act, and violation by you of those terms would lead, as night follows day, to your appearing in closed court charged with offenses under Section One of the Act."

Just as if he were falling, as if the ground opened under him, as if he could not help himself.

"What can I do?"

Far in the distance the dog was barking. Holt could see the leaping body and the snarling mouth, and George waving a stick at shoulder height, teasing the animal.

"You can help the man who murdered your girl to an early grave . . ."

The turmoil rocked in Holt's mind. She had been the girl with whom he had planned to spend his youth and his middle years and the last of his life.

"And you can assist your country in an act of vengeance."

There had been no mention of Ben Armitage, no mention

of an ambassador assassinated. But then the arm twist was on him, and Armitage was not personal to him.

The turmoil blasting him. He despised violence. He despised Jane's killer. But he had seen the eyes of the killer, he had seen the work of the gun of the killer.

"What are you asking of me?"

"That you join a team that will go into the Bekaa Valley in east Lebanon, that you identify Abu Hamid, the murderer of your girl."

"And then?"

"Then he is shot dead."

"And then we all just walk home?"

"You walk out."

"And that's possible?" Derision in Holt's voice, staring up into Martins's face, into the smoke cloud of the fire.

"If you've the courage."

"Who do I walk with and who fires the shot?"

"A man who is expert at crossing hostile territory, a man who is expert at sniping."

"One man?"

"So you're better off that way. He'd be better off alone, but you are the only man who saw the target. You have to go."

"Could it work?"

Martins waved at the billowing smoke. "We believe so."

"I'm a bloody puppet and you're a crude sod when it comes to manipulation."

"I knew I could depend on your help, Holt. . . . We'll have some coffee."

"I don't have the chance to say no."

"We'd be disappointed if you did . . . I'll make the coffee. He's a first-class man that you'll be traveling with, quite excellent. He goes by the name of Noah Crane."

"*Cataracta* is the Latin word for 'waterfall.' Cataract is what you have in your right eye, it is an opacity of the crystalline lens of the eye. At your age it is not at all surprising that you display the early stages of what we call the senile cataract."

To the ophthalmic surgeon he was simply another patient. The examination was over. After the explanation, a check would be written out at the reception desk. He knew the man was from overseas, he assumed that he was required for diagnosis, a second opinion, not for treatment.

The patient lay back in the padded examination chair. He showed no emotion.

"In the cataract-affected eye there is a hardening and shrinking at the heart of the lens which in time will lead to the disintegration of the lens. The cataract itself will lead to a deterioration in your short sight. Now, Mr. Crane, a cataract can be treated, but regrettably there looks like being another complication . . ."

They had been through the symptoms before the detail of the examination. Noah Crane had laconically described the frequency of the headaches while the viewing power of the eye was stretched, and the multiplication of bright lights in the distant dark. He had said that he saw better at dusk.

"The complication behind the cataract is—and I would have to carry out a further examination to be certain—that the retina of your right eye is probably diseased. I don't beat about the bush with my patients. Disease of the retina negates the type of successful surgery that we can carry out to remedy the cataract."

"How long do I have?"

"You have years of sight."

"How long do I have with my sight as it is?"

"You have no time. Your sight is already deteriorating. Everyone's is, of course, after a certain age. Mine is. Yours is. Without the problem of the retina I would say we could get you back to where you were a couple of years ago, but we have the retina, and that means your sight will gradually diminish . . . I should have qualified that. The affliction is purely in the right eye. Your left eye is in excellent shape. Do you work indoors?"

"Outside."

"Then you should not be unduly pessimistic. Outside you

will be using your long sight, shortsightedness is not so important. . . . You should see a surgeon when you return home."

"I understand that there's a place in Houston . . ."

"But the American techniques of treatment are unproven. You could spend a great deal of money, Mr. Crane, a huge sum, and have no guarantee of success."

The chair straightened to upright. Noah Crane sat for a moment with his head bowed and his hands clasped together. He could aim only with his right eye. He could not tell the ophthalmic surgeon that although he worked outside it was short-range vision that mattered to him, was what his life depended on. No long-range vision was required to peer into the magnification of the scope sight. He climbed out of the chair, he walked out of the room.

So he knew. He had asked and he had been told. Time was slipping from him.

In the street he felt the bitter cut of the wind. The wind lashed from a side street into Wimpole Street. He wore light trousers and a light shirt that was open at the neck, and a light poplin parka. Too many clothes for home in Kiryat Shmona at the base camp, not enough clothes for London in spring. In a small grip bag were all his possessions. A change of clothes, a wash bag, and a photograph in a leather wallet of his mother and her sister, and a small brown envelope. No other possessions, because everything else this man used was the property of the Israeli Defense Force.

He walked across central London, and then across the bridge to the railway station. He had seen his mother's sister, he had negotiated his price in the bare room on the third floor of Century, and the sight of his right eye was ebbing from him; he had no more business in London. He was ready to take the train.

The light was failing in the room, the shadows leaping from the fire. Percy Martins stood with his back to the flames.

"Crane being recruited was a master stroke. . . . You'll learn, Holt, that when the Service wants something it gets it. When the Service wants a man, it gets that man. You're to be a team, a two-man team. Neither of you can fulfill your task without the other. Crane cannot identify our target without you, you cannot eliminate the assassin without Crane. Two men with one aim, that's the way it has to be."

Holt was less than six feet from Martins, taking what heat he could that was diverted around the flanks of Martins's legs. He wondered why the man spoke as if lecturing to a full briefing room.

"Noah Aharon Crane is 48 years old. I expect that's a relief, eh? No worries about keeping up with an old timer like that. His father was a British soldier stationed in Palestine at the outbreak of the Second War, married locally, got himself killed in Normandy.

"By the time he was 18 he had spent his childhood in Israel, and his adolescence in the UK. He joined the 2nd Battalion of the Parachute Regiment, that was 1959. He served with the Regiment in Borneo and Aden and in Northern Ireland, he made it to sergeant and his records speak of a first-class soldier. But his mother died in 1971, and for reasons that are close to him, Crane left the British Army, flew to Israel and joined up with what they call the Golani Brigade. The file indicates that he had a sense of guilt at not having visited his mother—who was Jerusalem born and bred—for many years during the last part of her life, that a sense of blame took him back to her country. As an infantry man he earned a glittering record after his induction into the IDF. He was with the Golani at the retaking of Mount Hermon in 1973, he was in Lebanon in '78, he was a member of the assault squad on the old Crusader castle of Beaufort in '82. He was good enough to be a regular, he was hardened by combat experience, but he seems to have next to no interest in promotion. In fact it is difficult to locate what interests outside the IDF he does have. His only living relative is his mother's sister, living somewhere in north London. He has never married. He refuses leave. There are men like that in our army, every fighting machine throws them up. They are difficult, awkward men. In time of war they are a godsend, in time of peace they are assholes for nuisance value . . . I'm digressing . . . after the capture from the Palestinians of the Beaufort castle, twelfth century in origin but an excellent artillery spotting position, a particularly bloody battle, Crane's unit was pushed north and east into the Bekaa Valley, and he stayed there. He stayed put. He became a fixture for three years of Israeli presence there. Some inspired staff man back at the Defense Ministry seemed to have it locked into his head that the Bekaa represents a back door to Damascus, a way round the Golan Heights. By the time that Israel abandoned its positions and retreated, Noah Crane had acquired as much knowledge of that valley as any man in the IDF. It is our assessment that he, alone, can get into the Bekaa, do a job of work, and get out."

"Is this sanctioned by government?"

"Official Secrets Act, Holt—sanctioned from on high."

"You said 'difficult' and 'awkward.' "

"You'll cope."

Holt stood. "I never had a chance, did I?"

"Of course you didn't. You have become, Holt, an instrument of government policy."

"And if I was to say I was frightened?"

"Frightened? You ought to be grateful. It was the girl you were screwing that was shot, Holt. I'd have thought you'd have been jumping at the chance to get stuck in."

"I'll do it," Holt said.

"Don't make a big song and dance about it," Percy Martins smiled.

"I will go into the Bekaa Valley and I will identify a Palestinian terrorist so that he can be killed with the sanction of my government."

"We don't play fanfares round here."

"And when I come back I will scrape my knuckles raw on the end of your nose."

A wider smile from Percy Martins. "You do just that."

Late afternoon came, and the crowds of the capital's workers were streaming toward the rail termini and the bus stops and the Underground platforms. It was the time of day when the Director General usually slipped anonymously into the Whitehall entrance of the Cabinet office to take the discreet tunnel to Downing Street.

The Prime Minister read the list. "Arson attempt on Israeli Tourist Office, Fatah responsible. Failed assassination attempt on Iraqi ambassador, Fatah responsible. Gun attack on El Al bus with fatalities, Wadia Haddad group responsible. Letter bomb sent to Iraqi embassy, source unknown. Iraqi arrested while carrying explosives and on way to IRA link-up, source unknown. Own goal as bomb explodes at hotel, Wadia Haddad group responsible. Shooting of Israeli ambassador, Abu Nidal responsible. Arson at Jewish Club, source unknown. Bomb explodes near Bank Leumi of Israel, source unknown. Bomb explodes near Marks & Spencer's main branch, source unknown. Thwarted attempt to buy sophisticated military sabotage equipment, PFLP General Command responsible. Bomb explodes at Jewish-owned travel business, source unknown. Interception of explosives courier, Abu Nidal responsible. Attempt to place live bomb on El Al jetliner, Syrian Air Force Intelligence responsible. . . . It's a truly sickening list."

"That's just Arab terrorism in London, Prime Minister, in the last several years. On top of that we should add attacks on British nationals abroad—the machine gun attack on the women and children of our servicemen in Cyprus—grenade attacks on hotels used by British tourists in Greece—that's a whole other list, which ends with the deaths of the ambassador and Miss Canning."

"Sir Sylvester Armitage was a fine man, a great servant of his country."

"Whose death should be avenged."

The Prime Minister hesitated. The suggestion had been made, but the decision was the Prime Minister's alone.

"It can be done?"

"A small surgical operation into the Bekaa Valley? Yes, it can be done."

"How many men?"

"Just two. A Jewish Briton who is familiar with the ground,

skilled in covert work and a marksman, he will travel with young Holt who will identify the target."

"So few?" the Prime Minister murmured. "Would there be Israeli assistance?"

"Inside Israel, yes. Inside Lebanon, we would assume that also, yes." The Director General stood at his full height, avuncular and confident. "But it would be our show, Prime Minister."

"Against the man who pulled the trigger on our ambassador?"

"Indeed that very man. . . . We would be acting in the very theater where *others* talk about acting. We would not be scattering bombs over an international city in the hope they might find a target. We would be going for one man with whom we have a known score to settle."

"A marksman and a spotter," the Prime Minister mused. "Would they get out?"

"We've chosen the best possible soldier for the job."

The decision to be taken alone. The memory of sitting in a country church, hearing the tears of Armitage's granddaughter, of watching a coffin carried along the aisle, bedecked with spring flowers. The memory of many outrages, of television news clips of broken shop fronts, of blood smears on inner London pavements, of bodyguards crammed into armor-plated limousines.

"Bring me his head," the Prime Minister snapped.

The curtains were drawn, the fire smouldered.

Holt sat on a sofa. The light in the room was low as two of the five bulbs in the ceiling formation were dead.

Percy Martins was saying, "The Yanks cannot actually put this sort of operation together. You don't believe me? Well, I'll tell you. Their Special Forces have an annual budget of over a billion dollars, can you imagine that much money spent on one division-sized unit? No good, though. They have the Delta Force, and the helicopter Task Force 168, and the Air Force Special Operations Wing, but they're no damned good. They're more interested in saucy cap badges and expenses. Do you know that when they wanted to drop a squad on a hijacked liner in the Mediterranean, the Pentagon had to give permission for half the squad to leave United States territory, and why? Because the squad was under investigation for fiddling expenses. Their kit doesn't work. They're too late on the scene. The Germans are fine, up to a point, but at Mogadishu when they stormed an airliner it was Britons who can-opened the plane for them and chucked in the stun grenades. When the Italians have a problem they get on the phone pretty damn quick and call up help from us . . ."

Holt wondered how Martins had ever made it into the Secret Intelligence Service. He thought he'd be better employed running the social calendar for an Ex-Servicemen's Club.

". . . When my Director General was on the phone just now he was really chortling. A dog with two bones."

"Is that all you care about?"

"Showing that we can do a job well, yes, I do care about that."

"So you can crow to the Americans, is that why I'm being chucked into Lebanon?"

"You're not being chucked, you volunteered. In case we misunderstand each other, young man . . ." Martins was striding the carpet, talking to the ceiling gloom and the cobwebs that were beyond the reach of Mrs. Ferguson's feather duster. "In case we don't follow each other, let us be clear on something. You have been fortunate enough to have been chosen to carry out an operation of infinitely greater importance to your country's needs than anything you would have achieved in years of a career in the Diplomatic Service. Instead of a lifetime on your butt concocting reports that will have appeared better written and a month earlier in half of our daily newspapers, you are going to *do* something. You are going to *achieve* something about which you will be justly proud for the rest of your life."

There was the growl of a car engine. There was the scrape of the tires on gravel. Holt heard the bellow-bark of the dog.

He stood and went to the window. He pulled the curtain back. He saw the taxi pull up under the front floodlighting that beamed off the porch roof. The passenger must have passed his money inside the taxi, because when he climbed from the back the taxi drove away.

It was obvious to him that he was looking at the man called Noah Crane. He could be clearly seen in the light from the roof. He was a fleshless man. Skin on bone, physically nondescript, rounded shoulders, a cavern for a chest, and spindly arms. The wind flattened his cotton trousers and showed the narrow contours of his leg muscles. Cropped hair in a pepperpot mixture of brown and gray stubble, and below were hollow cheeks. Leather-tanned skin over a jutting thin jaw lay tight on a beaked nose.

Holt watched as Noah Crane made no move toward the front door but gazed instead over the black shadow gardens, assimilating his whereabouts. The front door opened. The dog came out fast, and Holt could hear George yelling for it to stay, stop, stand. The dog went straight to Crane. Holt heard George shout a warning that the dog could be evil. The dog was on its back, and Crane crouched beside it. The dog had its four saucer paws in the air, and Crane was scratching the soft hair of its stomach. Crane picked up his grip bag and came evenly, not hurrying himself, up the porch steps, and the dog was licking his hand.

That was the truth for Holt. The dog recognized authority. When he came away from the window, Holt realized that he was alone, that Martins had left the room, gone to the hall to meet Crane. The dog had found the power and authority of the man. It was the moment when young Holt knew into what pit he had fallen, how deep was the pit, how steep were the sides. It was the moment that young Holt knew he stared at the face of a killer. It was the moment that young Holt knew the dangers, the hazards of the Bekaa. He thought that Crane was unlike any man he had seen before. Something easy and untroubled about the way that Crane had walked up the old flagstone steps of the porch. He remembered how he had mounted those steps himself, in trepidation, anxious to please, fearful of what awaited him. Crane had come up the steps like a hangman, like an untroubled executioner.

God, but he was so frightened . . .

"Don't be childish, Holt."

The squeak of the swinging door.

The light flooding in from the hall.

"Holt, I'd like you to meet Noah Crane," Martins said.

Holt stood his ground, incapable of moving. He was taller than Crane, and he probably carried twenty pounds more in weight. He felt he was a beef bullock under market examination. Crane looked at him, head to toe. Holt wore a pair of well-creased slacks and a clean white shirt and a tie and a quiet check sports jacket, his shoes were cleaned. He felt like a schoolboy going for a first job. Crane wore dirty running shoes, his shirt was open three buttons from the neck. Expressionless eyes. Crane turned to Percy Martins. Martins stood beside him, playing the cattle market auctioneer.

"That's him?"

"That's young Holt, Mr. Crane."

"Any military time?"

"No, he hasn't been in the armed services."

"Any survival training?"

"There's nothing like that on his record."

"Any current fitness work?"

"Not since he came back from Moscow, not that I know of."

"Any reason to take him other than the face?"

"He saw Abu Hamid, Mr. Crane, that's why he's traveling."

"Any leverage put on him?"

"It was his girl friend who was killed, he didn't need persuading."

"Any briefing given him on the Bekaa?"

"I thought it best to wait until you joined us."

The accent was London. Not the sharp whip of east, but more the whine of west London. Crane spoke to Martins from the side of his mouth, but all the time his eyes stayed locked on Holt. Crane came close to Holt. Close enough for Holt to see the old mosquito scars under the hair on his cheeks, close enough for Holt to smell the burger sauce on his breath, close enough for Holt to feel the coldness of his eyes.

It came from down by the side of Crane's thigh, no backlift, without warning. A short arm punch with the closed fist up into Holt's solar plexus. The fist pounded into Holt's jacket, into his shirt, into his vest, into his stomach. Gasping for breath, sinking toward the carpet.

Holt was on his knees.

"Nothing personal," Crane said. "But your stomach wall is flab."

Holt thought he was going to throw up. His eyes were closed tight shut. He could hear their voices.

"If he's not fit he's useless to me on the way in, useless on the way out."

"We'll get him doing some exercises."

"Too right."

Holt used the arm of a chair to push himself back to his feet. He forced his hands away from his stomach. He was swallowing to control the nausea. He blinked to keep the tears from his eyes.

"I don't apologize, Holt. If I have a passenger then I don't succeed. If I don't succeed you'll be dead. I just might be dead with you."

"I won't be a passenger," Holt croaked.

Major Zvi Dan waved the station officer to a chair. Pig hot in the room with the table fan burned out.

The walk from his car into the building, and then the trek down the corridors had brought the first sweat drops to the station officer's forehead.

"I'm sorry, but again they say they will not."

"Shit."

"I explained that the request for reconsideration came from the Director General of SIS—I knew what the answer would be. That's the Israeli way. We make decisions and we stick with them."

The station officer bit at his lip. "I think I knew that would be the answer."

"Before they make you their errand boy, have they any idea in London of what would be involved, logistically, in a helicopter pickup deep in the Bekaa?"

"Probably not."

"Then you should tell them."

The station officer reached for his notepad from his briefcase, he took a ballpoint from his shirt pocket.

"Fire at me."

"First, what is involved in a pickup where there are no missiles, where there is only small-arms fire. You will have stirred a hornet's nest the moment the killing is made. A similar situation last year—we lost a Phantom over the hills close to Sidon. We had a pilot on the ground with his electronics giving us his position. By fixed wing and by Cobra helicopters we put down a curtain of bombs and cannon fire around him, through which no human being could move. We did that for ninety minutes until it was dark. Phantoms coming in relays, gunships overhead the whole time. Do I have to tell you how many aircraft, how many copters that involved? Overhead we had a command aircraft the entire time. When we had night cover we flew in a Cobra to pick up the pilot, with more Cobras creating a sanitized corridor through which it could fly. At the pickup there was no time to land, the pilot had to reach for the landing skids, hold onto them while he was lifted off and flown to safety. That is what's involved when there's no missile umbrella."

"They'll get it in London." The station officer was writing, grim faced.

"But in the Bekaa you are under the missile umbrella. The Bekaa is protected by the SA-2 Guideline for high-altitude intruders, by the SA-8 Gecko for medium-altitude intruders, by the SA-9 Gaskin for low level. If you put a helicopter in when there is a state of high alert, then you must also put in aircraft to protect it. Those aircraft in turn must be kept safe from the missiles. For that degree of protection you have to be prepared to assault the missile sites.

"In 1982 we destroyed the missile sites in the Bekaa. To achieve that we had to do the following. We had to launch drones to fly where we thought the missiles were positioned, the drones have reflectors that make them show on the radar like full-sized piloted aircraft. When the Syrians switched on their radar fully and prepared the missiles, that was disclosed by the EC-135, a converted Boeing airliner, and the E2C Hawkeye. When we had exactly located the missile sites and had confused them with electronic jamming, then we hit them from the air with the Maverick missile, and the Walleye bomb that goes to the source of the missile's energy unit. . . . It was a big operation. You follow me? All that *had* to be done. On top of all that we were also obliged to fight off the Syrian interceptors. It was quite a battle . . ."

"I hear you."

"My friend, that is what is involved. That is what we have had to consider when you made a request for an airborne pickup in the Bekaa."

"No helicopter lift . . ."

"How could there be? It is not even our operation."

"Then they have to walk out."

"Our marksman and your eyewitness, and the hornet's nest stirred . . . Do you think in London that they appreciate the teeth of the Bekaa?"

"Too late whether they do or don't, they're committed."

From a drawer in his desk Major Zvi Dan took a single plate-sized photograph. He told the station officer that the small pale patches in the magnified heart of the photograph were the tents of what was believed to be a Popular Front training camp for raw recruits. He went to his wall map and read off the coordinates for the position of the camp.

"We believe that is where you will find your man. It is a long way to walk to, a long way to walk back from."

The station officer dropped his notebook back into his case. He leaned over. "Crane is your soldier."

"He is seconded to you. He is paid by you. It is your operation."

The station officer thanked his friend for the photograph.

"I'll pass it on. Thank you, Tork."

"I thought you should know immediately, Mr. Fenner. They'll be on their own in Lebanon."

They talked on a secure line. Henry Fenner, number two on the Middle East Desk at Century, and Graham Tork, station officer in Tel Aviv.

"I'll pass it on, but it's not my concern."

"Aren't you running this, Mr. Fenner?"

"I am not. The Old Man's given it to Percy Martins."

"Is that a joke . . . ? He must be ready for going out to grass."

"I tell you, frankly, I'm not that sorry, not after what you've told me. And did you know that Hereford turned it down flat? For your ears, Mr. Anstruther agrees with me, it's a no-no-hoper. My advice, meant kindly, is keep your distance. If Martins is going down the plug, where he should have gone years ago, make sure you don't go with him. Bye, Tork."

"Thank you, Mr. Fenner."

In his office in the embassy, the station officer replaced his telephone. What a wonderful world . . . Anstruther and Fenner, high fliers on the Middle East Desk, giving him the nod and the wink. He had met Percy Martins on his last journey to London, thought he must have come out of the ark. He thanked the good Lord that he was posted abroad, that he didn't go each morning to a desk at Century.

He wondered if the young man, Holt, knew the half of it, and hoped to God that he did not.

It was the crisp snap voice that woke Mrs. Ferguson. She stirred in her bed. Her eyes clearing, she peered at her alarm clock on the table beside her. It was twenty-two minutes past six o'clock, it was eight minutes before her alarm would ring.

She had good hearing, she could hear the words.

"At your age a fit soldier can do fifty sit-ups a minute, you managed ten. On your push-ups a fit man can do thirty, you did eight. On your squat-thrusts you need to do twenty-five, you got to six . . ."

She gathered her dressing gown around her shoulders, stiffly levered herself off the bed. She went to the window.

"You'll get fit and quick, or you're a burden to me . . ."

She saw Holt, wearing vest and underpants, lying spread-eagled on the terrace, his chest heaving. Mr. Crane was standing over him and holding a stopwatch.

"Now you do sprints, three times forty meters."

She half hid her face behind the curtain. She saw Holt attempt to sprint between the edge of the terrace and the nearest rose bed, running like a drunk or a cripple, but running, not giving up.

"I reckon round this lawn six times is a mile and a half. If you do it in anything around eleven minutes that's excellent, anything over sixteen minutes is not good enough. . . . Get on with it . . ."

Holt was still running by the time Mrs. Ferguson had washed and dressed and applied the thin pencil of lipstick, still on his feet, still moving forward.

8

A light wind caught at the tent flaps and swayed them. There were bell tents for the recruits. From the tent area a clear track had been trodden to a single smaller tent, and there was another path to the cooking area where a sheet of rusted corrugated iron, nailed to four posts, served as weather protection for the fire. Eight tents for the recruits, and a smaller tent for Abu Hamid and for Fawzi when he was there, and the cooking area, they were all in a tight group. Away from the tents and the cooking area, thirty yards away, was a stall with three sides of draped sacking that served as the latrine pit for the camp.

Near to the tents for the recruits were air-raid trenches that had been cut down through the topsoil and into the rock strata. They had been dug deep, approached by wooden slatted steps and covered over with tin to make a roof and then the displaced earth and stones. In one last trench slit a door had been made to fit close against the heavy wood of the surrounds, and in this trench were stored the Strela ground-to-air missiles that were a part of the camp's defense system. Further away, closer to the perimeter of the camp, were three separate 14.5mm ZPU-4 anti-aircraft multiple guns. The inner perimeter of the camp was marked by a close coil of barbed wire on which had caught fragments of paper and cardboard, and into which had been thrown the debris of old ammunition boxes and packing cases. The outer perimeter was a ditch, hewn out by bulldozers, and with steep enough sides to hinder the progress of a tank.

To the west of the camp was the wall of the side of the Bekaa, to the north three miles away was a small Syrian camp housing a company of regular commandos, to the east was the full flat stretch of the width of the valley floor, to the south was a Shi'ite Muslim village.

The camp had been sited 24 miles from the southern extremity of the Bekaa. At its nearest point, the Israeli border was 36 miles from the camp. It was considered a safe haven.

Abu Hamid hated the place, hated the dirt and the filth and the smells of the camp. He hated the recruits who were his responsibility. He hated the flies in the day, and the mosquitoes that came at dusk from the irrigation ditch beyond the perimeter, and the rats that swarmed at night from the coiled wire. He hated the food that was cooked dry under the corrugated iron roof and over the open wood fire. He hated the relaxed calm of Fawzi who was the Syrian spy in place to watch over him. He hated the boredom of the training routine. Most of all he hated the isolation of the camp.

He had requested of Fawzi the necessary pass that would have enabled him to get to Damascus to see his Margarethe. Of course, the requests were not refused. Nothing was ever refused by the Syrians, the requests were only diverted, there was just the hinted promise that later everything would be possible.

For two weeks he had been a prisoner.

In two weeks he had not seen Major Said Hazan, nor had he seen any of the big men of the Popular Front. Of course, he knew that the Doctor, the inspiration of the Popular Front, could not travel into the valley, could not expose himself that close to the territory of the Zionist enemy, but there were others that could have come, others who could have demanded of the Syrians the right of access to himself and to the new recruits.

The place was hell to him. And there was a worm that ate at his confidence. Abu Hamid had performed a service to the Palestinian cause, to the government of the Syrian Arab Republic who were the sponsors of that cause. The service was secret, could not be spoken of. That was the worm. Of course, the recruits knew that he had taken part in the battles of 1982 in Tyre and Sidon and Damour and in West Beirut. But the recruits too, every last one of them, had been inside one or more of those battles. As young teenagers they had carried back the casualties, carried forward the ammunition. The young teenagers had been left behind in the Rachidiye camp and the Ein el Helwe camp and the Miye ou Miye camp and the Sabra and the Chatila camps when the fighters had been given safe passage by foreign peacekeeping troops and sailed away. The kids had stayed, under the Zionist occupation. They showed him a degree of respect for having been to the military academy at Simferopol and having passed out as top officer cadet, only a degree of respect. If only they had known . . .

"When can we go to Israel?" was their sole concern. "When can we fight the real war?" the recruits pleaded with Abu Hamid. "When can we show that we have no fear?"

Abu Hamid had known men who had gone to Israel, fought the real war, shown that they had no fear. He had known them in the camps before the Israeli invasion of Lebanon in 1982. He had seen them go. He had never seen one of them return.

One fact alone mitigated the hatred he felt for this filthy, stinking camp. It was a secret to his recruits, but he had proved himself at Simferopol, and he would never be required to prove himself again. It would never be demanded of him that he should go through the security zone into Israel.

A very secret thought. A thought that he would never share.

They were coming down the gentle lower slope of the valley wall. The recruits were in a loose formation, twenty ranks of three abreast, and Abu Hamid played the part of a noncommissioned instructor at the military academy and strode at the side of them and shouted for the step to be maintained. The recruits were singing, with fervor, an anthem of the Popular Front, a song of killing and victory. The anthem was of death, was of battle, but the valley was a place of peace. From the elevation of the track, looking out across the cultivated floor of the valley, and across the sharp ridge lines of the irrigation ditches, and the light sweep of the unsurfaced road that fed their camp, Abu Hamid could see a scene of undamaged tranquillity. There were women from the Shi'ite village pruning in the grove of olive trees, more women bent among the marijuana crop. There were men working between the lines of the vineyards, more men shepherding flocks of sheep toward brighter pastures among the gullies in the rock scrub. Smoke spirals drifted into the air above the commandos' camp.

He could hear birds singing. He could see two jeep vehicles kicking up short dust storms as they approached the camp along the unsurfaced road.

They came down the hillside. They reached the gate of the camp, the gap in the coiled wire, when the nearest of the jeeps was a hundred yards from the perimeter.

Abu Hamid gave his orders. The RPG-7 launchers to be returned after cleaning to the underground armory. The rifles to be cleaned and inspected. The cooking for the midday meal to be started.

He waited at the entrance of the camp. The first jeep ground to a stop in front of him. The second jeep had pulled up fifty yards further down the track. The engines were switched off. Both jeeps carried the red and white flashes of the military police of the Syrian Army on their dust-coated flanks. He saw that the driver of the near jeep wore the white helmet of the military police, he saw Fawzi climb out from the passenger seat. Fawzi had been away for three days and three nights. He saw the grin, the expectant pleasure on Fawzi's face. Fawzi acknowledged Abu Hamid, a casual waft of the hand, then walked to the back of the jeep, threw it open.

The woman was chicken trussed. She was carried easily by Fawzi from the back of the jeep. Her ankles, below the hem of her long skirt, were bound many times with the sort of twine that is used to bind straw or hay for cattle fodder. Her wrists were handcuffed behind her back. Fawzi carried her over his shoulder. She did not whimper, she did not writhe. Abu Hamid could not see her face which lay limp against the chest of Fawzi. She had no headscarf, her long hair was dirt-streaked, the pale soil of the Bekaa smeared into the black tresses. He saw the military policeman, the driver, stay in his seat, light a cigarette. He followed Fawzi into the camp, behind the unmoving legs of the woman. The woman had no shoes and the soles of her feet were raw and blood-caked. Abu Hamid's finger flicked at the scar well in his cheek.

Beside the tents, Fawzi heaved the woman to the ground. She fell hard, on her hip and her shoulder. No sound from her lips, only the heave of her lungs to replace the breath punched from her body.

Abu Hamid swallowed. The recruits were gathering, forming a hesitant circle around Fawzi and Abu Hamid, and the woman. Fawzi was panting, but silent, preparing his speech. Abu Hamid saw the face of the woman. He thought that her nose was broken because of the twist of the point of her nose as if it were putty and could be moved easily sideways. Her eyes were closed, perhaps she did not care to open them, perhaps the bruising was too heavy for her to be able to open them; there was dark vivid bruising on the soft sallow skin. He could see that the buttons of her heavy blouse had been torn away, he could see the sears on her throat and on the upper skin of her breasts. Abu Hamid thought that she had been burned with cigarette butts. He was struggling to suppress his vomit nausea.

"This woman is Leila Galah," began Fawzi. "Her parents live in Nablus, in the Occupied Territory. She herself comes from the Bourj el Barajneh camp in Beirut. She is twenty-three years old. She left the Occupied Territory seven years ago to join the Popular Democratic Front—all this she has told us."

No one looked at Fawzi. Every eye in the circle of recruits was fixed on the still body of the woman lying at Fawzi's feet.

"Also she has told us that for two years she has been an agent of the Zionist enemy . . ."

Abu Hamid heard the anger growl from his recruits. He heard the sucked breath. He saw the smile sweeping Fawzi's face. He wondered if the woman heard her denunciation.

"She has told us that she is a spy."

Abu Hamid had gone, after the evacuation from Beirut, to the port of Aden, the capital city of the People's Republic of South Yemen. He and friends had once gone in a fishing boat out to sea, beyond the sight of land, and they had tossed over the side a sack of offal and entrails, and when the sharks had closed on the blood-soaked meat, they had fired at them with their automatic rifles . . . for sport. He could remember the surging interest, the relentless approach of the sharks to the meat and the blood and the skin. The woman was the meat, that she was a spy for Israel was the blood scenting the water, the recruits were the sharks of the scarlet-streaming Red Sea.

"From her own mouth, she is an agent of the Shin Bet. She has taken the shekels of the Israeli security service. She has betrayed her name, the name of her father and of her mother. She has betrayed her own people, the Palestinian people. She has betrayed you, the fighters and defenders of the Palestine revolution."

The circle was closing, tightening. The growl had become a scream. Abu Hamid looked from the face of the woman to the faces of the recruits. Eyes ablaze, mouths cracked with hate, fists clenched tight and shafting the air in fury. He saw himself walking across the street in front of the Oreanda Hotel of Yalta, and discarding the light parka that covered the Kalashnikov. He saw himself gazing at the features of the girl as she came through the door that was held open for her by the man who was his target. He saw himself raising the extended shoulder stock to fit hard against his collarbone. He saw himself squeezing the trigger of the Kalashnikov . . . He thought he was going to vomit . . . He saw the girl flying back, lifted from her feet, flailing against the body of the target, and then the target going down. He had felt no rage . . . He had not felt the tempest emotion of the recruits.

He thought the woman was beautiful, even with the bruises and the burns. He saw the dignity of her quietness, her silence in pain.

"She was arrested by the agents of the military eight days ago. She has been interrogated, she has made a full confession of her criminal betrayal, she has been sentenced by a tribunal. She is to die."

Because he wanted to be sick, because he thought the woman was beautiful, because the target was bound tight and not free to walk through the glass doors of the Oreanda Hotel, because there was not the adrenaline excitement of the escape from the streets of Yalta, he knew the squeal of weakness in his body.

Abu Hamid shouted, "We will kill the spy pig."

The shout was the hiding of his weakness.

The baying for blood boiled around the woman. The shout of Abu Hamid for the right to slaughter her, the shouts of the recruits for the right to participate in the letting of blood.

Fawzi stood now over the top of the trussed woman. His straddled legs were over her hips. The woman showed no fear. The woman was a clinging fascination to Abu Hamid. Why did she not beg?

". . . Because she endangered you, it will be you that carry out the sentence of the tribunal."

Why did she not spit at her tormentors? Why did she not shriek in fear?

"Remember this. You are here under the protection of Syria. You are safeguarded by the vigilance of the Syrian security service. There is no safety for traitors in the Bekaa. Traitors will be rooted out, destroyed."

Inch by inch, stamped foot by stamped foot, the circle was closing on the trussed woman. Abu Hamid gazed into her face. For a moment he saw a flicker of animation from her eyes, he saw the curl of her lips. She stared back at him. If it had been himself . . . If it had been Abu Hamid tied at the ankles, handcuffed at the wrists, waiting for the lynch death, would he have been able to show no fear? Abu Hamid understood the power of Syria over the recruits of the Popular Front. A spy had been brought for them to revile, to massacre, just as the Syrians had provided the chickens for those same recruits to despoil at the Yarmuk camp. The power of Syria mocked them, made scum of them. The means of their learning was a bound and handcuffed woman. She stared back at Abu Hamid. At last he saw the contempt in her eyes, the sneer at her mouth.

Abu Hamid wrenched back the cocking arm of his Kalashnikov.

Into the contempt and sneer of the woman's face he fired a full magazine. He raked the body of the woman long after the life had been blitzed from her. The gunfire boom had died, died with the life of a woman branded a spy. The barrel of the rifle hung limp against his thigh and his knee. The body was a mess of blood and cloth and flesh. The circle had grown, had widened. The recruits had seen the trance in which Abu Hamid had fired—none had felt safe to stand close to the shooting. He saw the tremble at Fawzi's jaw.

He walked away. He left the circle and the Syrian and the body of the woman. He walked to the wire coil at the perimeter.

Down the unmade track, leaning on the bonnet of the second jeep, was Major Said Hazan.

Major Said Hazan was clapping the palms of his hands, applauding.

Abu Hamid turned away. He walked to the far side of the camp. The moment before he was lost behind a wall of tent canvas he looked back to where he had shot the woman. He saw the bouncing shoulders and the leaping heads, and he knew that the recruits danced on the bloody corpse of the woman who had been a spy for Israel.

He went behind the tents and vomited until his stomach was empty, until his throat burned.

He wiped his lips with the back of his hand, then he went through the camp entrance gap and down the track.

He gasped the question to Major Said Hazan.

"Why was she here?"

"The Israelis always want to know what is the situation in the Bekaa."

"Why my camp? Why the camp where I am?"

"Chance, nothing more than chance."

"Was she searching for me?"

"You should not acquire for yourself too great an importance. You are as a flea on a dog's neck. Your bite has been felt, but you cannot be found . . ." The voice of Major Said Hazan steeled. "Why did you not permit your young men to execute the spy?"

"It is my role to lead, to lead by example," Abu Hamid said.

"A fine answer . . . in a few days you will be brought to Damascus."

He saw the smooth skin of Major Said Hazan's face wrinkle in the attempted warmth of a smile.

"Why did you choose me for Yalta, Major?"

"I knew of you."

"What did you know?"

"Had you ever killed, Hamid, before Yalta?"

He blurted, "I fought at Bent Jbail in 1978. I was young then. I fought in 1982. I was at Tyre and then at Sidon and then at Damour and then at Beirut city. Many times . . ."

"Answer the question I asked."

"I have fought many times."

"The question is so very simple. Had you ever killed, Abu Hamid?"

"I have fought the Israeli . . . of course, I have killed the Israeli . . ."

The calming voice. The voice of endless patience. "Had you looked into a man's eyes, a man who is alive, looked into his eyes and then killed him? Tell me, Abu Hamid."

He could not control his stammer. "When you are fighting the Israeli you cannot stand about, look for a target . . . It is necessary to use a great volume of fire."

"Into his eyes, and then killed him?"

"If you are that close to the Israeli you are dead."

"Seen the fear in his eyes, because he has the certainty you will kill him?"

"Once." Abu Hamid whispered.

"Recall it for me."

The words in a rush, a torrent flow. "When we had left Beirut, after we had evacuated, we went to South Yemen. We were allowed to take out only one small bag and our rifle. The great men of the Arab world let us be humiliated, after we had fought with sacrifice the battle of the whole Arab world . . ."

"In South Yemen . . ." An encouragement, not a rebuke.

"We were in a tent camp, I had a transistor radio and one day my radio was taken. I found the thief. I went into his tent. He was playing a cassette tape on my radio. First he laughed at me, I waited until he was crying—yes, until he was certain, and then I shot him."

His hand was taken, gripped between the stumps and the thumb. He closed his eyes. He felt the brush of the silk skin across his face. He felt lips that had no moisture kiss his cheek.

"I had heard of it. It was why I chose you."

For a long time he watched the dust cloud spurting up from the back wheels of the jeep as it drove away.

The merchant had been through two roadblocks of the Syrian Army. He traveled the route every Monday and Saturday from Beirut, and returned by the same road to the capital every Tuesday and Sunday. He was well liked by the commando sentries. The main trade of the merchant was in small electrical components, anything from light bulbs and plugs to drums of flex wire to parts for the small generators that provided much of the power in those areas of the Bekaa that were off the two main roads and distant from the main supply. The merchant always offered the soldiers insignificant gifts, crates of soft drinks, throw-away lighters. Beside the wind-blown, weather-blasted and cardboard-mounted photograph of the stern-faced President of the Syrian Arab Republic at the roadblocks he had made his small talk, offered his passes for cursory inspection, and been waved on. He was lighter in his load by two cartons of Camel cigarettes.

The merchant drove south, taking the straight main road, the eastern side of the Bekaa. His car was a Mercedes, eleven years old and with 180,000 kilometers on the clock. The backseat had been torn out to provide him with additional carrying space for his wares. He always drove slowly, and would tell the sentries at the roadblocks that he thought his motor was on the last legs and close to collapse. He always made a joke of it. The snail speed of the laden, rust-coated Mercedes was a familiar source of amusement. By traveling slowly the merchant observed so much more.

He was south of the village of Haouch el Harime, he was north of the small town of Ghazze. He slowed the car, drove off the tarmac and came to stop on the hard shoulder. He walked from his car to a small clump of olive trees. He pulled down the zipper of his trousers. While he urinated he had the time to check that the old upturned bucket beside the tree in front of him had not been moved since the previous time that he had checked. There was no need for him to check the hidden space under the bucket. If the bucket had not been moved then no message had been left. He shuddered. If any man had watched him, from a distance with the aid of binoculars, he would have thought that he merely finished by shaking clear the remnant droplets. He shuddered in sadness and in fear.

The merchant had known since his last journey back from the Bekaa to Beirut that an agent had been held. The conversations at the roadblocks had given him the bare information. The unmoved bucket told him which agent had been taken. The spy would not know the identity he assumed, but the spy could have revealed the location of the dead letter box under interrogation. He turned. If any man watched him through the magnification of binoculars he would have seen the merchant pull back up the zipper of his fly before shambling back to the Mercedes. He would not again break his journey by the clump of greening olive trees.

The merchant drove on through Ghazze, and took the winding road south of Joub Jannine that climbed the Jabal Aarbi hills, until he came to the village of Baaloul. At the village he was welcomed like a hero because he brought a new magneto for the petrol-driven pump of the community's drinking well. In the morning, after talking late with the villagers, after sleeping in the concrete block house of the headman, he would go south again. He would drop his own message beyond the town of Qaraaoun, and then swing first west and then north for his return to Beirut.

The merchant was a man of middle age, grossly overweight, a man of Moroccan origin and of the Jewish faith, a citizen of the state of Israel, and in the employ of the Mossad.

In the house of the headman of the Shi'ite village of Baaloul, the merchant had slept poorly. His mind could not escape from the vision of a tortured colleague, of the fate of a captured agent.

Major Zvi Dan said, "We cannot confirm that the recruits are at the camp, nor that they are under the command of Abu Hamid."

"You didn't tell me that you were trying to confirm it," Tork said.

"We were trying to, but sadly we did not succeed. We had an agent in that region, but the agent has been taken . . ." Major Zvi Dan sighed, as if this were a matter of personal grief.

"You had someone in that camp?"

"We had an agent in the area."

"That's insanity. You may have alerted them, blown the whole show."

"We committed a valued, trusted agent, now lost. Don't shout at me."

"Shit . . . you may have blown it, Zvi."

"Wrong. The information requirements given to the agent were vague and covered various areas. Whatever those pigs beat out of her will not identify our target."

"*Her?* You sent in a woman?"

Major Zvi Dan slammed his fist onto his desk. "Spare me your British chivalry crap. We are at war. We use what we have. Old men, women, children, what we have. You miss the point."

"The point being . . . ?"

"My friend, you may make all your preparations, you may—Crane may and the boy may—walk into the Bekaa, take up a sniping position above the camp, and find that your target isn't there, perhaps never was there. That is what I tried to save you, that chance."

"I'm sorry," the station officer said softly.

"For what?"

"That you lost your agent."

"Friend, do not be sorry for me. Be sorry for her, a human being taken by animals. I will have lost a skirmish, she will lose her life, maybe already has."

"London will be grateful," the station officer said softly.

"That'll be nice," Major Zvi Dan said, "but I don't want their gratitude. What I want is that your people will very seriously weigh the risks before it is too late. Tell them, so that they understand about real war."

"I'm better than I was." The sweat soaked into his tracksuit top. "Can't you admit I'm improving?"

"Your sit-ups are average, your push-ups are average, your squat-thrusts are average. And all the time you're yapping, you're losing strength," Crane said. "You're still a passenger, Holt, so work."

"I'm fit, and you haven't the decency to admit it."

"Is that right?"

"Too damn right. You've such a bloody ego on your shoulders that you can't admit that I'm fit to walk with you. I know your sort, Crane, you're the sort that hasn't the bigness to admit that I've done well."

"Done well, have you?" Crane smiled grimly.

Holt gazed up at the wall of the house. He saw Mrs. Ferguson's face at the upper window. She was always there when he was performing his morning exercise ritual, when he went for his shower she would go down to the kitchen. The start of every day.

"I tell you what I think, I think I'm a bloody sight fitter than you are . . ." Christ, that was stupid. "I'm sorry," he said, sagging back on the damp slabs.

"Wait there." Crane snapped the instruction. He strode away, into the house.

Holt lay on his back. The sweat was cooling on his skin. His anger cooled too, but he knew what had scratched him. Planning and logistics were between Percy Martins and Crane. They huddled in front of the living room fire, they pored over the maps and over the inventory of required equipment, and over the aerial photographs. Never was Holt asked for his opinion. He *was* the bloody passenger. He had not even been shown the aerial photographs of the camp. He had not been lectured on the Bekaa, what he would find there. He had not been told how they would go in; he had most certainly not been told how they would get out.

George was standing a few yards from Holt and watching him. He had a sly smile, as if there were some sport to be had. The dog was sitting beside George, quiet for once, interested. Martins had followed George out of the house. He was sniffing at the air as if that would tell him whether it would rain this day. Neither George nor Martins had the time of day for Holt. Something they thought bloody clever was being cooked. Holt stood. He rocked. His legs felt weak. Of course he was weak, he had done the circuit of the sit-ups, push-ups, squat-thrusts, he had done the triple sprint, he had done the endurance run. He breathed deep, he pulled the oxygen back into his body, down into his lungs, deep into his bloodstream . . .

Crane came through the French windows, out onto the patio. He carried an old rucksack and a set of bathroom scales. He put the scales down and walked into the garden. George was laughing quietly. Martins had the look of a headmaster who has to punish a boy caught smoking—this hurts me more than it will you. Crane was in the rockery, tugging loose the stones. Crane loaded stones into his rucksack. When he had brought it to the scales Holt saw that it weighed five and a half stones, seventy-seven pounds. Crane swept the rucksack onto his shoulders.

"You say that you are fitter than I am. When we are in the Bekaa this is what I carry, and you will carry the same. Now we shall go six times round the lawn, the endurance . . . but you won't have the weight, and I shall beat you."

"I already apologized."

"I don't hear you." Crane growled.

Holt led the first time round. He tried to run easily, loosely, he tried to save himself. Past the decaying summer house, past the bare beech tree, past the rose beds, past the rhododendron jungle, past the straggling holly hedge, past the patio where George was smiling, where Martins was still looking pained. All the time the pounding feet of Crane behind him.

The second time round, Holt led.

The third time round, Holt led. The third time round hurt him, because he tried to increase his speed. Ten years since he had run competitively, school sports, and even then he hadn't cared for it. Stepping up the stride, trying to break Crane, trying to open the gap. Legs hurting, guts hurting, lungs hurting, and all the time the stamping tread of the man behind him, and the bastard carried seventy-seven pounds' weight on his back.

The fourth time round, Holt led. As though they were held together by elastic, when Holt lengthened his stride, Crane stayed with him. When Holt slowed then Crane stayed back. The fourth time round and Holt understood. He was a plaything.

The fifth time round, Holt led. His own breath coming in hurt surges, his legs leaden, his head rolling. Crane was behind him, struggling more now, but in touch. No chance now of Holt running him out. Survival was the game. Survival was keeping going. Survival was pride. He could not win, he knew the bastard would take him on the last circuit. Jane's face was in his mind. Jane's face back in his mind after being gone, absent, for days . . . Jane, darling, lovely Jane . . . Jane whose body he had known . . . Jane who was going to share his life . . . Jane who was watching him . . . Jane who was now safe . . . He was screaming, "Why did you have to stand in front of the old fool?" Couldn't hear his own voice. Could only hear the beat of Crane's feet, and the wheeze of his breath.

The sixth time round, Holt led. He led at first. He led past the summer house. He led past the beech tree. He led past the rose beds, but Crane was at his shoulder. He led past the rhododendrons, but Crane was beside him, only fractionally behind. He saw Crane's face. He knew he had lost when he turned his jerking head to see the composure of Crane's face. Past the holly hedge and he was following Crane home. His legs were jelly. When he reached the patio, Crane was already unslinging the rucksack. He lay on the grass, beaten.

"Put those stones back where I found them," Crane said. "Then go take a shower."

The dog was licking his face, large and gentle strokes of the dog's tongue. The patio was empty. Crane and Martins and the grinning George had left young Holt to his self-pity, to his picture of his girl. He retched, he had nothing to lose. It was raining. At first he could not lift the rucksack. He crawled to the rockery, dragging the deadweight behind him with the dog nuzzling at his ears. He tipped the stones out of the rucksack onto the wild strawberry strands.

The dog followed him inside and he didn't care that the dog, with muddied feet, was not allowed in the house, didn't give a damn.

Holt stood at the door of the dining room.

Martins and Crane sat at a table at the far end of the room. Crane was wiping the perspiration from his neck with his napkin.

His voice was a stammer, the weakness of it betrayed him. "Why, Mr. Crane? Why was that necessary?"

"So you get to understand my meaning of fitness."

"What happens if I am not fit?"

"On the way in, you slow me down because I have to travel at your speed. On the way out if you are not fit, I ditch you. And if I ditch you, you're dead or you're captured. If you're captured you'll wish you were dead."

Martins said, "You're making a fool of yourself, Holt."

"I'm not your son, *Mister* Martins. Don't talk to me as if I were your poor bloody son."

"Watch your mouth, and remember that I was a field operative for the Service before you were born. I won't get another show like this, I'm going to make damn certain this one works. So get a grip on yourself. She was your girl, and you never heard me say it would be a picnic. And get that bloody dog out of here."

9

It was a miserable drive for Holt.

He was relegated to the front seat with George at the wheel and taciturn. Martins and Crane were in the back of the old Volvo, and behind them, separated by stout wire mesh, was the Rottweiler. George was disgruntled because Martins had told him that the state of the car was a disgrace and had refused to leave until the sides had been hosed down and the floor mats shaken out and the ashtrays emptied. Martins was deep in his papers and Crane slept beside him with the ease of a man who catches his rest where, whenever, he can find it.

George drove well—as though it were the only thing he was good at—and he concentrated on the road ahead. Holt was on his own again.

But then for eleven days he had effectively been on his own, and he had given up the struggle to be party to the planning of the operation. He could cope. He was good at being alone, had been since childhood. Childhood in a country general practitioner's home, with Mum doubling as receptionist/secretary and nurse, had dictated that there were long times during the school holidays when he was left to his own devices. Being alone was not being lonely, not in Holt's book. Being alone, being able to live in a personal capsule, was fine by Holt. Noah Crane was another loner, Holt thought; they should have had a rapport, except that

Crane was too damned good at being alone to share even a common purpose. It had been good last night in the drawing room, after another awful Mrs. Ferguson supper, when Martins had launched into a sermon about "the long arm of vengeance" and "the moral evil of terrorism," about "those who have deeper convictions, stronger wills, greater determination, will surely triumph," about "the satisfaction of going the other side of the hill to strike with a mailed fist." High-grade crap, and Crane had shown what he thought of it. He closed his eyes and fell asleep. They should have been friends, young Holt and old Noah Crane. That they were not friends was a pity, nothing more, and he'd get there, sooner or later, if it killed him.

He knew they were going to an army camp. He didn't know more because he hadn't been told, and by now he had stopped asking. For a change it was a crisp and clean morning, bright and fine. A good morning for a walk on the wilderness wildness of Exmoor, even a good morning for sitting next to George who spoke not a word and sucked peppermints. They went west across Salisbury Plain, past the ancient hulks of Stonehenge, across the great open spaces that were crisscrossed with tank tracks, past small stone villages with neat pubs and Norman churches. The first time in eleven days he had been away from the crumbling damp pile and the overgrown garden that was encircled by the ten-foot-high chain-link fence set along concrete posts. Thank God for it, being away. They came to the small, bustling town of Warminster and they followed the red-painted signs toward the military camp.

They were checked at the gatehouse. They were saluted as they drove through. Holt didn't turn to see, but he fancied from the rustle of movement behind him that Martins would have given the sentry an imperial wave of acknowledgment. They pulled up outside a square red-brick building.

They were escorted to an upper room that was filled with the warm smell of fresh coffee, all except George. They were in the military world. Friendly handshakes, warm greetings. There was a long heavy box on the floor, half pushed under the table from which the coffee and biscuits were served.

The cups and saucers were back on the table. Three officers in smart pressed uniforms and polished boots, and Martins in a tweed suit, and Holt wearing his sports jacket, and Crane in the same trousers and the same poplin parka that he had worn since he had arrived. Ready for business.

"How many marksmen?"

"Just one," Martins said. "Mr. Crane is the marksman."

Holt thought the soldiers had assumed that he, Holt, was the marksman. Surprised, they stared at Crane. Another day that Crane had not bothered to shave.

"What weapon are you familiar with, Mr. Crane?"

"More weapons than you've handled," Crane said, indifferent.

Holt saw the glint in the officer's eyes. "I see. Let me put it another way. What sniper weapon are you most familiar with, Mr. Crane?"

"Galil 7.62-millimeter semi-automatic."

"We think ours is better."

"I don't need a sales pitch—I'm using yours because that's what I've been told to use."

Holt chuckled out loud, involuntarily, couldn't help himself, then bit his lip to silence. He wondered if the man had been born to whom Crane could be civil.

Martins said, "It's a British show, British equipment will be used."

Holt reckoned he had the drift. British equipment to be used, and no one too sorry if after a successful snipe the British equipment could be left behind. British ammunition cases . . . a calling card for the Syrians.

The case on the floor was pulled clear of the table. Holt saw the rifle lying on its side in a cut-out bed of foam rubber. The rifle was painted in green and brown shades of camouflage. He saw the telescopic sights snug in their own compartments.

For the officer it was a labor of love. "It is the Parker-Hale M-85 bolt action, detachable box magazine, militarized bipod with provision for either swivel or cant adjustment. It will travel with a six-by-forty-four daylight scope sight, and also the passive night vision job. We reckon it, in the right hands, to have a hundred percent success ratio at a first shot hit at anything under 650 yards, but the rear aperture sight has the capability of up to 975 yards."

"What's the weight?"

"With one magazine full and the telescopic sight it comes out at a few ounces under fourteen pounds . . . Going far, is it?"

"Not your concern," Martins said.

"Far enough for the weight to matter," Crane said.

"You want to fire it?"

"Prefer to fire it than have lunch."

"Then you'll want some kit."

"Right, and I want kit for him." Crane jerked his thumb at Holt, then turned to him. "Go and have the best shit and the best piss you've had all week, and get back here smartish."

Holt would have been gone ten minutes.

He came back into the room. Crane already wore camouflage battledress and his clothes were in a neat folded pile on the edge of the table. Crane tossed a tunic and trousers to Holt, pointed to a pair of boots and a pair of heavy khaki socks.

They walked for half an hour till they reached a place that satisfied Crane. Out of the camp, away up on the plain, beyond the red flag flying a warning of live shooting. They settled into beaten-down bracken. Crane said that Holt wasn't to talk, wasn't to move. Hundreds of yards ahead of them, across a shallow valley of young trees, Holt could just make out the barricade of sandbags and in front of it the human-shaped target.

Five hours and thirty-five minutes after they had taken their positions, Holt lying half a body length behind Crane and a yard to his right, the marksman fired.

One shot. No word, no warning that he was about to shoot.

Holt's legs were dead, his bladder was full, his mind was numbed.

They lay in the bracken a full ten minutes after the single shot, then Crane stood and walked away with the rifle on his shoulder, like he had been out after wood pigeon or wild duck.

Holt stumbled after him, bent to massage the circulation back into his legs.

Crane had his head down, was walking into the wind. "The way you fidgeted we wouldn't have lasted an hour."

"For God's sake, I hardly moved."

"*Hardly* isn't good enough, not in the Bekaa."

They were picked up by a waiting Land Rover and driven back into the camp.

By the time that Holt and Crane had peeled off their battledress, the human-shaped target had been carried into the room.

Holt saw the single bullet hole. The hole was central upper chest. A group formed. Two of the officers and Crane and Martins, with an inventory sheet, ticking off a list. The talk was in a jargon shorthand which Holt did not understand. As he dressed he found that his eyes always strayed back to the single hole on the target, a single killing shot. God, he could hardly tie his shoelaces. And he was making a mess of knotting his tie. He had his shirt buttons out of kilter. As if at last it were serious . . . as if every other thing since the steps of the Oreanda Hotel had been a cartoon for a comic paper.

Grown men discussing in low voices the grained weight of specific bullets, and the holding capacity of a Bergen, and night walking speeds, and the quantity of "compo" rations required. Grown men talking through the logistics of a killing snipe . . . that was bloody serious, young Holt.

The third officer stood beside him.

"We let you loose for an hour then we went onto the hilltop above and had a look for you. How far were you apart?"

"Why?"

"We saw you pretty quick, we never saw him. Was he far away?"

"Pretty far," Holt lied.

"It was a hell of a shot, 750 yards. Incredible. You know in one week in Belfast I once had seven hits, all between 600 and 1,000, but I knew the weapon, always used the same one. I tell you, to get a perfect hit with the first shot with a new weapon, unbelievable."

"Perhaps he just likes killing people," Holt said.

"Don't we all? My sweat is that all I get to blow away these days is pheasants . . . I envy you. I envy him more."

"Then you're out of your mind."

"Just trying to make conversation," the officer smiled.

Across the room the murmur of voices was uninterrupted. Holt caught occasional phrases, descriptions. Something called a Rifleman's Assault Weapon, something about low day/night signature, something about standoff demolition, something about minimal training, something about a Rifleman's Assault Weapon being right for young Holt. But Crane shook his head, didn't look at Holt, just indicated that he wanted none of that for Holt.

Holt's hands flickered uselessly at his tie. The officer knelt in front of him and without fuss tied Holt's shoelaces.

"You're fortunate to be with him. Marksmen are a rare breed. They tend to survive. Wherever you're going, whatever the opposition, they'll regret that guy ever turned up. Good luck."

"Mr. Crane doesn't trust luck."

"I hope you win."

"I'm scared out of my mind."

The officer looked embarrassed, finished with the shoelaces, stood and smiled awkwardly.

When they went down the stairs, out to the Volvo, George was holding the Rottweiler back from the opened hatch of the car and three private soldiers under the supervision of the quartermaster sergeant were loading equipment, wooden and cardboard boxes and two Bergens. When they had finished, George had to rummage in the load to make a space for his dog.

Martins signed three sheets on the quartermaster's clipboard.

The officers waved them away, waved to them until they were round the corner, gone from sight.

Out onto the main road.

George driving fast. The dog snoring again.

"You're off tomorrow, Holt," Martins said.

He didn't ask whether he could telephone his parents when

he was back at the house, tell them he'd be away for a few days.

He didn't even ask what was a Rifleman's Assault Weapon, and why it needed minimal training and why it was not right for young Holt.

He thought about a young man from the far side of the world, a young man of his own age. A young man with a crow's foot scar on his left upper cheek.

They drove in silence.

It was evening when they reached the house.

George was left to park the car, unload the equipment, exercise the dog. Martins hurried to the telephone. Crane said he was going to have a shower. It was as if they all had too much work on their hands to concern themselves with young Holt, so scared he could scream and starting the journey for the Bekaa the next day. Everyone too busy.

Holt sat in the living room, turned the pages of a magazine, didn't read the text, didn't register the photographs.

He heard Martins stamp into the room.

"It's too damned bad. She is becoming quite impossible . . ."

He didn't take the cue, didn't ask what was bad, who was impossible. Too bitter to be feed man for Percy Martins's little act.

"She is cooking for a dinner in the village hall, not for us. We come second to the village hall social evening. Sometimes that woman goes too far."

"I fancy a night out," Holt said.

"A cabaret at the village hall? That's a poor joke, Holt."

"It's all a piss-poor joke, Mr. Martins. I fancy a night out."

"Now, wait a minute . . ."

"Alone. Don't worry, Mr. Martins, I won't run away. You can tell the horrible people who run you that young Holt says you've done a hell of a good job in trapping him."

"Don't you understand, it's for your country."

He had drunk seven pints of best bitter. He had drunk three whiskey shorts.

He stood on the stage.

The comedian was long away. The magician had packed and gone.

There was an untouched pint and another whiskey on top of the piano.

The clock on the square tower of the village church that was across the road from the hall chimed the strokes of midnight.

He had given them his whole repertoire. He had led them in his *South Pacific* selection, his Presley impression, his Jim Reeves collection. He had them going with his choruses, he had them clapping to the hammer thump of the pale young rector on the piano beside him.

He rocked on his feet. His face was flushed. He could hear the shouting and the cheering from the audience. He understood his audience. It was an audience that he recognized from his village at home. They were the farm workers and their wives, and the Post Office staff and their wives, and the council workers and their wives, and the builders and joiners and their wives. Because he had drunk too much he had pushed his way forward and climbed the steps to the stage after the magician had taken his bow, he had offered himself when he had thought the evening was flattening out.

"Give us one more, young 'un." The shout from the back, from the darkness beyond the footlights and the smoke haze.

The rector shrugged. Holt whispered in his ear.

Holt sang.

> *"Wish me luck, as you wave me goodbye,*
> *With a cheer, not a tear, make it gay.*
> *Give me a smile,*
> *I can keep all the while,*
> *In my heart while I'm away.*
> *Till we meet once again, you and I,*
> *Wish me luck, as you wave me goodbye . . ."*

How many of them knew where the Bekaa Valley was? How many of them had any idea what the Popular Front for the Liberation of Palestine was? They joined in for the chorus.

> *"Wish me luck, as you wave me goodbye,*
> *Cheerio, here I go, on my way.*
> *Wish me luck, as you wave me goodbye . . ."*

Holt was not aware of the spreading quiet. His song, his voice filled his head. A young man saying his farewells, heading for the Bekaa with a marksman who could kill with a state-of-the-art rifle at 750 yards. A young man who had been told he was going to the Bekaa to have a man killed for his country. Did any of them care? Small safe people, living small safe lives, in a small safe community. A lone voice, and a piano, desperate for tuning, echoing through a tin-roofed village hall in the English countryside.

> *"Wish me luck, as you wave me goodbye.*
> *Wish me luck,*
> *Wish me luck,*
> *Wish me luck . . ."*

As the morning sun, brilliant bright, hugged the rim of the valley, the jeep pulled away from the camp.

No heat yet in the air, and Abu Hamid was cold in the passenger seat. He did not know for how long he would be in Damascus, he had not been told. He knew only that he was escaping from the camp and the firing range in the wadi cut into the hillside, and that, along with the possibility that he would have the chance to be with Margarethe, was sufficient to lift his spirits.

While they still crawled over the ruts and stone chips of the unsurfaced road he saw the cluster of dogs.

He knew at once. He should have stood over them when they dug the grave. Slowly they passed the dogs. There were six, seven of them, perhaps more. There was no window on the side of the jeep. He heard the snarling, selfish anger of the dogs. The dogs were pulling, snapping, tugging at the dark-stained bundle. Beside him the driver grinned. They drove on. The fighting dogs were left in the dust thrown up by the wheels of the jeep.

They crossed the valley. They were waved through the checkpoints. They reached the fast, tarmacadamed road to Damascus.

What the wandering Lawrence called a pearl in the morning sun is a vast archaeological treasure ground. It is also the oldest continually inhabited city in the world. The present population, numbering 7,000,000, are the successors of those who first settled south of the Jebel esh Sharoi, east of the Jebel Khachine, 5,000 years ago. Damascus has seen the worship of pagan gods, and of the Roman Jupiter. Damascus was the settling place of Saint Paul and the budding spirit of Christianity, it was the center of the world of Islam, it was a great city of the Ottoman despots, it was a fiefdom of European France. Now it is a bastard mixture of cultures. On the broad French-style boulevards of Damascus walk the covert fundamentalists of the Muslim faith, discreet and quiet-living Jews, Sunnis, ruling Alawites from the northern coastline, Soviets from the east, eye-catching prostitutes aping what they believe is the Western way of provocation. The regime, which is bankrupt and sustained by loans from the oil-rich Gulf, is headed by a man whose air force career was undistinguished, who had levered himself to Defense Minister in time for the catastrophic defeat at the hands of Israel in 1967, who had then climbed to President in time for the greater military disaster of Yom Kippur. The regime lives on a foundation of terror and repression. There are eight separate organizations responsible for internal and external security. The security men are the new masters of modern Damascus; they and their regime are without mercy. Orders are issued for public hangings on the portable gallows in Semiramis Square. Orders for 200 supporters of the Muslim Brotherhood to be brought by the lorry load to the center of Aleppo and executed by firing squad. Orders for 300 Islamic fundamentalists to be taken from the Tadmor prison in Palmyra to a trench dug by bulldozers, and there to be buried alive. Orders sent to Hama, after the suppression of revolt, for the killing of 15,000 males over the age of ten. Orders for torture, orders for murder. Mercy is a stranger in Damascus today; perhaps it was always so.

He knew enough of the geography of Damascus to know that they had entered the southern district of Abu Rummaneh.

He was being taken to the Air Ministry complex. They were approaching the Avenue El Mahdy. The driver said nothing. Abu Hamid was familiar enough with men such as his driver. A Palestinian learned in Damascus that he could expect no warmth from a Syrian, not unless he had favors to offer.

He had never before been to the Air Ministry complex, sprawling, five stories high; he had had no reason to.

Close to the Air Ministry, Abu Hamid saw the security presence on the pavements. Young men in street clothes lounged under the trees, leant on the lamp posts, sauntered beside the road. All the young men carried Kalashnikov rifles. When he had first lived in Damascus he had heard the rumors. Even out at the Yarmuk camp he had heard the explosions in the night of roadside bombs detonated against six army lorries in different locations and, so the rumors said, 60 had been killed; a car bomb in the city center, and 40 killed. He understood why the security men lounged on the street corners, leant against the lamp posts, sauntered on the pavements.

There was a concrete chicane pass inside the gates of the Air Ministry. Abu Hamid was dropped off in front of the gate. He still had his leg in the jeep when the driver gunned the engine. Bastard . . . He hopped clear. He endured the suspicion of the sentries, shining helmets, immaculate uniforms. He felt unclean from the dust of the Bekaa. He could smile as he was body-searched. If there were a car bomb at the Air Ministry then it would be the supercilious sentries at the gate that would catch the flying axles and radiator and gear housing.

He was escorted inside. It had taken twenty-five minutes to establish that he was expected.

A new experience for Abu Hamid, walking the scrubbed, airy, painted corridors and staircases of the Air Ministry. The first time he had ever stepped inside such a place. A new world to him. At the end of a long corridor was a gate of steel bars, guarded. The gate was opened, he was taken through, the gate clanged shut behind him. Into an inner sanctum.

He could shiver, he could wonder what was wanted of him.

A door subserviently knocked by his escort. A uniformed clerk greeted Abu Hamid, ushered him inside, crossed to a door beyond a huge desk, knocked. A shout. The space of the room emerged in front of him.

In all the years of his young life Abu Hamid had never seen such luxury. He stared around him. His eyes roved from the whispering hush of the air conditioning machine in the wall to the heavyweight softness of the leather sofa to the teak table to the sparkle of the decanter and glasses to the fitted pile carpet to the hi-fi cabinet to the dull true silver of the photograph frames . . . could not help himself, a child in a glittering treasure land.

He saw the welcome smile of Major Said Hazan. The major was far back in a tilted chair, his polished shoes on the polished desk top. The major was waving him inside, waving with his stumped fist for him to cross the carpet pile in his dust-laden boots. Abu Hamid knew the man who sprawled in the depths of the sofa. He knew the man only by a given code name. He knew that the man was designated as the head of the military wing of the Popular Front. He knew that the man was believed to be at least number three and possibly number two in the command ranking of the Popular Front. He knew that the man had once himself opened a package sent from Stockholm to the offices of the Popular Front in Beirut . . . that was many years before, but many years did not restore a right arm taken off at the elbow, nor three fingers amputated from the left fist, nor smooth away the wounds of the shrapnel in his neck and jaw.

"Of course you know our Brother. You are welcome, Hamid. I hear good things of what you are achieving with the young fighters. I hear only good things of you . . ."

He stared at them both, in turn, these veterans of the war against the state of Israel, and the scars of their war. A ruined face, a lost arm and a lost grip of fingers. Was that how he would end? A face that his Margarethe would shrink from, hands that could not caress the white smooth skin of his Margarethe . . .

"Come, Hamid, sit down."

The door was closed behind him. He sat on the edge of the sofa, he felt the leather sink under him.

"I have sad news for you, Hamid. Your commander in Simferopol has gone to a martyr's resting place, but he died in his uniform, his life was lost in the service of Palestine . . . A car accident . . . most sad. We all grieve for his passing."

No expression was possible on the unlined skin of the major's face. Abu Hamid saw no change in the eyes or at the mouth of the Brother. The understanding came as a fast shaft. The commander and Abu Hamid and Major Said Hazan had been the only persons directly involved in the shooting at Yalta. Three persons, now two persons.

"I want two men, Hamid. I want two of your best recruits."

Abu Hamid looked across the width of the sofa to the Brother. Their eyes did not meet. Again he understood. They were the proxies, the Palestinians. He was learning, sharply, quickly.

"What skills would the two men have?" Abu Hamid's recruits were raw, not yet expert in weapons or explosives.

"Courage, commitment. They will join others. You will go back to the Bekaa this morning. You will choose the two men. You will take them to the Yarmuk tomorrow . . . What is it, Hamid? I can see your impatience. Anger, is it? Or passion, is it? Tomorrow, Hamid, you will have the time to attend to your lady. Today the revolution has need of you . . . your best men, remember."

"It will be done, Major."

Holt had a sore head. He walked half a pace behind Martins and Crane. It was a part of the airport that was new to him. He hadn't been to Israel before, nor had he been to South Africa, so he had never come this way. It was the airport high-security corridor, quarantined from "ordinary" flight passengers, reserved for the two flights thought to be most greatly at risk from terrorist attack. He had seen it on television, of course, but the sight of the police and the dogs and the Heckler and Koch machine pistols still startled him. Policemen patrolling and parading in front of him with attack dogs on short leashes, with machine pistols held in readiness across their chests. He wondered how long they would have, how many fragments of seconds in which to beat off an attack. He wondered how long it would take them to snap out of the Musak-swimming calm of the corridor, how long to get the safety to Off, to get the finger from the guard to the trigger. He wondered how they slept at night, how they rested, relaxed with their kids. And if he found the man in the Bekaa, and Crane shot him, would that make their lives easier?

They settled into the chairs of the departure lounge, the same departure lounge in which, months before, an alert El Al security man carrying out the final personal baggage checks had been suspicious of a bag carried by a 32-year-old Irishwoman, Anne Murphy. When the security man emptied the bag he believed it still too heavy. When he stripped up the bottom of the bag he found underneath three pounds of oily soft orange-colored plastic explosive, manufactured in Czechoslovakia. The potential of the explosive was equivalent to the simultaneous detonation of 30 hand grenades. The explosive, the timer, and the detonator had been supplied to a plump-faced Jordanian called Nezar Hindawi by senior officers of Syrian Air Force Intelligence. It was intended that the pregnant Miss Murphy would be blown out of the sky along with all the passengers and crew, that the disintegrating aircraft would crash in the mountains of Austria, that all evidence of guilt should be destroyed.

Holt's mind was dead to his surroundings. His head ached from the excess of alcohol that he had consumed the night before. But sitting in that same departure lounge should have made him think of those events. In reprisal the government of the United Kingdom had broken diplomatic relations with the Syrian Arab Republic. Sir Sylvester Armitage had gone into the folklore of Foreign and Commonwealth with his booming "Bloody Nonsense." Sir Sylvester Armitage had been targeted, and Miss Jane Canning had walked in front of him onto the steps of the Oreanda Hotel in Yalta. The beginning of this story was in this departure lounge, leading to Gate 23 of Terminal One, months before. Holt sat with his chin on his chest and the throb in his temples. Crane sat and slept. Percy Martins sat and pondered the final elusive clues of the day's crossword.

A little before 5:00 A.M., in a deep gray dawn haze, a British Airways Tristar slammed down onto the tire-scarred runway of the international airport east of Tel Aviv.

It was just 29 days since a trio of British diplomats had boarded an aircraft at Moscow's Vnukovo Airport for a flight to the Crimea.

10

In the same jeep, with the same silent driver, Abu Hamid escorted his two chosen recruits to the Yarmuk camp.

Both were seventeen years old. All of the way back from Damascus the previous day he had considered which of his sixty he should proposition.

Mohammed was the most obvious choice because he was always the loudest to complain at the boredom of the training, to harangue his fellow recruits of time wasted when they should have been carrying the war into the Zionist state; he would eat, chew, choke on his words. The second, Ibrahim, had been brought to Abu Hamid's notice by the murmured accusation that he was a thief, that he pilfered the paltry possessions of his fellow recruits. Well, he could thieve to his content in the state of Israel. The choice had been made by Abu Hamid alone. He had found Fawzi gone when he had returned to the camp. Gone smuggling, the bastard, gone to organize the early summer cropping of the hashish fields, to gather his cut from the merchants who traded in transistor radios and Western liquor and fruit and vegetables out of the Bekaa. He had seen both men separately in his tent. He had spoken to them of the glory of the struggle against Israel, and of the love of the Palestinian people for the heroism of their fighters, and of the money they would be paid when they returned. Both men, separately, had agreed. Easier for Abu Hamid than he could have dared expect. The exhortation and the bribe, good bedfellows, working well together. He had wondered if they were frightened, if they dreamed of death. He wondered if the one guessed that he had been chosen because he had made a bastard nuisance of himself in the tent camp, the other because he was whispered to be a thief.

Abu Hamid cared not at all what they knew.

The jeep was stopped at the entrances to the Yarmuk camp: the sentries radioed to Administration for an officer to come.

Abu Hamid whistled quietly to himself. He had the statistic in his head, their chance was 1 in 100. A 1-in-100 chance of his seeing them again.

It was the Brother who came to the gate. Abu Hamid saw the loose empty sleeve of the Brother's jacket. He told the Brother the names of the two men that he had brought, he watched as the Brother peered inside the jeep at the two men, weighing them. The Brother gave Abu Hamid two sealed envelopes, then politely asked Mohammed who was the boaster and Ibrahim who was the thief to come with him.

He watched them go. He watched the barrier lift for them, fall after them. He saw the camp swallow them.

He tore open the first envelope. The form carried the heading of the Central Bank of Syria. It told him the number of an account in which the sum of five thousand American dollars had been lodged in his name. His chortling laughter filled the front of the jeep. Abu Hamid owned nothing. He had no money, no things even that were his own. He felt his chest, his lungs expand with the excitement; his head sing. He ripped open the second envelope. A single sheet of paper, a handwritten address.

He pushed the form of the Central Bank of Syria into the breast pocket of his tunic and buttoned it down, he thrust the address into the driver's face. The driver shrugged, started the engine, turned the wheel.

When Abu Hamid looked back at the gate he could no longer see the backs of the Brother or of Mohammed and Ibrahim.

He was driven into the center of Damascus.

The jeep driver seemed to pay no attention to traffic lights at Stop or to pedestrian crossings. Away from the wide streets, into the warren alleys of the old city. Past the great mosque, past the colonnade of the Roman builders, past the marble Christian shrine to John the Baptist. Through the narrow roads, weaving among the cymbal-clashing sherbet sellers, past the stalls of spices and intricate worked jewelry, past the tables of the money changers, past the dark recesses of the cafés, inside the vast sprawl of the Suq al Hamadieh. Only military vehicles were allowed inside the tentacles of the *suq* lanes, and only a military vehicle would have had the authority to force a way through the slow shuffling morass of shoppers, traders. He supposed he could have bought a street, he thought he could have cleared a table of jewelry, a shop window of stereo equipment, a clothing store of suits; he had in his tunic breast pocket a bank order form from the Central Bank of Syria for five thousand American dollars. He could have bought flowers for Margarethe, champagne for Margarethe. He could take her to restaurants, the best, and order a feast of *mezza* and the *burgol* dish of sweet boiled crushed wheat and the *yalanji* dish of eggplant stuffed with rice and the *sambosik* dish of meat rissole in light pastry and unleavened bread and as much *arrack* as they could drink before they fell.

He could buy her what she wanted, he could buy himself what he wanted. He had been paid for the success at the Oreanda in Yalta.

The driver stopped. He pointed. He pointed down an alley too narrow for the vehicle. He wrote on the paper beside the address a telephone number to call for transport back into the Bekaa.

Abu Hamid ran. Shouldering, pushing, shoving his way through the throng.

He saw the opened door, the stone steps.

He ran up the steps. The wooden door faced him. The handle turned, the door swung.

"Well done, sweet boy, well done for finding me."

His Margarethe, in front of him. Her fair hair flopped to her shoulders, her body sheathed in a dress of rich wine-colored brocade. His Margarethe standing in the heart of a quiet oasis, in a room of cool air, standing in the center of a faded deep sinking carpet, standing surrounded by hanging dark drapes and the heavy wood furniture, intricately carved. He thought it was the paradise that the Old Man of the Mountains had spoken of, the paradise of the Assassins.

"Wasn't I good to find it, wasn't I good to find such a place for us?"

No questions in his mind. No asking himself how a foreigner with only the handout crumbs from the table of the regime could find paradise, quiet, clean comfort, among the alleys of the *suq*. He was kissing her, feeling the warm moisture of her lips, scenting the hot skin of her neck, clutching the gentle curves of her buttocks then her breasts.

The news was bursting in him. He stood away from her. He beamed in pride. He pulled the form from the Central Bank of Syria from his pocket.

"A piece of paper . . ."

"Read the paper."

He saw the moment of confusion, then the spread of concentration, then the drift of disbelief.

"For what?"

"It is *five thousand dollars*, for me."

"For what?"

"For what I have done."

"It's a joke, yes? What have you done?"

"Not a joke, it is real. It is for me. It is the paper of the Central Bank of Syria."

"You have not done anything, sweet boy. You are a revolutionary soldier . . . why is this given to you?"

Abu Hamid stood his full height. He looked up, into the eyeline of Margarethe Schultz. He said sternly, "For what I have done this is the reward of the Syrian government."

She blinked, she did not understand. "You have done nothing. You came to Syria, you lived in a camp. You went to the Crimea, you were one of many, you came back. Now you are in a camp in Lebanon. What in that history is worth five thousand dollars?"

"It is payment for what I have done for the Syrians."

"Sweet boy, you are a fighter of the Palestine revolution, not an errand boy of the Syrians."

"You insult me. I am not an 'errand boy.' "

"Hamid, what did you do for the Syrians?"

She was close to him, she stroked the hair of his neck.

"Hamid, what did you do?"

"I cannot . . ."

"Damn you, what did you do?"

"Don't make . . ."

"What?"

It came in a blurted torrent. "In the Crimea I killed the ambassador of Britain, I killed also one of his aides . . ."

"For that they pay you?"

"For that they reward me."

She stood straight, contemptuous. He saw the heave of her breasts under the brocade of her dress.

"Which is more important to you, the revolution for Palestine, or dollars earned as a hireling?"

He said meekly, "I was going to buy things for you, good things."

"I fuck you, sweet boy, because I believe in you I have found a purity of revolution."

He handed her the bank order for five thousand American dollars. He watched as she made a pencil-thin spiral of it, as she took from the table a box of matches, as she lit the flame, as she burned the wealth he could barely dream of.

"You are not a hireling, sweet boy. In the purity of fire is the strength of the struggle of the Palestinian people."

She lifted her dress, pulled it higher, ever higher. She showed him the spindle of her ankles, and her knees, and the whiteness of her thighs, and the darkness of her groin, and the width of her belly, and the operation scar, and the weight of her breasts. She was naked under her dress. She threw the dress behind her.

She took him to her bed. She took the clothes from his body, kneeling over him, dominating. She straddled his waist.

When he had entered her, he told her of the woman who had been a spy, the woman he had shot. As he told her of the killing, she pounded over him, squealing.

Later, when he rested on the bed, when she had gone to the bathroom to sluice between her legs, he would reflect what her ardor for the clean struggle, the pure revolution, had cost him.

Abu Hamid lay on his side on the bed. If an *Arab* girl had burned five thousand American dollars he would have killed her. He worshiped this European. Could not understand her, her love of his revolution, but could worship her. And she had waited for him, he thought she was a dream of pleasure.

Her soft voice in his ear. "Will they hunt you?"

"Who?"

"The English whose ambassador you killed, the Israelis whose spy you killed."

"In Damascus, in the Bekaa, how can they?"

"You will not be forever in the Bekaa. You will take the battle of the Palestine revolution into Israel."

If he told her of his fear, then he would lose her, he would be the assassin dismissed from paradise. He lied his courage.

"I believe in the inevitability of victory."

She kissed his throat, and the hairs of his chest. With her tongue she circled the crow's foot scar on his left upper cheek.

He was a good-looking boy, blond sun-bleached hair, a wind-tanned face. The uniform looked well on him.

He wore jauntily the sky-blue beret of a soldier on United Nations duty, and his shoulder flash denoted that he was a private soldier of NORBAT.

He was Hendrik Olaffson. He was 23 years old. He was a nothing member of the Norwegian Battalion serving with the United Nations Interim Force in Lebanon. He had been eight months with NORBAT in the northeastern sector of the UNIFIL command.

Intellectually he was a nothing person, militarily he was a nothing person. To Major Said Hazan he was a jewel. Only to Major Said Hazan was Hendrik Olaffson any different than the thousands of private soldiers making up the UNIFIL force from France, Ireland, Ghana, Fiji and Nepal, men stationed in a buffer zone separating southern Lebanon from northern Israel.

At the NORBAT checkpoint on the Rachaiya to Hasbaiya road, it was usual for the UNIFIL troopers to talk to the travelers as they searched the cars for explosives and weapons. The common language of conversation was English, and it was unusual for the troopers to find a traveler who spoke English as well as they did themselves. From a first conversation four months earlier had come the promise of a small quantity of treated marijuana. Enough for one joint each for Hendrik Olaffson and the two soldiers who shared the next night sentry duty with him. The traveler was regularly on that road, the conversations were frequent, the marijuana became plentiful.

In due course Major Said Hazan, who received a report each two weeks from the traveler, had learned of the political views of Hendrik Olaffson. One quiet day at the roadblock the traveler had heard the gushed hatreds of Hendrik Olaffson. The hatreds were for Jews. The hatreds went far back beyond the life of Hendrik Olaffson, to the early life of his father. The grandfather of Hendrik Olaffson had been on the personal staff of Major Vidkun Quisling, puppet ruler of Norway during the years of German occupation. In the last days, as the Wehrmacht had retreated, the grandfather of Hendrik Olaffson had taken his own life, shot himself, spared a postwar tribunal the job of sentencing him. The father of Hendrik Olaffson had been brought up as a despised, fatherless child in Oslo and had died young, consumptive and without the will to live. Many years ago. Too many years for any stigma to survive on Hendrik Olaffson's record. But the boy burned with what he believed to be the injustice that ruined his family. All this had been vouchsafed to the Arab traveler at the roadblock.

He drove a three-ton Bedford lorry, painted white, marked with the sign of UNIFIL. He drove the lorry from the Lebanese side of the security zone that was patrolled by the IDF and their surrogates, the Christian South Lebanese Army, through the zone and into Israel. A UNIFIL lorry was not searched.

He drove the lorry from the NORBAT area to collect 15 soldiers from his country's contingent who had been enjoying four days' rest and recreation in Tel Aviv. On the way south, in darkness close to Herzilya which was a northern suburb of the coastal city, Hendrik Olaffson dropped off the two recruits who had been selected by Abu Hamid. They had traveled in the back of the lorry hidden behind packing cases.

Of course Hendrik Olaffson was a jewel to Major Said Hazan. The major believed he had found the crack in his enemy's armor, a crack he could exploit.

When they ran from the road, into the night, when they watched the disappearing taillights of the white lorry, it was Ibrahim who led, Mohammed who held the strap of the grip bag.

"Your man isn't the great communicator, our man hasn't much to say for himself. They're an odd pair of birds," the station officer said.

Major Zvi Dan shrugged. "Whether they can talk to each other is hardly important. What matters is whether they listen to each other. What is critical is that they have respect for each other."

"When I saw them at the hotel yesterday, and the day before, the impression I had is hardly one of respect. Our man's very quiet, like he's out of his depth and doesn't know how to get into shallow water. Crane speaks to him like he would to a child."

"Respect is difficult when the one has so little to contribute."

The station officer glanced down at his watch. "This Percy Martins will be here soon, he's a crochety old wretch . . . The word from London is that he was damn near on bended knee to the Director to get this trip . . . He's bringing Crane."

"And your young man?"

"That pleasure must still await you, Crane's sent him to the beach for a week, and told him he'd kick his ass if he got sunburn."

"Mr. Fenner is not coming to grace your mission with his presence?"

"Staying in London, sadly." The station officer did not expand, did not feel the need to explore the grubby departmental laundry with his friend.

The girl soldier who did the typing and filing in the outer office put her head around the door. Dark flowing hair, sallow skin, tight khaki blouse. The station officer wondered how elderly crippled Zvi Dan attracted such talent. "Martins has arrived," she said languidly.

Holt lay on the beach.

There was a hotel towel over his legs, draped up to the swimming trunks he had bought at the hotel shop. He wore a shirt, with the sleeves down. He checked the time every half an hour, so that he could be certain that he kept to the schedule Noah Crane had given him. Half an hour with his skin exposed lying on his back, half an hour with his skin covered lying on his back. Half an hour with his skin exposed lying on his stomach, half an hour with his skin covered lying on his stomach.

It was the third morning. He was settling to the routine.

The first morning he had been allowed to stay put in his bed. The last two mornings his alarm call had gone off beside his head at 5:30. Breakfast was tea, toast. Out onto the beach, a lone figure working at sit-ups, push-ups and squat-thrusts, and then repeated sprints, and then the endurance run. However bad the endurance run had been on the soft grass of the country house, it was hell's times worse on the dry sand of the beach. Exposure to the sun all morning, then a salad and cold meat lunch, and then the repetition of the exercises in the full heat, and then recovery on the beach. A final repeat of the exercises as the sun was dipping. After that, the time was his own, that's what Crane had said.

So young Holt had stayed the daylight hours on the beach in front of the row of tower block hotels.

But he had started to walk the streets of Tel Aviv in the

evenings, after he had showered the sand and the sweat off his body, before he was due to attend dinner with Crane and Martins.

He thought Tel Aviv ugly and fascinating.

Perhaps there had never been time at the country house for him to consider what he would find there, but nothing about it was as he had expected. He had walked the length of the seafront promenade, past and beyond the hotels, past and beyond the fortified American embassy, past the scorched grass of Clore Park, he had tramped to the old Arab town of Yafo. He had walked down Ben Yehuda, past the small jewelry shops and the shops that sold antique Arab furniture. He had walked back on Dizengoff, past the plastic-fronted pavement cafés. He thought it was a country of beautiful children, and a country of olive-green uniforms and draped Galil and Uzi weapons. That the state was not yet 40 years old was apparent to Holt from the ramshackle development of building, fast and unlovely construction. Dusty dry streets, unmended pavings, peeling plaster on the squat blocks of apartments. He thought he understood. Why build for the future when your country is targeted by long-range Scud missiles, when your country is nine, ten, eleven minutes' flying time away from hostile air bases, when your country is flanked by enemy armies equipped with the most modern of tanks, artillery and helicopters?

When he worked at his exercises, when he walked the streets, then his mind was occupied. When he lay on his back or his stomach on the beach, when he lay on his bed after supper, then his mind swam with the character of Noah Crane.

He hated to think of the man. He had tried with eagerness, with humor, with achievement to break into the shell defense of Noah Crane. God, had he failed.

"I find the attitude of the Israeli Defense Force quite incredible," Percy Martins said.

"Not incredible, entirely logical," Zvi Dan said quietly.

"This ground was all covered in my report, Mr. Martins," the station officer repeated soothingly.

"It is most certainly not logical that the Israeli Defense Force will offer no facilities for extracting Crane and Holt."

"Mr. Martins, if we wished to make an incursion into the Bekaa we would do so. It is you who wish to do so."

"There has to be a plan for the extraction of these two men in the event of difficulties. They have to be able to call by radio for help."

"Israeli lives, Mr. Martins, will not be put at risk for a mission that is not ours."

"Then I will go higher in the chain than you, Major Dan."

"Of course, you are free to do so. But may I offer you a warning, Mr. Martins? Create too many waves and there's a possibility that the cooperation already offered you will be reduced . . . but you must decide for yourself."

"Dammit, man, would you turn your back on them, would you see them die out there?"

Percy Martins took the handkerchief from the breast pocket of his suit jacket. It did not seem strange to him that he wore a suit of light green tweed plus matching waistcoat with the room temperature close to 100 degrees Fahrenheit. It was one of perhaps six more or less indistinguishable suits that he always wore, winter and spring and summer and autumn, except on Sundays. There was a watch chain across the buttons of the waistcoat, given him by his mother after his father's death, and the timepiece was more than sixty years old and kept good time if it was wound each morning. He mopped the perspiration from his forehead. He disapproved of the designer safari suit in which Tork was dressed, and he disapproved more of the lack of support he was getting from his colleague. His career in the Service had been a lifetime of struggle. His response to all obstacles was to lower his head and raise his voice. There was not one colleague in Century who could level against him the accusation of subtlety.

"I have to believe, Mr. Martins, that the hazards of a mission into the Bekaa were fully evaluated."

The station officer saw Percy Martins blanche. He saw the tongue flick across the lips.

"We *must* have backup."

The station officer had been long enough away from Century to recognize the signs. He felt as if he had eavesdropped a conversation on the upper floor of Century. Naturally, the Israelis would jump to the bidding of the men from the Secret Intelligence Service. Take it for granted that the Israelis would be grateful to help in every possible way.

"I think that what the major is trying to say, Mr. Martins, is . . ."

"I know bloody well what he's trying to say. He's trying to say that two men would be left to rot because the Israeli Defense Force is not prepared to get off its backside and help."

Major Zvi Dan said, "Mr. Martins, allow me to share with you two facts of life in this region. First, for years Israel has pleaded with Western governments to take action against international terrorism, and for years we have been rebuffed. Now, you are in our eyes a Johnny-come-lately, and you expect after years of rejecting our advice that we will suddenly leap in the air at your conversion and applaud you. We think of ourselves first, ourselves second, ourselves third, it is what you have trained us to do. Second fact: in Lebanon in the last five years we have lost close to 1,000 men killed. If our population were translated to that of the United States then we would have lost more men killed in five years than died from enemy action in the whole of the Vietnam war that was of double the duration. If our population were that of the United Kingdom, then we would have lost, killed, some 17,000 soldiers. How many have you lost in Northern Ireland, 400? I think not. How many were killed in the South Atlantic, 350? Not more. Mr. Martins, had you lost 17,000 servicemen in Northern Ireland, in the South Atlantic, would you rush to involve your men in further adventures that would end in no advantage to your own country? I think not, Mr. Martins."

Percy Martins sat straight backed.

"In the event of a crisis the abandonment of those two men would be contemptible."

"Not as contemptible as the appeasement of terrorism that has for years been the policy of your government, of the governments of the United States, of France, of Germany, of Greece. We have offered and already given considerable cooperation. You should make the best of what you have."

There was the scrape of the chair under Percy Martins. He was red-faced from the heat, flushed from the put-down. He stood, turned on his heel. No handshakes, no farewells. He strode out of the room.

A long silence and then the major said, "Before he leaves, I should see Noah Crane."

The station officer reached for his hand, clasped it, shook it in thanks.

They took a bus through the snail-slow raucous rush hour of the late afternoon. She clung to him to avoid being pitched over in the jerking progress of the bus. They raised eyes. Margarethe was the only woman on the bus, and a white woman at that. Her Arabic was uncertain, good enough for her pithy comment about the coming role of women in a socialist democracy to be heard, good enough to check the blatancy of the gaze she was subjected to when her hands were held behind Abu Hamid's neck.

She had been coy. She had not told him where she was taking him. It was three days after he had found her in the shaded room above the alley in the Suq al Hamadieh. It was the first time in three days that he had left the room, the first time in three days that he had dressed, the first time in three days that he had moved more than a dozen paces from the disheveled bed.

He was returning to the Bekaa in the morning.

She released her hands from his neck. She pecked at his cheek. She horrified the men on the bus. He loved her for it. He kissed her. He offended the passengers and gloated.

He showed, in public, for all to see, his love for a woman, for an infidel.

They stepped off the bus.

A dark wide street. High walls to the sides of the dirt walkway along the road. He did not know where they were. She held his hand. She led him briskly.

The gate was of thin iron sheet, nailed to a frame, too high for Abu Hamid to see over. She pulled at a length of string that he had not seen and a bell clanked. A long pause, and the gate was scraped open.

She led him forward. They passed through a gloomy courtyard. She had no word for the old man who had pulled back the gate for her. She walked as though she belonged. They climbed a shallow flight of steps, the door ahead was ajar.

Through the doorway, into a cool hallway, on and down a dim lit corridor, into a long room. His shadow, her shadow, were spreadeagled away down the length of the room. He saw the blurred shape of a robed woman coming toward him, and the woman took the hands of Margarethe in greeting and kissed her cheeks.

He saw the lines of tiny cot beds that were against the walls on both sides of the long room. His vision of the room cleared. He saw the cot beds, he saw the sleeping heads of the children. Margarethe had slipped from his side. She moved with the woman, deep in whispered conversation, Margarethe using her flimsy Arabic in short pidgin sentences; they paused only in their talk to tuck down the sheets that covered the children, to wipe perspiration from the brow of a child with a handkerchief. He looked down on the faces of the nearest children, took note of the gentle heave of their breathing, of their peace.

From the far end of the room she summoned him. Without thinking he walked silently, on the balls of his feet.

A child coughed, the woman in the robe slid away from Margarethe, went to the child.

Margarethe said, "It is where I work, it is the new place that I work."

"Who are the children?"

"They are orphans."

He saw the robed woman lift the child from the cot and hug it against her chest to stifle the coughing fit.

"Why did you bring me?"

"They are the orphans of the Palestine revolution."

He looked into her eyes. "Tell me."

"They are the future of Palestine. They were orphaned by the Israelis, or by the Christian fascists, or by the Shi'ite militias. They are the children of the revolution. Do you understand?"

"What should I understand?"

He saw the woman return the child to the cot bed, and smooth the sheet across its body.

"Understand the truth. The truth is these children. These children lost their parents at the hands of the enemies of Palestine. These children are truth, they have more truth than the baubles that can be bought with five thousand American dollars . . ."

He closed his eyes. He saw the flame crawling the length of the spiral of paper.

"What do you want of me?"

"That you should not be corrupted."

He saw the radiance in her face, he saw the adoration for the great struggle to which she was not bound by blood.

"You want me dead," he heard himself say.

"The man that I love will not be a hireling who kills for five thousand American dollars."

"You know what is Israel?"

"The man that I love will have no fear of sacrifice."

"To go to fight in Israel is to go to die in Israel."

"The man that these children will love will have only a fear of cowardice."

"To go to Israel is to be slaughtered, to be dragged dead in front of their photographers."

"These are the children of the revolution, they are the children of the fallen. They must have fathers, Hamid, their fathers must be the fighters in the struggle for Palestine."

"Have I not done enough?"

"I want you to be worth my love, and worth the love of these children."

She took his hand. He felt the softness of her fingers on his. She shamed him.

"I promise."

"What do you promise, sweet boy?"

"I promise that I will go to Israel, that I will kill Jews."

She kissed his lips. She held his hand and walked him again down the room, past the long rows of sleeping children.

They settled to sleep in a grove of eucalyptus trees near to the north bank of the Hayarkon river. They were at the very edge of the Tel Aviv city mass.

They had eaten the last of their food on the move, as they made their way through Herzilya and Ramat Ha-Sharon.

They had the map of the streets. They would start early in the morning. They had decided it would take them more than an hour and a half to walk from where they were to the bus station off Levinsky on the far side of the city.

With the food gone, the grip bag contained only the three kilos of plastic explosive, plus the detonator and the wiring and the timer. As they lay under the ripple rustle of the trees, Mohammed and Ibrahim talked in whispers of what they would do with the money they would be paid, what they would buy in the stores of Damascus when they returned.

A light wind brought the scent of oleanders in bloom and the rumble of the lorry traffic in from the street. They were sitting near to the door of the dormitory room, their backs against the wall.

Margarethe said, "When I am here I am at peace."

Abu Hamid said, "I have no knowledge of peace."

Lying on her lap, huddled against her breast was a girl child who had vomited milk. On his shoulder, his hand gently tapping its back, was a boy child now quietened from crying.

They were in darkness. The shaded nightlight was at the far end of the room.

"When you were like them, was there no peace?"

He whispered, "There was no peace in the tent camps. When I was like them there were only the camps for refugees, for my people who had fled from the Israeli."

"But you had what they do not have, you had the love of your mother."

"Who struggled to survive with a family in a tent."

"What is the future of these little ones, my sweet boy?"

"Their future is to fight. They have no other future."

"What do you remember of when you were a child?"

He grimaced. "I can remember the hunger. I can remember the drills to get us to run fast to the ditches so we would be safe if their aircraft came."

She watched the boy child's fingers clutch and free and clutch again at the collar of Abu Hamid's tunic. She asked, "You surely do not regret being a fighter?"

"I do not regret it, but I never had the chance to be otherwise. So, there are Palestinians who have gone to the Gulf and to Saudi and to Pakistan and to Libya, and they work for the people there. I do not have that chance. Margarethe, I can write only my name. I can read a little, very little . . . I tell you that in honesty. I cannot go to Bahrain or Tripoli to work as a clerk. There is no employment for a clerk who can read very little. There were not schools at the tent camps which taught reading and writing and making arithmetic. We were taught about the Israelis, and we were shown how to run to the air-raid shelters . . ."

She saw the boy child's fingers grasping at his lips and his nose. He made no attempt to push the boy child's fingers away.

". . . and if we have not succeeded in our lifetimes in freeing our homeland from the Israelis, then these little ones also must be taught to be fighters. We cannot turn our backs on what has happened to us."

"You said two hours ago that you had done enough."

"Do you try to make me ashamed?"

"You are a fighter, that is why you have my love."

The boy child's fingers had found the small wellhole of the crow's foot scar. There was a gurgle of pleasure. He suppressed the memory of the stinging pain as the artillery shell shrapnel had nicked across his left upper cheek, the memory of the last days of the retreating battle for West Beirut.

"It is all I know. I know nothing of being a clerk."

Major Said Hazan made up a rough bed of blankets on the leather sofa in his office, then undressed.

When he had folded his clothes, when he stood in his T-shirt and shorts, he went to the Japanese radio behind his desk and tuned to the VHF frequency of the Israeli Broadcasting Corporation. He smoked another cigarette. He searched his way through the file on his desk, the file that obsessed him. He listened to the news broadcast in the English language. It was a powerful radio, it guaranteed good reception.

The radio, in his opinion, broadcast a news bulletin of irrelevant crap. It said that "orthodox" Jews in Jerusalem had again been stoning bus shelters that carried advertisements showing women in bathing suits. The pipeline feeding the Negev irrigation system from the Sea of Galilee had closed down because of shortage of water. The triumph of a rabbi who had come up with the solution of self-propelled tractors to work on the Golan Heights during the fallow year when the Commandment dictated that a farming Jew should not work his fields. The rate of inflation. The public squabbling between Prime Minister and Foreign Minister. New figures showing the decline of young people seeking a kibbutz life. The performance of a Tel Aviv basketball team in New York . . . But the bulletin pleased him.

If the recruits had been taken he would have heard it on the radio. The IBC was always quick to report explosions, arrests. If they had been taken it would have been on the radio that evening. He switched off the radio and lay on the sofa.

Major Said Hazan laughed and the shiny skin on his face buckled in his mirth. His own secret, his own reason to laugh.

The secret of the timer was shared only between himself and the technician in the basement technical laboratory of the Air Force Intelligence wing. Not shared with the Brother of the Popular Front, not shared with the cattle who had been brought from the Bekaa. The cattle believed the timer was set for 45 minutes, the cattle believed they would be off the bus at the Latrun Monastery and that the explosion would follow when they were legging it hard to Ramallah, cross-country into the Occupied Territories. The setting of the timer was the secret he shared only with his technician.

When his laughter subsided, he concentrated on the file.

The first page of the file showed in detail a plan of the layout of buildings of the Defense Ministry on Kaplan.

Major Said Hazan was half in love with the file.

He was in T-shirt and running shorts and track shoes, and washing his stubbled face when the telephone rang in the bedroom. He wiped his eyes. Water splattered on the tile floor. The telephone yelled for him.

It was not yet a beard, just a dark rash over his coloring face.

He picked up the telephone.

"Holt?"

Crane's gravel voice in Holt's ear. "Get your clothes on, get downstairs."

"What's the panic?"

"We're going out."

"Where?"

"Traveling."

"What do I need?"

"Just yourself, dressed."

"For how long?"

"A few days."

"For God's sake, Crane, you could have told me last night . . ."

"You're wasting time, get down."

He heard the purr of the telephone. He slammed his receiver down. He chucked on his trousers and a shirt. Holt steamed. He had had dinner with the monosyllabic Crane and Percy Martins. Crane had hardly spoken beyond asking for the salt to be passed him, and sugar for his coffee. Martins had been bottling some private anger. Nobody had told Holt anything.

He ran down the service stairs and strode into the hotel foyer.

Up to Crane who was standing by the glass front looking out, bored, onto the street.

"Will you start treating me like a bloody partner?"

Crane grinned at him. "Come on."

They walked past the hotel's taxi rank. They walked all the way to the bus station. Crane had the decency to say that a walk would do Holt good if he was missing this morning's workout. Crane set a fierce pace. That was his way. Three times Holt tried to batter his complaint into Crane's ear, three times he was ignored.

It was a dingy corner of the city. Noisy, crowded, dirty, impoverished. And this was the new bus station. Holt wondered what the old one had looked like. Sunday morning, military travel day. To Holt, it seemed that a full half of Israel's conscript army was on the move. Young men and young women, all in uniform, all with their kit, most with their weapons, rejoining their units after the weekend. Crane moved fluently through the crowds, through the queues, as though he belonged, and Holt trailed behind him.

There were buses to Ashkelon and Beersheba and Netanya and Haifa and Kiryat Shmona and Beat Shean. Buses to all over the country. Buses to get the army back to work. So what the hell happened if the enemy came marching in at a weekend? Holt caught Crane, grabbed his arm.

"So where are we going?"

"Jerusalem, first."

"Why don't you tell me what we're doing?"

"Surprise is good for the human juices."

"Why don't we drive?"

"Because I like going by bus."

"When do we start being a partnership?"

"When I start telling you where you're going you'll start messing your pants."

Crane grinned, shook himself free.

He pointed to a queue. He told Holt to stand there.

Holt stood in the queue. It stretched ahead of him. He was wondering whether they would get two seats when the driver deigned to open the door of the single-decker bus. There were soldiers in front of him, men, women, there was a woman with four small children, two in her arms, there was an elderly couple arguing briskly.

There were two young men.

There were two young men who looked, moved, seemed different. Holt could not say how they looked, moved, seemed different. He was the stranger . . . Light chocolate skins, but then the Arabic Jews had light chocolate skins . . . Long dank curly hair, but then there were Arabic Jews of that age who would be in their last year of school, or who had some exemption from the military . . . Nervous movements, anxious glances over the shoulder, snapped whispers to each other . . . looking, moving, seeming different. And then the queue started to move, and the soldiers were surging and the woman was shouting for her stray children, and the elderly couple were bickering away their lives.

Alone in the queue, Holt saw two young men who looked, moved, seemed different.

He was a stranger. He took nothing for granted. He saw nothing as ordinary.

He watched. He was edging forward. He just knew that he would reach the steps into the bus, the driver, and Crane would not be back with the tickets. Holt moved a little out of the queue, so that he could watch for Crane more easily, so that he could shout to him to hurry. He was only half a step out of the queue. It gave him sight of one of the young men with his hand in a cheap grip bag, fiddling. He saw the frown of concentration on the forehead of one of the young men, and he saw the strain of the other young man who bent close to his friend. He saw that the two had their hands in the bag. Relief on their faces, hands out of the bag. He saw their hands clasp together, as if a bond were sealed, as if a mountain were climbed.

He was alone beside the bus, alone he saw them.

The taller of them slipped away. The shorter climbed the narrow steps onto the bus. Holt was looking for Crane—wretched man, as if the man enjoyed making Holt sweat . . . Holt saw the taller of the two young men standing at the ice cream kiosk. The one moment frantic because of something in a grip bag, the next moment buying ice cream . . . Crane walking unhurriedly back from the ticket booth, Holt waving for him to hurry.

He saw the taller man skipping across the road from the kiosk toward the bus.

The queue was formed alongside an all-weather shelter. A stout graffiti-covered brick wall masked the windows of the bus from Holt. He was buggered if he were going to stand like an obedient dog waiting on Crane. Holt was moving toward Crane . . .

He felt the hot wind. He heard the roar of the fire wind. He was off his feet, flying. Could not get his feet to the ground, could not control his body, mind, arms. Moving above the road, moving toward the ice cream kiosk. He could see the kiosk, he could see the taller man with the ice creams splattering across his chest. He felt the snap cudgel blow of the bricks at the back of his legs. He heard the thunder blast of the explosion.

Holt careered into the taller man, hit him full in the body, smashed against the splattered ice cream cones.

Eyes closed. The knowledge of fire, the certainty of calamity. Ears blasted, ringing from the hammer strike of plastic explosive.

The body was under him. The body of the taller man was writhing.

Holt did not understand. Explosion, fire, demolition, he knew all that. He did understand that the taller man on whom he lay had wriggled clear of his belt a short double-edged knife. Could not comprehend, why the taller man on whom he lay held the double-edged knife and slashed at him. All so bloody mad. Mad that he had flown, that he could not control his legs, that debris lay around them, that the taller man slashed at him with the bright blade of a knife. The knife was at full arm stretch. The taller man screamed in words that Holt did not know.

He saw the knife closing on him. He saw the old dirty running shoe. He saw the knife part from the fist, clatter away. He saw the tail end swing of Crane's kick.

Holt blurted, "His friend took the bag. He went to get an ice cream. He tried to knife me."

The breath was crushed out of Holt's chest. Crane had smother-dived onto him. He was gasping for air. He felt himself pushed aside, rolled away, and Crane had twisted the taller man onto his stomach and hooked an arm behind the back, held it, denying the taller man any freedom of movement. Holt saw the spittle in the mouth of the taller man and heard the frothing words that he did not understand.

Again the staccato explanation from Holt. "There were two of them in the queue. They had a bag. One climbed onto the bus, the other went for ice creams. I was just picked up, I was chucked across the road. I hit him, fell on him. He pulled the knife on me."

"Bastard terrorist," Crane said, a whistle in his teeth. "Arab bastard terrorist."

Holt looked into Crane's face. It was the eyes that held him. Merciless eyes. As if the anger of Crane had killed their life; ruthless eyes.

"He was shouting in Arabic at you," Crane said.

Crane moved fast. Holt left to fend for himself. Crane moving with the Arab propelled in front of him by the armlock, and Holt crawling to his feet and struggling to follow. Crane driving the Arab forward as if his only concern was to get clear of the bus station. Holt thought he would be sick. His foot kicked against a severed leg. He stepped over the body trunk of the elderly woman who had been arguing with her elderly husband, he recognized the shredded remnant of her dress. His shoe slid in a river of blood slime, and he careered sideways to avoid a young girl soldier who dragged herself across the road on her elbows and her knees, and who tried with her hands to staunch the blood flow.

There was the cut of the screams in the air, and the first shrill pulse of the sirens.

Holt lurched, staggered after Crane and the Arab. They were going against the tide surge of shoppers, shopkeepers, taxi drivers, passengers from other queues who ran toward the smoking skeleton of the Jerusalem bus.

A police car swung a corner, tires howling. Crane put himself into the road in front of it, forced it to stop. All so fast. Crane jabbering at the driver and his crew man and wrenching open the rear door and dragging the Arab inside after him, then reaching out to pull Holt aboard. The door slammed shut.

The police car reversed, turned, sped away. Holt smelled the fear scent of the Arab who was squashed against him, pressed between himself and Crane.

"Tell me I did well, Crane."

"Nothing to boast about."

"I did well."

"You did what any Israeli would have done. Nothing more, nothing less."

They had left him in the corridor that led down to the cellblock. He had been there for more than three hours. He was ignored. He sat on a hard wooden bench and leaned exhausted back against the painted white brickwork of the corridor walls.

Through all the three hours a procession of men passed up and down the corridor. There were soldiers, officers with badges of rank on their shoulders, there were senior policemen in uniform, there were investigators of the Shin Bet in casual civilian dress. He was never spoken to. He was brought no coffee, no tea. The heavy wooden door with the deep key setting and the small peephole was left empty. Holt heard the questioning, and he heard the thumping and the beating, and he heard the screams and the whimpering of the Arab. The screams were occasional, the whimpering was all the time. Holt could recognize the battering of the fists and the boots, could find images for those sounds.

Crane came out of the cellblock.

Holt stood. "I have to say, Mr. Crane, that whatever was done at the bus station I do not approve of the torture of prisoners . . ."

Crane stared at Holt. "There are five dead, two of them children. There are fifty-one injured, of whom eight are critical."

"You win against these people by a rule of law, not a rule of the jungle."

"Is the need for a rule of law taking you into the Bekaa?"

"Abu Hamid in the Bekaa is beyond the law, this man is in the custody of the law."

"Neat, and pathetic. Whether or not you'll be alive in two weeks' time may well have depended on the thrashing that Arab shitface is getting right now."

"How?"

"I fancy coffee."

"How?"

"Because we've kicked him and belted him and he talked to us. Abu Hamid selected him for the mission. He was a Popular Front recruit at a camp run by Abu Hamid. Considering the state of his hands he's drawn us a damn good layout of the camp and he's done us quite a good map of where the camp is. Fair exchange for handing out a thrashing, don't you think, knowing where to find Abu Hamid in the Bekaa?"

"I just meant . . ."

"Close it down, Holt. I don't think I fancy walking into Lebanon with you bleeding a damn great trail of your sensitivities."

"I hear you," Holt said.

A police car drove them back to the bus station.

The building was Beit Sokolov, on the far side of the road and down the hill on Kaplan from the Defense Ministry complex.

The chief military spokesman was a barrel-chested bustling man, wearing his uniform well, showing his para wings on his chest. He strode into the briefing room.

He walked to the dais. His entry quietened them. He faced his audience. They sat below him, pencils and pens poised over the blank sheets of their notepads. They were the military correspondents of the Israeli Broadcasting Corporation and *Maariv* and *Yediot* and the *Jerusalem Post*, and the bureau chiefs of the American and European broadcasting networks, and the senior men of the foreign news agencies. He checked around him. He was satisfied there were no microphones to pick up his words.

"Gentlemen, on a matter of the greatest importance to us, a matter directly affecting the security of the state, we demand your cooperation. Concerning the terrorist bomb explosion in the New Central bus station this morning, you will be handed our statement at the end of this informal briefing. The statement will say that two members of the Popular Front for the Liberation of Palestine terrorist organization were involved in the planting of the bomb, and that *both* died in the explosion. Your reporters may, in conversation with eyewitnesses, bring back stories of one terrorist being arrested and driven away from the scene of the explosion. We demand that that information does not appear. It is of the uttermost importance that the terrorist leaders who dispatched these two men do not know that we are currently interrogating one survivor. A matter of life and death, gentlemen. Any attempt to smuggle information concerning this survivor past the censors, out of the state, will lead to prosecution and harshest penalties of the law. Questions . . ."

The bureau chief of the Columbia Broadcasting System drawled, "Have we gotten involved in another bus ride cover-up?"

The military spokesman had anticipated the question. Four years before, four Arabs from the Gaza Strip had hijacked a crowded bus in southern Israel, and threatened to kill the passengers if 25 Palestinians were not released from Israeli prisons. The bus had been stopped, and stormed. Two Arabs had died in the military intervention, two others had been seen being led away by the Shin Bet into the darkness at the side of the road. In a field, out of sight, these two were bludgeoned to death. Senior officials of Shin Bet were subsequently granted immunity from prosecution, and resigned.

"The move is temporary. There will be no cover-up because the survivor is alive. Within a month he will be charged with murder and will appear in open court. Questions . . ."

The senior Tel Aviv–based reporter of the Reuters news agency asked, "Will we ever be told what it is that is a matter of life and death?"

"Who can tell?"

The briefing was concluded.

Within fifteen minutes the IBC had broadcast the news that according to the military spokesman it had now been ascertained that two Arabs, thought to be the bombing team, had died in the explosion.

Because of the deformity of his features it was difficult for the other officers in the room to ascertain the feelings of Major Said Hazan.

The major had pulled his chair away from his desk. He was bent over his radio set, listening intently, as he had been for every one of the news broadcasts from Israel that morning.

He switched off the radio. He resumed the course of the meeting. He knew the scale of the casualties. He knew the fate of the two recruits. He knew that the trail of evidence to the Yarmuk camp on the outskirts of Damascus was cut.

More martyrs for the folklore of the Palestine revolution, more casualties for the enemy that was Israel.

The station officer rang Major Zvi Dan immediately after the news broadcast.

"I just want, again, to express my gratitude. If they had known there was a survivor . . ."

". . . They would have moved the camp, the contact would have been lost. We have given you the chance, we hope you can use it."

11

They had slept in a hostel for soldiers in transit.

No explanations from Crane, and Holt was less bothered at the silences with each day he spent in the man's company. He was into the rhythm of tagging along, speaking when he was spoken to, following Crane's lead.

They had had fruit and cheese for breakfast. He thought his beard was beginning to come, slowly enough, but starting to appear something more than just a laziness away from the razor. When he had stood in front of the mirror, when he had taken his turn at the washbasin, when he had looked at himself, then he had wondered how Jane would have liked his beard . . . only a short thought, a thought that was cut before being answered because Crane had been behind him and told him to put away his toothpaste, told him to get used to life without a toothbrush. No explanation, just an instruction.

It beat him, why they could not stay in a hotel when they had all the expense money available to pay for a suite at the Hilton, why they had to sleep in a hostel at eight shekels a night.

He had reflected. His mind had cast back to the Crimea journey, to the field of the Light Brigade on which he would have walked with Ben Armitage.

"Ours not to reason why."

That was life with Noah Crane.

"Ours but to do and die."

Pray God that was not life with Noah Crane.

When he had finished his breakfast Crane stood and walked away from the table. He wouldn't wait for Holt to finish what he was eating. Holt stuffed two apples into his trouser pockets, grabbed a slice of cheese and followed him out. At a table in the hallway Crane put down his bank notes, and waited for his four shekels of change. No tip.

They walked. Crane said that Holt was missing his morning exercises, so they wouldn't take a bus. Holt was used now to Crane's stride, his cracking pace. They started from old Jewish Jerusalem, with the walls of the old city behind them and the golden semi-orb of the Dome of the Rock. If he ever returned to London . . . of course he would . . . When he returned to London no one would believe he had been in Jerusalem and never visited the old city, never walked the route of the Cross. And he was fitter. He could tell that, he was beginning to match Crane stride for stride. Away along wide streets, under gently leaved trees, over steep hills, and into new Jewish Jerusalem, through suburbs of villas constructed of clinically cut sandstone.

They were on the fringe of the city, they climbed the last hill.

They were overtaken by the tourist coaches as they approached the memorial.

"Yad Vashem, Holt," Crane said. "It's where we remember the six million of our people that the Hun slaughtered."

"History makes man complacent, doesn't get people forward. Take the Irish . . ."

"Don't give me university crap. Isaiah 56:5. 'Even unto them will I give in mine house and within my walls a place and a name better than of sons and daughters: I will give them an everlasting name, that shall not be cut off.' We do remember what happened to our people. If we ever forget them then that will be the day that the same can happen to us."

"I don't believe history tells us . . ."

"Holt, six million of our people went to the gas chambers and the furnaces. They didn't fight, they lay down. Because we remember what happened, today we will always fight, we will never lie down. I don't want a debate, I'm just telling you."

They went into the low-ceilinged bunker that was the heart of the memorial. They stood at the rail, they looked down on the stone floor in which were carved out the names of the 21 largest concentration camps. Further from the rail were fading wreaths, and near to the back wall of rough-cut lava rocks there burned a flame. Holt was the tourist, he gazed around him, as if he stared at the Kremlin cupolas, or the arches of the Colosseum, or the Arc de Triomphe, or the Statue of Liberty. He turned back to see if Crane was ready to move on. He saw the gleam of a tear rolling on Noah Crane's cheek. He could not help himself, he stared blatantly. He read the names . . . Treblinka, Auschwitz, Dachau, Belsen, Lwow-Janowska, Chelmno . . . He stood behind Crane so that he should no longer intrude into the privacy of his vigil.

Abruptly Crane swung away, marched out into the sunlight. They walked quickly.

Crane leading, Holt following.

They walked through a garden parkland that was laid out in memory of Theodor Herzl, the originator of the concept of a Jewish state. They went past the young sprouting trees and bank beds of flowers, and down avenues of bright shrub bushes. When they had crossed the parkland, when they looked down the hillside, Holt saw the terraced rows of graves with their slab stone markers. He stood on the high ground, he left the neat chip stone paths to Noah Crane. It was a personal pilgrimage. For a long time he watched the slow lingering progress of Crane among the graves.

Holt brushed the flies from his forehead. He was being given a lesson, that he was aware of. He thought that Crane did nothing by chance.

At the far end of the graveyard, Noah Crane looked up, shouted to Holt, "They're all here, Holt, the high and mighty and the unknowns. Men from the Stern Gang, from the Liberation War of '48, Sinai, Six Days, Yom Kippur, Netanyahu who led the raid to Entebbe, Lebanon, all the men who've given their lives for our state. We value each one of them, whether he's a hero like Netanyahu, whether he's a spotty-faced truck driver who went over a mine in Lebanon. Whatever happens to me in the Bekaa they'll get me back here, that's the best thing I know."

"That's mawkish, Crane."

"Don't laugh at me. This isn't a country that's going soft. You know, Holt, in the President of Syria's office there is one painting, one only. The painting is of the Battle of Hattin. You ever heard of that battle, you with all your history? 'Course you haven't . . . At the Battle of Hattin the great Saladin whipped the ass off the Crusaders. The President of Syria aims to repeat the dose. He aims to put us to the sword, and the rest of us into the sea. Got it?"

"Got it, Mr. Crane."

"It's not my intention to end up here, Holt."

"Glad to hear it, Mr. Crane."

"So you just remember each damned little thing that I tell you, each last damned little thing. You do just as I say, without question, no hesitation," Crane's voice boomed on the hillside. "That way I might just avoid the need of them cutting a hole for me."

"Let's hope we can save them the trouble, Mr. Crane."

Later, toward the end of the morning, with their kit, they were dropped off at the start point chosen by Noah Crane.

They were going walking in Samaria, north from Ramallah toward Nablus, in the Occupied Territories.

Via a scrambled telephone link, Percy Martins reported their progress to the Director General.

From Tork's office in the Tel Aviv embassy he spoke directly to the nineteenth floor at Century. By protocol he should have talked to Fenner. He hoped, fervently, that Fenner would hear he had bypassed him.

"Crane's taken the youngster for a few days into the Occupied Territories to get him thinking the right way, used to the equipment, used to the movement."

"And then they go?"

"They're going to be picked up near Nablus, they'll be taken to Kiryat Shmona, rest up for a few hours, then off."

"What state is the eyewitness?"

"Holt's in a good state. He'll do well."

"How are they coming out?"

"They're going to have to walk out."

"Haven't you bent a few backs?"

"God knows, I've tried, but they're going to have to walk out."

"Anything new?"

"We have a fix on a training camp that is being run by Abu Hamid. We know exactly where to go for him."

"The Prime Minister wants it for Sylvester Armitage's memory. I want it for Jane Canning's memory. I'm relying on you, Martins."

Martins, hired hand, third man on the Desk, first time running his own show, said defiantly, "You can depend on us, sir."

Crane was on watch, Holt drowsed.

For Holt, the night march with the laden backpack was the most exhausting experience of his life.

"They're going, Prime Minister, within a week."

"To bring me his head?"

"Regrettably not on a salver, but his head for all that." The Director General smiled.

"He's terribly lucky."

"Who is, Prime Minister?"

"This young man we've sent out there."

"The eyewitness."

"Exactly, terribly lucky when so few people of his age have the chance afforded them of real adventure."

"Let us hope he appreciates his good fortune, Prime Minister."

"I have to tell you, I would be less than honest if I did not. I am already savoring the moment when I can recount this small epic to our friends in the States . . ."

"Forgive me, but they have a long road to walk."

"If I do not have the head of this Palestinian wretch, then most certainly I will have another head. It's your plan and your advice I'm taking."

The Director General smiled comfortably across the Downing Street sitting room.

"It was a very fine calculation then, Prime Minister, and in a number of particulars it is finer still."

The Prime Minister was gathering papers. The meeting was over. "His head or yours. Good night."

The second night out, and they had not been walking more than an hour and a half, and it was the third time that Holt had fallen, pulled over onto the rocks by the weight of his pack the moment he had lost his balance.

He heard the stones rumbling away on the hillside. He could have cried in his frustration. He could hear the venom of Crane's swearing from in front.

Abu Hamid watched them coming.

He stood at the flap of his tent and studied the slow progress toward the camp of the girl who led the donkey, and behind it the crawling jeep. He could hear the soft cough of the jeep's engine as it idled. At that distance, even, more than half a mile, he knew that it was Fawzi's jeep.

She wore the floppy trousers of the Shi'ites, and the short cotton skirt, and the full loose blouse, and the scarf tied tight over her head and then wrapped across her mouth to mask her face. She dressed in the clothes of a village girl of the

Bekaa. The jeep was a dozen paces behind her, but she made no effort to quicken her pace, or to move aside.

Abu Hamid sucked at a hardly ripe peach, swirling his tongue over the coarse surface of the stone. He knew that in the Bekaa, under the eye of the Syrian Army, under the control of the Syrian intelligence agencies, nothing would happen by chance. He knew that it would not be by chance that a girl walked a donkey along the track that led only to the tent camp, and that the girl was followed by Fawzi's jeep. She was young, he was sure of that, he could see the smooth regular flow of her slim hips, the trousers and skirt could not hide the slender outline of the young body.

Abu Hamid took the peach stone from his mouth, threw it high into the coiled wire of the perimeter fence. He called for the recruits to come forward, to break from their meal, to get off their haunches, make a formation. He lined them up, three untidy rows.

He turned to face the entrance to the camp.

Now the jeep accelerated and swung past the girl. The donkey shied, and the girl held her course and seemed unaware of the jeep. She was lost for a moment in the dust thrown up by the jeep's wheels, and when she appeared again she still walked forward, light step, leading the donkey. Abu Hamid saw that the donkey had a pair of old leather pannier bags slung down on its flanks.

With a swaggering step Fawzi walked toward Abu Hamid. His hands rose to grip Abu Hamid's shoulders, he kissed him on both cheeks. Abu Hamid smelled the lotion that crept to his nostrils. Fawzi clapped his hands for attention, played the big man. For Abu Hamid it shamed the Palestine revolution that Fawzi and his clumsy conceit should have control of the recruits, of himself. He watched the girl and the donkey approach the camp entrance. Fawzi had his back to the girl and the donkey, as if their time had not yet come. Fawzi addressed the recruits.

"Fighters of the Palestine revolution, I have news for you of an epic attack by the Popular Front deep into enemy territory. A commando force of the Popular Front has traveled to the heart of the Zionist state, and in so doing has disproved the claim of the Zionists that their borders are secured. The target was the principal bus terminus in Tel Aviv. The attack was timed for last Sunday morning, at the moment when the maximum number of enemy soldiers would be boarding transport to return to their units. The Zionists, of course, have attempted to minimize the effectiveness of our commando strike by releasing ridiculously false figures of the casualties inflicted. Their lies will not deflect the truth. Forty-eight of their soldiers were killed, more than a hundred were wounded. The heroism of the commandos knew no limitations. They carried out, our men, an attack of greater pain to the enemy than the successful assault by hand grenade at the Dung Gate in Jerusalem against a military parade. Fighters, I said to you that the heroism of the commandos knew no limitations. I grovel in admiration at such heroism. The plan of the attack allowed for the commandos to place a bomb on the Tel Aviv to Jerusalem bus. The bomb was fitted with a timing device that would permit the commandos to leave the bus en route with the bomb left under a seat. That was not good enough, fighters, for these heroic commandos. They feared that after they had left the bus that there would be a small chance of the discovery of the bomb that would negate the attack. Such heroism, fighters . . . The commandos were governed by total commitment to the cause of the Palestine revolution . . . They set the timer early. They stayed with the bomb until it exploded. By their selfless action they determined that there was no possibility of the bomb being discovered and rendered harmless. For the success of the revolution they gave their own lives. Fighters, the strike force of the commandos came from this camp. They were your brothers in arms. Fighters, Mohammed and Ibrahim were of your blood. They shared your hardships, they shared your food, they shared your tents. They were given the chance to wage total war against the enemy, against your enemy, they did not fail the cause of the Palestine revolution."

Abu Hamid stood numbed. The man who was an incessant pain in the ass was now a hero. The thief was now a martyr.

The girl with the donkey walked slowly through the entrance gap in the wire.

The recruits gazed awestruck at Fawzi. They had clung to each word he had spoken. As if each man yearned for himself the admiration now settled on Ibrahim and Mohammed.

The girl now stood beside Fawzi. She held loosely in her hand a length of rope that was fastened to the bridle. The donkey was old and patient.

Fawzi looked to the girl with pleasure.

"Without great courage, without great bravery, the Palestine revolution will not be won. But we have the courage, we have the bravery, and so the victory of the revolution is inevitable. Look at her, fighters, look at her and rejoice in the courage and bravery of the revolution. She is sixteen years old, she is in the full flower of youth. She has no ambition other than to give her life, her breath, her spirit, to the revolution."

Abu Hamid stared at the girl. He could not tell whether she heard Fawzi. Her face was blank, her eyes were dead. He had seen men who habitually smoked the poppy, or dragged on cigarettes made from the marijuana crop, and their eyes, too, were dead, their faces were without expression. He could not say whether her love was for the revolution or whether it was for the poppy and the hashish fiber.

"This girl is going alone to the security zone. Without the support of comrades, with the help only of a fervent faith in the ultimate success of the revolution, she is going into the security zone with her donkey. The donkey is her friend. The donkey has been with her since she was a child at her mother's breast. In the bags carried by the donkey will be one hundred kilos of industrial dynamite. Do you understand me, fighters? This girl will go to the checkpoint at the entrance to the security zone, where there are the Israeli surrogates of the fascist South Lebanese Army, and the Israelis with their personnel carriers, and the torturers of the Shin Bet. When she is among them she will fire the explosives. They will go to their hell, she to her paradise."

His eyes never left the girl. She was a wraith. What Abu Hamid could see of her face was dry and pale. He could not see fear, he could not see boredom. Could it be real? Could a girl have such love of martyrdom that she would lead a donkey laden with explosives among the enemy, that she would obliterate herself and her enemy? He knew of the Shi'ite car bombers, the heroes who had plowed their vehicles into the American embassy, and the French embassy and the Marine camp in Beirut. He knew of the car bomb that had been driven against the walls of the Shin Bet headquarters in Tyre during the enemy's occupation of the city. He knew that the cars approaching the security zone were treated with such suspicion that a better chance now existed for approaching close with a donkey or a mule or a packhorse. Could a girl have such little love of life?

"She is an example to us all. By seeing her, by knowing of her, we are honored. She visits you in order that you may be encouraged by the memory of her bravery, when the time comes for you, yourselves, to go south and fight the enemy who denies you your rightful homeland. Show her your love, show her your admiration."

Abu Hamid raised his fist in the air. White knuckles, the fist punching.

"Long live the Palestine Revolution."

The recruits shouted their answer, echoed his words.

"All glory to the martyrs of the Palestine Revolution."

The cheering soared.

"Strength to the enemies of the state of Zion."

"Courage for the fighters whose cause is just."

The girl did not smile. Slowly she rolled her head so that she gazed flatly at each and every one of the recruits who yelled their support of her. She turned. She seemed to speak a word into the ear of the donkey. She stood for a moment in profile to Abu Hamid. He saw the bulge, he saw the weight forward and low on her stomach. He knew she was pregnant. She led the donkey away and out of the camp. The recruits cheered her all the way, but she never looked back.

Abu Hamid dismissed the recruits and they stood silently at the camp gate as the girl and the donkey became small figures on the rough track.

Fawzi beamed. He walked to Abu Hamid.

"She is to go through all the villages between here and the security zone. It has a great effect on the villagers, just as she has made a great impression on your men. When she has made her attack, a film of her will be shown on the television, it is already made."

"Is she . . . ?"

"Drugged? You surprise me, Abu Hamid . . . She is a fighter, she is like yourself."

Fawzi drove away in his jeep. He caught up the girl and her donkey before they reached the tarmac road.

When he strained his eyes, Abu Hamid could see them. A girl and a donkey, and just behind them the jeep of the Syrian Army.

They worked hard at their training that morning. No backchat, only studied concentration. They worked at the lesson of the platoon in attack on a hillside against a defended position, with the support of .50 caliber machine guns and RPG-7 launchers.

That morning Abu Hamid did not find the need to repeat any part of his teaching.

Holt drank his water. It was a new discipline to him, to ration himself. He must have looked with obvious longing at his water bottle, because he was aware of the smear of amusement at Noah Crane's mouth.

The merchant braked, slowed his Mercedes.

Ahead of him, down the straight road running from north to south under the east slope of the Bekaa Valley, was a column of Syrian Army trucks. The trucks, more than a dozen of them, he estimated, had pulled across onto the hard shoulder of the road. He came forward slowly. Always his way to pass a military convoy slowly, so that he could see what the convoy carried. And always better to go slowly past the Syrian military, with the window wound down the better to hear any shouted instructions—they would only shout once, they would shout and if their shout was ignored they would shoot.

There was a jeep stopped at the head of the convoy, and

he saw a very fat young lieutenant talking, arm waving, to another officer. Heh, who was he, Menachem, to laugh at the grossness of a young soldier? The merchant weighed on the scales some 260 pounds . . . He saw a young girl leading a donkey.

The girl and her donkey were at the far end of the convoy, coming past it. He drove onto the same hard shoulder, he switched off his engine. No one looked at him. He listened but there was no shouted instruction. The canvas roofing of the lorries had been rolled down. He saw that they carried troops. A dozen lorries could carry two companies of infantry, the mental arithmetic was second nature to the merchant. The troops crowded to the sides of the lorry and watched the girl and her donkey come alongside them, move forward. Faintly, he could hear the shouting voice of the gross young lieutenant who had gone from the side of the officer and now offered explanation to the soldiers. As the girl led her donkey past each truck, so the soldiers cheered her.

Deep in his mind where the truth of his existence was hidden, the merchant swore. He recognized the signs, and it would be two days before he was again in a position to make a drop. A long time ago he had been offered a radio. He had declined, he had said he would not be able to learn how to use it, and anyway he had known that a signal sent to Israel was a signal sent also to the men of Syrian Intelligence. He preferred the dead letter.

The bomber would be paraded through the Bekaa. The bomber would be used to jolt the commitment of the young. He could see that the bomber was herself scarcely more than a child.

The merchant, Menachem, saw his controller, Major Zvi Dan, rarely. Never more than twice a year. The last time, smuggled by the IDF through the night across the border, he had talked to Zvi Dan about the bombers.

The bomber was just a slip of a girl. He could piece together what Zvi Dan had told him, late and over whiskey, about the bombers.

"You know, Menny, the IRISHBAT found a car bomb in their sector, abandoned. They made it safe, and then they looked to see why it was abandoned. You know why, Menny? It was abandoned because it had run out of petrol . . ." The merchant could remember how they had laughed, hurting their stomachs laughing. "They are not all suicide people, we had one who came up to the checkpoint and surrendered, and said that the girl who was with him had already run away. Do you know with another, Menny, the bastard Syrians gave him a flak jacket to wear and they told him that way he would survive the explosion of his own car, and in the car was more than 150 kilos of explosive. More recently, they have taken to a remote firing. The bomber goes to the checkpoint, but the detonation is remote, from a command signal, from a man who is hidden perhaps a kilometer away. That is because they know that not every recruit wishes to hurry to martyrdom. We have learned, Menny, that the bombers are not so much fanatics, as simple disturbed kids. There was one who was with child and did not dare face her father, there was a boy who had quarreled with his father and run away, there was one whose father was accused by the Syrian military of crimes and who volunteered to save his father from prison. Believe me, Menny, they are not all Khomeini fanatics. Most are sick kids. We know, we have captured eleven of the last sixteen sent to the security zone. I tell you what is the saddest thing. They make a film of the kids, and they show it on the television, and they make great heroes of the kids. There is a village in the security zone where live the parents of a boy who drove the car for one of the big Beirut bombs, and now it is like his home is a tourist attraction, and his father is a celebrity, and the kid's picture is everywhere on the walls. Heh, Menny, what sort of cretin takes a holiday in south Lebanon? Only a Jew, if the discount is good." More laughter, more whiskey. A conversation of many months back.

There were times, in the loneliness of his subterfuge life, that the merchant doubted his own sanity. There were times when his mind ached for a return to the buoyant, carefree students on the campus in the Negev desert. He saw the girl leading the donkey. Zvi Dan had told him that the men of Syrian Intelligence scoured the villages of the Bekaa for kids who would drive a car bomb, for kids who would lead a donkey bomb. He thought that the girl and the donkey and the heavy bags slung on the rib cage of the beast were an abomination. One day he would go back to his students . . . on a day when there were no more donkey bombs, no more car bombs, Menachem would go back to his lecture room.

Whatever he saw, whatever its importance, he would not break his routine. It would be two days before he could report the coming threat to a roadblock leading into the security zone.

She had passed the parked lorries. He could hear the shuffle of her feet, the clip of the donkey's hooves. He saw the sweating lieutenant amble toward his jeep. For the soldiers the parade was over.

He saw the face of the girl, devoid of expression.

He shouted through his opened window.

"God is great."

They were high above the village. Crane had pointed to it on his map, 'Aqraba. Holt watched through binoculars as the kids launched their rocks and Molotovs at the troops. It was like something he had seen on the television from Northern Ireland. From their vantage point, Holt not daring to move for fear of Crane's criticism, they watched a daylong battle between the kids and the soldiers, fought in a village square that was wreathed in tear gas, and in the alleys behind the mosque. Sometimes, when the fight went against the soldiers, Holt heard Crane's chuckle. Sometimes, when the soldiers caught a youth and battered him with their rifle butts, Holt ground his teeth.

He heard the voice in the corridor, and the clatter of feet.

Martins tidied the newspaper. He had been through yesterday's *Times*, and the *Herald Tribune*, and that day's *Jerusalem Post*. Read them all from cover to cover, right down to the cost of a ten-year lease on a two-bedroomed flat in West Kensington, to the discounts available in a jewelry store's winding-up sale in Paris, to the price of a secondhand Subaru car in Beersheba. He was nagged by frustration. Martins could recognize that he was the outsider, he was an intrusion in the smooth dealings between Tork, station officer in Tel Aviv, and his local contacts.

He tidied his paper. He scraped out the debris from the bowl of his pipe into the saucer of the coffee cup that he had been given three hours before. He ignored the No Smoking sign stuck onto a window of the station officer's room.

The door opened. Martins saw the station officer blink as the smoke caught his eyes. Sod him . . . The station officer tugged in with him a shallow long wooden box, olive-green. No greeting, not as yet. The station officer's priority was to get to the window, shove it open, then to the air conditioner, switch it off.

"Been able to occupy yourself?" the station officer asked curtly.

"I've passed the time. What have you brought?"

"A rifle."

Martins tried to smile. "A present for the Ayatollah and the mullahs?"

"I beg your pardon?"

"Just a joke."

"Actually it is the rifle for Crane."

"We brought Crane's rifle out from England—rather a lot of paperwork."

"It wasn't the rifle he wanted."

"Why didn't the bloody man say what he wanted? He test fired the Parker-Hale, he didn't complain."

"Perhaps you never asked him what he wanted. Perhaps you just told him what he was getting."

"The man's impossible."

"Just doesn't waste time arguing. What he would have told you he wanted *if* he had been asked was a model PM from Accuracy International, small firm down in Hampshire."

"How did it get here?"

"Israelis picked it up yesterday, shipped it out in their DipCorps bag to save time, avoid the export license. I collected it this morning."

Martins puffed, "That makes me look a complete fool."

The station officer asked, "Would you like some more coffee?"

"There are more important things than coffee. If it has not escaped you, I am in charge . . . Damn it, man, I didn't know you were smuggling a rifle out of the UK, I don't know where Holt and Crane are, I don't know when the jump-off is, I have not been given access to the latest intelligence on the camp."

"Unfortunate."

"Meaning?"

"You're going to have to live with it."

"I'm a senior man in London, Tork . . ."

"And this is Israel. Sorry . . . Decision taking is in Crane's hands, and stays there. Crane will decide on the jump-off, on the route. He will make the decisions because he is going to be in the Bekaa, and we are not, for which in all sincerity I thank God."

"You and I are going to have to get one or two things straight."

The station officer glanced up, heard the rasp in the voice. He thought a man who wore a three-piece suit in the heat of Israel to be a fearful ass.

"As I understand it, Mr. Martins, you got the job, were sent out here, because there were no decisions to be taken—sorry."

"Fenner told you that . . . ? Well, you've got a nasty surprise coming to you. Control of this mission has been entrusted to me by the Director General, and I mean control. And one more thing: There is more to the work of the Service than the analyses that you fill your day in writing. I've read some of your stuff—15 pages on the future of the Coalition here, eight pages on the prospect of a right-wing backlash, 21 pages on future settlements on the West Bank, all the sort of crap that Fenner wants, the sort of gibberish that keeps Anstruther happy."

"I am sorry if my material is too *complex* for you, Mr. Martins."

"You can think of it as complex if you wish, Tork, but you'd better get it into your head that this mission into the Bekaa is of infinitely greater importance to the interests of the United Kingdom than the trivia with which you spend your days, and if this goes wrong, for your lack of cooperation, I'll have you gutted," Martins said.

The station officer peered down at him. Twice in the last week his wife had asked him whether they were not duty bound to invite Mr. Martins, out from London, to their flat for dinner. Twice the station officer had told his wife to forget it, leave the man to his hotel room. The station officer fancied he could hear the boast chat in London on the upper floors of Century. Problems, why should there be problems? Difficulties? Difficulties only existed to be overcome. A good show, a super big show.

As if it were a gesture of defiance, Martins shoveled tobacco from his pouch and into the bowl of his pipe.

"I'm going to be in Kiryat Shmona."

"What for?"

"Because I'm bloody well responsible."

"Once they're over the frontier, once they've gone there's nothing you can do."

"I have to be somewhere, and that's where I mean to be," said Martins.

The station officer considered the alternative. He thought of having him fretting in his office for the next week, perhaps longer.

"I'll take you up."

Rebecca was the personal assistant to the major. She had been with him for more than two years. Major Zvi Dan liked to say, when he introduced her, that she was his eyes and his ears, that she alone understood the mysteries of the now computerized filing system. She was blessed also, he claimed, with an elephantine memory. At the end of each working day he would share with her his thoughts, his newfound information, and they would be stored electronically in the computer and mentally in her head.

Rebecca sat in the front passenger seat of the pickup truck. She was out of uniform. She wore jeans and a blouse of brilliant orange. First she had smoothed her nails with a manicure stick, now she painted them purple, fingers and toes.

Rebecca was a fixture in Major Zvi Dan's life. Perhaps he relied too greatly on her, on her memory and her organizing skills. She bullied him—not that he complained other than to her face. She made him go to the doctor at Defense when his leg stump ached intolerably, she forced him to eat when the work load bowed him down, she came once a week to his bachelor flat, high and overlooking the Ramat Gan quarter, to collect his dirty clothes and take them to a launderette.

They had been parked at the side of the Nablus to Jenin road for a little more than an hour.

Rebecca glanced up occasionally from her concentration to amuse herself at the growing anxiety of Major Zvi Dan. The major paced around the pickup. He looked down at his watch. He fingered the automatic pistol that was tucked into the belt of his slacks. With binoculars he studied the pale rock-strewn hills, and the small terraced fields from which the stones had been lifted to make walls.

She heard the snort of Major Zvi Dan's exasperation. When they had first stopped, he had told her that within five minutes they would be making the rendezvous with Crane and the English boy. Five minutes drifting into more than an hour. He was cursing quietly, he was staring up the road, he was searching for the approach of two small and distant figures.

"You should get something done about those eyes, Major."

She heard the voice. She swung her head. Major Zvi Dan was rooted, peering down the rough hill slope that fell from the road. Small rocks only, low and hardy scrub bushes. She watched the head of the major tilt and twist as he tried to find the source. She could see no hiding place.

"Crane?" Major Zvi Dan shouted. "Get the hell up here."

The ground seemed to rise. The figure seemed to materialize. Where there was dung-gray rock there was a standing man.

"You need to get them looked at, Major."

She laughed out loud.

"Move yourself, Holt."

A second figure appeared. They stood together some fifteen yards from the road, level with the pickup.

They were in uniform, their skins were dirt smeared.

"I am a busy man, Crane. I have better things to do."

Crane came forward.

"You should meet Holt, Major."

Major Zvi Dan stared Holt up and down. "How's he done?"

"Acceptable."

"Is he good enough to go?"

"The first day he'd have had us identified three times. Second day once, third day once. He's just been under your glasses for an hour, that makes him acceptable."

"Get in the back," the major said coldly.

Rebecca watched. She saw that Crane carried his backpack easily, like it was a part of his body, along with the rifle with the elongated telescopic sight. She saw that the younger man came more slowly, as if the backpack were a burden, as if he had never before carried an Armalite rifle.

"What's your timetable, Crane?"

"Shit and shower first, long sleep. Tomorrow, aerial photographs and maps, pack the kit. Move tomorrow night."

She watched Crane climb easily into the open back of the truck, slinging his backpack ahead of him, she saw the young man struggle to scramble aboard and get no help.

The Mercedes was clean, the merchant carried the code in his head.

In the darkness of early night, before the stars were up, the merchant had lifted the bonnet of the car and loosened a battery cable.

He was a little off the main road. He was parked above the sparse lights of the village of Qillaya.

It was a routine for him. If he had been bounced by a Syrian patrol or by a group of Shi'ite militia, or by a band of the Hezbollah, then he would have had the explanation that his car's engine was broken, that he could not put it right in the darkness.

He wrote his message, a jumble of numerals on a scrap of paper.

He had to walk some fifty yards from the car to the angle of the road. There was always danger in these moments, on the approach to a dead letter drop. He could take every precaution during his traveling, during his halts, but the moment of maximum danger was unavoidable. If the dead letter drop was compromised he was gone. He was breathing hard. On the angle of the road was a rain ditch, cut to prevent the tarmacadam surface being eroded during the spring floods when the higher snows melted. In the ditch was a rusted, holed petrol drum. He left his messages in the drum, he received his messages from the drum. He was not more than 2,000 yards from the UNIFIL zone, there was a checkpoint of NORBAT 2,000 yards down the main road. He was eleven miles from the Good Fence, the Israeli frontier. He was a few minutes' walk, a few minutes' drive, from the sanctuary of the NORBAT checkpoint, from the safety of his country's frontier. It was always the worst time for him, when he was within touch of sanctuary, safety, when he was short moments from turning his back on the checkpoint and the Good Fence and starting the drive back into the Bekaa.

He had the paper in his hand. The merchant bent over the drum, searched for the hole into which he would place his coded report of the progress south through the valley of a girl with a donkey bomb.

The flashlight flooded his face.

He thought he was losing his bowels.

He could see nothing behind, around, the blinding beam of the flashlight.

He waited for the shot.

The urine was driving from his bladder.

"It's Zvi, Menny. Heh, I am sorry."

The flashlight went out. The merchant stood his ground, could see nothing.

There was an arm around his shoulder, stifling the trembling of his body.

"I think you pissed yourself. Heh, I am truly sorry. There was someone who had to see your face."

The merchant saw the shadow looming behind the shape of his friend, but the shadow came no closer.

The merchant whispered, "Couldn't you have used a night sight?"

"He wanted clear light on your face, it was important . . ."

For ten minutes the merchant and Zvi Dan sat by the rain ditch. The merchant made his report in incisive detail. Zvi Dan gave his instructions, handed over the package.

The merchant went back to his car. First he collected an old pair of slacks from the trunk and quickly changed into them, then he refastened the battery cable. He drove back to the main road and then on to the village of Yohmor where he would spend the night. In the morning he would advise the elders of the village on the spare parts they needed to buy for the repair of their communal generator, and how much those parts would cost.

Holt started up in his chair. He had been dozing. He was brought back to life by the thud of the boots on the plank slats of the veranda. God, and was he lucky to have dozed. Percy Martins was still in full flow and the station officer seemed to suffer from a private agony, and the girl was reading a Hebrew romance with a lurid cover.

The veranda was outside the officers' canteen at the army base. There were pots of flowers, and a jungle of vine leaves overhead, and there was coffee and Coca-Cola to drink if anyone could be bothered to go inside to the counter to get it for himself.

The girl was reading the book and ignoring Martins like Jane had been able to do when they were in his or her London flat and he was watching the cricket on television. The station officer hadn't quite the nerve to turn his back on the reminiscing. Martins was remembering his time in Cyprus, spook on the staff of Government House, recommending his old strategies for application in the Occupied Territories.

Holt looked behind him, turned in his chair. He could see that both the major and Crane were still wet from face washing, and he could see that it had been a fast job because there were still smears of dark camouflage cream under the earlobes and down at the base of their throats.

Crane said, "Long day tomorrow, Holt . . ."

Martins said, "Pleased you've returned from wherever, Major. Something I'd like sorted out. I am informed I have to sleep in a hotel. I would have thought you could put me up on camp."

Major Zvi Dan said, "Not possible."

The girl, Rebecca, said, "Do you like cocoa?"

Holt said, "Ages since I've had it. Quite."

Crane said, "Get to your bed, Holt. Now."

The station officer said, "I'm off early in the morning, back to Tel Aviv, I'll be gone before you've surfaced . . . Give it your best effort. Look forward to welcoming you back. Holt. Sergeant."

Holt stood and shook the station officer's hand, a damp hand and a limp grip. Crane wandered off toward the counter in search of food.

Percy Martins drummed his fingers on the table. "I would like to discuss the matter of my accommodation further."

The girl, Rebecca, was back in her book. Holt saw the mud dirt on the major's boots.

"Good night, all," Holt said.

He went to the room they had allocated him. A white-painted cubicle, with a bed and a table and a chair, and three hangers on a nail behind the door. He didn't bother to wash, and he wasn't allowed to use toothpaste. He peeled off his jogging shoes and his shirt and trousers. He switched off the light, flopped on the bed. He had slept fourteen hours the night before, and he was still tired. The day had been divided in two. There had been the kit part of the day, and there had been the route-planning part of the day. He didn't think it was from choice, he assumed it was from necessity, but at least Crane had talked to him, at him. Down the corridor was Crane's room, and next door to that the kit was laid out for packing in the morning. Crane had talked to him, at him, when they were with the Intelligence guys, when they were looking at the aerial photographs that footprinted the Bekaa.

He heard the knock at the door.

He didn't have the time to reply. The door opened.

He saw the silhouette of the girl against the lit corridor. He saw that she carried a mug, steaming.

Holt laughed out loud, "Not the bloody cocoa?"

She laughed back at him. The curtains were thin, and when she kicked the door shut behind her, the floodlights outside streamed through. He could see that she was laughing.

"It's the best thing to make you sleep."

"You're very kind."

"And you are going to Lebanon tomorrow, so you need to sleep." She sat on the bed. She wore a deep-cut green blouse, and a full skirt.

He thought her laughter was an effort. He thought she had sad eyes, and there were care lines on the edge of her mouth. He took the mug from her, held it in both hands, sipped at the thick stirred cocoa. He had not had cocoa since before he went to boarding school, since his mother used to make it for him on cold winter evenings when he was a small boy.

Holt tried to smile. "It's supposed to be a secret, me going into Lebanon tomorrow."

"My husband was in Lebanon. He went with the first push, and then he went back again in the last year of our occupation. After the first time he was a changed man. He was very bitter when he came home to me. Before he went he used to play the saxophone in a small jazz band where we lived. He never played after he came back. He was an architect, my husband. There were many casualties in his unit, tanks. I used to wonder what an architect, a saxophone player, was doing driving a tank in Lebanon. My husband said that when the IDF first went into Lebanon they were welcomed by the Shi'ite people, the people in the villages threw perfumed rice at the tanks, by the time they left that first time they were hated by the same Shi'ites. The mines were in the roads, the snipers were in the trees. He was called up again for Lebanon in '85, just before the retreat started. The leaders, the generals, of course they didn't call it a retreat, they called it a redeployment. He used to write to me. The letters were pitiful. He used to say he would never go back again, that he would go to prison rather than serve another tour in Lebanon. He used to say that the basic rule of survival was to assume the worst, at every moment, to shoot first. Lebanon brutalized him. A week before he was due to come out, from the second tour, he wrote to me. He wrote that they had painted on their tank the words, 'When I die I will go to Heaven, I have already been through Hell.' He was killed the day after. He was shot by a village boy near Joub Jannine. They knew it was a village boy because they caught him in their follow-up search, he was 13 years old. He was 13 years old and through hate he shot my saxophone player, my husband. That is Lebanon, Holt."

"I am sorry."

"It is the way of life for us. We are Jews, we are condemned to a permanent perdition of warfare."

"I'm sorry, but my viewpoint is from a long way away. I'm not trying to be an impertinent outsider, but I think you've brought much of it on yourselves. Again, I'm sorry, but that's what I feel."

"When you go into Lebanon you will be part of us. There is no escape from that."

"You know my quarrel, why I go?"

"I've been told. Your leaders, your generals, want a man killed. They need you for assistance at the execution."

"The man killed the girl I loved," Holt said. He raised the cocoa mug to his mouth. The cocoa spilled from his lips, dribbled down onto his newfound tan from the beach at Tel Aviv.

"Do you go into Lebanon for the girl that you loved, or for your leaders and your generals?"

Holt shook his head. He said softly, "I don't know."

"Better you go for your girl."

"Did he love you, your husband, when he died?"

"He wrote in his letters that he loved me."

"My girl, she snapped at me, the last words that she spoke. We were quarreling . . . Can you see what that means? The last time we spoke, the last memory I have of her, is of argument. That's a hell of a weight to carry."

"Close your eyes, Holt."

His back was against the pillow that was propped up against

the wall. His eyes closed. He felt her movement on the bed. He felt the softness of her lips on his cheek. He felt the moisture of her lips on his mouth. He felt the gentleness of her fingers on the bones of his shoulder.

"My husband, Holt, my saxophone player, he used to write to me from Lebanon that the feel of my mouth and my hands and my body was the only sanity that he knew."

With the palms of his hands he reached to the smooth angles where her cheeks came down to her throat. He kissed her, as if with desperation.

"Remember only her love, Holt. Make her love your talisman."

The memories were a riptide. Walking with Jane in the sunshine of spring on the moorland hills. Sitting with Jane in the darkness of a London cinema. Lying with Jane in the wet warmth of her bed.

His eyes were tight shut. He moved aside in the bed. He heard her peeling away her blouse, pushing off her shoes, dropping down her skirt. He felt the lovely comfort of her against his body.

He cried out, "It doesn't help her, cannot help her, killing him."

"Until he is dead you have no rest. Her memory will only be torment. Love me, Holt, love me as you would have loved her. Love me so that you can better remember her when you are in Lebanon."

When he woke, she was gone.

As if she had never been there. As if he had dreamed of Jane.

12

His eyes ached, his forehead hurt.

Crane had the maps in front of him, and the aerial photographs. An Intelligence officer took Crane through the photographs.

It was the close work that pained him, caused him to blink, but this close work was inescapable, critical. The pilotless drone had flown the previous day. The Delilah drone had flown from inside Israel, and taken a route north from Metulla and over Marjayoun in the security zone. The drone had clipped the edge of the NORBAT sector and flown on at a height of 15,000 feet toward Yohmor. By the time that it cleared Lake Qaraaoun at the southern end of the Bekaa Valley, the camera set in the belly of the Delilah was picturing the ground beneath. The drone's flight path had taken it along the western side of the valley, over small villages, over goat herds and the boys who minded them, over women hoeing the weeds out of the stony fields in preparation for the planting of corn crops, over the steep sloping tiled roofs of Shi'ite villages, over Syrian Army positions, over the main road running northeast from Khirbet Qanafar to Qabb Elias, over the small vineyards from which would come in the autumn the delectable bottles of Cabernet Sauvignon and Pinot Noir, over the Syrian headquarters garrison at Chtaura across the Beirut to Damascus road, and then east, and then south along the Bar Elias to Ghazze road. And, of course, Delilah, a speck in a clear midday sky, had passed over a tented camp that was surrounded by a fence of coiled barbed wire and a bulldozed ditch. The drone had been seen by many people. It had been seen by the boys with the goats, and by the farming women, and by the men sitting outside their village coffee houses, and by bored Syrian soldiers, and by Abu Hamid as he lectured his class in the workings of the DShKM heavy anti-aircraft machine gun, and by Fawzi as he negotiated a transaction with a headman, and by a merchant who drove an old Mercedes car. Seen by many people, but unremarkable to all of them. The drone flew twice a week, it was accepted.

The photographs had been taken especially for the benefit of Sergeant Crane.

He studied each one with the help of a stereoscope. It was the stereoscope that killed his eyes, brought the throb to the deep recess where his retina was diseased. Had to use the stereoscope, because that was the instrument that threw the flat vision of the photographs into a three-dimensional reality.

Crane spoke only rarely to the youngster. He thought of him as the "youngster." He believed that he was not a nursemaid, and his experience of handling novice troops had taught him that to talk too frequently was to confuse. He expected that Holt should listen, and above all that he should watch. Noah Crane did little by chance. He demanded that Holt should concentrate, watch everything, react on it, remember it.

Most times his conversation was with the Intelligence officer. He trusted the man. The planning of the route required trust, and the man had served him well. Most recently this gawky, spiderlike Intelligence officer had carried out the detail of the planning for the sniping of a Hezbollah unit commander. His care had earned the trust of Noah Crane. They talked in the Hebrew tongue. Crane had two maps on the table in front of him. The one he marked, bold lines for the route, decisive crosses for the stop positions; the other he left clean.

The Intelligence officer gathered up the photographs. Noah

Crane folded the map that was not marked. He spoke from the side of his mouth to Holt, staccato, as if it were obvious.

"See the way I fold it. The way I fold it doesn't show which section interests me, it concertinas out. And I never put my fingers on it. When we're out there, when we're using it, we will always use a pointer, like a stick, to indicate. We never leave marks on the map, finger marks."

"So that if we are captured they don't know what our target was?"

Crane said, matter of fact, "We don't talk about capture. Capture is not thinkable. It is in case we lose the map."

He saw the youngster look away.

He led Holt to the kit room, the room beside his own. He was a loner. For years, as a sniper, he had taken responsibility for himself, for his own skin. Noah Crane had never gone after promotion, he had shunned taking novice soldiers under his wing. He didn't bloody well know how to raise the spirits of the youngster, didn't bloody know. He could see the youngster was scared witless, standing close to him, walking close to him, but he didn't bloody well know how to breathe confidence into the youngster. And it worried him. He needed the youngster to begin well . . . and how? How to get the youngster doing it right. That was an agony to Noah Crane, a second agony to the pain behind the tiredness of his shooting eye.

Holt was young enough to be Noah Crane's son, and he had never fathered a son, never brought up a son. Course he didn't know how to communicate with the youngster.

He had laid the kit out in the same way he always did.

Two Bergen packs nearest the door, the kit stretching away.

"You'll know him, won't you?"

"I'll know him."

"I'd skin you, if we went that far and at the end you didn't know him."

"Mr. Crane, I see him just about every hour of my waking life. I see his face, I see his movement, I see him running. There's no chance, if he's there, that I won't know him."

"Not personal, I just had to be sure."

"Mr. Crane, has it ever crossed your mind that I might not be sure of you?"

"You cheeky brat, you know about nothing."

"I know about plenty. About the things normal people know. I'm just weak about going into other folks' backyards and killing people. . . . They don't do degree courses in that."

"Everything I do you copy. You do everything I say, and we'll make it back."

"I hear you, Mr. Crane, and is there something I can say?"

"What is it?"

"It would be great to see you smile, and to hear you laugh would be quite marvelous."

Crane scowled.

"We're taking more than we had on the warm-up hike. We're taking what I can carry, which means you have to manage with the same. We are taking five days' water, which is fifty pounds' weight. We are taking rations for five days. We will have first-aid and survival gear. We will have a sniper rifle with day vision and night vision sights, and we will have an Armalite rifle with six magazines. Watch the way I pack your kit, I won't pack it for you again. . . . It's not easy for me, you know, having a green ass."

"I'll do my best, Mr. Crane."

"Too right you will, 'cause I kick hard."

When the Bergens were packed, and the weapons had been cleaned one more time, Crane dressed in olive-green military trousers and shirt. He saw that Holt watched the way he pulled the sleeves down and buttoned them, hid the forearm skin. He saw the way Holt copied him as he threaded the hessian lengths of brown and yellow and black material into the rubber straps sewn into the uniform, to break down the body's outlines. He saw that Holt imitated him as he smeared the insect repellent cream on his face and throat, but not on his forehead. He could have explained that creams were never put on the forehead, because the sweat would carry it into the eyes, but he saw no point in explaining. The youngster just had to watch, copy, imitate. When Holt was dressed, he hoisted the Bergen pack onto Holt's shoulders, told him to walk around, told him to get the feel of the pack that was half as heavy again as the one that Holt had struggled with in the Occupied Territories. Six times round the room, and then the adjustments that were necessary on the straps. More adjustments for the waist belt. And adjustments for the sling strap of the Armalite.

Holt said, "Why haven't you given me a practice with the Armalite?"

"Because if our lives depend on you with the Armalite, then they're not worth much."

"I have to be able to fire it."

"If it has to be fired then it'll be me that's firing it. You're just there to carry it."

Crane reached out. He took the wristwatch off Holt's arm. For a moment he read the inscription on the back. "Our dearest son, 21st birthday, Mum and Dad." He felt a vandal. He tore off the strap. He looped a length of parachute cord through the slots, knotted the ends. With adhesive tape he fastened two morphine ampoules to the cord, one each side of the watch. He hooked the cord over Holt's neck, saw the watch sink with the ampoules down under Holt's shirt front.

Like he was dressing a kid for a party, he tied a dull green netted cloth around Holt's forehead. He stood back, he looked Holt up and down.

"You won't get any better," Crane said. He punched Holt in the shoulder, he made a rueful grin.

"If they ever audition for the lead in the Great Communicator, you'd be a certainty, Mr. Crane. You might even end with an Oscar."

"Let's move."

He thought the youngster was great, and he did not know how to tell him. He thought that he was not alone. He had seen the way Percy Martins looked at Holt, when Holt didn't see him. He thought they were both trying to reach the youngster, and both failing, both too bloody old.

Crane said, "You won't have noticed, Holt, but there is no magazine on the Model PM Long Range. It's one shot only. You don't get a chance to reload. You have one chance, one shot. I have to get into a five-inch circle at around a thousand yards with a first shot, an only shot."

He saw the sincerity in Holt's eyes. "That's why they had to dig out the best man, Mr. Crane. Thank God they found him."

They went through the door.

Holt's own clothes and Crane's were left folded in separate plastic bags, each with a name tag.

Loaded down by the Bergens they walked down the corridor, out to the transport.

Percy Martins was talking to him, pacing alongside Holt. He was following Crane out into the sunshine and toward the mine-proofed Safari truck.

"I'll be here, Holt, I'll be at Kiryat Shmona, and via Tel Aviv I'll have secure communications with London. Everything that I can humanly do for you will be done, rest assured on that . . ."

He saw the girl standing on the veranda of the officers' canteen. She wore scarlet this morning. He would like to have gone to her, kissed her his thanks for what she had given to him. She looked straight through him, as though he were a stranger.

"You're going to help to make the world a better and a safer place for decent folk, young Holt. Go in after that bastard and blow him away. Let them know that there are no safe havens, no bolt holes, that we can see them and reach them even when they're the other side of the hill. I'll be waiting for you."

"Great, Mr. Martins."

He followed Crane into the back of the Safari, the major gave him a hand up, pulled him over the tailboard.

"God speed . . ."

Holt didn't hear any more. The Safari lurched forward. Martins stood in the road, shouting silently, waving as if it were important, with the white plastic nose shield set as a bull's-eye in the center of his sun-red head, and the light catching the watch chain across his waistcoat. When he looked to the veranda the girl was sitting and her head was in her book.

He felt the sharp finger tap on his arm.

Crane said, "Forget it, right now you've more to think of than some doe-eyed fanny."

He didn't think any woman had ever loved Noah Crane. He thought Noah Crane was in pain because of the way that his face was screwed up, and his forehead was cut with lines. The back of the Safari was covered with a canvas roof and sides, and the three of them sat as close as was possible to the driver's cab. To other cars, to people walking on the road, they were unseen. Their own vision was through the open back. The major and Noah Crane sat on the slatted seats, facing inward, and Holt was down on the floor between them and sitting on sandbags. The sandbags covered the whole of the floor of the back of the Safari. Holt understood they were there to cushion a mine explosion. He smiled to himself, did not show his black amusement to the others. He had once read of a man who was shipwrecked and alone in a rubber dinghy, and the man had said that the worst aspect of his 100-day drift before rescue was when the sharks came under the dinghy and prodded the thin rubber base with their snouts. He wondered which would be worse, the snout of a tiger shark under his backside, or the blast of a land mine—great choice, beautiful options.

He held the Armalite rifle upright between his knees, and he didn't even know how to maintain it, how to strip it, how to clean it. He was young Holt. He was a young diplomat of Third Secretary grade. All so wretchedly unreal.

They went through the village of Metulla, and through the back of the Safari Holt saw that almost immediately they drove past a border checkpoint and through a wide-cut gap in a high wire fence. Crane reached out, no preliminaries, took the Armalite and with fast hand movements cocked it. Holt heard the clatter as the escort sitting in front beside the driver armed his weapon.

"Welcome to our security zone, Holt." The major seemed to smile, and he creaked his leg as he shifted to take more easily a Service pistol from the leather holster at his waist. "It is our buffer or protection strip. At the fence we have our last line of defense to keep the swine out of our country. At the fence we have the electronic beams, body heat sensors, TV camera fields, mined areas. But that is the last line. We try to halt them, the infiltrators, here in the security zone. You know we have around ninety attempts each month to get through the security zone but they don't get through. The security zone is of the greatest importance to us. We are indeed lucky, Holt, that we have in the security zone several thousand armed men of the South Lebanese Army, they are Christians who were isolated down here when Lebanon fragmented. We pay them hugely, much more than we pay our own soldiers, and because they have to fight for their own survival they protect us well. The security zone, Holt, is a place of enclaves. Apart from the Christian enclaves, there are groupings of Shi'ite Muslim, and Islamic Fundamentalist Muslim, and Hezbollah Muslim. The Shi'ites and the Fundamentalists and the Hezbollah have in common a hatred of everything Jewish and everything Christian. It makes for an interesting zone. But we have cut our funerals. The funerals of our soldiers were destroying our nation. The SLA now die on our behalf, handsomely rewarded for their sacrifice. Our men are more precious to us than shekels, we can pay the price."

They drove on. Over the lowered tailgate Holt saw that they were climbing through a dry and barren landscape. He saw roadblocks that they sped through without checking. He saw a Subaru sedan, with no identifying number plates, parked on the hard shoulder, and there were two men in civilian clothes sitting on the bonnet and one cradled a submachine gun on his lap and the other had a Galil rifle slung from his shoulder. The car was low on its suspension. He presumed they were Shin Bet, that the car was armor plated. They passed the turning to Khiam, and Holt saw the fences and watchtowers of what seemed a prison camp. They passed the turning to Marjayoun, which Holt knew was the principal Christian town in the zone.

They climbed.

The major and Crane talked fast now, in Hebrew. They talked over the top of Holt, as if he were not there, and twice the major leaned over Holt and tapped energetically with his finger at a piece of equipment on Crane's belt harness. It was the one piece of equipment that was not duplicated on his own belt harness.

The truck was slowing, changing down through the gears. There was the rocking motion of the vehicle as it pulled off the road, and headed up to a steep incline on a rough track.

They lurched to a halt.

"Where you walk from, Holt," the major said.

Crane disarmed the Armalite, cleared it, then handed it to Holt. He carried his Bergen and his Model PM to the tailboard, jumped down. The major clumsily followed him. Holt lugged his Bergen the length of the Safari and swung himself off the end. All three ran the few yards into a concrete and stone built observation post. It was early afternoon. It was sickeningly warm in the observation post, as though the reinforced walls held the heat.

He sensed the tension immediately.

There were two soldiers and an officer. There was a radio squawking with bursts of static, and one of the soldiers sat by the radio with his earphones clamped on his head and held tight by his hands. The other soldier and the officer raked with binoculars the ground ahead of their split-vision portholes.

He saw the major speak to the officer, saw the officer shake his head, resume his watch.

Holt came forward. He placed himself at the officer's shoulder. He stared out.

The checkpoint was about a hundred yards down the road, a chicane of concrete blocks positioned so that a vehicle must slow and zigzag to pass through. The road stretched away, winding and falling toward the green strip of the Litani River bed. The observation post was, Holt estimated, a hundred feet above the road. A great emptiness. A silence stretching up the road that led north. Down at the checkpoint he could see that the soldiers all peered up the road, some through binoculars, some holding their hands flat against their foreheads to protect their eyes from the sun.

"When do we go?" Holt asked, irritated because he was ignored.

"When it is dark," the major said, all the time gazing up the road.

"So why are we here so early?"

"Because the transport has to be back before it is dark."

"So what do we do now?"

"You wait, because I have other things to consider."

Holt flared, "Why can't someone tell me . . . ?"

"Leave it," Crane snapped.

He felt like stamping his foot, furious and apparently powerless. The officer had turned away from the vision slit he watched through, and had gone with quick, nervy movements to the table where the radio operator worked. The officer pulled a cigarette from a packet beside the set, lit it, puffed energetically on it, then offered a cigarette to him. Crane was looking at him. Sulkily he shook his head. Cigarettes were banned. Toothpaste was banned. Soap was banned. . . . Crane had said that cigarettes and toothpaste and soap were all banned because they left a smell signature. What the hell was a smell signature? What sort of language was that? *Smell signature.* He looked up, it was on the end of his tongue to argue what difference it would make if he had one cigarette.

They had their backs to him. He stared at the backs of the officer, and the soldier, and the major, and Crane. Hunched backs, heads pressed against the wood surrounds of the vision slits.

He could see over Crane's shoulder.

In the bright light of the afternoon he had to blink to make anything from the sunswept rocky ground and the narrow gray pencil line of the road.

The radio operator was scribbling, then tearing the paper off his pad, holding his arm outstretched for the officer to take the message.

He could see a girl leading a donkey.

The soldiers at the roadblock were running to take cover behind the blocks of the chicane, and two men were crouched in the cover of their car back from the roadblock.

Unbelievable to Holt. The soldiers had taken cover because there was a girl a thousand yards down the road leading a donkey. A girl and a beige brown donkey, and This Man's Army was flat on its face. A girl and a donkey, something out of a Sunday School lesson when he was still in short trousers. A small boy's idea of the Holy Land—bright and sunny, and yellow rock, and a girl with a donkey.

The major spoke to Crane. Crane shrugged, nodded. The major spoke to the officer. The officer went to the radio, took the earphones from the operator, spoke briefly into the microphone.

A girl coming up the road and leading a donkey. The only movement Holt could see through the vision slit. Crane had gone to the back of the observation post, was rooting in his kit. Holt saw two of the soldiers who had been behind the cement blocks were now scurrying, bent low, to get further back. All unbelievable. Crane pushed Holt aside, wanted the whole of the vision slit to himself, and he was jutting the barrel of the Model PM through the slit.

"For God's sake, Mr. Crane, it's a girl."

"Don't distract him," the major said quietly.

"So what in God's name is he doing?"

"Be quiet, please."

A girl with a donkey, something sweet, something pastoral.

Crane slid a bullet into the loading port forward of the bolt arm, settled the rifle into his shoulder.

"What in bloody hell gives? It's a girl. Are you sighting your rifle? Can't you see it's just a girl? Is this your idea of a test shot? . . ."

"Quiet," the major hissed. Crane oblivious, still.

"It's a bloody person, it's not just a *target* . . ."

Crane fired.

There was the rip echo of the report singing around the inside of the observation post. Holt's eyes were closed involuntarily. He heard the clatter of the ejected cartridge case landing.

He looked through the vision slit.

The donkey stood at the side of the road beside the small rag bundle that was the girl.

Holt looked at them, looked from one to the other.

"Bloody well done, so you've got your rifle sighted. Only an Arab girl, good target for sighting a rifle. First-class shooting."

Crane reloaded.

The donkey had moved a pace away from the girl's body, it was chewing grass at the side of the road.

"I didn't know it, Crane, I didn't know you were a fucking animal."

Crane breathed in hard. Holt saw his chest swell. The rifle was vice steady. Crane breathed out, checked. Holt watched the first squeeze on the trigger, saw the finger whitening with the pressure of the second squeeze.

Again the crash of the shot echoed in the confines of the observation post. Crane spurted out his remaining breath.

Holt saw the orange flame.

Holt saw the flame ball where the donkey had been.

There was a thunder rumbling. There was a wind scorching his face at the vision slit.

The donkey had gone. The girl had gone. There was a crater in the road into which a big car could have fallen. Holt stared. God, and he felt so frightened. He was naked because he knew nothing.

Crane ejected the cartridge case. His voice was a whisper, a tide turn over pebbles, a light wind in an autumn copse. "Did you watch me?"

"I'm just sorry for what I said."

"As long as you watched me, saw everything I did."

He had seen that Crane's head never moved. He had seen the breathing pattern. He had seen the way Crane's eyebrow and cheekbone merged into the tube of the telescopic sight. He had seen the two-stage squeeze on the trigger.

"I saw everything that you did."

The major said, "You are in Lebanon here, Holt, nothing is as it seems."

They were given tea.

Crane cleaned the rifle, unfastened the bolt mechanism to pull the cloth through the barrel.

Major Zvi Dan crouched beside Holt.

"I don't think, and this is not criticism, that you know anything of the military world."

"I'm not sorry."

"If you had been born an Israeli you would have been in the army."

"Not my quarrel."

"You may not think it your quarrel, but when you walk from here, when you walk away from our protection, then every man and woman and child in the villages and towns of the Bekaa would hate you if they knew of you. Would you believe me if I told you, Holt, that in the Bekaa they do not acknowledge the Geneva Conventions on the treatment of prisoners . . . ?"

Holt grimaced, he liked the man. "I believe you."

"I am so very serious. It is a place without conventions. There would be no officers to safeguard you. Your life would be worthless after the sport of torturing you."

Holt said softly, "I'm scared enough, no need to make it worse."

"I do not try to frighten you, I try only to stress that you should follow Noah, exactly follow him. Noah is a marksman, he is a sniper. Do you know that in your own army for many years sniping was frowned on? It was not quite right, it was even dirty. Examine the job of the sniper. He shoots first against an officer. When does he shoot the officer? He kills the officer when he goes for his morning defecation. The officer is dead, his men are leaderless, and they dare not leave their trench for the call of nature. They make their mess in their trench, which is not good, Holt, for their morale. The sniper is hated by his enemy, he is prized by his own forces who are behind him. Often they are far behind him, where they cannot be of assistance to him. It is a peculiar and particular man who fights far beyond help. Your Mr. Crane, who has never accepted a medal, is peculiar and particular. Follow him."

Holt sat on his backside as far as he could be from the

vision slits. For as long as he could avoid it, he wanted to see no more of a battlefield where the enemy was a young girl, and her arsenal was a donkey.

The aircraft was late.

The aircraft was at the end of its flying life. At every stop-over it required comprehensive maintenance testing. The aircraft was elderly because that way the premiums paid to Lloyd's of London by Middle East Airlines for comprehensive insurance cover could be kept to a reasonable figure.

The aircraft landed from Paris in the middle of the afternoon. It had come in over the sea, the view of Beirut had been minimal in the heat haze.

He was Heinrich Gunter, the passenger who was eager to be free of the passport queue in the bullet-pocked airport terminal.

He was forty-five years old, and this was the thirty-ninth visit he had made to Beirut since the shooting and shelling had started in 1976.

He was a middle-management employee of the Credit Bank of Zurich, and he was personally responsible for the administration of many millions of United States dollars invested with his bank by wealthy, quiet-living Lebanese entrepreneurs.

He was married, with three children, and he had told his wife that morning that Beirut was fine if you had the right contacts, made the correct arrangements.

He was expecting to be met. He was not to know that the airport road had been closed for three hours, that a rising of tension between men of the Druze militia and of the Shi'ite Amal militia had prevented his agent from getting to the airport to meet him.

He hurried away from the passport control. He collected his one suitcase that was adequate for a two-day stay, maximum. He moved through the frequently repaired glass doors at the airport's main entrance. He could not see his agent.

After waiting for 25 minutes, Heinrich Gunter agreed with

a persistent taxi driver that he would pay the fare asked, in hard currency. He was told that the driver knew a safe way, avoiding the area of tension, to the hotel into which he was booked. It was already a long day. A row with his wife over his breakfast because he was going to Beirut, an argument at Zurich airport because the Swissair flight was overbooked and he was a late arrival, drinks in the airport bar at Charles de Gaulle because Middle East Airlines was leaving late, more drinks on the flight because he was going to Beirut. It had been a long day, and he had been drinking, and he took the taxi.

Heinrich Gunter never really saw what happened. In the backseat of the taxi Heinrich Gunter lolled back, the whiskey miniatures of the Paris airport and the Middle East Airlines first-class cabin had taken a gentle and gradual toll.

By the time that his eyes opened, the taxi had been waved down to the side of the road, the back door had been wrenched open, a hand had grabbed for the sleeve of his jacket. The first thing he clearly saw was the barrel of a rifle half a dozen inches from his chest. The first thing he felt was himself being propelled out of the car. He lurched to the pavement. He was grabbed under each arm and rushed down an alleyway. He had seen a flash of two slimly built young men, each wearing a cotton imitation of a balaclava face mask, each carrying a rifle. In the alley a length of cloth was wrapped around his face, covering his eyes. He was kicked hard in the leg, the back of his head was cudgeled with the butt of a rifle.

There was no fight in Heinrich Gunter as he was dragged away.

He knew what had happened to him. He was sobbing as his shoes scuffed the surface of the alleyway. He had not even shouted for help. He knew he was beyond help.

Fawzi showed his papers to the NORBAT sentry. The papers identified him as a Lebanese dentist.

He drove out of the UNIFIL sector. The checking by the

sentry of his car had not been thorough. A thorough check would have discovered the dirtied overalls in which he had lain on the hillside a mile and a half from the roadblock. It would also have discovered a powerful pair of East German binoculars. Had the car been stripped to its panels, then the sentry would have unearthed the radio-controlled command detonator that would have fired the explosives in the pannier bags slung against the donkey's sides.

He went fast, angrily.

He had seen weeks of manipulation destroyed by a long-range marksman.

He had failure to report to Major Said Hazan.

He had seen the girl as a gem, and her long triumphant journey had been ended several hundred yards short of her target. Fawzi could taste the humiliation.

Percy Martins wrote his occupation as "government servant," and the reason for his visit as "vacation," when he filled in the registration form at the guesthouse.

He had not been asked where he wanted to stay. He had been driven from the army camp at Kiryat Shmona to the Kibbutz Kfar Giladi. He was not that disappointed. He was greeted at the reception desk as a VIP. His bag was carried. He was treated with respect. The guesthouse, six stories high, set in flowering gardens, appealed to him.

He was given his key.

"I was wondering," he said to the raven-haired, raven-eyebrowed receptionist, "would there be any fishing in these parts? Would one be able to hire a rod?"

Percy Martins was nothing if not a pragmatist. He understood that his marriage was in terminal collapse, that his relationship with his son was as good as finished. He could look clear-headed at his career, twice passed over for promotion to Deputy or In Charge of the Middle East Desk. But he was no longer wounded by setbacks. He could cope with his home life. He could live with what to other men would have been humiliation in the office. He could endure the taciturn Holt and the imperious Israelis. That is what he told himself. He said to himself, Sod the lot of them. He would bloody well go fishing.

"I would have thought there would be some trout in those nice little streams running down from Mount Hermon. Now trout isn't what I usually go for—I'm a pike man actually. I don't suppose you know about pike. If you're into trout then you would regard pike as something akin to vermin. You'll see what you can find out for me, of course you will. You're very kind."

With his key in his hand he trudged up the stairs to his second-floor room. He imagined himself ushering young Holt into the Director General's office, and of standing quietly at the back of the room. Very well done indeed, Percy. We are all proud of you.

He sat down on the bed. He unbuttoned the front of his waistcoat. He loosened his tie. Sod the lot of them. He held his head in his hands. Unseen, alone, close to tears.

There was a crushed ball of paper on the pile carpet beside the chair of Major Said Hazan. It was the clean sheet of paper he had crumpled with all the strength of his fist when the telephone call had informed him that the girl and her bomb had not reached target.

He had given his instructions. On the evening television news broadcast, transmitted by the Syrian state station, a statement would be made by the girl. She would talk of her commitment to a Lebanon free of Israeli terror, and of her commitment to the Syrian cause and the Palestine revolution. And then the news reader would give factual information of the heavy casualties inflicted on the IDF and their surrogate SLA by the sacrificial heroism of the girl.

The truth, and this was clearly recognized by Major Said Hazan, was an irrelevance. The northern boundary of the security zone was a closed area, there would be no independent witnesses. More of the Arab world would believe the claim of the Syrian state station than would believe the denial put out by the Israeli Broadcasting Corporation. The message would go on the airwaves that a young Muslim girl of exemplary purity had given her life in the struggle against the Zionist brutes—she had been photographed with care by the camera, her pregnancy would not be seen. It was the estimate of Major Said Hazan that a car bomb or a donkey bomb had more effect on the anxious sheiks and emirs and sultans of the oil-wealthy Gulf than any other lever for the extraction of funds. Great truth in the ancient Arab proverb, The enemy of my friend is my enemy, the enemy of my enemy is my friend. His country needed the funds of the Gulf. The route to those funds was through constant, daring attacks against Israel carried out by the young vanguard of the Arab peoples.

The truth might be an irrelevance, but he hated to know that the bomb had been stopped short of its target. The crushed, crumpled paper lay beside his feet.

He reached for the telephone. There were some who came to his office who marveled to find four telephones on the table beside his desk. A joke had once been made that he had only two ears, two hands. A poor joke, because his ears had been burned away, leaving only stumps, and the fingers of his right hand had been amputated. One telephone gave him access by direct line to the desk of the brigadier general commanding Air Force Intelligence. A second telephone gave him scrambled communication with military headquarters at Chtaura in the Bekaa Valley. A third telephone gave him an outside line, the fourth put him into the exchange system of Air Force Intelligence. He lifted the third telephone.

He dialed.

He spoke with silk. "Is it you? . . . A thousand apologies, I have been away, and since I have been back just meetings, more meetings. Too long away from you . . . How was he, my pet? . . . How was his spirit? How was his resolution? . . . My pet, you would lift the organ of the dead . . . Excellent. I will see you, my pet, as soon as I can turn away this cursed load of work. Goodbye, my pet."

There had been the knock at his door which caused him to ring off. He loved to hear her guttural foreign voice. He loved to linger with his thoughts on the smooth clean curves of her flesh . . .

He called for his visitor to enter.

Major Said Hazan stretched out his left hand in greeting. "My Brother, you are most welcome . . ."

For an hour he talked with this military commander of the Popular Front over the plans for an attack on the Defense Ministry complex in Tel Aviv. That section which housed the rooms of the Military Intelligence wing was ringed in red ink. They discussed the method of infiltration, and leaned toward a seaborne landing, and they pondered over the sort of man who might have the élan, the resolution, to lead such a mission.

After an hour Major Said Hazan had quite overcome his sharp fury at the failure of the girl and her bomb at the checkpoint in the security zone.

Far behind them, far from sight, came the dulled reports of the artillery, and far ahead of them there was the brilliance of the flares bursting and then falling to spread their white light against the darkness.

Holt tugged at the Bergen's straps, wriggled for greater comfort. They were outside the observation post.

Crane said, "I told you not to look at them."

Crane had his back to the flares.

"And you haven't told me what they're for."

"I'm not a bloody tourist guide."

"Why are they firing flares, Mr. Crane?"

"Because you're looking at the flares you're losing the ability to see in darkness. We have to pass through a chunk of NORBAT ground, so we are putting flares up for illumination between NORBAT positions and where we're walking, we're burning out their night vision equipment. Got it?"

"Would have helped if you had told me in the first place."

"Piss off, youngster."

"Let's get this show on the road, then."

They hugged each other. A brief moment. Arms around

each other, and the belt kit sticking into the other's stomach, and the weapons digging at each other's rib cages, and the weight of the Bergen packs swaying them.

They were two shadows.

The stars were just up. The moon would be over them at midnight, an old moon in the last quarter.

They crossed the road beneath the observation post. They headed into the darkness, away from the road, away from the slow falling flares.

They were gone from the safety of the security zone.

Nothing in his mind except concentration on his footfall and the faint shape walking in front of him. Nothing of Jane who had been his love through his life before, nor of the girl who had been his comfort the night before, nor of the leaders and the generals, nor of his country. Only the care of where he laid his boot, and his watch on Noah Crane ahead.

13

It started as a casual conversation.

At the airfield south of Kiryat Shmona there was a hut where helicopter passengers could wait, sit in comfortable rattan-style chairs, for their flight. There was a steward dispensing orange juice, there was a radio tuned in to the army station, there were some pot flowers which had even been watered.

The pilot came into the hut to advise Major Zvi Dan that there would be a short delay before he could lift off with the major and the major's assistant.

"Up to your ears?" the major asked.

The pilot knew Zvi Dan. The pilot sometimes joked that he was a bus driver, that Zvi Dan traveled more often from Tel Aviv to Kiryat Shmona than any grandmother in search of her grandchildren.

"I'm down the queue for refueling, for maintenance checks. Ahead of us are the choppers going tomorrow."

Because the pilot knew Zvi Dan, he knew also that the major worked in Military Intelligence. He could talk freely.

"Where?"

"Big show up the road."

"I've been out of touch." Zvi Dan sipped at the plastic beaker of juice.

"Bombers are going up the road in the morning, we're down for rescue standby."

"So we're in the queue, and what's new? That's the old army motto, Hurry up and wait."

Rebecca read her book, almost at the end, rapt attention.

"There's to be a big chopper force on rescue standby, it's a difficult target they're going for."

"How so?"

"The Bekaa, not under the missile umbrella directly, but the fringe area. It's not the missile that's the problem, the target's just small, and for small targets they have to line up more carefully, all the usual gripes from the bombers."

"What's the target?"

The pilot leaned forward, said quietly, "We were told that they had good interrogation of one of those shit pigs that did the bus station—well, you'd know more of that than me, that it was all hocus them both being killed. Seems they came out of a training camp in the Bekaa, that's where the bombers are going . . ."

Major Zvi Dan was rigid in his chair. His orange juice had spilled on his tunic.

"Heh, have I said something?"

He saw the major's back going out through the door.

Rebecca looked up, grimaced. She had not been listening. She went back to her book.

Major Zvi Dan, anger mad, pounded into the night.

He swung through the door of the airfield's flight operations room. He stomped to the chair of the flight operations officer. He pulled the chair round, swiveled it to face him.

"I am Major Zvi Dan, Military Intelligence. I am an officer with an A-level category of priority. On a classified matter of importance I demand an immediate takeoff for Tel Aviv."

He cowed the flight operations officer into submission.

He could barely believe it: Two men had started to walk toward the Bekaa, to walk toward a tent camp, to identify a target, to take out a terrorist, and the air force were planning to beat them there by two days and scatter the ground with cluster bombs. Right hand and left hand, light-years apart. Why couldn't his bloody country put its bloody act together?

He stormed back into the hut. He limped up and down the floor space, pacing away his impatience.

The pilot came in. "You put a bomb under somebody, Major. We have clearance for lift-off in ten minutes."

It was the same rhythm of advance that Holt had learned during the hike in the Occupied Territories. But that had been only rehearsal. Different now. In the Occupied Territories Crane had hissed curses at him when he kicked loose stones, when he stood on dry wood, when he stumbled and stampeded away small scree rock. On his own now, wasn't he? Had to make do without help. Not that he needed cursing when he scuffed a stone, he wanted to punch himself in frustration each time.

Holt knew that the pace that had been set was aimed to cover one mile in each hour. It had been dark at six, it would be light again at six. They had moved off an hour after darkness, they would reach their LUP an hour before dawn. He was unconsciously soaking up the jargon, a lying-up position had become LUP. Ten hours on the move, ten miles to cover. Stripped, Holt weighed 168 pounds. He carried a further 80 pounds' weight in his clothing, his Bergen and his belt. In addition he was ferrying the Model PM, because Crane had the Armalite. He remembered the race around the lawns of the house in England, when he carried nothing, when Crane had a backpack full of stones. Christ, there was a weight on his back, on his hips, on his arms.

The first hour he had kicked stones, the second hour fewer. They were in the third hour and he moved as Crane had shown him. His booted foot edged forward, found the ground, the ball of his foot rolled, tested. If the test was fine, if the stone held fast, then the weight followed. It was the rhythm of each pace, every footfall tested.

There was just the starlight for them to move under. Crane was fifteen yards in front. It was Holt's job to follow Crane's speed. Crane set the pace, Holt had to follow. Crane was an outline ahead of him, blurred at the edges by the hessian tabs on his body shape and on the bulk of his Bergen. All the time he had to be within sight of Crane, because Crane would not stop each few yards and turn to see if Holt kept contact.

A week before, before the hike into the Occupied Territories, Holt would not have credited that so much skill, so much care, would be involved in moving across ground at night.

It was indeed a rhythm.

It was the same rhythm from the moment they had crossed the road under the observation post, headed away.

Every 30 minutes they stopped. Holt would see Crane hold up his hand and then drift to the side off the line of march. A few moments of listening, looking into the darkness, with Crane and Holt sitting back to back, each covering a 180-degree arc of vision. No talking, no whispering, just the straining of the ears and the eyes. In the Occupied Territories, Crane had told Holt that they should always be low down when they were listening, looking, seeking for information that they were followed or that there was movement ahead of them. Crane had said that a dog or a cat had good vision at night because its low eyeline permitted it to see most shapes against a skyline in silhouette. In the short moments when they were stopped, Crane would check his map, holding over it the lens of his Beta light, powered by tritium, giving him the small glow that was hidden from view, sufficient for him to see by.

During the third hour they crossed the Litani River. Waist deep in fast water, going off rocks and climbing back onto rocks, so that they left no footprints in mud. There were no roads, and Holt saw that Crane avoided even rough tracks that could have been used by the villagers of Qillaya that was across the river to the east, or Qotrani that was beyond the hill summit to the west. It was strange to Holt how much he could see with the help only of starlight, something he had never thought to learn before. He supposed the trail they took might have been made by wild animals, perhaps an ibex herd, perhaps the run of the low-bellied hyrax, perhaps the regular path of a scavenging hyena or a fox.

North of the narrow road between Qillaya and Qotrani, in the fourth hour, they were high above the Litani, traversing a steeply sloping rock face. On the slope face they moved sideways, crablike. When they had to cross the upper lines of a side valley, Holt saw that Crane immediately changed direction as soon as they had been outlined. He had been told why they did not climb to the upper ridges of the hills, Crane had told him that the military were most likely to be on the high ground, basic officer training was to seek out the greatest vantage point. A hellish strain on Holt's leg muscles as he fought to hold his balance against the sway of the Bergen weight when they crabbed on the sloping, uneven ground.

By the fifth hour he was sagging down at the RP. The rally points, where they stopped for the few moments each half hour, seemed to him to be drifting further apart. He knew that was eyewash, he knew he was feeling the exhaustion of the night march. At the RPs he sat against Crane's shoulder, and had to be elbowed hard in the ribs to remind him that the stop at the RP was not for recovery, but for checking that the way ahead was clear, that the way behind was not compromised.

He was halfway through the first night, and there would be three nights of marching to get to the tent camp, and then there would be the stampede march back. God, and he was tired, and he was only halfway through the first night. He could hear his chest heaving, he could feel the gasping pant in his lungs. Silence from Crane, as though he were out for a stroll in the park. . . . Bloody man.

Rebecca drove from the Sde Dove Airport on the north side of Tel Aviv, across the city.

Major Zvi Dan sat beside her, still angry, silent. The streets were fully lit. Bright shop windows, pavement crowds, cafés packed. The anger corroded him. The old and the young strolling the streets, examining the windows, laughing and joking and singing, and two men not quite a hundred miles to the north were struggling in the darkness through rivers, over rock slopes, further and deeper into the territory of the enemy. The logic was gone from his mind, blown away by his temper. He wouldn't have said that he wanted the citizens of Tel Aviv to hot tail it to the synagogues and offer prayers, nor that they should shut their mouths, shut off their music, tiptoe down Dizengoff, but it fueled his anger to see so many who knew so little, cared less.

She dropped him on Kaplan, outside the David Gate of the ministry. She said something to him about what time she would arrive in the morning, but he didn't hear her. He ran, as fast as his imitation leg would allow him, toward the barrier and the night sentries. And he couldn't find his pass . . . and his pass wasn't in his breastpocket . . . and his pass was in his bloody hip pocket. He could have been the Prime Minister, could have been the Chief of Staff, he would not have entered the David Gate if he had not found his pass in his wallet in his hip pocket.

He was allowed through. They didn't hurry themselves. It was the way of sentries, little men with power, that they never scrambled themselves for a man who was hurrying.

He headed for the wing building occupied by the IAF staff.

And how his leg hurt him when he tried to run. . . . Into the building, another check on his pass. . . . Up the stairs and into the access corridor used by night duty staff, one more check on his pass . . . along the corridor and into the fluorescent-lit room that was the war management section of the Israeli Air Force. A big, quiet room, where the men and the women on duty spoke in soft whispers, where the radios were turned down, where the teleprinters purred out their paper messages. A room flanked by huge wall maps, and dominated in the center by the operational console table. It was from this room that the long-range voice contact had been kept with the Hercules transporters flying the slow lonely mission of rescue to Entebbe, and from this room also that the F-16s had been guided the thousands of miles to and from their strikes against the Palestine Liberation Organization headquarters in Tunis and the Iraqi nuclear OSIRAK reactor outside Baghdad. Those who worked in this room believed themselves to be an élite backup force to the élite arm of Israel's retaliatory strike capability.

Those who worked in the room looked first with puzzlement, then amusement, at the hobbling army major making his entry.

It was a room of great calmness. Low-key calmness was the strength of the men and women who supported the combat pilots. Major Zvi Dan had abandoned calmness. He was dirty, he was tired, his hair was disheveled.

All eyes were on him.

A girl officer, wearing lieutenant's insignia on her shoulder flaps, glided from a chair to intercept him.

"I need to see, immediately, the duty brigadier." Major Zvi Dan breathed hard. In no condition, not with the imitation leg.

"In connection with what, Major?"

"In connection with a classified matter."

"Believe it or not, Major, all of us who work in here have a degree of security clearance."

There was a tiny surf of laughter behind her. She was a pretty girl, auburn hair gathered high onto the crown of her head, a tight battledress blouse, a skirt that was almost a mini, and short white socks, carefully folded over.

"Please immediately arrange for me to see the duty brigadier."

"He is sleeping."

"Then you must wake him up," Zvi Dan growled.

"Regulations require that . . ."

Zvi Dan lowered over her. "Young lady, I was fighting for this God-forgotten country before you were old enough to wipe your own tiny butt. So spare me your regulations and go at once and wake him."

This last he bellowed at her, and she did. She spat dislike at him through her eyes first, but she went and woke the duty brigadier.

He was in poor humor. He was a tired, pale man, with gray uncombed hair and a lisp in his voice.

"Major, I do eighteen hours on duty on a night shift. During that time I take two hours' rest. My staff know that I am to be disturbed from that rest only on a matter of the highest importance. What is that matter?"

"You have a strike tomorrow against a Popular Front camp in the Bekaa, located at 35.45 longitude and 33.38 latitude."

"We have."

"It has to be canceled."

"On whose say?"

"Mine."

"The strike was authorized by the Chief of Staff."

"Then he didn't know what he was doing."

"Tell me more, Major."

"That camp must not be attacked."

"What is it? Do we have prisoners there?"

"No."

The duty brigadier gazed shrewdly at Major Zvi Dan, as if his annoyance was gone, as if now he was amused at the puzzle.

"Do we have a ground mission going in—which the Chief of Staff does not know about?"

"There is a mission. The Chief of Staff would not be aware of the fine detail."

"To that camp?"

"There is a mission in progress against that camp."

"An IDF mission?"

"No."

"Fascinating. . . . So, who can that be? The Americans, the doughnut boys?"

"The British."

"So the British have gone walking in the Bekaa, have they? How many of them?"

"Two."

"Two British are in the Bekaa. What have they gone to do, to pick grapefruit . . . ?"

"There is nothing in this matter that should amuse you." Major Zvi Dan stared coldly for a long time into the face of the duty brigadier. The coldness came from the freshness of his memory. Two men battleclad, their heavyweight Bergen packs, their bearded dark-creamed faces, their killing weapons. "In liaison with our Military Intelligence section, the British have two men walking into the Bekaa to get above that camp, to identify the assassin of their ambassador to the Soviet Union, to shoot that man."

"It is the policy of Israel, Major, the policy of the country that pays your wage, to hit the source fount of terrorism. From that camp an attack was launched against your country. It is expected and demanded of us that we strike back."

"You scatter a few bombs about, you may inflict casualties, you may not."

"It is expected of us."

"You will break up the camp. You will destroy a real chance of the killing of a single man whose death is important. Send that attack tomorrow morning and you ensure that two days later a brave pair of men will arrive at their target position to find nothing to fire upon. Brigadier, how many times do you kill the people you want killed, for all the Phantoms, all the bomb weight?"

"Thank you, Major."

"Which means?"

"That I shall wake the Chief of the Air Staff. Where will you be?"

He wrote on his notepad his extension number. He tore the page off, handed it to the duty brigadier.

"All night."

"I make no promises, I merely pass the problem higher."

The quiet returned to the room.

All of them, at their desks and their consoles and tables and maps, watched with the duty brigadier the flapping swing door, and heard the uneven diminishing footfall.

The girl officer asked, "What do we owe the British, sir, with their arms embargo, their criticism of us?"

The duty brigadier said, "The British were going to hang my brother in 1947 when he was in the Irgun. They reprieved him 48 hours before he was to go to the hangman. I was a small boy then. . . . The first people that I learned to hate were the British soldiers, who had captured and tortured my brother, and twenty years later I was a guest at their staff college, the staff college of the Royal Air Force. We owe them only what is best for us, and that decision mercifully is not mine."

In the small night hours, Major Zvi Dan's head lay on his hands that were spread on his desk.

The telephone was close beside him, and stayed silent.

The end of the seventh hour of the first night march, the time of the fourteenth rest moment at a rally point.

Above them, aloft on the steep slope, were the lights of the village of Meidoun. At the previous rally point Crane had shown the marking of the village on the map, used the Beta light for Holt to see it, and then Crane had shaken his head, as though the place was bad news. Holt knew that already Crane had broken one of his bible laws. The bible according to the prophet Crane stated that they should not pass within a thousand yards of a village. But no damned option. They had been moving on the slope below the village and above the Litani where it ran fast in a narrow gorge. They were sandwiched. It was a bastard place, and the rules were broken. On the far side of the gorge Holt could follow the movement of headlights snaking on the road, going north. To the west was a Shi'ite village, below them was the rushing river. To the east was the main military road.

Holt heard a stone fall. He heard a stone dislodged below him. After the long silence of the walk in the night his hearing was clearer than he had ever known. He froze. Crane, beside him, had half risen. Crane was now a bent statue. There were the sounds of more stones slipping on the slope below. Crane showed Holt the palm of his hand, the gesture that he should not move.

There were the sounds of a young shrill whistling voice, and then the sharp bark of a dog. The whistling and the barking and the falling stones were closer.

Crane's hand was on Holt's shoulder, urging him down, down until his face ate at the cool dust of the rock slope.

God, was this where it ended? Not a third of the way in,

not eight miles from the jump-off. Pray God that it didn't end because a village kid had gone after rabbits with his dog down to the scrub at the side of the Litani River. He tried to control the pace of his breathing. Breathing was another of the chapters of Crane's bible. Everything was down to control of breathing, keeping it regular, keeping it smooth, swallowing it down. He smelled the boy first, then he saw him.

The smell was of urine and animal fodder. It was a fecund sweet smell. No cigarette taste in his mouth, nor the cloy of toothpaste, nor the scent of soap on his face. He could smell the boy clearly moments before he saw him.

At first the boy was a shadow shape. The boy materialized as a wraith out of the darkness below, but coming fast, climbing easily on a steep pathway running down from the village to the river gorge. It was the moment it could all end. A shout would have been heard in the village, a scream would have roused the village. A fear yell would have brought the men of the village running, scrambling for their weapons. And there was the dog. The dog was close to the heels of the boy, skipping after him then stopping to sniff or lift a hind leg, then catching the boy. He knew that each village was an arsenal. Each village community would have automatic rifles and rocket-propelled grenade launchers and machine guns. He wondered if Crane had his hand on the whipcord handle of his knife. He could follow the line of the boy's climb, he saw that the boy with the dog at his heels would pass less than a dozen yards from them. He tried to slow his breathing, tried to master the battering heave of his heartbeat.

The boy was level with them, no break in his pace. The boy was unaware of them. Long seconds in the life of young Holt. Didn't want to look, didn't want to see. Had closed his eyes. Didn't want to know the moment of discovery if that were to be their fate. If Crane knifed the boy then the boy would be missed and searched for, and when he was found then the trail of his killers would be tracked. The rock that seemed to penetrate into the flesh of his groin grew sharper, more cutting with each moment that he lay prone on it. He was against Crane's body and there was not the slightest flicker of movement. His bladder seemed to have filled to aching point. There was the first whisper of cramp behind his knee. There was a dried leaf teasing at his nostril. He wanted to pee, wanted to jerk his leg straight, wanted to sneeze, and if he wet himself or moved his leg or sneezed then the mission was gone before it had begun.

He heard the growl of the dog.

The boy was above them, going quickly. The boy called for the dog to catch him.

Holt fractionally opened his eyes. The dog was two, three yards from them. The dog was thin as a rake, brindle brown he reckoned, and back on its haunches in defense, and growling at Crane.

The boy threw a stone, and called louder for the dog.

The growl was a rumble of suspicion. His bladder was bursting, cramp pain spreading, his sneeze rising.

The dog yelped. The second stone thrown by the boy hit it square in the neck.

The boy raised his voice to shout for the dog to come.

He heard the sounds going away. He heard the sounds of the boy and his dog dwindling away up the hillside path. He lay on his face. He felt only exhaustion, he felt too tired to know relief.

He felt Crane's hand on his shoulder pulling at him to get upright.

Crane's mouth was at his ear, a near silent whisper, "We've time to make up."

"Did I do all right?"

"That wasn't militia, not soldiers, just a kid. That was nothing."

Crane rose to his feet, headed away. Holt let him go fifteen paces then took his own first step.

He remembered the words of the song, mouthed them silently to himself:

Wish me luck, as you wave me goodbye,
Wish me luck, wish me luck, wish me luck . . .

And he seemed to hear her voice.

"Don't be childish, Holt."

He thought that he hated himself. He could have seen the boy knifed to death. He had never seen the face of the boy, he did not know the name of the boy. He was totally ignorant of the boy, and he could have cheered if Crane had felt the need to slide his short-bladed knife into the stomach of the boy, if Crane had drawn the sharp steel across the throat of the boy. If the boy had turned off the path, if the boy had come to see why his dog growled, then Holt would have cheered the boy's murder. As if a sea change had passed through him, as if he were no longer the man who had complained to Noah Crane about the torture of a Palestinian. He was dirtied in his soul.

He could remember, like yesterday, when he was ten years old, three days past his tenth birthday, and he had been walking with a holiday friend beside the river that ran close to his home. He had found a fox with a hind leg held by the thin cutting wire of a rabbit snare. There had been a blood smear around the wire, a little above the joint of the hind leg of the dog fox where the wire had worked deep through the fur and skin. Below the wire the hind leg hung at a silly angle. He had known, and he was only three days past his tenth birthday, that the dog fox was beyond saving because the leg was impossibly damaged. And he could not have freed it anyway because the dog fox snarled its teeth at him and at his friend, and would have bitten either of them if they had come close enough to release the other end of the wire from the hazel stump around which it was wound. They had taken smoothed rocks from the river shore, and they had thrown them at the fox until they had stunned it, could approach it, and with more stones they had battered the fox to death. All the time that he had killed the fox he had cried out loud. He could still remember how he had cried, child-like, in his bedroom that night. And now he could have cheered if the boy had been knifed.

He followed Crane. More of the Crane bible. He kept his eyeline to the right of Crane so that the moving shape was in the periphery of his vision. Crane had said that that way he would see better.

He was learning. He was changing.

Every late spring and every late autumn the ambassador of the United States entertained the Prime Minister of the United Kingdom to dinner in the splendor of the official residence in London's Regent's Park. For those two evenings of the year the lights blazed, the drink flowed, the hospitality was warm. It was the style of these two evenings that the Prime Minister would attend in the company of selected Cabinet ministers with responsibilities particularly affecting relationships "across the drain," along with principal industrialists with commercial links to the United States. On the American side a secretary of state would make the flight across the Atlantic. They were social occasions primarily, but permitted the free exchange of ideas and views.

A warm damp night. A fog rising from the park's grasslands. The mist outside was thickened in the driveway by the exhaust fumes of the chauffeur-driven cars. The night air was rich with good humor, noisy with guests making their farewells.

The Prime Minister warmly shook the hand of the ambassador.

"A wonderful evening, as always."

"A good night for a celebration, Prime Minister."

Below the steps the Branch men surrounded the Prime Minister's car, the lit interior beckoned. There was the warble of the radio link in the police backup car. If there was a weakness in the makeup of the evening it was that the ambassador and the Prime Minister had sat at dinner at opposite ends of the table, had barely exchanged words.

"You have the advantage over me, what is there in particular to celebrate?"

"An American triumph in the war against terrorism. We're very proud, I've wanted to tell you all evening."

"What triumph?"

"We have an air force base at Vicenza in northern Italy. Two nights ago our base security, American personnel, picked up a Lebanese male on the perimeter fence. He was in a hiding place and checking out the wire security with a PNV pocketscope. Sorry, that's Passive Night Vision. Our guys whipped him straight inside, straight into the guardhouse."

The Branch men fidgeted. Other guests stood respectfully out of earshot and in line to offer their thanks.

"What do the Italians say?"

"There's the beauty of it. About now my colleague down in Rome will be informing the Italians that our captive is currently on a USAF transport and heading Stateside. No messing up this time. But I'm jumping . . . I haven't got to the choice part."

The guest line grew. The Prime Minister's driver switched off the engine of the Rover.

"The choice part is this . . . TWA flight 840, Rome to Athens in the spring of '86, an explosion at 15,000 feet takes a hunk out of the fuselage through which four passengers are sucked. Three of those four are American citizens. The source of the explosion was under a seat occupied by a Lebanese woman who had hidden the explosives before getting off in Rome. Okay, you're with me? Best part. That woman boarded at Cairo for the leg to Rome. She was seen off by a male, tagged as Palestinian, we have his description, we have his fingerprints on the ticket stubs left at Cairo TWA check-in. We have him as the organizer, and the woman just as the courier. That man is one and the same as the joker on the fence at Vicenza. The prints match. That bastard is up in a big bird right now, Prime Minister, he's going to Andrews base, then a tight little military cell. That's why you can join me in celebration."

"Remarkable," the Prime Minister said softly.

"You'll remember what the President said. He said to these swine, 'You can run, but you cannot hide.' That's what we're proving. It's the first time we're able to put deeds to words, make action out of talk. We reckon this to be the turning point in the war against international terrorism. You're not cold, Prime Minister . . . ?"

"Not cold."

"It's the first time this has happened, and it's the first time that counts. Sam leads the way, Sam is first in, that's our celebration."

"A fine stroke of luck," the Prime Minister said distantly.

"In this game you earn your luck. Look, we've known for a year this man was in and out of Lebanon, in Damascus or in the Bekaa Valley. We went through all the military evaluations about getting a force into the Bekaa to drop him there. Can't be done, no way. The Bekaa would swallow a Marine division, that was our best advice, and even if we got in we'd never get out."

"You're very well informed."

"Secondhand, my number three here was in Beirut previously . . . we would have faced the risk of prisoners being paraded through Damascus, hell of a mess. Going into Lebanon wasn't on . . . that's diversion. It's being the first that matters. Prime Minister, not at your expense of course, but we're feeling very comfortable at this moment, very bullish. You see, what really matters is not just confronting these people, it's putting them into court. Assassination is small beer when set against the full rigor of a court of law."

The Prime Minister smiled congratulation, and walked away down the steps to the car. The engine coughed, the doors slammed shut. The car pulled away, trailed by the backup.

The Prime Minister's age showed, the tiredness of office and responsibility. There was a long sigh of weariness.

"Inform my office to have the Director General stand by. I'll be calling him from Downing Street as soon as I get there."

The Prime Minister sagged back in the seat. The Branch man in the front passenger seat relayed the instruction.

"What have you to do?" the private secretary asked quietly.

"I just have to cancel something. Nothing for you to worry about."

He had been dreaming of the fish he would catch, in the sleeping recesses of his mind was the recollection of the conversation he had had in the guesthouse bar with a tractor driver from the Kibbutz Kfar Giladi. Not a fast river to fish in, but a fish farm pond, not flies nor lures for bait, but worms from a compost heap. And to hell with tradition. Percy Martins dreamed of tight lines . . . until the bell exploded in his ear, like a big rainbow jumping.

He groped, he found the light. He lifted the telephone.

"Martins."

"Is that a secure line?"

"No."

"DG here."

"God . . . good evening, sir."

"Good morning, Percy. Our friends, where are they?"

"Gone."

"Can you reach them?"

"No."

"Why not?"

Martins sat straight up in his bed. "Because sir, they have no, ah, telephone. As it is they are carrying in excess of eighty pounds' weight. I would hazard, sir, that you or I could barely lift eighty pounds' weight, let alone walk a long way with it."

"Thank you, Percy. That's all the detail I need. Just confirm for me that you've some means of communicating with them in case you wanted them back in a hurry."

"That's not on, sir. In fact it's quite out of the question. We've no means at all."

"Thank you, Percy. Keep up the good work. And goodbye."

Martins replaced the telephone. He switched off his light.

He could not find again for his mind the pleasure of an arching rod. He thought of two men struggling through the night, moving further from safety, and he was damned pleased those two men carried no radio transmitter/receiver, were beyond recall.

Slowly, like a cat beside a fireplace that is minutely disturbed, Major Zvi Dan opened his eyes. He looked from just above his hands across the room.

The girl, Rebecca, sat on the one easy chair in the room, a new book was in her hands.

"Message?"

She shook her head.

He grimaced. "There is nothing more I can do. If I go higher then I antagonize."

"You have to wait. Coffee?"

He moved his hand, declined. They would not be drinking coffee, Noah Crane and Holt who were heading toward the Bekaa.

"If they hit the tent camp, I quit. If they bomb that camp, they'll have my resignation."

She looked at him curiously. "Why does it matter to you?"

"Because . . . because . . ." Major Zvi Dan rubbed hard to clear his eyes of sleep. He coughed at the phlegm in his throat. "Because . . . because of that boy, because of Holt. He shouldn't be there, he is not equipped to be there. It would be a crime if we screwed up their effort."

He let his head fall back to his hands. His eyes closed. Beside him the telephone stayed silent.

"Prime Minister, they cannot be recalled because they have no radio transmitter/receiver. Each of them, without a radio transmitter/receiver, is carrying in excess of eighty pounds' weight. I would hazard that you or I could barely lift eighty pounds' weight, let alone walk across country with it."

The Prime Minister sat in a thick dressing gown before the dead fire in the private sitting room. The Director General had lit his pipe, was careless of the smoke clouds he gusted around the small room.

"They are not carrying a radio because a radio and reserve batteries would have increased each man's weight burden by at least ten pounds. In addition, radio transmissions, however carefully disguised, alert an enemy. . . . Am I permitted to ask you what has undermined your enthusiasm for this mission?"

The Prime Minister fumbled for words, stumbled in tiredness. The conversation with the American ambassador was reported. The Prime Minister slumped in the chair.

"I want them called back."

"And you cannot have what you want."

Four o'clock in the morning. The chimes of Big Ben carried on the squalling wind, bending around the great quiet buildings of Whitehall.

"I was talked into something that I should never have allowed myself to accept."

"We are an independent country, we are not beholden to the opinions of the United States of America."

"I was beguiled into something idiotic, by you."

"You told me that then you would claim my head." The Director General had no fear of the head of government. A wintry smile. "Would it be your head you are nervous for?"

"That's impertinent."

"Prime Minister, it would distress me to think that the sole reason for your authorizing this mission was to enable you to brag to our cousins over the water."

"You have made me a hostage."

"To what?"

"To the fortune, the fate, of these two men. Think of it, think if they are captured, think if they are paraded through Damascus, think what the Syrian regime can make of that, think of the humiliation for us."

The Director General stabbed the air with his pipestem. "You listen to me. This is nothing to do with point scoring over our American allies, with boasting to the Oval Office. . . . Listen to me. Your ambassador was assassinated. That would be enough, enough to justify much more destructive a response than this mission, but Miss Jane Canning was one of mine. Miss Jane Canning too was murdered. I do not tolerate the murder of one of mine. The arm of my vengeance reaches to the other side of the hill, reaches to the throat of a wretched man who was stupid enough to murder Miss Jane Canning. Do you hear me, Prime Minister?"

He towered above the Prime Minister. He glowered into the face of the Prime Minister. He sucked at his pipe. He reached for his matches.

"How soon will I know?"

"Whether it is Abu Hamid's head that is on a salver, whether it is my head or yours?" The Director General chuckled. "Three or four days."

He let himself out. The Prime Minister thought the door closing on his back was like the awakening from a nightmare.

Exactly an hour before dawn they reached the first lying-up position.

The LUP had been chosen by Crane from the aerial photographs. The photographs of this stretch of upper ground high over the Litani and the village of Yohmor had shown no sign of troop tracks, nor of grazing herds. There was a mass of large, jagged wind- and snow-fractured rocks.

They went past the LUP, moved on another two hundred yards and then looped back in a cautious circle. According to Crane's bible, the way to make certain that they were not followed.

Amongst the rocks Crane helped Holt to ease off the Bergen. For an hour they sat back to back, alert, listening and watching.

Crane whispered, "I suppose you think you've earned some sleep."

Holt was too tired to punch him, too exhausted to laugh.

The dawn came fast, a spreading wash of gray over the rough ridges of Jabal bir ed Dahr. A new morning in Lebanon.

14

Abu Hamid stretched, spat onto the dirt floor beside his camp bed, and shook himself awake.

The light knifed through the poorly fastened join in the tent flaps. He glanced across the short interior, saw that Fawzi's bed had not been slept on.

There was never any explanation of Fawzi's coming and going. Abu Hamid spat again, then untied the strings that held the flaps together. He yawned, arcing his head back. He had slept for seven hours and was still exhausted. He had slept but not rested because his mind had turmoiled through the night, scattering thoughts with the drive of an old engine. His mind had clanked with memories spread out over many years of his life.

The sun beat into the tent. His opening the flaps was a signal for the flies to begin their daily persecution. From under his bed he took his personal roll of lavatory paper. He had so little in the world that was his own, he valued his personal lavatory paper so greatly. He set off for the latrine.

The fire was alight in the cooking area. There was the rich smell of a slowly simmering meat stew, and the dry aroma of cooking bread. He had chosen well with their cook, a good boy who earned his absence from the firing range and from the daylong exercises out on the hill slopes and the wadis. He might make every last one of them a fighter, except the cook. The cook would never be a fighter against Israel, but not one of the other recruits would prepare goat stew like this boy. He deserved to be left to forage for wood, to snare rabbits, to dig out a cold store, to go to the village to buy vegetables. He walked by the cooking area. He dipped a finger into the slow-bubbling whirlpool of the pot. He bowed his head, he made a play of his satisfaction, and the cook inclined his head with a wide grin to take the compliment.

There was a line of recruits waiting outside the latrine's screen. From yards away Abu Hamid could hear the howl of the flies.

His memories were of what he had been told of the times long past, the times before he had been born, of his grandfather who had been a corn merchant, sufficiently successful to have owned a villa near to the sea in Jaffa, the town that was now called Yafo by the Zionists and which had been swallowed in the spread of Tel Aviv. From the time he was a small child he had been told of his grandfather's home in what was now Israel. His father had told him that the building was now a restaurant serving Italian food. In his family there had been no photographs of the house, but he had been told that the rooms led off a small courtyard that in the times long past had been shaded with a trellis of vines. He had told his father once, years back, that he would one day set foot in that house, he would stand in that courtyard or he would die on the route to that house. His father had shrugged, muttered the words "If God wills . . ." and kissed his cheek as he had gone away to the ranks of the Popular Front.

His inherited memory told him that his grandfather and his grandmother, and his father and his mother, and his uncles and his aunts, had been put out of their homes in Jaffa in 1948 when the war had gone against the Arab armies. The house of his grandfather was left behind, the grain storage warehouse in the docks had been forsaken and was plundered to feed the flood of Jewish settlers arriving from Europe.

Abu Hamid arrived at the line waiting to use the latrine. He went to the front of the line, he stood at the head and he yelled for the recruit inside to stir himself and get out.

His grandfather and the tribe that he led had settled in a

refugee camp on the hills above Jericho in the winter of 1948. He had learned of the hunger and cold and lack of shelter in the camp on the West Bank of the Jordan River, of the lack of funds from the government of the boy king Hussein, of the lack of materials provided by the fledgling relief organizations. His parents had been married in Jaffa, little more than children, his father had worked for his grandfather in the accounts office of the business, but their own first children had not been born until they had reached the damp cold of the refugee camp. He had been told that he had been born in 1960 in a tent, that his mother had nearly died of pneumonia after his birth.

The recruit came out of the latrine. The smell billowed with him, as if released from behind the screen. He took a deep breath, hurried inside. He squatted over the pit. He held his breath. He clutched the roll of soft yellow paper.

The first memories were of the refugee camp. Of the fierce heat of the summers when the sun spread down from clear skies onto the dust and the rock of the hillside, the chill and rain and winds of winter when the pathways of the camp were river races and the cesspool drains overflowed, and there was no school for the kids and no place for them outside the wire on the edges of the camp. There was a memory that was clear, of the fighting on the hills above the camp when he was seven years old, and the sight of the Jordanian troops in retreat, and the billowing dust clouds of the Israeli tanks and half tracks in pursuit. Sharp memories now of his grandfather leading his tribe a further step away from the house that was now an Italian restaurant. They had joined the refugee swarm—his feet blistered and his belly swollen in hunger—that had crossed the Allenby Bridge over the river Jordan, under the guns of the Israelis, and climbed to new tents in a new camp, on the outskirts of the city of Amman.

There was the gleam of two pinheads of brightness. Two ruby-red lights beaming at him. The lights were in the shadow fold of the screen where it reached the ground around the pit. He knew what he saw but he peered with fascination, compulsion, down at the lights until he saw the yellowed stumps of the bared teeth and the gray needles of the whiskers. A rat. The breath burned out of his body. He had to gulp again for air, foul air within the screen. He watched the rat, he prayed the rat would not go behind him where he would not be able to see whether it came closer to the dropped trousers at his ankles.

He picked at the scar well on his face. He was afraid of the beady eyes of the rat. With his trousers at his ankles he did not have the freedom to kick out at the rat.

He remembered the school in the camp called Wahdat. He could remember the encouragement of the blond-haired teacher from Switzerland, and the care of the lady from France who ran a clinic in Wahdat. He could remember the day that the tanks of Hussein had battered into Wahdat. He was ten years old, his memory was quite clear. He could picture in his mind the tortoise shapes of the tanks grinding into Wahdat, blasting at the schoolhouse which was built of concrete and therefore defended by the Palestinian fighters, hammering at the clinic because that too was defended as a fortress. They were Palestinians, they were Arabs, they were the citizen families of Wahdat. Their enemy was not the Israelis, their enemy was the army of an Arab king.

He moved slowly. He thought that a sudden movement might startle the rat, provoke it.

They were memories that had denied him rest when he had slept in his tent. Ten years old, and a refugee again. His grandfather did not lead the tribe out of the Wahdat camp, his grandfather was buried in a shallow grave on the edge of the camp, one among many. His father led the exodus of the family away from Amman. The ten-year-old boy was of an age to know the glory of the struggle as fought by the Popular Front of Dr. George Habbash. The Popular Front had brought the aircraft of the imperialist enemies to the desert landing strip at Ga'khanna, they had brought to Jordan the airliners of the Americans and the British and the Swiss. A boy of ten years could understand the success of the Popular Front in capturing airliners of enemies, but a boy of ten years did not understand that such a capture could be regarded as a legitimate provocation by the King of Jordan, justification for terminating the state within a state, the

Palestinian autonomy inside the kingdom. His grandfather was dead, his grandmother was blinded, the family tribe was again destitute, again uprooted.

Abu Hamid was pale faced when he emerged from the latrine. He left the rat to eye the next man. He walked away toward the perimeter fence, sucking in the clean air. And it was the same each morning. Each morning he thought he would be sick, throw up in front of the recruits, when he came out of the latrine.

Memories of the family settling in another tent on the edge of the Rachadiye camp outside the Lebanese coastal city of Tyre. The family tribe was a rolling stone, tumbling from a tent at Jericho to a tent at Amman to a tent at Tyre. By the time he was age 15, by the time that Abu Hamid took the oath of the Popular Front, his unseeing grandmother had died. It was the end of 1975. He knew all the events of that year. He knew of the martyrdom of the comrades who had captured the Savoy Hotel in Tel Aviv and given their lives at cost to the enemy. He knew of the heroism of the commando who had killed and wounded nearly a hundred enemy with his bomb in the café by Zion Square in Jerusalem. He knew of the men who had captured the OPEC conference and turned the eyes of the world on the suffering of the Palestinian people.

He gazed out over the quiet hillside beyond the perimeter fence. He watched the stillness. He listened to the silence. So great a stillness, so great a silence, as if the possibility of warfare did not exist.

His memories told him of the dispersal of his family tribe. He did not know where were his uncles and his aunts, his cousins, his nephews and his nieces. He knew that his brother, two years older than himself, had died fighting the Israelis in 1982 at Sidon. He knew that his sister had been wounded at Damour that same bitter summer. He knew that his parents were besieged by the Shi'ite militia in the camp at Rachadiye.

He walked slowly along the perimeter fence. He saw the rat holes and the paper rubbish caught on the coiled wire. Since he had joined the Popular Front, twelve years ago, he had suffered the dream. The dream was to walk the street in Jaffa until he came to the house that was now an Italian restaurant. The dream was to put out of his grandfather's house those who had made a home into a restaurant, put them out on the street and there bayonet them. The dream was to take the hands of his father and mother and to lead them from Rachadiye to Jaffa and to take them to the house that had been his grandfather's and to give them the key and to tell them that what was rightfully theirs was theirs once more.

The dream was in his mind as he walked the fence. When he had the dream he had strength. The girl had given him the strength to dream of the house in Jaffa. The girl had taken the promise from him, the promise to go to Israel, the promise to kill Jews. As if he had never wavered. Margarethe had fashioned the courage for him to dream of walking on the street in Jaffa. He saw her in the badly lit dormitory for the orphans.

He was jolted from his thoughts.

He had stumbled against the rail post that marked the entrance to an air raid bunker.

Abu Hamid looked at the filled sleeping bag at the bottom of the steps, he saw the black hair that was the crown of a head peeping from the bag.

His anger flashed. He thought a recruit was hiding in the bunker to avoid duties. He scratched up a handful of small stones, threw them down on the head. He heard the oath, he watched the convulsive movement, he saw Fawzi's face.

He almost laughed, whatever his own instinctive anger had been was nothing set against the disturbed fury of the Syrian officer.

"I thought you were a malingerer," Abu Hamid said. "I did not think to find our political liaison hiding in an air raid bunker."

"That stuff's in my eye."

"You sleep better there than in a bed?"

"Are you a fool or are you still asleep?"

"Are you telling me that if I don't take my sleeping bag into a bunker then I am a fool?"

Fawzi wriggled his shoulders clear of the bag. He was shouting up from the dank dark of the bottom of the steps. "I was back late last night. I walked into this place, like it was a hotel on the Beirut Corniche. Try getting out of your bed in the night, hero, and try checking your sentries. Try counting how many are asleep. I walked in here, if I had been an enemy you would have been dead."

Abu Hamid sneered, "I thought we were under the protection of the omnipotent forces of the army of the Syrian Arab Republic. Do you think so little of that protection that you sleep in a bunker?"

"When I sleep in this camp, now that I am back with you, I will sleep in a bunker until . . ."

"Until what?"

"Until the air raid."

"What air raid?"

"Then you are a fool, Abu Hamid, you are stupid."

"Give me the breadth of your wisdom."

"Even a fool knows there will be an air raid . . . Six days ago a bomb was exploded at the bus station in Tel Aviv . . . A fool knows that each time there is a major attack inside Israel that they retaliate with their aircraft, or has Abu Hamid forgotten? We have not yet had the air raid, but do not think the Israeli sleeps, he never sleeps. The Israeli will bomb us. The Israeli has to find a target. I do not want to be woken to the sound of you idiots trying to launch Strelas, trying to fire the DShKMs. I want to be able merely to crawl a few meters into the depths of a bunker should they strike our camp. Until they have bombed only an idiot would choose to sleep in a tent."

The fight was gone from Abu Hamid. He asked quietly, "Why our camp? They died, both of them, they were not interrogated."

"I am just careful, because I am careful I will live to be an old man. It is my intention to die in my bed, Abu Hamid."

He saw the surprise cloud fast across the face of the old man on the steps of the Oreanda Hotel. He saw the shock spread into the eyes of the girl who walked in front of him.

He could not know whether he was marked, whether he was identified. He trembled.

"If we hide in holes in the ground we show them our fear."

Fawzi rolled his bag, climbed the steps, belched. "And that to me is a small matter."

"Then you are a coward."

"Then I am a survivor."

Abu Hamid gazed into the clearness of the skies. He saw an eagle wheel, high on a thermal draft. He saw the peace of the valley.

The telephone rang.

Rebecca reached for the receiver.

She wrote on her notepad. She never spoke. She put down the telephone.

"The Chief of the Air Staff will see you in his office, immediately," she said. "And for love's sake, tidy yourself."

"So they both died, brave boys."

"They died in the cause of freedom."

The Arab traveler shrugged. He leaned against the wall of sandbags. The marijuana had been passed, a package hidden in rolled newspaper, for circulation among the NORBAT platoon.

The traveler and Hendrik Olaffson talked quietly. The other troops manning the UNIFIL post were engaged in searching vehicles. They talked without being overheard.

"From our position we were able to see the girl who came with the bomb on her donkey, yesterday. She had not come through our check, she must have skirted us and gone across country, but we could see her getting toward the SLA and Israeli block. I tell you this, friend, they were waiting for her. That is certain. Even before she came within sight they had moved their people back behind the fortifications, as soon as she appeared, when she was hundreds of meters away, they were all behind cover. For certain they were waiting for her, ready for her."

"A sweet child of courage."

Hendrik Olaffson murmured, "They had a marksman in position. We worked it out afterward. They shot her at a range of at least one thousand meters. One bullet, one firing, she went down. Then one more shot to detonate the donkey. It was incredible shooting."

"You are observant, friend."

"More, I have more to tell you."

"Tell me."

"Last night, just after dusk the Israelis fired many flares to the west of our OPs. There was no artillery, just flares. Now that is not usual for them. Yes, often it is flares and then artillery, but this time only the flares."

The traveler gestured with his hands. "I am just a humble traveler of the road while you, friend, are a trained and educated soldier. What does the firing of the flares tell you?"

The young Norwegian leaned forward. He did not say that the explanation offered for the firing of the flares was the opinion of his company commander, a regular officer with the rank of captain and fourteen years in the military. He gave it as his own. "They blinded our equipment. If they believe there is an incursion of the Palestinians or the Hezbollah then they would also have fired shells. They made useless our night viewing. My assumption, they acted to prevent us seeing what they were doing. Why should they do that? My assumption again, they were passing through the NORBAT area. I offer you something else. During the night no transport left the checkpoint for Israel, so there is no indication that men coming from Lebanon were awaited and then taken back to Israel. I believe that the Israelis were inserting a squad *into* Lebanon."

"You believe that?"

"I am certain of that."

"Friend, you are a great help to the cause of freedom."

After he had drank the dregs of a mug of thick, sweetened tea, the traveler waved his farewell.

The marijuana was dispersed among the NORBAT men

at the checkpoint, hungrily broken down for sale onward among those men of the battalion who needed the treated weed to make bearable service with UNIFIL.

Hendrik Olaffson was becoming by the standards of a private soldier in the Norwegian army a wealthy young man. There was money in excess flowing inside NORBAT, there were only occasional four day visits to Tel Aviv and more frequent evening visits to northern Israel for the soldiers to spend their wages. He kept his money, Norwegian bank notes, hidden in a slit in the base of his kitbag.

He had neither a sense of guilt, nor any fear of discovery.

"That's him."

"You are certain?"

"It is the one against the sandbags."

"No doubts."

"I am certain."

For three days the two men from Shin Bet had escorted the tall Arab teenager, Ibrahim, from vantage point to vantage point on the extremes and slightly into the UNIFIL sector controlled by NORBAT. The Shin Bet men were both fluent Arabic speakers, both armed with Uzi submachine guns. All the time one of them was linked by handcuffs to Ibrahim.

They were a kilometer and a half from the NORBAT checkpoint, on rough raised ground, and across a valley from the sandbagged position.

It was of no surprise to the Shin Bet men that the teenager was eager to cooperate in their investigation. It was their experience that the fervor of an attacking commando was quickly dissipated by the despair brought on by capture. The interrogators who had beaten, kicked, punched the initial information out of Ibrahim had been replaced days before. They had done their work, they were not a part of the new scene around the teenager. In his early statements, between the screams, of course, Ibrahim had told the interrogators how he and Mohammed had reached Israel, had told them of the UNIFIL lorry. For the last three days, aided by high-powered Zeiss binoculars, the two Shin Bet men and their prisoner had scoured through the magnifying lenses for the driver of the UNIFIL lorry.

The binoculars showed a well-built and pleasant-faced young soldier, with a shock of fair hair streaming from below a jauntily worn blue beret.

"Absolutely certain?"

"That is the one who drove the lorry to Tel Aviv."

They praised the teenager. They made him believe they were his friends. They made a pretense to him that his future might lie other than in a maximum security wing of the Ramla prison.

They led him back into the security zone. They drove him into Israel with his head masked by a blanket. When they had returned to their base, reported their findings, a second team was infiltrated forward to maintain surveillance from a distance on the Norwegian soldier.

"I gather that last night, Dan, you went barging into Air Operations, demanding that a mission be canceled."

"Correct, sir."

The Chief of Air Staff looked coolly at Major Zvi Dan. "I assume this was not a flippant request."

"It is critical that the mission be canceled."

"They fly in ten minutes . . ."

"Criminal."

". . . unless I am given reason for cancellation. You have one minute, Dan."

Major Zvi Dan looked at the face of his watch. He waited for the second hand to climb to the vertical.

"First, a raid on the camp from which the bus station bombers were launched will tell the Popular Front military command that at least one of their men has been captured and successfully interrogated, which would lead to the dispersal of the camp. Second, such a dispersal would mean the disappearance of Abu Hamid, the Popular Front commander at the camp. Third, last night a two-man team left Israel to walk into the Bekaa with the specific and only task of sniping Abu Hamid who was the murderer, with Syrian connivance, of the British ambassador in the Soviet Union. Fourth, the team is British, and our country needs friends where it can find them. If we foul that mission we hardly have Great Britain in our palm. Fifth, a planned snipe offers a greater guarantee of taking out a known and effective terrorist whereas an air strike may kill some second-grade recruits but offers no certainty of success. Sixth, I would hate two very brave men, one a Jew, to walk into that danger for nothing . . ."

He paused. The second hand of his watch crawled again to the vertical.

He breathed in deeply.

The Chief of the Air Staff reached for his telephone, lifted it, waited for a moment for it to be answered. He glanced at the major, his smile wintry.

"The tasking of callsign Sierra Delta 6, the target should be the second option."

The telephone was replaced.

"Thank you, sir."

"You should not thank me, you should thank your own major general. Last week I attended a briefing given by our head of Intelligence. In his address he referred back to what he had said at the time of the synagogue massacre in Istanbul, where 22 Jewish lives were taken by the Abu Nidal group. At the time he said, and he repeated it for us, 'You cannot lash out blindly. This is not a war of days, weeks, even months; those responsible will be pursued to the ends of the earth. But we must have a clear address before we act, then act we will.' I appreciated what he said . . . You have an address, you have a name. I pray to God that you can deliver to that address."

Major Zvi Dan ducked his head in acknowledgment.

He walked out of the office. He felt a huge exhaustion sweeping over him.

Holt lay in the rock cleft and slept. He was huddled tight, a fetus in the womb, his knees up and as close to his chest as the bulky shapes on his belt would allow. The sun was rising, close to its zenith, but he had discarded none of his clothes, nor his chukka boots. A lightweight blanket was laid over him.

He was too tired to dream. He lay in the black abyss of sleep.

From a short distance the fact that two men rested up in the rock cleft could not have been spotted. Neither could it have been seen from the air as this small gap in the yellowed rock was covered by a drape of olive-green scrim netting. His Bergen pack was beside his shoulder, he was not allowed to sleep against it for fear that his body weight could damage the contents.

Holt woke when Crane shook his shoulder.

There was the moment when he did not know where he was. There were the few seconds of slow understanding. Not in his bed in the doctor's house on Exmoor, not in his bed in the London flat, not in his bed in the Moscow apartment, not in his bed in the Tel Aviv hotel. Crane's hand was relentless on his shoulder, urging him awake.

Because they were trapped under the scrim net, the fumes of the hexamine solid-fuel cubes permeated to his nostrils. The fumes told Holt where he was. The first time on the hike in the Occupied Territories that he had known the hexamine stench under the scrim netting he had nearly gagged. He heard the bubbling of the water.

"Time for a brew-up, youngster."

He saw the two teabags cavorting in the boiling water.

"How long have I been out?"

"I let you have two hours, you looked like you needed two hours."

"I can do the same as you."

"No chance," Crane dismissed him.

They spoke in low whispers. Each time Crane spoke Holt had to lean toward him to understand what he said.

Crane passed him the canteen and began to anoint himself with the mosquito cream. Holt drank fast from the scorching tea, burned the soft tissue on the inside of his mouth, gulped. While he was smearing the cream onto his skin surfaces, Crane was tracking with his binoculars backward and forward searching over the ground below them, around them.

"Clear?"

"So far."

Holt handed back the canteen. "I want to pee, where do I go?"

"You don't just go for a walk."

"Where?"

"You roll on your side, you undo your flies, and you piss. Simple."

"Then I have to sleep on it, and sit on it."

"Then you get to learn to piss when it's dark, before we settle and before we move off. That's when you piss and that's when you crap, like I showed you . . . and wake me in an hour, and don't do anything stupid. Just do what I've told you."

"If I've had two hours' sleep you can have two."

"You think I'll sleep two hours knowing you're watching my back?"

Crane was gone. Blanket over his head, curled into a ball, breathing regular, the low growl of a snore.

God, and it was blessed uncomfortable in the cleft. He must have been dead tired to be able to sleep on those rocks, and a separate ache was in every inch of his side, in his shoulder and in his ribs and in his hip and in his thigh.

Before, before he had known what it was to walk through a night and to get to a lying-up position for the day, he would have thought that night was the enemy and daytime was the ally. Not anymore. Night was the friend, darkness was the accomplice. At night and in darkness he could melt into the shadows, he was on his feet and able to move. Daylight was the bastard, in daylight he was trapped down into the cleft of two rocks and he couldn't stand and he couldn't walk. The cover was waist high, and if he stood or he walked then he would be seen. For a long time he looked across the few inches at Crane. Christ, wouldn't he have liked to have woken him, talked to him? Not half a chance of that. Just time for a few words in the moments between sleeping and sentry duty, and another few words before moving off, and another few words before lying-up for daylight. It was a bastard . . . and he watched the calm heave of Crane's breathing.

First job of the day. Crane's bible. Holt laid out the six magazines for the Armalite which were carried between them. Only five were loaded. Holt's job was to change the thirty rounds of ammunition from one magazine to another, so that each time he carried out the maneuver a different magazine would be left empty. Crane's bible said that magazines left full led to the weakening of the spring. Crane's text said that most firing failures were in fact magazine failures. The first time in the Occupied Territories it had taken Holt close to an hour to reload the 150 rounds; now he was going at twice that pace.

Second job of the day. Clean with dry cloth and graphite grease the outside surfaces of the Armalite and the Model PM. Crane's text said that cleaning oil should never be used because it would leave a smoke signature of burned-off oil in the firing heat. He checked that the condoms were tightly fastened over the barrels of the two weapons.

He was painfully hungry. Might have sold his mother for a bar of chocolate; well, pawned her for sure. Crane's bible said no sweets to suck, because when you sucked sweets you also bit them, and when you bit them you made such a noise in your head that you knocked out your hearing; no boiled sweets. He had had a biscuit and a piece of cream cheese before going to sleep. They would have their main meal at the end of the afternoon, Crane had said. The old goat had said it would be a proper bloody feast. Crane had said that it was a good thing to be hungry, that hunger bred alertness.

He heard them a long way off. He thought he could hear the aircraft from a hell of a long way off because he was so hungry.

Through the squares of the scrim net he thought he could

see the silver shapes leading the run of the vapor trails, flying south to north. It was strangely disconcerting to him to know that Israeli aircraft were overhead, flying free, while young Holt was down on his backside in the cleft in the rock. He watched the trails until they were gone from sight.

He had the binoculars. He looked down on the village of Yohmor. He could see the men moving listlessly between the houses and the coffee shop in the center of the village. He could see children scampering down to the Litani River to swim and dive. Between the rock cleft and the river he could see a lad herding sheep, tough little blighters and surefooted, scrambling toward a small plateau where water must be held, or where there must be a spring, because there was green on the handkerchief of level ground.

Beyond Yohmor, higher up the far valley, was the winding road. It was the dirt cloud that he noticed first, and then the rumble of the engines traveled across the valley to him. Six tank transporters, each loaded, and a couple of lorries and a couple of jeeps. Through the glasses he studied the tanks. With the glasses he could see the unit markings on the turrets. He had never seen tanks before, not the 60-ton main battle tank jobs. He saw the long lean barrels of the tanks. Holt seemed to crush himself down against the rock base of the cleft. Over the battlefield had flown two pairs of multimillion-pound strike aircraft, across the battlefield were being hauled six tank monsters. They were the bloody currency of the battlefield. Holt wasn't. Holt was just ordinary. Holt didn't even know how to fire a damned Armalite . . . Crane slept. Holt hadn't known anyone before who could sleep as easily as Crane. Right, the man kicked, and he stirred. Right, the man snored. But he slept.

Crane coughed, guttural. He turned from his side to his back and then shook himself, coughed again. Holt would speak to him about that. Crane moved onto his other side. Have to speak to the prophet Crane about making so much noise coughing. Holt would enjoy that. He'd enjoy it, because he could pull a suitably aggrieved face and say in all seriousness that Crane's coughing was putting the mission in jeopardy . . .

So still.

Holt not moving. Holt grabbing to halt his breathing.

Not daring to move, not daring to breathe.

Crane's heel had moved the stones.

Holt watched the snake emerge from its disturbed hole.

Crane had been lying on the stones, and hidden under the stones had been the snake.

Holt had a knife in his belt, he had the binoculars in his hand.

Crane's body rolled.

If Crane sagged again on to his back then he would lie on the snake.

Holt had had all the books when he was a kid. Holt knew his snakes. There were snakes on Exmoor, kids always knew about snakes.

Saw-scaled viper, *Echis carinatus*. Vicious, a killer, common all over North Africa, the Middle East, across to the subcontinent.

The snake slithered slowly over the rock at the small of Crane's back.

God, don't let him roll. God, don't let the old goat cough.

The snake was a little less than two feet long. It was sandy brown with pale blotches and mahogany-brown markings.

Holt saw the flicker of the snake's mouth.

He thought Crane slept deeply. He thought that if he called to him to wake that he would start in a sudden movement. He couldn't lean across to him, couldn't hold him as he woke him, because to lean forward would mean to cover the snake with his body.

The damn thing settled. The bloody thing stopped moving. Sunshine filtering through the scrim net. Two warm stones for the snake. Holt thought the snake's head, the snake's mouth, were four or perhaps five inches from the small of Crane's back.

Couldn't go for his knife. To go for his knife was to twist his body, to unhook the clasp that secured the knife handle, to draw the knife out of the canvas sheath. Three movements before the critical movement, the strike against the neck of the snake. Couldn't use his knife.

Crane grunted. Holt saw the muscle tighten under the light fabric of Crane's trousers. The old goat readying himself to roll, the prophet winding himself up to change position.

The bible according to Crane. When you've got something to do, do it. When you've got to act, stop pissing about.

Holt looked at his hand. Quite surprised him. His hand was steady. Shouldn't have been, should have been shaking. His hand was firm.

Do it, stop pissing about.

The snake's head was over a stone. He marked the spot in his mind. The spot was an inch from the snake's head.

One chance for Holt. Like the one chance that Crane would have when he fired.

His hand was a blur.

The binoculars were a haze of movement.

He felt the bridge of the binoculars bite against the inch-thick body of the snake.

All the power he had in him, driving against the thickness of the snake at a point an inch behind the snake's head. The body and the tail of the snake were thrashing against his arm, curling on his wrist, cold and smoothed dry. The mouth of the snake was striking against the plastic covering of the binocular lenses. He saw the spittle fluid on the plastic.

When the movements had lessened, when the body and the tail no longer coiled his arm, he took his knife from his belt and sawed off the head of the snake at the place where it was held against the stone by the bridge of the binoculars.

The head fell away. With his knife blade Holt urged the head down between the stones.

He was trembling. He saw the blade flash in front of his eyes. He could not hold the blade still. His hands were beginning to shake.

His eyes were misted.

Holt heard the growl whisper.

"Can I move now?"

"You can move."

"What was it?"

"Saw-scaled viper."

"I can move?"

"You can get into a dance routine if you want to."

Crane's head emerged from under the blanket. Steadily he looked around him. Holt saw that when Crane focused on the snake's body, sawn to a stump, that he bit at his lip.

Holt moved the stones with the tip of his knife blade, exposed the snake's head, and the bite on Crane's lip was tighter.

"Do you fancy a brew, youngster?"

Holt nodded.

"Youngster, don't let anyone ever tell you that you aren't all right."

15

When they had eaten, when they had wiped clean their canteens and stowed them again in their belt pouches, Crane talked.

His voice was always a whisper, low pitched. There were times that Holt interjected his questions and in the excitement of the communication he lost control of the pitch in his chords and then Crane would silently wag a finger to show his disapproval. But the disapproval was no longer the put-down. It was as if young Holt had proved himself in Crane's eyes.

They sat back to back. With the food eaten the daytime sleeping was finished. Their heads were close, mouth to ear in close proximity. The debris of the food wrapping had been collected by Holt and put into the plastic bag reserved for rubbish. It would be dark in an hour, when it was dark they would wait a further hour to acclimatize their eyes and ears to the night, then they would move off.

Crane faced down into the gorge, and watched the main road leading into the Bekaa. At their next lying-up position they would be overlooking the valley. Holt's attention was on the steep slopes above and to the west, looking into the sun that would soon clip the summits on the Jabal Niha and the Jabal al Barouk that were six thousand feet above sea level.

They were for Holt moments of deep happiness.

Mostly he listened, mostly Crane talked, whispered.

Crane talked of sniper skills, and survival skills, and of map-reading skills and of evasion skills. He took Holt through the route of the coming night march, his finger hovering over but never touching the map. He showed him the next LUP, and he showed him then the track they would follow for the third of the night marches, and where they would make the final LUP on the ground above the tent camp. He showed him by which way they would skirt the high village above the valley of Khirbet Qanafar, how they would be sandwiched between Khirbet Qanafar and the twin village of Kafraiya; he showed him where, above them on the Jabal al Barouk, was positioned the sensitive Syrian listening and radar post. He showed Holt, on the map, from where he would shoot, with the sun behind him, with the sun in the eyes of those in the camp.

Happiness for Holt, because he had won acceptance. He was trusted.

"And you want him dead, Mr. Crane?"

"Just a soldier, being paid to do what I'm told."

"Being paid a hell of a lot."

"A chicken shit price for what I'm doing."

"I'm not being paid," Holt said.

"Your problem, youngster."

"I saw your room back at base camp, I couldn't see what you'd spend your money on."

Crane smiled, expressionless, but there was a sharp glint in his eyes. "Too long to tell you about."

A curtain fell in that moment, then Crane's face moved. Holt saw the flicker of regret. He thought a scalpel had nudged a root nerve.

"Have you ever been paid before, to kill a man?"

"Just taken my army pay."

"Have you killed many men, Mr. Crane?"

"Youngster, I don't notch them up . . . I do what I'm paid to do, I try to be good at what I'm paid for doing."

"Is it a few men, is it a lot of men, that you've killed?"

"Sort of between the two, youngster."

Holt watched him, watched the way he casually cleaned

the dirt out from behind his nails, then abandoned that, began to use a toothpick in his mouth.

"Is it different, killing a man in battlefield conditions to killing a man that you've stalked, marked out?"

"To me, no."

"Do you think about the man you're going to kill at long-range? Do you wonder about him, about whether he's guilty or he's innocent?"

"Not a lot."

"It would worry me sick."

"Let's hope you never have to worry yourself. Look at you, you're privileged, you're educated, you're smart, people like you don't get involved in this sort of dirt . . ."

"This time I have."

". . . most times people like you pay jerks to get these things done. Got me?"

"But don't you feel anything?"

"I kind of cover my feelings, that way they don't get to spit in your face."

"What's your future, Mr. Crane?"

Again the quiet smile. "What's yours, youngster?"

Holt was watching a bird like an eagle soar toward the summits above him. A beautiful, magnificent bird. He thought it must be from the family of eagles. No flap of the wings, just the drifting glide of power, freedom.

He grinned, "I suppose we get out of here?"

"Or I wouldn't have come. I don't buy one-way tickets, I came and I aim to leave."

"I'll go back to England, then I have to make the big decision of where the next move is. I can stay in Foreign and Commonwealth, as if nothing had ever happened, as if Jane Canning hadn't existed. Or I can quit . . . I could walk out on them, I could teach, go into business. Now, I don't know. Where I came from is rough, wild country. It's at peace. Nothing ever happens down there. In our village, if they knew I was in Lebanon, well, half of them wouldn't know where it was."

"You're lucky to have options," Crane said.

"What's your future?"

"I'm getting old for this rubbish."

The bird was brilliant against the fall of the sun. The light in the gorge behind him was graying. The bird was the size of the lofty buzzards that he knew from Exmoor.

"What does an old sniper do in his retirement?"

"Sits at the pavement cafés on Dizengoff, listens to all the talk, and has nothing to say. I can't boast about my work, my work never existed. An old sniper in retirement, youngster, is a lonely bastard."

"Come to England."

Crane snorted.

"Where I live, you'd like that."

"Leave it, Holt."

He persisted. "It would be fantastic for you." He smiled as he planned Crane's retirement. "You could work for the water people, a bailiff on the salmon runs. You could be a gamekeeper. It's a huge park area, they need rangers for that . . ."

"You're all right, youngster, but not all right enough to organize me."

"You'll have the money to set yourself up, you could buy . . ."

"The money's spoken for."

He searched for the bird, couldn't find the damned thing. His eyes raked the crest of the hill. He looked into the sun. He cursed. Eternal damnation in Noah Crane's bible was to look directly into light, self-inflicted blindness.

Crane said, "It's a difficult walk tonight, youngster. It's where we can hit Syrian regular army patrols, or Hezbollah, or just Shi'ite village trash. Tonight it starts to get serious."

"I hear you, Mr. Crane."

There was the start of a blister coming on his left heel; Holt didn't mention it, nor did he speak of the sores coming on his shoulders from the Bergen straps. He started to change the rounds in the magazines for the Armalite.

Later, when it was fully dark, he would move away from the rock cleft and squat down, and then he would learn to wipe his backside with a smooth stone. Bloody well looking forward to that, wasn't he?

The deal was struck in the hallway of the house, not that Heinrich Gunter knew of this transaction.

Heinrich Gunter, banker from Europe with a fine apartment and a salary and pension scheme to match, lay tightly bound on the cellar floor below the hallway. He knew he was in a cellar because almost as soon as he had been brought in from the street he had been bustled down a stairway. He was still blindfolded. His wrists were securely tied behind his back. There was lashed rope biting into the skin of his ankles. He had lost his spectacles when he had been hauled out of the taxi. His tongue could run on the chipped edge of his broken tooth, behind the swelling of his bruised lip.

In the hallway of the house, Gunter was sold on. There was a gentle irony that among the men who regarded the United States of America as the Great Satan the currency of the transaction should be American dollars, cash.

For 25,000 American dollars, the Swiss banker became the property not of the freelancing adventurers who had kidnapped him, but of the Party of God, the Hezbollah.

The money was passed in a satchel, hands were shaken, kisses exchanged. Within a few minutes, the time taken to swill a bottle of flat, warm Pepsi-Cola, the cellar had been opened, and Gunter lifted without ceremony or consideration up the steps, into the street, down into the trunk of a car.

He was in darkness, in terror, half choking on the exhaust fumes.

Because the information provided by the traveler moved raw and unprocessed by any other Intelligence officer direct to the desk of Major Said Hazan, the call that he made gave him pure satisfaction.

In the Syrian Arab Republic of today there are many competing intelligence agencies. That, of course, was the intention of the President, that they should compete, that each should derive pleasure from a coup. It is the belief of the President that competing powers deny any single agency too great an influence. Too considerable an apparatus might threaten the stability of the President's regime. But the President had been a pilot, and in the Syrian Arab Republic of today the intelligence-gathering organization of the Air Force ranks supreme.

Major Said Hazan used his second telephone. This telephone was the one with a scrambler device and gave him a secure line to the military headquarters at Chtaura on the west side of the Bekaa.

"The interception of the girl with the donkey leads us to believe that the enemy has an agent free in the Bekaa, also that this agent has frequent communications with a controller. An especial vigilance is required . . ."

He drew deeply on his cigarette. He smoked only American Marlboros that were brought to him, free of charge, by the toad Fawzi. Major Said Hazan thought of him as no better than a reptile to be squashed under foot because he had never faced combat. He brought Major Said Hazan cigarettes and much more in return for his license to move backward and forward between Beirut, the Bekaa and Damascus. The toad was a kept man, as much a harlot as his own foreign sweet pet.

". . . We also have reason to believe that some 24 hours ago the enemy infiltrated a group from a checkpoint northwest of Marjayoun into the NORBAT area between the villages of Blat and Kaoukaba. It is to be presumed that this group has gone through the NORBAT sector and will be moving toward the Bekaa. Maximum effort is to be given to the interception of this group."

In front of him the desk was clear. His papers, and most particularly the plan of the Defense Ministry on Kaplan in Tel Aviv, were locked away in his safe. His evening was free for his sweet pet. The good fingers of his left hand toyed with the clip fastening of the leather box. He thought the pendant, the sapphire jewel and the diamond gems would be beautiful on the whiteness of her throat. The pendant had cost him nothing. There were many merchants in Damascus who sought the favor of Major Said Hazan.

"I would stress that both these matters have the highest priority. We shall be watching for results."

He saw nothing strange, nothing remotely amusing, in the fact that he handed down instructions for action to a full brigadier of the army. Major Said Hazan was Air Force Intelligence.

If the spy were caught and the incursion group intercepted it would be the triumph of Major Said Hazan. If they were not caught it would be the failure of headquarters in the Bekaa.

Now for his sweet pet, the only woman who did not stare at him, did not flinch.

They came back by truck.

Abu Hamid was the first off the tailboard. As the chief instructor, he had the right to wash first.

He was filthy. The dust caked his face. His uniform denims were smeared black from handling the collapsed beams that had caught fire.

He had seen the results of air raids in Tyre, Sidon, Damour and in West Beirut, but that had been years before. Many years since he had stood in a line of men manhandling the sharp debris of fallen concrete. Many years since he had helped to maneuver the heavy chains of the cranes that alone could lift whole precast floors that had fallen in the blast of the high explosive.

They had been ten miles to the north. They had tunneled into a ruin in the village of Majdel Aanjar. Once the building had been a hotel; until that morning the building had been the sleeping quarters of a unit of the Struggle Front. They had been among many, digging at the rubble, gently pulling out the bodies. There had been squads of the army with heavy lifting equipment, there had been the local people, there had been men of the Democratic Front and the Abu Moussa faction and from Sai'iqa. Those from the Democratic Front and the Abu Moussa faction and Sai'iqa had been trucked in as much to help in the recovery of the casualties as to witness the damage done by the air strike of the enemy.

When they had finished, when the light was failing, Abu Hamid had called his own recruits together. Forcefully lectured them on the barbarity of the Zionist oppressors, told them that their time would come when they would be privileged to strike back.

He was heading for his tent, he was shouting for the cook to bring him warm water, he was intent on dragging off his clothes. He rounded one of the bell tents.

He saw Fawzi sitting in front of the flaps of his own tent.

Abu Hamid said, "From what I saw you could have been sleeping in the bunker and you would not have been saved."

Fawzi said, "Tonight I sleep in our tent, the Zionist gesture has been made."

"It was horrific. Pieces of people . . ."

"We are lucky that our comrades martyred themselves, or it would have been us."

Abu Hamid said, "We are the more determined, we will never give up our struggle. Tell that to them in Damascus."

"Tell them yourself, hero, there is transport coming for you in the morning."

Inside his tent, Abu Hamid stripped off his filthy clothes. He stood naked. The galvanized bucket of warm water was brought into his tent. He thought of the orphan children. He thought of the mutilated bodies. He could not believe that he had ever hesitated through fear. He thought of his grandfather's home. He thought of the blood that would gush from a bayonet wound.

"I don't have any feelings for him," Holt said.

"For who?" Crane helped him to ease the weight of the Bergen high onto his shoulders.

"For Abu Hamid. I don't loathe him, and I don't feel pity for him."

"Better that way."

"If I'm going to help to kill him, then I should feel something."

"Feelings get in the way of efficiency," Crane said.

They moved out.

There was a faint light from the stars to guide them.

It was the boast of the Israeli technicians who worked in the small fortified listening post astride the top of the third-highest peak of the Hermon range that they could eavesdrop the telephone call by the President of Syria from his office in Damascus to his mother, telling her when he would call to take a cup of lemon-scented tea with her.

The listening post of prefabricated cabins and heavy stone fort circles was 7,500 feet above sea level. In the Yom Kippur War it had been captured. The girl technicians had been raped, slaughtered. The boy technicians had been mutilated, tortured, murdered. On the last day of the fighting, after a battle of intense ferocity, the listening post had been recaptured. The listening post was of immense strategic and tactical value to the military machine of Israel. Beneath its antennae was the most sophisticated electronic intelligence-gathering and signals equipment manufactured in the United States of America and in the state's own factories. The listening post was situated some 35 miles from Damascus, and some 40 miles from Chtaura on the western side of the Bekaa Valley.

The Hermon range marked the northeastern extremity of Israelite conquests under the leadership of Moses and Joshua. The eyes of Moses, the ears of Joshua, that was how the present-day technicians regarded their steepling antenna towers concreted into the bedrock of the mountain top.

The problem lay not with the interception of telephone and radio messages from Damascus to military headquarters at Chtaura, more in the analysis and evaluation, carried on far behind the lines inside the state of Israel, of the mass two-way traffic.

In full flow, untreated data swarmed from Damascus and the Bekaa to the radials of the antennae before the computers of the Defense Ministry on Kaplan attempted to make sense from the jargon of coded radio messages, scrambled telephone conversations.

Some communications received by the eyes of Moses and the ears of Joshua were more complicated in their deciphering than others. A telephone call from Damascus to Chtaura via a scrambled link offered small scope for interpretation. But radio messages fanning out from Chtaura to battalion-sized commando units stationed at Rachaiya and Qaraaoun and Aitanit gave easier work to the computers.

The orders coming from Chtaura to Rachaiya and Qaraaoun and Aitanit made plain to the local commanders that their origin was Damascus. The orders were acted upon.

That night, patrols were intensified, roadblocks were strengthened.

It had been the intention of Major Zvi Dan to work late in his office, to delve into the small hillock of paper that had built up on his desk while he had been in Kiryat Shmona.

Behind him was a wasted day. He had failed to beat off the lethargy that had clamped down on him after the tension of his early morning battle to have the air strike diverted. He was slow with his work, but he would work through the night, and then return to Kiryat Shmona in the morning. The girl, Rebecca, had gone home. Sometimes when she was gone he felt as crippled by her absence as he was crippled by the loss of his leg. He read for the third time the evaluation by the Central Intelligence Agency, newly arrived, of a preliminary debrief of a Palestinian captured in northern Italy. Israel for so long had stood alone in the front line of the war against international terrorism that it amused him to notice how the Western nations were now queuing to demonstrate their virility.

He could remember the carping response of those same nations when the IAF had intercepted a Libyan-registered Gulfstream executive jet en route from Tripoli to Damascus. Intelligence had believed Abu Nidal to be aboard. The previous month the jackals of Abu Nidal had killed and wounded 135 civilians at the check-in counters at the airports of Rome and Vienna. Those Western countries had issued their sanctimonious disapproval because the intelligence had been ill founded. He could recall numerous instances of public criticism from the government of the United Kingdom for Israeli retaliatory strikes, yet now they had men slogging into the Bekaa . . . Of course it had been bluff. He would never have resigned. Of course he would just have gone back to his desk and started to work again, had the jets hit the tent camp. He knew no life other than the life of defending his country; had he been a Christian—and he had many friends who were Christians—then he would have said that that was the cross he had to bear.

He wondered if the Americans had the guts to stand in the front line. He thought of the thousands, tens of thousands, of American citizens living abroad who would be placed at risk when a Palestinian went on trial in Washington, went to death row, went to interminable lawyers' conferences, went to the electric chair.

There was a light knock on his door.

He started. He had been far away.

He was handed a folded single sheet of teleprinter paper.

The door closed.

He read the paper.

He felt it like a blow to his stomach, like the blast that had carried away his leg.

He reached for his telephone, he dialed.

"Hello, This is Zvi. You should come to my office straightaway . . ."

He heard the station officer wavering, there were people for dinner, could it wait until tomorrow?

"It is not a matter for the telephone, and you should come here immediately."

Men from the Shin Bet watched the Norwegian leave his company headquarters. He was clearly visible to them through the scope of the night sight. They saw that he had changed from his uniform fatigues into civilian dress. In a white T-shirt and pale yellow slacks, the young man showed up well in the green wash of the lens. They watched him, with three others, climb into a UNIFIL-marked jeep and head south toward the Israeli border.

The car took side lanes to skirt Syrian Army roadblocks on the highway leaving Beirut. From a post that was jammed sturdily through the top gap in the front window flew the flag of Hezbollah. On a white cloth had been painted the word "Allah," but the second "l" had been transformed to the shape of a Kalashnikov rifle. The car used a rutted, deserted road and climbed, twisted, toward the mountains to the east.

The station officer read the teleprinter sheet. At home the local wine had been flowing free. His suit jacket was on the back of the chair. He took off his tie, loosened his collar.

"Shit . . ."

He did not concern himself with the demand for "especial vigilance" for a spy in the Bekaa. He read over and over the order that "maximum effort is to be given to the interception of this group."

". . . So bloody soon."

"For Crane it would be natural to assume that the enemy is alert." Major Zvi Dan hesitated. "But he has Holt."

"And the boy's green. I shall have to tell them in Century . . ."

"Tell them also that there is nothing you can do, nothing we can do."

It would be two hours before the station officer returned, sobered, to his guests.

His message, sent in code from his embassy office, reported the probability, based on intercepted Syrian Army transmissions, that the mission of Noah Crane and Holt was compromised.

He thought that he had made a fool of himself at the fish pond.

The first fish was exciting, the second fish was interesting, the following 34 fish were simply boring. If he had not pulled out the pellet-fattened trout then they would have used a net for the job.

But time had been killed, and it had been made plain to him that he was denied access to the Intelligence Section at the Kiryat Shmona base, and that news—whatever it might be—would reach Tel Aviv first.

He had taken a bath. He had put on a clean shirt and retrieved his trousers, pressed, from under the mattress of his bed. Percy Martins had smoothed his hair with his pair of brushes.

Dinner in the dining room. Trout, of course. A half a bottle of white Avdat to rinse away the tang of the artificially fed rainbow.

Before dinner and after dinner he had tried to ring the station officer. No answer from his direct line at the embassy. No help from the switchboard. Inconceivable to him that the station officer would not have left a contact number at the embassy's switchboard, but the operator denied there was such a number. He walked to the bar. He could read the conspiracy, those bastards at Century in league with that supercilious creep, Tork, a mile off. They had shut him out. Actually it was criminal, the way that a man of his dedication to the Service and his experience was treated. The Service was changing, the recruitment of creatures like Fenner and Anstruther, and their promotion over him, that showed how much the Service had veered off course. Good work he had put in over the long years of his time in the Service. He had had his coups, and damn all recognition. He reckoned that his coups, their full extent, had been kept from the Director General . . . if the Director General only knew the half of it, Percy Martins would have been running the Middle East Desk long since, sitting in Anstruther's chair, kicking the ass off Fenner. He would have bet half of his pension that the Director General had never been told that he had crowned his Amman posting with, as near as dammit, a prediction that the Popular Front were about to launch a hijack fiesta. In his three years in Cyprus he had actually gone to his opposite number at the American shop, warned him of the personal danger to the ambassador, all there in his report—he bet the Director General had never been told, certainly never been reminded when the ambassador had been shot dead. First categoric and specific news of the Israeli nuke program out of Dimona, that had been his climax on a Tel Aviv tour—he hadn't had the credit, the credit had gone to the Yanks. God, and he had made sacrifices for the Service. Sacrifices that started with his marriage, followed with his son. He hadn't complained, not when he was given his postings, not when his wife had said she wasn't going Married Accompanied, not when his son had grown up treating him like an unwanted stranger. A record of total disappointment at home, and he had never once let it show, hadn't let his work suffer.

Holt and Crane into the Bekaa, Percy Martins's last big one, by Jesus, he would not let the last big one go unnoticed on the nineteenth floor of Century.

He had a good record, nothing to be ashamed of, and less recognition for it than the man who sat behind the reception desk at Century. Meanwhile he was stuck in a kibbutz, where there was no fishing, where there was no access to a damn good mission going into Lebanon. Of course, he should have insisted that there was proper preparation of the ground rules before he ever left London. And no damned support from the station officer. The station officer's balls would be a decent enough target when he made it back to Century . . .

He had signed his bill, should have had a full bottle of Avdat but he had never gone over the top with expenses, he had strolled to the bar.

Percy Martins had never been able to understand why so many hotels dictated that drinking should be carried out in semidarkness and to the accompaniment of loudspeaker music. There were Americans in the shadows, from the air-conditioned bus that had arrived in the afternoon. He preferred solitude to them. Blue rinse, check trousers and damn loud voices for both sexes. The Americans had all the tables except one. Two men sat at the table, and bloody miserable they seemed to Martins because in front of each of them was a tall glass of fresh-pressed orange juice. Not young and not old, the two men. Obviously Israelis. One wore an old leather jacket, scarred at the cuffs and elbows, the other wore a bleach-scrubbed denim jacket. They were not talking; they looked straight ahead.

And there were the young Scandinavians. He knew they were Scandinavians, impossible language they were speaking, like English taped and played backward. And drinking, and loud. All that Martins associated with Scandinavians.

There were four of them. He had the choice between several loud American women and their husbands, the teetotal Israelis, and four merry Scandinavians. They were at the bar, they were ordering another round. He assumed them to be UNIFIL. At the bar he nodded to them, made his presence known, then ordered himself a beer.

He had drunk half his beer, not made contact, when the young man closest to him lurched backward on the punchline of a joke, stumbled against Martins's elbow while he was sipping, spilled a mouthful down the laundered shirt.

It was the beginning of the conversation. Handkerchiefs

out, apologies first in Norwegian and then English when Martins had spoken. Introductions.

He learned that the young man who had jogged him was Hendrik. He learned that Hendrik was with UNIFIL's NORBAT. He learned that Hendrik and his friends were allowed one evening a week in Kiryat Shmona.

He was rather pleased. A stained shirt was a cheap price to pay for introductions.

A replacement beer was called for by Hendrik.

"You are English, Mr. Martin?"

"Martins. Yes, I am English . . . Cheers."

"Here for holiday?"

"You could say I am here for a holiday, Hendrik."

"For us it is not a holiday, you understand. No holiday in south Lebanon. What does an Englishman find for a holiday in Kiryat Shmona?"

"Just looking around, just general interest . . . Your glass is empty, you must allow me."

Martins clicked his fingers for the barman. Had he looked behind him, he would have seen that the two glasses of orange juice remained untouched, that the Israelis leaned forward, faces set in concentration. Four beers for the soldiers, a whiskey and water for Martins.

"So how do you like it here, Hendrik, serving with the United Nations?"

"Are you a Jew?"

The young man's face close to his own. "Most certainly not."

"The Jews treat us like filth. They have so great an arrogance. They make many problems for us."

"Ah, yes. Is that so?"

His whiskey was less than half drunk, but the barman had reached for it, prompted by one of the soldiers. The glass was refilled.

"That's most civil of you. You were saying, Hendrik . . ."

"I was saying that the Jews make many problems for us."

"Not only for you, my boy," Martins said quietly, the first trace of a slur in his speech.

"Every day they violate the authority of the United Nations."

"Is that so?"

"Every single day they come into the UNIFIL area."

"Indeed? Do they indeed?"

"They come in and they make trouble, but it is us who have to mend the damage."

"Absolutely."

There was an appealing candor to the young man, Martins thought, compared to his own callow son, miserable little brat, without a polite word for his father.

"That's very decent of you . . ." The whiskey glass was gone again. Percy Martins felt the warm careless glow in his body.

"They've always made trouble, the Jews. Since way back, since before you were born, my boy. Part of their nature. Now, don't get me wrong, I'm not an anti-Semite, never have been, but by God they tax my patience. They always have done, damn difficult people to do business with when you need cooperation."

"Business or holiday?"

Martins leaned forward, avuncular, confiding. "A little more business than holiday."

"What sort of business?"

Martins swayed, "Careful, my boy. Over your young head . . ."

He seldom drank in London. A pint in the pub or a quick Scotch when he slipped out of Century in the evening to get some fish and chips or a takeaway pizza before going back to work late. He kept no alcohol at home. If he left alcohol in the house it would be drunk by his wife, or by the boy when he was home from college. But this was a first-class young man, with a good reading of events, a very level-headed young man. God, why did they have to have that bloody music? And why did those bloody Americans have to address each other as though they were in the next state?

"Like last night."

"Sorry, my boy, what was last night?"

"They sent an infiltration team through our lines . . ."

Martins reeled back. "How did you know about that?"

He was close to losing his footing. He hung on the edge of the bar.

"They sent an infiltration team through last night."

Martins shouted. "I bloody heard you, don't repeat yourself. I asked you a question. How did you bloody know what happened last night?"

He was not aware that his raised voice had quietened the Americans. He did not see the man behind him, the one who wore the leather jacket, slide from his chair, go fast for the door.

"Why do you shout?"

"Because I want an answer, my boy."

"To what, an answer?"

"How you knew about an infiltration team moving off last night."

"Does it concern you?"

"Your answer, I want it."

His vision was blurred. He could not register the curious concentrated interest of the boy Hendrik.

"An Englishman, on holiday—why does an infiltration concern him?"

"It bloody well concerns me, how you knew."

"You are drunk, mister."

In front of him the young man turned away, as if no longer interested. Martins caught at the white T-shirt, spun him round.

"How did you know about the infiltration last night?"

"Take your hands off me."

"How did you know . . . ?"

There was quick movement. As though the Norwegians were suddenly bored with the elderly Briton. Martins's shout still hung in the air as they pushed past him, away from the bar, out through the swing door.

The music played was ragtime.

The man sitting at the table behind abandoned the two orange juices, hurried out through the door to drag his colleague off the telephone.

There was the sound of the UNIFIL transport roaring to life in the car park.

"What did he say, Hendrik, that pissed fart?"

Hendrik Olaffson drove. "Heh, thanks for pulling the asshole off me."

"What was it about?"

He spoke slowly. "He was English. He said he was a tourist, but he did not dress like a tourist and there is no tourism here, that is the first. Then the second, he went stupid when I said that the Israelis had infiltrated through our sector last night. He said, 'How did you know about an infiltration team last night?'—those were his words."

A voice from the darkness in the back of the jeep. "Hendrik, is it possible that the British have pushed an infiltration group through our sector, going north?"

"Into the Bekaa? It would be madness."

"Madness, yes. But worth much weed, Hendrik . . ."

They were laughing, full of good humor.

They were waved through the checkpoint at Metulla.

In the foyer of the guesthouse of the Kibbutz Kfar Giladi, the receptionist passed the man who wore the frayed leather jacket her guest book. Her finger pointed to the name and the signature of Percy Martins, British passport, government servant.

They were moving on an animal track. He thought it could be a goat track. There were wild goat loose on Exmoor and Holt knew their smell. He reckoned it was a regular track. It was the fifth hour of the night march and the old moon was up, in the last quarter which was the best time for night infiltration according to Crane's bible. Maximum safe light for them to move under, and it was a hell of a job for Holt to follow the track. Would have been impossible for him if he had not had the guiding wraith of Crane ahead. Damned if he could figure how Crane could have been able to identify the animal track from the high-up aerial photographs.

The fifth hour, and the march was now going well. Two hours back it had not been good, they had scampered across the tarmac road in their path. A bad bit, the road, because they had had to lie up for a quarter of an hour before moving into the open, and in the waiting Holt had felt the fear pangs. Gone now, the fear, gone because the road was behind them and below them. The hillside was steep, and much of the time Holt walked crab style going sideways, because that was the easiest way with the weight of the Bergen. The Bergen should have been easier. He was a gallon of water down, ten pounds' weight down, didn't seem to make any difference. He was feeling good and the blister hadn't worsened, and he thought he could live with the sores under the backpack straps. He was the son of a professional man, he had been to private school, he was a graduate in Modern History, he had been accepted via the "fast stream" into the Foreign and Commonwealth Office. And no bloody way any of that had fitted him for crab walking along a hillside in south Lebanon, no bloody way it would help him if the blister on his heel burst, if the sores on his shoulders went raw.

He thought he was beginning to move by instinct. He thought he was getting into the rhythm of the march.

He tried to think of his girl. So hard to see his girl in his mind, because his mind was taken up with footfall, and lying-up positions, and water rations, and watching and following Crane up ahead. The old goat on an old goat track . . . Hard to think of Jane. It seemed to him like a betrayal of her memory, of his reason for being there. She was just a flicker in his mind, like the bulb going in a fluorescent light. The good times with Jane, they didn't have anything to do with changing the ammunition twice a day in the magazines, nor with squatting in the lee of a rock after dark using smooth stones to wipe his backside, nor with cleaning his teeth with a pick because paste left a smell signature, nor with carrying a Model FM long-range sniper rifle that gave one chance, one shot. He could feel his Jane. She could be against his skin, like the pain of the pack straps was against his skin, like the heel of his right chukka boot was against his skin, he could feel her, but he could not see her. Each time he tried to see her then he reckoned it was the girl, Rebecca, that he saw.

He didn't know whether Crane had quickened his pace, or whether he himself was slowing. Feeling Jane's body against his skin, seeing Rebecca's body against his skin. That was a bastard, like he was selling his Jane short.

He was struggling to keep pace with Crane, he was struggling to see the soft face, lips, throat, eyes of his girls.

He kicked the stone.

The track was not more than foot wide. There was a sloping black abyss to his right. His left hand was held out to steady himself against the rock slope soaring above him.

He had gone straight through the stone. He had not paused, he had not tested the ground under his leading foot. He had begun to move by instinct.

The loose stone rolled.

The stone slid off the track.

The stone seemed to laugh at him. The stone fell from the track, and bounced below, and disturbed more stones. More stones falling and bouncing and being disturbed.

He stood statue still. The vertigo seemed to pull at him, as if trying to topple the weight of the Bergen pack down into the abyss, after the tumbling stones.

Snap out of it, Holt. Get a grip, Holt. No room in his mind for his girl, any girl. No room for pack strap sores, nor heel blisters. Get yourself bloody well together, Holt. He jerked his foot forward. He rolled the sole of his boot on the ground of the track ahead. Tested it, eased onto it. First stone he had kicked all night. Crane hadn't stopped for him. Crane's shadow shape was smaller, moving away.

All the time the echoing beat of the stones skipping, plummeting, racing, below him.

He was into his stride again when the flare went up.

A thump from below and behind. A white light point soaring . . . Crane's bible. Trip-wire ground-level flare, freeze into tree shape and sink ever so slow. High-level flare, drop face down like there's no tomorrow.

The moment before the flare burst into brilliance, Holt was on his face, on his stomach, on his knees.

The flare when it burst seemed to struggle against gravity. It hung high. A wash of growing light on the hillside. The epicenter was behind him, but he could sense the light bathing his hands and the outline of his body and his back, and niggling into his eyes. He lay quite still. Ahead of him he could see the exposed soles of Crane's boots.

The flare fell, died.

There was a hiss from Crane. Holt saw the fast movement of Crane's arm, urging him forward. He was half upright, and Crane was moving. He was trying to push back the weight of the Bergen holding him down, and the weight of the Model PM, and the weight of his belt kit.

Crane gone. Blackness where there had been light. Should have bloody closed his eyes. Shouldn't have let the light into his eyes.

The second flare was fired.

Holt dropped. Eyes closed now, squeezed tight.

Trying to do what Crane had told him, trying to follow verse and chapter of Crane's bible. Nothing over his ears, his hearing was sharp, uncluttered. He heard the voices below. No bloody idea how far below. Voices, but no words.

When the light no longer hurt his eyes he looked ahead. The flare was about to ground. The path ahead was clear. He could not see Crane.

There were two more flares.

There were bursts of machine gun fire against the hillside. The strike of the tracer red rounds on the hillside seemed to Holt to have no pattern, like it was random firing. He had grown to know the jargon. He reckoned it was *prophylactic* firing. He wondered to hell whether they had *thermal imagery* sights, whether they had *passive night* goggles. There was movement below him. He thought he heard the sounds of men moving in the darkness, scrambling on the slopes. He could hear the voices again. Christ, he was alone. His decision, alone, to move or to stay frozen. His decision, whether to reckon he was invisible to the men below so that he could move, whether the firing had been to flush him out into the view of the TI sights and the PN goggles.

Hellishly alone. He could not crawl, if he crawled he would make the noise of an elephant. If he were to move he had to get to his feet, he had to walk upright, slowly, weighing each step.

He lay on his face. He thought of how greatly he depended on the taciturn goading that he had from Crane. He pulled himself up. He listened to the voices and the movements on the hillside. The thought in his mind was of being alone on the hillside, of being discovered, of being apart at that moment from Noah Crane.

The aloneness drove him forward.

There was no more shooting. There were no more flares. The voices faded, the footfalls died.

He tried to remember how far it would be to the next halt position. He tried to recall the map that Crane had shown him before they had moved off. They were now in the sixth hour. Holt had not taken much notice of the map, didn't have to, because he had Crane to lead him.

Alone, Holt resumed his night march.

It might have been five minutes later, it might have been half an hour, he found Crane sitting astride the animal track.

He could have kissed him.

Crane whispered, "Syrian regular army patrol."

Holt spoke into Crane's ear. "Routine?"

"They're not usually out at night. Usually tucked up, holding their peckers."

"Why would they have been out?"

"You're the educated one, youngster."

"Were they waiting for us?"

"You went to university."

Holt hissed, "Tell me."

"Just not certain that one kicked stone was it, but waiting."

"Are we blown?"

Holt saw, in the fragile moonlight, Crane's smile without

humor. "They're behind us, there's only one sensible way to go."

They moved off.

He was unaware of his shoulder sores and of his heel blister. Holt was aware only of each single, individual footfall.

They bypassed the sleeping village of Aitanit, and the silent village of Bab Maraa, they climbed high to avoid the village of Saghbine where dogs broke the quiet of the night.

Below him to the east was the moon-draped flatness of the floor of the Bekaa Valley. Holt thought of the valley as a noose.

16

In front of him, below him, in brilliant sunshine, lay the valley.

He could see right across to the gray-blue climb of the far wall. In the soft haze it was hard for him to make out clean-cut features in the wall. Behind the rising ground were the *jebels* that marked the line of the border between Lebanon and Syria. With difficulty, he could make out the far distant bulk of the Hermon range.

Holt and Crane had reached the lying-up position in darkness, and Holt had taken the first guard watch, so that he had taken his turn to wrap himself in the lightweight blanket and tried to sleep under the scrim net while the dawn was spreading from the faraway hill slopes. Crane must have let him sleep on beyond his hour. They were above the village of Saghbine. Crane had set his LUP in an outcrop of weathered shapeless rock over which the scrim net had been draped. Holt knew that Crane's bible decreed that they should never make a hiding place in isolated, obvious cover, but there was a scalped barrenness about the terrain around them. The nearest similar outcrop would have been, he estimated, and he found it difficult to make such estimates over this ground, at least a hundred yards from their position. Lying among the rocks, in the filtered shade of the scrim netting, he felt the nakedness of their hiding place. It seemed impossible to him that they should not be seen should an enemy scour the hillside with binoculars. But Crane slept and snored and grunted, like a man for whom danger did not exist. There was room between these rocks, under the scrim netting, for the two of them only if they were pressed against each other.

Their valley wall, on which jutted the occasional rock outcrop, shelved away to the floor. He could see that the rock of the sides gave way to good soil at the bottom. The fields were neatly laid out, delineated by the differing crops. The valley walls were yellowed, browned, the valley floor was a series of green shades, and Holt could make out the flow of the Litani winding, meandering, in the middle of the valley, and he could see also the straight-cut ditches that carried the irrigating life run of water from the river into the fields. He played a game to himself and tried to make out the produce of the handkerchief fields. He could see the posts supporting the vines that were just beginning to show their spring shoots, and the cutback trees of the fruit orchards, and the hoed-between lines of the grain crop, and the more powerful thrusting traces of the marijuana plants, and the white streamers of the plastic tunnels under which the lettuces flourished.

Holt thought that luxury was a warm bath, and a razor, and a tube of toothpaste . . .

What few trees there were, pine or cypress, were in small clumps on the valley floor. He reckoned the village of Saghbine was about a mile away below them. The village was clear enough through the binoculars, but it was hard for him to make out the individual buildings when he relied only on his eyesight. He was interested in the village because in his imagination he exchanged the village houses for the aerial photograph he had seen of the camp, and he tried to imagine how it would be when they came to lie up a thousand yards from the camp. Terrifyingly open . . . If the camp had been where Saghbine was . . . if they had had to maneuver to within a thousand yards of Saghbine and rest up through long daylight hours . . . he couldn't see how it could be done. And Crane, snoring and nestling against him, just slept, slept like tomorrow was another day, another problem.

The village was a sprawled mess of concrete block homes and older stone buildings with a mosque and minaret tower in the center. The high-pitched chanted summons to prayer from the minaret tower reached him.

"Fancy a brew?"

Crane had an eye open. Snoring one moment, thinking of tea the next. Holt thought that Crane might just turn over and give up the ghost if the crop failed in Assam and Sri Lanka.

"Wouldn't mind."

"Done the magazines?"

"Done them."

"What's new?"

"Place is like the grave."

Crane stretched himself full length. Holt heard his joints crack.

"Then you're a danger to me, youngster."

"How come?"

"Because, youngster, when you start thinking the Bekaa is quiet as the grave then that's the time you start to get careless."

"I just said the place was pretty peaceful, which it is."

Crane took the binoculars. Tea was going to have to wait. Holt bridled, and Crane didn't give a damn.

Crane started by looking south.

"Pretty peaceful, eh, that what I heard? Back where *you* kicked the stone last night, where they fired the flares, there's troops out there. Pretty blind if you didn't see them, but they're there . . ."

His head turned, his gaze moved north.

". . . There's a kiddie with some sheep, or didn't you see him? He's a mile back, not much more, he's about four hundred feet below us. He'll be watching for hyena because he's got lambs with him. If he sees anything that adds up to hyena then he'll yell, bet your backside . . ."

Again the twist of the head. Crane peered down at the village.

"Gang of guys going into the mosque for a knees-down, or didn't you see them? They're in fatigues, or didn't you see that? They'll be Hezbollah, or didn't you know that? If the troops find a trail, if that kiddie spots you when you go to scratch your ass, then the God men'll be up here, too damn right."

"I hear you, Mr. Crane."

"So, don't go giving me crap about it being quiet."

"It looked quiet."

"Looked? Heh, watch the kiddie . . ."

Crane passed the binoculars to Holt. He gestured where Holt should look. To himself, Holt cursed. When the boy and the sheep were pointed out he saw them. Could have kicked himself. The boy with the sheep wore flopping dun-colored trousers and he had a gray blanket over his shoulders, and the sheep and the lambs were dirty brown-white with black faces. He hadn't seen them, wouldn't have seen them without the prompting.

"I'm sorry."

"Doesn't help you, youngster. Waking up is what helps."

Holt watched the boy with the sheep. It was as if he were dancing to the music of a flute. Private dancing, because the boy was sure that he was not watched. The boy tripped in the air, and his arms circled above his head, skipping from foot to foot, bowing to something imaginary.

Crane whispered, "If he stops his act, if he starts running, then I get the shits. Do I piss you off, youngster?"

Holt grinned. "Why should you do that?"

"I'll give you a lecture. The troops back there, they hate you. The kiddie with the sheep, he hates you. The guys in the mosque, they hate you. Out here, I'm the only one on your side. Don't get a clever idea that somehow because you're a Brit, because you're not Yank and not Jew, that the troops and the kiddie don't hate you. Our problem was, before we came here in '82, that we never worked out just how much they'd hate us. When they started to mess with us we kicked their asses, we blew up their houses, we carted their guys away to prison camps. They hate us pretty deep. They're dangerous because they've this martyr crap stuck in their skulls, aren't afraid of biting on a .762 round. Fight them and you're in a no-win, you kill them and you've sent them to the Garden of Paradise which they don't object to. They go in hard. Kill 'em, and more come, there are more queuing up to get to that Garden. They made our life a three-year misery for sinners when we were in the Bekaa. They sniped us, they mined us, they never let go of us. Bombing them is the same as recruiting them. And they don't fight by your nice rules. When I'm in the Bekaa I forget everything, every last thing, that I learned about Hearts and Minds when I was in the British Paras. Treat each last one like he's an enemy, like he wants your throat, that's what I learned here. Don't ever hesitate, just kill, because they have no fear. The girl with the donkey, she had no fear . . ."

"Do you have fear, Mr. Crane?"

"Only when I've got you hanging on my tail, telling me it's all peaceful."

The chanting from the minaret had stopped. In the fields work was resuming. Holt could see the women with their hoes, forks, spades, shovels.

Crane grabbed the binoculars from Holt.

He gazed down at the approach road into Saghbine.

He seemed to smile.

There was a billow of dust on the road. Crane passed the binoculars back to Holt.

Holt saw the car with the dust streaming from its wheels.

"Don't ever forget what that car looks like."

"Why?"

"Because I say don't ever forget that car."

The car was an ancient Mercedes. Holt thought it not much less than a miracle that it still moved. The panels were rusty ocher. The front fender looked to have been in an argument. There were white smears of filler in the roof. He could see packing cases in the back, that the seats behind the driver had been stripped out. At his angle he could not see the face of the driver, only the width of his gut.

"I see the car."

"About time you learned how to make a brew. Get on with it."

The phone trilled on Major Zvi Dan's desk. Rebecca picked it up.

She listened, she passed it to him.

She saw the annoyance, because he liked to be told first who was calling him.

"Dan here . . . What name? Percy Martins. Yes, I am aware of the presence of Percy Martins at Kfar Giladi . . . What do you mean, is he sensitive? . . . No, I will merely confirm that he is sensitive, but also that his role in Israel cannot be regarded as the legitimate business of the Shin Bet . . . I don't believe you . . . You have to be joking . . . I had a flight for this evening—but I'll drive . . . listen, listen, everything to do with that man is sensitive . . . three hours."

He replaced the telephone. His head sank into his hands.

Rebecca looked at him. "Is it bad?"

"Unbelievable." As though the wound were personal to Major Zvi Dan.

"Is it bad for the young man?"

"The roof is falling in on him."

Mid-morning, and Percy Martins lay in the bed in his darkened room. He had bawled out the woman who had come to clean and change his bedclothes, sent her packing. He had ignored his wake-up call. There was a drumbeat behind his temples. He knew there was a calamity in the air, couldn't place the source of it. He seemed to think that if he got up and washed and shaved and dressed, then he would get to the bottom of the catastrophe . . . and he didn't want to. He shirked the discovery.

While he remained in his room, while he lay in his pajamas, he was unaware that a man from Shin Bet sat on a chair beside the staircase where he could look down the corridor, watch the door of Percy Martins's room.

A quiet morning in the NORBAT sector.

The troops had checked and searched only four cars and two cartloads of market produce in the previous three hours.

The sun was sprawled in the skies, a lethargy hung over the roadblock, a shimmer burnished up from the roadway. Two of the Norwegians dozed in the oven area under the tin roof that topped their sandbagged position, a third played patience at the lightweight table beside the entrance to the position.

Hendrik Olaffson, smartly turned out in a freshly laundered uniform, carried his NATO self-loading rifle easily on the bend of his elbow. He stared up the road. He watched the bend. He waited to see if the traveler would come to visit.

He realized they had taken a diversion.

The driver of the jeep turned frequently to give the face of Abu Hamid a sharp glance, as though he were the possessor of a private joke. The driver had few teeth. A grin for Abu Hamid to see, and foul breath seeping through the gaps above and below the few there were. Abu Hamid was not familiar enough with Damascus to know where they went. He would not ask why they had taken a diversion from the usual roads they used to get from the Beirut road across the city to Air Force headquarters, would not give the bastard the satisfaction.

They were in narrow streets. Abu Hamid thought the driver a lunatic. He had the belt on, and that had been a sign of fear, and he knew that he would be ignored if he asked the bastard to go more slowly, or to pay heed to the pedestrians and cyclists. He would just give the bastard pleasure if he told him to pay attention to the traffic signs.

In surges that shook Abu Hamid, lurched him forward against the belt, the jeep hammered down narrow streets, scattered women with their shopping bags, grazed a cart drawn by a ragged, thin horse.

They came into a square. The square seemed overhung, squashed in, by the buildings around. It was a dark square because the buildings were tall and cut out the sun. Abu Hamid thought that only at the middle of the day would the sun fall into the cobbled center of the square. There were balconies at many levels of the surrounding buildings, with washing suspended from them, and the stucco façades were peeled raw.

He felt the tug at his sleeve. He realized the driver had slowed. He saw the squinted amusement in the driver's eyes. The driver jabbed with the nicotined tip of his finger, showed Abu Hamid that he should look to the center of the square.

He was not prepared.

He retched, choked, he tried to swallow down the bile that pitched into his mouth.

There were three men suspended from the gallows beam.

It was late morning. There was the bustle of traffic, and the cries of the hawkers, and the shouts of the traders, and there were three men hanging from three ropes from the scaffold. Their heads were hooded, their arms were pinioned behind their backs, their ankles were tied with rope. He knew they were men because under the long white robes in which they were draped he could see the ends of their trousers, and he could see also that they wore men's shoes. There was no movement in the three bodies because no freshness of wind could enter the confines of the square. Fastened to the robes on each man was a large black-painted sign. The driver split his face in a delighted grin.

"You like it?"

"Who are they?"

"Can you not read?"

"Who are they?"

"They are Iraqis."

"What did they do?"

"Who knows what they did? They were accused of 'jeopardizing state security to the Israeli enemy.' They are Iraqis, they let off bombs in Damascus, they killed many people . . ."

The jeep idled past the rough-cut, fresh wood gallows. Abu Hamid stared. He saw that the shoelace of one man was undone, that his shoe was all but falling from his foot. A fast flash thought for Abu Hamid. He saw a man in terror, crouched on the floor of a cell. He heard the tramp of feet in a passageway. He felt the shame of a man who was to be taken out to be hanged in a public square and whose fingers would not allow the small dignity of retying his shoelace.

"... That is what I heard, that they set bombs in the city. The government says they are agents of Israel. Who am I to say they are not? They were hanged at dawn. You like to see it?"

The driver chuckled. Abu Hamid saw the stains at the groin of each man. Abu Hamid nodded dumbly.

"It is good," the driver said. "It is not often that they hang the enemies of the state where we can see them. It should be more often . . ."

The driver slammed his foot down onto the clutch, went up through his gears. He hit the horn.

They went fast out of the square. Within a few minutes they were back into the system of wide boulevards that were the public face of Damascus. They were heading for the Air Ministry headquarters.

"Did Major Said Hazan give orders that I was to be brought this way, that I was to see them?"

Abu Hamid saw the black tooth gaps, and the yellowed stumps, and he heard the cackle of the driver's mirth.

"Ourselves, we are not sure of him," the Brother said.

"He has proven himself."

"We are not certain of his determination."

Major Said Hazan wriggled in his chair. He fancied he could still feel the sharpness of her nails in the skin at the small of his back. The skin on his back and down over his buttocks was of an especial sensitivity, because it was from there that the surgeons had taken the live tissue for grafting onto the uncovered flesh of his face. "He was the top student in Simferopol, and in the military academy he showed us the extent of his determination."

The Brother shrugged. It was many years since the Popular Front had been able to take decisions for themselves.

"If you are certain . . ."

"It is what I have decided."

Major Said Hazan went to the door of his office. In the outer office he saw the young Palestinian sitting with his head drooped. He thought the young man seemed tired. He made his pretense of a welcoming smile, he waved Abu Hamid into his office.

"You had a good journey, Hamid?"

"I had a good journey," Abu Hamid muttered.

"You saw the sights of Damascus?"

"I saw the hanged bodies."

Major Said Hazan stretched out his arms, rolled his shoulders. "We are like an old city, Hamid, with enemies at every gate, but if we are ruthless in our struggle our enemies will never scale our walls nor force our gates. Please, Hamid, be seated."

Major Said Hazan took from a cabinet refrigerator a chilled bottle of fruit juice and poured it for Abu Hamid. He went back to his desk, he took from a drawer the plan of the Defense Ministry on Kaplan, and spread it over the surface of the desk. With the heel of the hand that had no fingers he smoothed the plan flat.

"You are a fortunate young man, Hamid. You have been chosen ahead of others. You have been chosen to strike a great blow for your people . . ."

The Brother said, "We ask you to lead an attack into Israel."

Major Said Hazan watched the young man's jaw tremble. He saw that the soles of his boots fretted on the pile of the carpet.

There was a syrup in the voice of Major Said Hazan, "You hesitate, Hamid, of course you hesitate. You wonder to yourself, are your shoulders sufficiently broad to carry the weight of such responsibility? Your immediate concern is whether you have the competence to carry out a mission of this importance . . . Hamid, because you hesitate there might be others who would take such hesitation as a mark of cowardice, not I. Hamid, it is I who have faith in you. I could not believe that you have less courage than a girl child who would walk against her enemy with a donkey and with explosives."

He saw Abu Hamid's eyes waver, stray to the Brother.

"I would refuse to believe that you had less courage than had Mohammed and Ibrahim, chosen by yourself, for the glory of carrying a bomb onto the Jerusalem bus . . ."

He saw that the young man now held his head in his hands.

". . . Look at me, Hamid, look at my face. I carry the scars of being in the front line of the struggle against Israel. I would not be among those who might say that because you hesitate you do not have the courage to follow where I lead . . ."

He saw Abu Hamid's head rise. He held him, eye to eye.

"I know, Hamid, that the money draft of the Central Bank of Syria has never been cashed. I know, too, that in the presence of the orphans of the Palestine revolution you pledged your loyalty to the struggle . . ."

He saw Abu Hamid's eyes gape open. He saw the confusion spread.

"Because I know everything of you, I have chosen you."

"We ask you to lead an assault against the Defense Ministry of the Zionist state," the Brother said.

"You would go from here to the bed of your girl. You are the modern day inheritor of the mantle of the Assassins, Hamid. You are honored among your equals, you are loved by the weak and the young and the aged who cannot fight, but who stand behind you, who pray for you."

"We have to have your answer, Hamid," the Brother said.

"You would go from the bed of your girl, from the perfume of her body . . . There is a clear choice, Hamid. Either you are worthy of the love of your people, or you are branded a coward. You would not prove me wrong, Hamid, I who have trusted you."

Major Said Hazan saw the trance in the eyes of Abu Hamid. He knew that he had won. He wondered why the shit-scared bastard took so long to clear away his hesitation. It did not concern him that Abu Hamid would be shit scared when he led his squad against the Defense Ministry in Tel Aviv. No way out, no escape then, a rat under a boot, and the rat would fight. The rat would claw and bite for survival. Shit scared was desperate, shit scared was good. He thought the boy would fight well.

"I will," Abu Hamid said.

It was over. Major Said Hazan said that the Brother could take Abu Hamid for an initial planning briefing, that he should stay the night in Damascus, that he should return to the camp in the Bekaa and choose ten men who would accompany him into Israel.

Major Said Hazan turned briskly back to his desk. "I have work," he said curtly.

He had eaten only bread in the last 24 hours, he had drunk only water. He was moved in the black trunk of a car, his eyes hidden in darkness by the hood, every few hours. He spoke no Arabic, so he did not understand the low voices of his captors. Heinrich Gunter, trussed, strapped, blind, had long since ceased to concern himself with the outside world, the world beyond the trunk of a car and the basement of a building. He no longer thought of his wife and his children, nor the actions of his government, nor the position that his bank would have taken. If his hands had been free, if his tie had still been around his throat collar, he would have attempted to end his life. He knew enough to recognize that he was the classic kidnap victim. He was the man who had disregarded the warnings, who had thought that he had arranged the safe passage into the city.

Rolling painfully in the trunk of the car Gunter knew the pit depths of despair. He could think of no corner into which he could crawl in his mind, where he would find comfort. He could think of no power to help him. Into the coarse material of the hood he sobbed his tears. He had seen on the television back at home the photographs of the men held hostage. Cheerful, smiling faces from family snapshots and company archives of journalists and businessmen and priests and academics. He had also seen the photographs of those few who had returned from captivity, haunted men whose cheeks had sunk and whose eyes were buried in dark sockets. The rare few who had been brought out to freedom.

But Gunter no longer cared about the many who were

held, or the few who had been freed. He did not believe in the possibility of freedom, he believed only in the blessing of death.

In the middle of the day, when the car had halted, bumped off a road, he was given food. The hood was lifted an inch or two. Bread was fed to him, given him in small pieces, each piece replaced when he had chewed and swallowed.

He had no idea where he might be, what part of Lebanon he was in, and it did not seem to him to matter.

Holt played the chef. It had been a bit of a joke between them that Holt had been allowed to plan the menu for the main meal of the day.

His gut ached with hunger. More of Crane's bible. The bible said it was good to be hungry. If you were hungry you weren't drowsy. If you were drowsy you were halfway to being ambushed.

Crane sat under the scrim netting with his legs folded and his back straight and the binoculars at his face. Holt was on his hands and knees over the hexamine tablets heating in their frame, and on the frame the canteen of water boiled. Crane's bible said that the hexamine tablets were the only source of fire they could use, anything else would give off a smoke signature and a smell signature. Two tablets the size of the firelighter pieces that his mother used at home to get the sitting room logs alight.

They were going to have a hell of a good meal. Had to be a good meal. God alone knew where they would be in 24 hours' time. Overlooking the camp, that's where they should be all through tomorrow, watching for Abu Hamid on the binoculars. Crane's plan said they should go for a dusk shot. Holt couldn't imagine having much room for stewing up a meal, or much appetite for it, when the time was getting close for action with the Model PM. So a good meal, that afternoon, a long rummage round the Bergen for the ration packs, all that was choice and best in the sachets.

Holt heard the low whistle between Crane's teeth. He looked, he saw Crane had the binoculars away from his face, that his lower lip was bitten white by his upper teeth. Crane saw Holt's attention, relaxed his mouth, returned the binoculars to his eyes. Holt looked away.

It wasn't the first time, nor the second nor the third that Holt could recall the sight of screwed-up pain on Crane's forehead, in Crane's eyes, at Crane's mouth. He looked away. He didn't want to look into Crane's face because he was afraid.

It was the best menu he could manage.

Not a prawn cocktail or marinated mackerel for *hors d'oeuvre*, but a sachet of isotonic powder mixed with water to give a lemon-tasting vitamin boost. Not a bisque or a consommé for the soup course, but a short and stubby stick of pepperoni to chew. Not steak and chips or lamb cutlets for *entrée*, but the boiling water into the plastic sack that held the dehydrated chicken and rice flakes. Not a strawberry flan or a sherry trifle for dessert, but a granola cereal bar that seemed to explode and expand and bulge the mouth full. Not coffee to wash it down, but a brew with a teabag. And a piece of chewing gum to wind up the feast. That added up, Holt reckoned, to a hell of a meal.

He had the powder ready mixed, he had the pepperoni laid out, he had the granolas ready. When he had mixed the chicken and rice they could get stuck in while the water heated for the teabags.

Holt looked up. He saw Crane's head, bowed, his eyes closed tight. Shouldn't have bloody looked . . .

"Dinner is served, Mr. Crane."

He saw the face snap back to life, saw Crane grin, as if there was no problem.

"Brilliantly done, young Holt."

They ate. Holt was learning from watching Crane. The isotonic drained, and the sachet held upside down over the mouth for the drips, and the pepperoni lingeringly held on the tongue for the spice taste, and the fingers wiping the remnants of the chicken and rice from the sides of the canteen, the tea drunk.

"What's your problem, Mr. Crane?"

Crane twisted his head, as if he were caught on the wrong foot. "I've got no problem."

"Give it to me."

"Being in fucking Lebanon, is that a problem . . . ?"

"If you've got a problem then I've a right to know."

Crane snarled, "Being here with you, that's enough of a problem."

"Mr. Crane, we are together and you are in pain. It seems to me you have a pain in your eyes . . ."

"Get the canteens cleaned, get the rubbish stowed."

"If you have a problem with your eyes then I have to help."

Crane was close to him. Holt saw the anger in his face.

"How are you going to help?"

Holt shook his head. "I don't know, but I . . ."

"What do I need eyes for?"

"For everything."

"To shoot, crap kid. I need eyes to shoot. I need eyes that can put me into five inches at a thousand yards."

"What is it with your eyes?"

Crane slumped back. He rubbed the back of his hand across his eyes, like he was trying to gouge something out of them. "Disease of the retina."

"Can you shoot?"

"I shot at the roadblock."

"You had two hits at the roadblock."

"I don't know why, truly. Okay, I had two hits, but she wasn't going anywhere. I suppose it didn't matter. Perhaps that's why I had the hits . . ."

"Is that why you took the job, for the money, for treatment?"

"There's a place in Houston. They have a one-in-five success rate, that's one more than anywhere else. It's my shooting eye, youngster."

"Mr. Crane, if you can't shoot, then what's going to happen?"

Holt looked into Crane's right eye. He saw the blood red veins creeping toward the iris.

"Bet your life, Holt, I'll shoot one last time."

Holt wiped out the canteens. He cleared up the rubbish

and put it in the plastic bag. He rubbed down the Model PM and the Armalite. He changed the ammunition rounds in the magazines. He felt the light had gone out. He smeared insect repellent cream onto his cheeks and his throat and onto the backs of his hands. He felt that he had been tricked. He took off his boots and peeled down his socks so that he could renew the plasters across his blister. They had given him a man who was over the hill. He let a glucose tablet dissolve in his mouth. He had gone into the Bekaa with a marksman whose sight was failing. That was a good laugh.

"It's worse, isn't it, worse than it's been before?"

Crane nodded.

Inside the perimeter of the base camp at Kiryat Shmona, in a position far removed from the sight of the camp's main gate, were the prefabricated offices used by the Shin Bet. In previous times the principal occupation of the Israeli internal security apparatus had been to watch over the Arab population of the West Bank of the Jordan River. Since the invasion of Lebanon in 1982, the main thrust of Shin Bet work had been in the northern frontier and the security zone. Building had not kept pace with the development of the new and onerous duties. It was as if the prefabricated, sectionalized buildings represented a pious hope that the diversion of resources to matters affecting Lebanon was merely temporary. A hope only. The men of the Shin Bet found their resources absorbed by the fierce thirst for violence and revenge among the Shi'ite villagers of the security zone and the countryside to the north. There was no sign that the crowded offices in the base camp would in the near future be emptying.

Major Zvi Dan had left Rebecca outside, left her to sit in the afternoon sunshine on a concrete step. He was in a cubbyhole of a room with three officials of the Shin Bet. He brooded miserably that in their temporary quarters they had failed to install a halfway decent coffee machine.

He was hellishly tired from the drive out of Tel Aviv.

"... So that is the situation, Major, concerning the Norwegian soldier and the situation concerning the Briton, Martins."

"Martins is mine."

"The case of Private Olaffson is a very delicate matter."

"I don't know what you do. While he is in the UNIFIL area we have no jurisdiction over him, and the UNIFIL command will not respond favorably to a request that he be interrogated."

The senior Shin Bet man tidied his papers together. "This Olaffson, he drove the two Popular Front bombers to Tel Aviv?"

"Confirmed."

"He knew their mission?"

"Probably not, but he would have to have assumed that they were heading toward a terrorist target."

"Then Private Olaffson will have to discover at first hand what is a terrorist target."

Major Zvi Dan was passed the report compiled by the two agents who had tailed Olaffson to the guesthouse of the Kibbutz Kfar Giladi, who had sat in the bar, who had listened to the conversation between the Norwegian soldier and a member of the British Secret Intelligence Service.

He read fast. He winced.

"Martins I will deal with."

"Friend, you are a warrior of the cause of freedom."

"I only tell you what I heard."

"Repeat it for me, friend."

"He said, 'How did you know about an infiltration team moving off last night?'—that was what he said." Hendrik Olaffson spelled it out. He spoke slowly. He gave time for the traveler to write the words on a sheet of paper.

The traveler put away his paper. He took the hands of the young man and he kissed him on each cheek.

"It is worth something?"

"It is worth much," the traveler said. "We will show you our gratitude."

When he had gone, the four soldiers at the checkpoint huddled together. They talked about quantity, they talked of the monies that could be charged for the quantity of hashish that would be supplied as a matter of gratitude.

Far away across the valley, invisible among scrub bushes, a photographer bent over the camera on which was mounted a 2,000mm lens and carefully extracted a roll of film.

Martins had made himself a prisoner in his room, he had not drawn the curtains back. Through the center gap he had seen the start of the day and the middle of the day and then the end of the day. It was dark now and he had abandoned his unmade bed and sat crosslegged on the floor, his back against the furthest wall from the door. He knew they would come for him. He wore his suit trousers and his shirt and his socks, and he had not shaved. Though he had eaten nothing during the day he felt no hunger. He was cocooned in pity for himself.

When there came the knock at the door he flinched. Not the chambermaid's inquiring tap, but the thump of a closed fist on the door panel.

He didn't reply.

He watched as the door crashed open, and as the man whose shoulder had been against it lurched into the room. The man wore a leather jacket, scuffed at the wrist and the elbows. He knew the man from somewhere, his jaded memory could not tell him from where. There was another man framed in the doorway. Slowly, Martins pushed himself upright. There were no words necessary. Martins went to his disturbed bed and bent to find his shoes. He wondered if they knew yet at Century. He wondered how many of them would be celebrating his fall from grace.

He walked to the door. As they moved into the corridor the man who wore the leather jacket laid his hand on the sleeve of Martins's shirt and he shook it away.

There was one of the men ahead of him and one behind. He walked free of them. He felt a great tiredness, a great sadness. They went out into the fresh air, onto the fire escape. Martins understood. If he had been the man in the leather jacket he would have done the same.

He was driven to the base camp at Kiryat Shmona. There was a standard procedure used. He had ducked into the backseat of the car and been waved across toward the far door. He knew the door would have a locking device. The man with the leather jacket sat beside him. He thought that this was the way a traitor or a dangerous criminal or a sex offender would be dealt with. He stared straight ahead of him. He shook his head when the man in the leather jacket offered him a cigarette.

Once in the camp he was taken into a small, bare room. He sat at a table. He stared across the surface of the table at Major Zvi Dan. Two men sitting on hard chairs separated from each other by a narrow plastic-topped table. He heard the door close behind him.

Martins thought he had never stared into eyes so filled with contempt.

"Are we to be taped?"

"Of course."

"I don't think that's really appropriate."

"Mr. Martins, in your position you should not presume to tell me what is appropriate."

"I should not be treated as an enemy agent." He felt the confidence slowly ebbing back to him. He sat straighter in his chair.

"That is how we view you."

"That's preposterous."

Major Zvi Dan spoke very quietly, he spoke as though he were nervous that he might lose control of his temper. "You have behaved like an enemy agent. You have endangered lives."

"Rubbish. I was merely foolish. I drank too much."

"You endangered the lives of Holt and Noah Crane and at the very least you put their mission at risk."

"Quite ludicrous. I was drunk, men get drunk. I was indiscreet, it happens. Whatever I said would have been gobbledygook to that Scandinavian, he wouldn't have understood a word of it."

"You passed information of vital importance to the enemy."

"The enemy?" Martins snorted. "Your sense of the theatrical does you credit, Major. I was talking merely to a private soldier of the NORBAT . . ."

"To an agent of the enemy." There was the appearance on Major Zvi Dan's face that he thought he was talking to an idiot, a retarded creature. He spelled out each word. "A bomb exploded in the central bus station in Tel Aviv, you may remember. Holt and Crane will not have forgotten. Two terrorists were responsible. The terrorists traveled into Israel via the Bekaa Valley in Lebanon . . ."

"Don't give me a yesterday's newspaper lecture."

". . . in Lebanon. They were brought through the UNIFIL sector, through the security zone, across the border, hidden in United Nations transport."

"So?"

"Your private soldier drove that transport."

"God . . ." The breath seeped from Percy Martins.

"Your private soldier, to whom you confided the existence of an infiltration team, is an agent of the enemy."

"Christ . . ." Martins slumped. He felt the looseness in his bowels, a feebleness in his legs. "I don't suppose . . . he didn't understand . . ."

"It is our belief that the information you provided him with is already en route to Damascus."

Martins said, "You cannot know that."

With great deliberation, Major Zvi Dan lifted from the floor a brown paper envelope. From the envelope he spread out on the table a series of photographs. His finger settled on one, and he pushed it toward Martins.

Martins saw the back of the head of the UNIFIL private soldier. He saw a man leaning forward to kiss the cheek of Olaffson.

"It is how they show their gratitude," Major Zvi Dan said.

"I couldn't have had any idea," Martins said.

"You were drunk, you knew nothing." The savage reply.

"What can I do?"

"If you are not too proud to pray, you can pray. You came here in your naïveté to play a game of political chess. You came here to further your career. Now all you can do is to pray for the lives of the men you have criminally endangered."

"Will you tell them in London?"

"That they sent an idiot here? Maybe they are all idiots in London, maybe they all seek to play games."

"What do you propose to do with me?"

"You will be confined in the camp area, where you can do no further damage."

"And afterward?"

"Afterward you will live with your shame."

"What have I done?"

"You have confirmed to the Syrians that there is a mission. You have told the Syrians of British interest in that mission. If the Syrians can make an equation between the mission and the killings at Yalta then they will know the target. They will remove the target from view, and also they will ambush your man and my man. If the Syrians make the equation then the mission is lost, our men are lost."

Martins murmured, "God, I am so sorry."

"Pray that the Syrians are as idiotic as you are . . . Myself, I do not think it likely."

There was the scratching of Major Zvi Dan's chair as he stood up. The door opened. The two men led Martins away to confinement, his head sagging.

They had studied the map, they had covered the trail they would use and the positions of the rally points.

"How long tonight?"

"Eight hours."

"And then the camp?"

"In eight hours we should be above the camp, youngster."

"How are the eyes?"

"Just stick to worrying about yourself, whether you'll recognize the target. I don't need your worry."

"You should come back with me, Mr. Crane, afterward, back to England."

"You talk too much, Holt."

"I've done nothing in my life. If I'd done everything you've done in your life there's nothing I'd want more than to go away, bury myself, live on the moor, walk beside the rivers, know the peace of where I live. I haven't earned that peace, Mr. Crane. You have."

"Is it that good there?" Crane asked.

"You could walk free. The animals are free, the people are free, the light and the air are wonderful. No rifles, no fighter-bombers, no bloody minefields, you deserve that peace, Mr. Crane. Will you think about it?"

"Might just."

They had the Bergens high on their backs. Holt let Crane get fifteen yards ahead, then moved out after him. The start of the last night march.

As a matter of routine, Major Said Hazan received in the early evening a report covering the previous 24-hour period as prepared by army headquarters at Chtaura. He read every detail of the report, as he always did. Far down in the list he read that a patrol in position west and south of the Bekaa village of Aitanit had fired flares in response to unidentified movement further west of them. The report stated that a follow-up search in daylight centerd on an animal track, but had failed to provide evidence that would justify further sweep searches of the area.

The major went to his wall map. He put a red-headed pin into the map over the area of the UNIFIL sector through which it had been reported that an infiltration had been made. He drove in another red-headed pin at the point of the unconfirmed contact with the patrol. He stood back. He extended a line from the infiltration point to the supposed contact. They were going north, the shortest possible route into the foothills on the west side of the Bekaa.

In the valley, marked on his map, were the camps of 18 different Syrian Army concentrations, and in addition the camps of the Popular Front, the Democratic Front, the Abu Moussa faction, the Sai'iqa group, the Struggle Front. There were also the villages used by the Hezbollah, and the houses occupied by the men of Islamic Jihad. There were the communities that played host to the Revolutionary Guards who had sat in the Bekaa unmoving after their dispatch from Iran. In all, indicated on his map, there were 43 locations that could prove of interest to an infiltration team of the enemy.

At the moment he was helpless. But he was a man of patience.

In the camp the cook's fire guttered. The cook thought that in the morning he would use the last of his wood to prepare the breakfast, that he would spend the morning scavenging for more.

17

It was a crisp, sharp night.

The heat of the day had dissipated into the rocky slopes. In the night there was a fresh wind that caught at the sweat that ran in rivers on the throat and chest of young Holt. The pace of the night march was no greater and no less than it had been on the two previous nights, but he sweated, as he thought, like a pig. The pace of the night march remained, give or take a few yards or a few minutes, at one mile in one hour. The going should have been easier because each man was lighter from the consumption of water, close to half of the water had been used, but still he sweated in the cool of the night march. He felt as if, along with the perspiration, the strength oozed from his body. When they reached there, when they were on the high ground overlooking the tent camp, Holt thought he would be reduced to a wrung-out rag. There were no more kicked stones, there were no cracked twig branches, there was no scuffling through sun-crisped leaves. Each step was concentration, each short checked stride was care.

Crane was a shape ahead of him. It was a blurred shape that only came to life at the rally points when Crane stopped and squatted and Holt reached him to slump beside him. They did not speak at the first rally points of the night. They sat and allowed their leg muscles to soften and Holt let his mind wander from the concentration and care and exhaustion of the march. There were no words, no whispers, because Holt did not have to be told that they were now deep behind the lines. It was all in his head, it had all been told him and was remembered. They were moving north on the hill slopes between the valley floor and the peaks of the Jabal al Barouk. On the Jabal al Barouk was a state-of-the-art Soviet-built complex of radar dishes and antennae manned by the Syrian Air Force. Sensitive country. The dishes and antennae were protected from surprise attack. Scattered round the air defense and signals listening equipment would be, according to Crane's bible text, the GS-13 divisional-level surveillance radars operating from 50-kilowatt power packs and with a 12-kilometer competence to detect personnel and a 25-kilometer range for seeing the movement of vehicles. Moving on the slopes above the valley and below the installations on the summit of Jabal al Barouk, Crane led Holt in darted spurts as a sailor would tack before the wind. They changed the angle of their progress every 50, 60 yards, as if by that maneuver Crane believed he could throw the attention of a drowsing ground surveillance radar-screen operator. Of course, it would have been faster to have moved lower down onto the gentler slopes of the valley sides, but Crane had explained at the last lying-up position that further behind the Syrian positions the risk increased of blundering into mine fields, of drifting into the wadis where the antipersonnel mines would be set around the heavy pressure antiarmor concentrations. That night, on the marches between the rally points, Holt learned much. He learned of the methods of evasion from the dishes of ground surveillance radar, and of the way in which the cover of the terrain could be used to prevent discovery of their progress at the hands of thermal imagery equipment. He learned of the hazard of a low-flying aircraft, droning above them without even navigation lights, when Crane had plotted the aircraft's path and scuttled to get clear of its flight line in case it carried infrared targeting screens.

They moved on. Holt could not assess the threat. He could only remember the warnings that had been given him in a gravel whisper before they had left the lying-up position. They lurched from rally point to rally point. The exhaustion spread through Holt's legs, through his back, through his shoulders. His recovery in the short breaks at the rally points became steadily less restorative.

He understood why the exhaustion seeped through him . . . He was helpless . . . He was led on and on by a man with disease clawing at the retina of his right eye. He was with a marksman who had taken a contract in order to finance a one-in-five-chance operation to reverse the decline in the sight of the shooting eye. He himself was blind, his king's good eye was done for . . . and he had to live with it. In the first part of that night's march, up to the first rally point, he had felt a bursting anger toward Crane. The anger was gone, knocked away by the tiredness in his legs, the soreness of his feet. He felt a sort of sympathy. But it was bloody pointless, feeling sympathy for Crane. Sympathy was no salve for the disease in the retina.

They went west and high to bypass the village of Ain Zebde. They would climb to avoid the village town of Khirbet Qanafar. Beyond the glow of Khirbet Qanafar, two and a half miles ahead, they would come down the hill slope until they overlooked the tent camp.

It was late into the evening.

The city was a mysterious place of flickering headlights and of candle-thrown shadows.

Another power cut in Damascus. The cutting of the electricity supplies was more frequent that month, a cut would last five hours and there was nothing remarkable in that. The traffic moved through a wraithlike haze of exhaust fumes. The cafés were lit by the wavering flames of the candles. Abu Hamid saw that few of the cafés had lanterns lit. There was a shortage of oil for the power station, also a shortage of paraffin for the public.

His mind was bent by the weight of detail forced upon him by the Brother. Through the afternoon, through the evening, he had listened and attempted to absorb the attack plan against the Defense Ministry on Kaplan as described to him by the Brother. He had been allowed to write nothing down, everything he had been told had to be committed to memory. He knew the numbers of the men involved. He knew the firepower they would carry. He knew the harbor from Cyprus out of which he would sail, he knew the times of the tide changes that would dictate the time of sailing. He knew the speed at which the coastal tramp ship would travel. He knew of the diversionary tactic that had been planned to draw away the patrolling missile boats. He knew of the two closed vans that sympathizers would drive to the shoreline at Palmahim, south of Tel Aviv. He knew of the driving time from the shoreline to the buildings on Kaplan. He knew of the defenses of the ministry complex.

Through the cacophony of the horns, through the darkened traffic lights, through the swirling crowds of the *suq*, the jeep pressed its way toward the alley.

The jeep shuddered to a halt. The headlights lit a drover who flailed at the back of a horse that refused to pull further a cart laden with vegetables. From the way the horse refused to ground its left front hoof, Abu Hamid thought the horse to be lame. The jeep driver was shouting at the drover. The drover was shouting at his horse. He slipped open his door. He slammed the door shut after him. He was gone into the night, into the flow of the crowds. He was no longer the Palestinian who had been chosen to sail onto the beach at Palmahim which was south of the city of Tel Aviv. He was no longer the man on whose forehead the spot of the martyr had been painted. He could have turned, he could have cut into the narrow lanes. He could have fled. He was a moth, the alley was the lamp, the woman was the light.

When he knocked at the door, she opened it to him. She wore the loose dress of an Arab woman.

He saw the soft whiteness of the skin on her throat. He saw the curved fullness of her breasts and of her hips. He saw the hands that reached for his face in welcome.

She was Margarethe Anneliese Schultz.

At Wiesbaden in the Federal Republic of Germany, in the computerized records section of the *Bundesamt für Verfas-*

sungsschutz, the printout directly relating to her history, biography and activities would, on a continuous roll of paper, stretch to 235 inches. That part of the Federal Internal Security Office devoted in its work to the destruction of urban guerrilla movements inside the state was indeed familiar with Margarethe Anneliese Schultz.

She was now 33 years of age. She had been born the only daughter of a pastor serving a small community a few kilometers to the north of Munich. As an only daughter she had been a spoiled and privileged child. Early in her life she had learned the art of winning her way either by tantrums or by sweet smiles. Within the budget of her parents' household her every whim had been granted.

Excellent grades in her final school examinations led to her admission as a student of social sciences to the Free University of West Berlin. Her father had a married cousin living in the city. Her father had believed that it would be a good thing for the young girl to continue her education away from home, while at the same time remaining under the eye of the family. It had been the summer of 1974 when Margarethe Anneliese Schultz had left home with her two suitcases to take a train to Frankfurt, and another train to West Berlin. That late summer the Federal Republic recovered from the excesses brought on by victory in the World Cup soccer tournament, and awaited the death of a judge shot dead at his front door, and the death of Holger Meins from self-inflicted starvation, and the sentencing of Ulrike Meinhof.

From the day they waved their goodbye, as the long-distance express train pulled away from the platform at Munich's *Hauptbahnhof*, Doktor and Frau Schultz had not set eyes on their beloved daughter. One letter only had been received by them, written a week after her arrival in West Berlin. Margarethe Anneliese Schultz had within a month of her arrival in West Berlin dropped out of her course, dropped into underground cover. She had been recruited into a cell of a Red Army faction that sought to revive the drive of armed insurrection on behalf of an oppressed proletariat as first initiated by Ulrike Meinhof and Andreas Baader and

Jan-Carl Raspe and Gudrun Ensslin and Holger Meins. In a world of heady excitement she became a part of the small core of revolutionaries living in sympathizers' apartments, stretching her legs to the newest young man who carried a Firebird 9mm Parabellum pistol, eating in restaurants on the proceeds of bank robberies, moving in stolen BMWs and Mercedes sedans.

Her parents had reported her missing to the Munich city police.

Eight months after she had left them, men of the "PoPo," the political police, had called on the pastor, had interviewed him in the living room of his home, and after 35 minutes had left him in prayer on his knees and with the comfort of his wife.

The pastor's daughter was a bank robber. The pastor's sweet child had driven the getaway car from a robbery in which a policeman had been fatally shot. The pastor's angel was on the list of those hunted by the political police, the criminal police and the security police.

Her induction had been through a working circle, photography. It had been her initial role to photograph targets for assassination, targets for bombing. Her hand was steady. Her photographs were crystal sharp in focus. The years passed. The Red Army Faction slaughtered the high and the mighty of the state. The capitalist exploiters were cut down. Chief Federal Prosecutor Siegfried Buback, executed. Chief Executive of the Dresdner Bank Jurgen Ponto, executed. Military attaché to the FRG embassy in Stockholm Baron von Mirbach, executed. President of the Federation of Industries Hanns-Martin Schleyer, executed. The government stood firm. The killings did not win the freedom of the founding fathers and mothers of the movement. There was a week when despair became a plague. A Lufthansa holiday jet hijacked to Mogadishu in the African state of Somalia was retaken by the intervention of the *Grenzschutz Gruppe Neun*. The principal imprisoned activists hanged or shot themselves in their cells. The movement sagged under the failure of action and the loss of the star participants. Margarethe Anneliese Schultz, her face on the wanted posters, her name on the charge sheet of a federal court, her future likely to be 20 years behind bars, drove into Switzerland, took a train to Italy, bought an airline ticket to Damascus.

She threw off the cause of the bovine proletariat of her homeland, she embraced the cause of the Palestinian people. She was careful with her favors, she dispensed them only where they could be of advantage to her.

She had sought out a protector, a man of such influence that she would not be repatriated to the maximum security women's prisons of West Germany.

He was a repulsive bastard, the major in Syrian Air Force Intelligence, but he had influence. She warmed his bed. She worked hard to please him. In obedience to the wishes of Major Said Hazan, she had, many months before, given herself to a young Palestinian fighter of the Popular Front.

The pendant hung at her neck.

The pendant was a sapphire held by a fastening crescent of diamonds.

The pendant hung at her neck from a gold chain of close, fine links.

He heard the words. The drooled words slipping from the rebuilt mouth of Major Said Hazan . . . "in the presence of the orphans of the Palestine revolution you pledged your loyalty to the struggle" . . . He heard the words that had been used to taunt him.

The chain that supported the pendant lay on the smooth skin of her throat.

She was kissing his mouth, and the lobes of his ears. She told him of her love. The flatness of her stomach undulated against his groin. The warmth of her breasts drifted through the cotton of his shirt.

Abu Hamid, standing just inside the room, leaning back against the closed door, hearing the muffled raucous sounds of the *suq*, knew that he would kill the girl he had loved.

He was calm. He felt no fear. It was not as it had been when the woman who was a spy for the Israelis had gazed back in contempt into his face. It was as it had been when he had gone to seek out the man who had stolen his transistor radio. It was as it had been when he had eased himself up from the bench outside the Oreanda Hotel, when he had walked, filtering between the traffic, toward the hotel steps. As it had been when he had raised the assault rifle to confront the old man and the young woman pushing through the glass swing doors.

Major Said Hazan had played with him as a child. The toy that had won him had been the breasts and the cleft of Margarethe Schultz. He held her in his arms. He smelled the cleanness of her hair and the dry pleasure of her body.

"I love you, brave boy."

"As you love him?" Abu Hamid murmured from the pit of his throat.

"I love you for your courage, brave boy."

She arched her head upward, she stretched to kiss his forehead. Her neck was pulled taut. The pendant seemed to him to dance on her skin, and the candlelight caught the kingfisher brilliance of the sapphire and flashed upon the wealth of the diamonds.

"As you love him?"

He held the back of her head in his left hand, the fingers tight into the looseness of her hair. He held the back of her neck in his right hand, the fingers twined into the slender strength of the chain.

"I love only you, brave boy."

She had not looked into his face. She had not seen his eyes. She had not seen the smile curve at his lips. He thought of her cheeks against the reconstructed atrocity that was the face of Major Said Hazan. He thought of the fingerless hand groping to the smoothness of the skin of her thighs.

The fingers of his left hand that were tight in her hair jerked Margarethe Schultz's head back. He saw the shock sweep into her eyes. With his right hand he tore the pendant from her throat, snapping the chain clasp on her neck. He bent her head down so that it was lower than the level of his waist, so that she could see only his feet. In front of her, between her bare feet, between his boots, he dropped the pendant. He stamped on the sapphire, on the diamonds of the crescent. He thought of how she had shamed him from taking money, how she had burned the letter from the Central Bank of Syria. She had taken a pendant of sapphire and diamonds, she had taken the body of Major Said Hazan. He ground with his heel into the carpet. He heard the wincing gasp of her breath as he moved his foot aside, forced her head lower so that she could see the shattered pendant.

She had taken the love of Abu Hamid. She had taken his pledge that he would go into Israel, take the war into Israel, take his death into Israel.

When he pulled her head up, when she could look into his face, she spat.

She snarled, "You are scum . . . You are not even a good fuck, not even as good as him . . ."

He saw her eyes bulging toward him. He saw the blue sheen at her lips. He saw her fingers scrabble to hold his wrists. He saw her tongue jumping from her mouth.

When he let go of her throat, when she slid to the carpet, he crouched over her.

He could hear the choking of his tears. He lay across her. He could feel the wetness of her skin where his tears fell.

Percy Martins was on his bed.

It was hours since he had walked around the bare room. He had only had to walk round once to understand the nature of his confinement. Behind the curtains over the windows he had found the metal bars. He had noted that there was no light through the keyhole of the door. He had heard the coughing of a man in the corridor.

He was on his bed.

He was close to sleep when he was roused into alertness by the muffle of voices behind the door. He heard the rasp of the turning key. He sat upright on his bed.

It was the girl, Zvi Dan's assistant, Rebecca. She carried a mug of tea. He could see that it was freshly made, that it steamed in her hand. She passed him the mug.

"That's uncommonly civil of you."

"It is nothing."

"Why?"

"I thought you had been kicked, I thought they were queuing to kick you again. There were plenty of them in line to kick you."

"People like to kick a fool, when a fool is down." Martins drank the tea, scalded the roof of his mouth.

"Kicking you does not help Holt."

He gazed into her face.

"I suppose it's stupid to ask, but there hasn't been any news?"

"There could only be news from the Syrian radio. We are monitoring their transmissions, there has been nothing on their radio."

Martins slumped back onto his bed. "The waiting, it's so bloody awful, waiting for news of catastrophe, and for the inevitability of disgrace."

"What are your feelings for Holt?"

"He's one of the finest young men I've ever met, and I never got round to telling him."

She turned away, went out through the door. He heard the key turn. He lay in the darkness and sipped at the hot sweetness of the tea.

With three men to escort him Heinrich Gunter stumbled, tripped through the darkness over the rough ground on the slope of the hillside.

He was handcuffed to one man.

He had been given back his shoes, but they rubbed and calloused his feet and it was more years than he could remember since he had last worn lace-up shoes without socks. He had been given back his shoes, but they had retained his shirt and his suit jacket and his trousers. He wore his vest and his underpants that now smelled and over his shoulder was draped a coarse cloth blanket.

Where they had left the car, his photograph had been taken. All very quick, and he had hardly been aware of the process. The hood had been snatched up from over his face, the light had blasted him. Time for him to identify the gun barrel that had been the sharp pain under his chin, and the face mask of the one who held a camera level with his eyes. Two workings of the camera, and the flash, and the hood retrieving the darkness and falling. The taking of his photograph had disturbed him. As if the photograph brought him back toward a world that he understood, a world of ransom demands and bribery, and of newspaper headlines and radio bulletins, and of the government in Bonn, and of the helplessness of the world that he knew. The taking of the photograph had forced his mind to his family, his wife and his children, and his home. Forced him to think of his wife sitting numb in their home and of the dazed confusion of his children.

It was easier for him when he was in their world, not his own, when he lived the existence of his captors. Their world was the gun barrel and the handcuffs, taking a hooded hostage across the rough sloping ground below the Jabal al Barouk.

Crane froze.

Holt, behind him, had taken three more steps before he registered Crane's stillness.

Crane held the palm of his hand outstretched, fingers splayed, behind his back, so that Holt could see the warning to stop.

It was the fifth hour of the night march. Holt was dead on his feet. The moon, falling into the last quarter, threw a silver light on them.

Crane, very slowly, sunk to his knees and haunches. A gentle movement, taking an age to go down.

Holt followed him. The Bergen straps cut into his shoulders. Pure, blessed relief, to sink low and not to have to jar the Bergen on his back.

Crane turned his head, his hand flicked the gesture for Holt to come forward.

Holt sensed the anxiety growing in his body. When Crane had first stopped he had been walking as an automaton, no care other than not to disturb a loose stone or tread on a dried branch. Gone from him, the sole concentration on his footfall. He came forward, he strained his eyes into the gray-black stillness ahead, he saw nothing. He found that his hands were locked tight on the stock of the Model PM and the bloody thing was not even loaded and the flash eliminator at the end of the barrel was still covered with the dirt-stained condom. Hell of a great deal of use young Holt would be in defending the position . . . He was close to Crane, crouched as he moved, close enough for Crane to reach back and with strength force him lower.

Crane had him down, pushed Holt so that he lay full length on the narrow track.

Holt heard the stone roll ahead of them. A terrible quiet was in him, the breath stifled in his throat. A stone was kicked ahead of him. They shared the path. So bloody near to the tent camp, and they shared the track. Crane was reaching for his belt, hand moving at glacier speed.

They shared the bloody path. All the tracks in south Lebanon, all the trails running on the hill slopes of the west side of the Bekaa, and they, by God, shared it. Holt breathed out, tried to control himself, tried not to pant.

He heard the voices, clear, as if they were beside him.

Words that he did not understand, a foreign language, but a message of anger.

He could see nothing, but the voices carried in the night quiet.

A guttural accent, speaking English, seeking communication.

"I cannot see, I cannot know what I hit."

"More careful."

"But I cannot see . . ."

Holt heard the impact of a kick. He heard the gasp, muffled, then the sob.

"I cannot see to walk."

A noise ahead as if a weight were dragged, and new voices, Arabic, urging greater pace. Holt did not understand the words, knew the meaning.

Crane had the pocket night sight to his eye. He rarely used it. Crane's bible said that reliance on a night sight was dangerous, hard to switch back and forth between a night sight and natural night vision. They were making as much noise ahead as Holt had conjured up on the first of the night march tests in the Occupied Territories—so bloody long ago, back in the time before history books.

Holt thought the man who complained, who could not see, might be German or Austrian or Swiss German. There was a stampede of stones away from the path, and the sound of another kicking, and the sound of another whimper. He thought they were moving faster, he thought the noises moved away.

Holt waited on Crane.

He heard the call of a hyena above. He heard the barking of a dog behind and below from among the village lights of Ain Zebde. He waited on Crane.

Methodically, as was his way, Crane replaced the pocket night sight in the pouch on his belt.

"It's a European," Crane whispered.

"What's a European doing . . . ?"

"God, didn't you learn adding at school? There are three hoods with a European prisoner on our track. A European, with a bag over his head, who cannot see where he's going, with Arabs, that adds to the movement of a hostage."

"A hostage . . ." Holt repeated the word, seemed to be in awe of the word.

"Moving a hostage on my bloody route." A savageness in Crane's whisper.

"What do we do?"

"Keep going, have to."

"Why, have to?"

"Because, youngster, we have a schedule. We have an appointment. We have to move behind them, and move at their pace. I don't have the time to lie up. And I'm better keeping them in sight, I'm better knowing where they are."

"A hostage?"

"That's what I said."

"Definitely a hostage?"

"He's tied to one of them. He's got a European accent. He's short of trousers, just a blanket over him. We're in an area of Syrian control, so they move him at night. They'll be from Islamic Jihad or Hezbollah, they don't trust the shit Syrians any more than I do . . . Don't kick any bloody stone, youngster."

Carefully, with so much care, Holt pushed himself upright. He stood. All the time he could hear the fading sounds of movement ahead. He let Crane move off, get the fifteen paces in front. He struggled to ease the pressure of the straps on his shoulder.

Best foot forward, on a shared path.

He could not help himself. He should have concentrated solely on each footfall. There should have been nothing else in his mind, no chaff, no clutter, nothing other than the weight of the ball of his foot testing for the loose stone, for the dried branch, for the crisped leaf.

The chaff and the clutter in his mind were the thoughts of love and vengeance.

He had told his girl, his Jane Canning who was the personal assistant to the military attaché, that he loved her. A long time ago, he had told his girl that he loved her. His girl was ashes, he did not even know where the parents of his girl had scattered her ashes. Too distant from them to know whether they had taken her ashes to a seashore or taken them to a heathland of heather flowers or taken them to the serenity of a woodland. His girl was ashes, gone, dust, earth. So many things that he could remember of her. Meeting in the canteen at the School of East European and Slavonic Studies and thinking she was stunning. Waiting for her when she was late and the tryst was the pavement outside the Odeon cinema in Leicester Square and hoping to God that she hadn't stood him up. Coming to her own bachelor girl flat, with a bunch of freesias and a bottle of Beaujolais and wondering whether he would get back to his own place before the end of the weekend. Holding her and kissing her when she had told him that she had landed Moscow for a posting, and wasn't it marvelous because he was headed there in a few weeks' time, and cursing that for those few weeks he would be without her and she would be without him. Scowling at her because she had put him down forever and ever, amen, in the corridor of the Oreanda Hotel in Yalta . . .

"Don't be childish, Holt."

He had told his minder, his Mr. Martins who worked the Middle East Desk of the Secret Intelligence Service, that he wanted vengeance. Bloody light-years ago. He would know the man that they called Abu Hamid the moment that he could focus the lenses of the binoculars upon him. No doubt. He had seen the man they called Abu Hamid for nine, ten seconds. He didn't believe he would ever forget the face and the crow's foot scar. Bloody light-years ago he had wanted vengeance, he had told Martins that he wanted the eye and the tooth, both. He thought that his desire for vengeance was sapped, he thought that he had simply never had the guts to walk away from Mr. Martins in England, to walk away from Mr. Crane in Israel. He thought that he was on the west slopes of the Bekaa because he had never had the guts to turn his back on something as primitive as vengeance. He thought that he would in no way benefit from the sniping of Abu Hamid. He knew that nothing would change for Jane, nor for her parents either, even if they would ever know. And would anything change for him?

"I'd want him killed."

They were at the seventh rally point of the night.

It was where Crane had told him they would spend the few minutes of rest. An exact man was Crane, each rally point reached on time, the perfect instrument of vengeance.

Holt huddled against Crane. The wind caught at the sweat running on his body and chilled him.

"Can I talk?"

"Whisper, youngster."

"Where are they?"

"Ahead, perhaps a quarter of a mile."

"And it's a hostage?"

"What I reckon."

Holt swallowed hard. He caught at the sleeve of Crane's tunic shirt.

"He's more valuable."

"Riddles, youngster."

"A hostage is more valuable than sniping Abu Hamid."

"You know what you're saying?"

"There is more value in bringing back a hostage alive than in leaving Abu Hamid dead behind us."

"I didn't hear that." Crane tugged his sleeve clear.

"To bring back a hostage alive, that is a genuine act of mercy."

"Then you're forgetting something, youngster."

"I am not forgetting a fellow human being in danger."

"Forgetting something big."

"What is bigger than rescuing a man from that sort of hell?"

"Your promise, that's what you're forgetting."

"A hostage is alive, a hostage is an innocent . . ."

Crane turned away, his voice was soft and cut the edge of the night wind. "I gave my word, youngster. I don't play skittles with a promise."

"A hostage is worth saving. Is Abu Hamid worth killing?"

"I gave my promise. Pity you don't see that that's important."

"They aren't worth it, the people who've got your promise."

"Time to move."

"A hostage's freedom is worth more than your promise."

"I said it was time to move."

Holt stood.

"If I ever get out of this I'll hate you, Mr. Crane, for abandoning a hostage."

"If you ever get out of this, youngster, it'll be because of my promise . . . Just stop pissing in the wind."

Crane searched the ground ahead with the pocket night sight. They moved off. The gap between them materialized. Holt could hear the distant sounds ahead of the progress of a hostage and his captors. To the east of them, below them, was the village town of Khirbet Qanafar. They went quiet, traversing the slope side of the valley wall. When they next stopped they would be at the lying-up position overlooking the tent camp.

In the village town of Khirbet Qanafar the merchant lay on a rope bed and snored away the night hours.

Many years before, when he had first forsaken his lecture classes at Beersheba and moved into his clandestine life in Lebanon, he had found sleep hard to come by, he had felt the persistent fear of discovery. No longer; he slept well covered by a blanket that he fancied had come from the headman's own bed.

Beside the chair on which were laid his outer clothes, the merchant had spread out two plastic bags of the sort that were used to carry agricultural fertilizer. On these empty bags he had laid all the working parts of the pump engine that brought up water from one of Khirbet Qanafar's three irrigation wells. He had dismantled the pump engine during the late afternoon and early evening, then he had eaten with the headman and the headman's sons. In the morning, after he had woken and washed and fed, he would begin to reassemble the pump engine. He knew the reassembly would take him many hours, perhaps most of the day. He knew that in the dusk of the following day he would still be at Khirbet Qanafar. It was all as he had planned it. Crane would snipe at dusk. He slept easily, he was in position, as he had been told to be.

But how much longer, how many more years, could a university lecturer play the part of a merchant in spare parts for electrical engines and sleep in the bed of an enemy?

When he felt the softness of her body turn to cold, Abu Hamid rose to his feet.

The candle had gone, but the electricity supply was restored and light was thrown into the room from the alleyway.

She lay at his feet. Only an awkwardness about the tilt of her throat and the lie of her head.

He went to the window. He edged the thin curtains aside. He saw the jeep parked at the end of the alley. There was the auburn glow of the driver's cigarette.

He had been briefed on the plan for the attack against the Defense Ministry on Kaplan. They asked him for his life, and for the lives of the men who would travel with him. Of course, they would watch over him.

He lay on her bed. He smelled the perfume of the sheets and the pillows. He remembered the small, groping hands of the boy child she had placed with gentleness on his shoulder.

Heinrich Gunter was pushed down onto his hands and his knees. As he propelled himself forward over the rough rock floor he sensed the damp mustiness of the cave.

All according to Crane's bible. They moved through the lying-up position then doubled back to circle it.

They settled. Away below them were the lights of the camp, and the chugging drive of the generator carried up to their high ground.

18

Flooding it with gold light, the dawn slipped over the rim of the far valley wall.

It was as if the valley exploded in brilliance, with the low beams of the sun's thrust catching the lines and colors of the Bekaa. At dawn, at a few minutes before six o'clock, the valley was a place of quiet beauty. The sun caught the clean geometric lines of the irrigation channels, it flowed over the delicate green shades of the early growth of barley and wheat, it bathed the rough strength of the gray-yellow rock outcrops, it glinted on the red tile roofs of Khirbet Qanafar, it shone on the corrugated iron roofs of a commando camp. The sun laced onto the windshield of a traveling car. The sun pushed down long shadows from the bodies of a flock of sheep driven by a child toward the uplands of the valley to the plateau where it would be cooler when the sun was high. The sun burnished the scrubbed whiteness of a flag that carried in its center an outline of the Zionist state that was overpainted with crossed rifles with fixed bayonets.

And the sun, striking out, gave a shape to the conical tents of the camp.

The camp was no surprise, it was familiar from the aerial photographs.

There was the wire perimeter. There was the antitank ditch. There was the cluster of large sleeping tents. There was the latrine screen. There were the holes in the ground of the air raid pits, and of the armory. There was the tent of the commander, set aside. There was the roof above the cooking area.

The generator had been switched off at the first surge of daylight, as if light were only needed as a protection against the dangers of the night. A complete silence at the tent camp. The only movement was the turn and wheel and casual stamp of the sentry at the entrance to the camp, and the hustling of the cook as he revived the fire after the night, and the drift toward the sun orb of the wavering smoke column, and the flag fluttering out the emblem of the Popular Front.

Above the camp, at a place where the steeper sides of the valley wall flattened out to offer a more gentle slope to the floor of the Bekaa, the ancient ice age movements had left a gouged-out overhang of rock. The space under the lip of the protruding rock was shallow, not more than three feet deep, but the overhang ran some ten feet in length. The overhang was unremarkable. In the half mile or so to either side of this particular formation there were another nine similar devastations of the general line of the ground fall.

The overhang of rock was the place chosen by Crane for the final lying-up position.

Crane asleep.

Holt on watch.

The sun lifted clear of the Jabal Aarbi on the east side of the Bekaa. It was extraordinary for Holt how fast the cleanness of the light began to diffuse into haze. The sun was climbing. He tugged his watch out from under his tunic top, checked the time. Crane was sleeping well, like he needed to sleep. He would liked to have left Crane to sleep longer, to have the chance to rest the eye and to bring back strength into his muscles and calm into his mind. The watch was the taskmaster. He would be chewed out if he allowed Crane to sleep beyond his allotted time. He touched Crane's shoulder. Since they had reached the lying-up position he had slept for an hour, and Crane had slept for an hour. But the sun was now up, and the camp was stirring. He could not think when they would next sleep.

Crane awoke.

God, and did he do it easily? For Holt it was a miracle of the world, Crane waking. A fast rub of the eye, half of a stifled yawn, a vicious scratch at the armpit, a scowl and a grin, and Crane was awake.

There were small figures moving from the tents, there was the first tinkle of a transistor radio playing music and traveling against the wind.

"Did you sleep all right?"

"I slept fine . . . what's moving?"

"Starting to be shit-shower-shave time down there. You know, Mr. Crane, it's fantastic, us being here, them being there. I mean, it's what you said would happen, but until I was here perhaps I didn't ever quite believe it."

"You think too much, youngster, that's the problem of education."

"How's the eye?"

"Worry about yourself."

Holt heard the pitch of Crane's voice drop, he saw him turn away. Crane's tongue was rolling inside his cheeks, like he was cleaning his teeth with his tongue, like the action was a toothpaste substitute.

"What else is moving?"

"A boy over there with sheep, there . . ." Holt pointed to his right, through the scrim net that masked them. "Bit of traffic on the road. Nothing else. When do I start looking?"

The binoculars were in Crane's Bergen. Crane shook his head. "Think about it, youngster. Where's the sun? The sun's straight into us. You put the glasses up and you'll risk burning your eyes out, and you'll risk a lens flash. Neither's clever. You don't do any looking till the sun's a hell of a lot higher. Patience, youngster."

"Mr. Crane . . ."

"Yeah."

"Mr. Crane, what happened to the hostage?"

There was a tremor of annoyance across Crane's mouth. "What's it to you?"

"I just wanted to know."

"Are you going to make a thing about it, are you going to puke over me?"

"What happened to him?"

Crane whispered, "There's a cave a quarter of a mile back, that's where they went. We passed about a hundred yards higher. I'd say it's where they're going to hold him. Sometimes it's Beirut where they hold them, sometimes it's out in the Bekaa . . . would be better in Beirut, won't be a hotel out here."

"Mr. Crane . . ."

"Yeah."

"When we've sniped, when we're heading back . . ."

"No."

"Nothing we can do?"

"You want to get home, or you want to die? If you want to go home you walk right past the cave, if you want to die you call for tea and scones . . . Sorry, youngster."

Holt hung his head, his words were a murmur, the wind in the scrim netting. "Seems dreadful to leave him."

"Heh, Alexander the Great came through here, Nebuchadnezzar was here, the Romans had a go at it. There were the Crusaders and the Turks and the French and the Yanks and the Syrians, and my people had a try at it. Everyone's had a go at civilizing this place, and Lebanon saw them all off. That's just fact, that's not education. And it's fact that you can't change things, Holt, not on your little educated own. You can't change a damned thing . . . forget him."

"It's rotten to turn our backs on him."

Crane looked for a moment keenly at Holt, didn't speak. He untied the laces of his boots, then pulled the laces tighter through the eyes and made a double bow. From a pouch in the Bergen he took a strip of chewing gum. He lifted the Armalite onto his lap. Holt watched him. Crane had his face against the netting and his eyes roved across the vista in front, down toward the camp. Crane's hand settled on Holt's shoulder.

"You'll be all right, youngster."

Holt gagged. "What are you doing?"

"Scouting, going to find myself a hide further down."

"You said that where we'd be lying-up would be a thousand yards."

"I want six hundred," Crane said.

"Is it the eye?"

"I just want six hundred."

"Can't you do it at a thousand?"

"Leave it, Holt." Close to a snarl.

Holt shook his head, didn't believe it. According to Crane's bible there should be no movement by daylight. According to Crane's text not even an idiot tried to move across open ground after dawn, before dusk. According to Crane's chapter the team never split. According to Crane's verse a thousand yards was best for the sniper. He couldn't argue. He stared at Crane. It was as if his fear, wide eyed, softened Crane.

"I'm not gone long, an hour, maybe a little more. In an hour you start to use the glasses . . . They're all shit down there, they can't see their assholes right now. On my own, just myself, a buzzard overhead won't see me. I find the place at six hundred yards, and I'm back. You spot the bastard for me, we mark him, we follow him, we get to know him. Late afternoon, sun's going down, sun's behind us, sun's into them, that's when I move again. One shot at six hundred. I stay put, you stay put, till it's dark. I come back for you, and we move out . . . Got it, youngster?"

"Got it, Mr. Crane." There was a reed in Holt's voice, like he was a child, afraid to be alone.

The scrim netting was slowly lifted, and then Crane was gone.

There was a crag boulder to the right of the overhang, and Holt saw the shape of Crane, his outline broken by the camouflage tabs, reach the boulder.

He did not see him afterward.

Holt screwed his eyes tight. He peered down onto the desolate and featureless ground between himself and the tent camp and he could not find a movement. He could not credit that Noah Crane, on that landscape, had vanished.

Fawzi blinked in the sunlight. He stretched, he yawned, he pulled his trouser belt tighter.

He had slept well, heavily. The smile came to his face. He had much to be cheerful about. He was casting aside the sleep, he was basking in the sunlight and the memory of the previous evening. Last year's harvest, well-stored and well-dried leaves, and well packed. Much to smile about, because there were five packages in the locked rear of his jeep and each package weighed ten kilos, and each kilo was top quality.

The posting in the valley as liaison officer to the recruits' camp had this one salvation, constant access to the old and new marijuana crop. He had done well in the weeks that he had spent setting up the camp and then introducing it to these boys of the Popular Front. His money was in dollars. Cash dollars, bank notes. For dollars an understanding could be negotiated with the customs officials at the airport. His dollars in cash, less the price of the understanding, could be carried in his hip pocket and in his wallet, to the cities of Rome and Paris and Athens. They were the holy cities he would make his pilgrimage to, when the creep Hamid had gone with the chosen ten to Damascus for the final preparation before the flight to Cyprus and the sea journey to the shoreline of Israel.

Much to be cheerful about, and the most cheering matter for Lieutenant Fawzi was that this would be his last day and his last night in the suffocating tedium of the Bekaa.

There was a queue of recruits waiting to be served by the cook. He ordered an omelet, three eggs. He said that he wanted coffee. He went back to his tent, pulled out a chair from inside, waited for his food to be brought to him.

The smoke, pungent from the dew-damp wood, played across his nostrils.

He held the binoculars as Crane had taught him. His thumb and his forefinger gripped the far end of each lens, and the outstretched palms of his hands shielded the polished glass from the sun.

Holt had stopped looking for Crane. He lay on his stomach, quite still, only allowing his head to move fractionally as he raked over the faces of the magnified figures moving lethargically between the tents.

He had covered the line in front of the cooking area, and the line in front of the latrine screen. He had followed the men as they emerged from their tents, until they ducked back into them.

He could not believe that he had looked with the power of the binoculars into the face of Abu Hamid and had not known him. He had seen no man with a crow's foot scar on his cheek. He had seen no man walk with the rolling gait of Abu Hamid crossing the street in front of the Oreanda Hotel. He could remember the long sitting wait on the hard bench in the corridor leading to the cellblock of the police station in Tel Aviv. He could remember the beating given freely to the bomber. What if the man had lied? . . . What if the man had lied to save his skin from the fists and the boots? . . . The doubts crawled in him.

What if he had traveled to the Bekaa and Abu Hamid was not at the camp? What if he had traveled to the Bekaa and could not recognize Abu Hamid?

For the fourth time he started his search at the southern perimeter wire of the camp, and traversed north, searching for the face, and doubting.

He had laid her body on the bed.

He covered her body with the sheet and then the bedcover. He pulled the sheet high enough to obscure the bruising at her throat.

He had taken a flower from the vase by the window, a rose. He laid the flower on the bedcover across her breast.

He closed the door behind him. He walked down the steep steps and out into the noise and crush of the alley. He walked very straight, he walked with the purpose of a young commander who had accepted a mission of leading an assault squad against the Defense Ministry on Kaplan.

Abu Hamid climbed into the passenger seat of the jeep.

Holt set the binoculars down on the rock dirt beside his hands. The valley shimmered in the heat below him. The sun burned a whiteness from the tent tops, and flickered at those strands of the wire that were not rusted. Nothing wrong with the binoculars, he had seen the dart of the rats at the bottom of the wire. He was learning the life of the camp. The men were sitting in a half circle, swatting off the flies, watching a hugely fat young man demonstrate the stripping down and the reassembling of a machine gun. He could not see all of their faces, not at this moment, but he had checked each of the faces before they had sat down, and he had checked the face of the uniformed instructor. It had been a desperation to see if there was a crow's foot scar on the left upper cheek of the instructor, a last throw. The cook was on his knees blowing at the fire. Only the cook and a sentry at the entrance to the camp and a man asleep in a chair by his tent were not involved in the class session. He had come so far with Crane, three nights' march, a squashed-in lifetime, and Abu Hamid was not there. His head and his body ached and his whole heart sank in despair.

Major Zvi Dan went into the hushed, badly lit room that housed the communications center.

He closed the door gently behind him.

It was a world where no voice was raised, where none of the men or women in uniform moved other than at a studied pace. The room was an empire of electronics. There was the purr of the teleprinters and the greenwash screens of the visual display units and the faint whisper of the recording equipment. Because of the nature of events, because Crane and Holt had walked into the Bekaa, transmissions from the Syrian military that were intercepted by the antennae of Hermon would be relayed to the communications center at Kiryat Shmona.

In a lowered voice he asked the communications captain if there was any information he should have. There was nothing.

Major Zvi Dan tore a sheet from the small notepad that he carried in his tunic breast pocket. On the paper was written the figures identifying an ultrahigh-frequency radio channel. He asked that from the middle of the day that frequency should be continuously monitored.

Still he watched the camp. He played through in his mind what Crane would say to him, how he would reply. Definitely he's not there . . . Maybe he's a bit changed . . . If he was there I'd know him . . . If he had a beard . . .? I'd know him . . .

Nothing further to look for at the camp. The men were at the machine gun still, three at a time, practicing what they had learned. Mr. Crane would have been disgusted. The fire in the cooking area was out, and the cook fellow was washing stainless steel dishes, and the sentry walked backward and forward across the road track to the camp looking as though he were asleep. The camp had nothing for him.

With the binoculars he tried to find Crane.

Couldn't find him, just as he could not find the man he'd come so far to see killed.

Holt was desolated, he had never been so alone.

"If there is no one else to whom you will communicate your information, then you have to wait."

The traveler settled deeper into the comfort of the armchair. The outer office was cool, pleasantly furnished. He had walnuts in a bag, their shells already cracked. "My information is only for Major Said Hazan."

The clerk did not trouble to hide his contempt. The man stank, was dressed like a peasant. His shoes had brought the street dirt onto the carpet.

"He has gone to a meeting, I do not have a time for his return."

"Then I shall wait."

The pieces of walnut shell flaked to the carpet. The traveler made no attempt to retrieve them. He chewed happily on the crisp interior.

Holt saw the dust plume spitting from behind the wheels of the jeep. He reached for the binoculars. He saw the markings above the jeep's engine, presumably Syrian Army. He saw that a single passenger sat beside the driver.

His sight became a blur. Holt's head slashed sideways, away from the road view, away from the jeep. The magnified vision leaped from the roadway to the camp, from the tents to the camp entrance, from the sentry to the cook.

The cook had come out of the camp. He had skirted the wire. The cook now climbed the slope on the west side of the camp. Holt could see that he was scavenging. In the hugeness of the binoculars' tunnel vision the cook seemed about to step into the overhang of rock. Holt could see that he whistled to himself. He watched him smile, pleased, because he had found a length of dried wood. He watched him tuck the length of wood under his arm and climb again. He watched him, slowly and unhurried, hunting for more wood, and climbing the slope.

Holt did not know where Noah Crane hid.

At the entrance to the camp Abu Hamid jumped clear of the jeep and strode through the gap in the wire. The jeep reversed away.

He saw Fawzi's lesson. He thought that Fawzi would have messed his trousers if he had ever been called on to fire a heavy machine gun in combat. His throat was dry. He walked to the cooking area. He saw the dead fire. No coffee warming. High on the hill slope above the camp he saw the cook foraging for wood.

The vision of the binoculars roved.

The cook had an armful of wood, so much now that he had wavered twice as if uncertain whether more was needed.

The open falling ground was devoid of cover except for long-dead trees lying strewn and ossified. The sun had burned the bark from them.

The deep, clumsily dug ditch.

Refuse bags and the sheets of discarded newspaper, trapped on the coiled wire. The men were all sitting, bored and listless, no longer attentive to the gesturing officer in front of his class.

The new arrival . . .

The new man in the camp walked to stand behind the sitting instructor, listened for a few moments, turned away.

The binoculars followed him.

Something in the stride, something in the bearing. The twin eyepieces were rammed against Holt's eyebrows and cheekbones. He had seen the right side of the face, he had seen the full of the face, he had seen the short curled hair at the back of the head.

The new man now seemed to walk aimlessly. A tent floated in front of him. Holt swore.

The man reappeared, doubling back, smoking. Left side of the face.

Holt could hardly hold the binoculars steady. Breath coming in pants, hands trembling. He gulped the air down into his lungs. He forced the air down into his throat, breathing as a sniper would, winning control of his body. Crane's bible, breathing critical.

He saw the man's left hand raised to his face. He saw the finger peck at a place on the left cheek. He saw the hand drop.

Holt saw the crow's foot scar.

The breath shuddered out of his chest.

The vision of the binoculars bounced. The tunnel of sight bounced, fell. He had seen the crow's foot scar. The shadow pit of the well of the scar, four lines of the scar spreading away from the dark center.

The cook . . .

The cook still coming up the hill, bending here and there for a piece of wood, carefree.

Abu Hamid . . .

Seen beside the other men in the camp, Holt thought Abu Hamid was taller than he had remembered him, and thinner, and his hair was longer and falling to the olive-green collar of his fatigue top. All doubt was gone. He felt a huge surge of exhilaration—and he recognized it, a sudden, sharper, stronger fright. But Noah Crane and young Holt had done it, they had walked into the bloody awful Bekaa Valley, and they had found him. They had him at close quarters, had traced him behind the lines, on the other side of the hill. And where the hell was Noah Crane?

The cook . . .

The cook had set down his gathered bundle, and come higher. He would collect another armful and then go back for the first. The cook meandered on the hillside, searching.

Abu Hamid . . .

Abu Hamid walked among the tents. To Holt he seemed a man without purpose. Sometimes he would insinuate himself close to the officer who lectured the young soldiers. Sometimes he would turn and walk away as if the lecture bored him. He flitted, he was aimless. Holt, in his mind, saw Jane and the ambassador. He saw the blood rivers on the steps of the hotel. He saw the white pallor of death on her face, on his face. He wondered if there was indeed a sweetness in revenge, or whether it would merely be a substitute, saccharine dose . . . He knew the excitement at the discovery of Abu Hamid, he could not imagine whether he would find pleasure, fruit, satisfaction in Abu Hamid dead. He had never hurt a human being in his life, not even at school, not even in a playground fight. No answers.

The cook . . .

As if struck by an electric shock, the cook jerked backward, scattering the branches of wood behind him. Crane appearing, seeming to thrust himself up from under the feet of the cook. Holt saw everything. The tunnel of his binoculars was filled with the cook trying to heave himself backward, with Crane rising and groping and grasping for him. The cook screamed, a shrill, carrying scream. The scream winnowed over the hillside. The scream was clear to Holt who was four hundred yards from the cook, to the tent camp that was six hundred yards from the cook. Holt heard the rising cadence of the scream. He saw the flash of the blade. He saw the body of Crane merge with the body of the cook. He heard the scream cut, snuffed out.

Fawzi's words had been lost. The recruits had first stiffened, swung, then jackknifed to their feet. They had seen the cook on the hillside, seen him try to twist away, break into flight. They had seen the assailant. They had heard the death of the scream. Abu Hamid charged from in front of his own tent toward the class, toward the DShKM heavy machine gun.

Holt lay on his stomach pressing his body as far as he could back into the recess of the rock overhang. He saw the brightness of the blade, and he saw the cook crumple to his knees, then slide to his face. He realized at once the enormity of it. Their cover was gone. He was hiding, but Crane had no hiding place. He thought the cook might even have stepped on Crane, he thought the cook had been close enough to Crane to have actually put his boot onto the back of Crane's camouflaged head or the back of Crane's camouflaged body.

Holt watched Crane. The hugeness of the tunnel vision seemed to give him an intimacy with Crane who was four hundred yards further down the hillside. He believed he could see the turmoil of decision in Crane's features. Crane looked back down the hillside, down the slope toward the tent camp. Holt followed his eyeline, flashed the tunnel view of the binoculars toward the tent camp. The recruits were streaming toward the entrance between the coiled wire. Back to Crane. Holt saw the hands of Noah Crane fumbling at his waist, then he saw him crouch. Sharp movements now, decision taken, mind made up. Crane back onto his feet. Holt saw that he no longer wore his belt. He peered again to be sure. Crane no longer carried his belt on his waist. According to Crane's bible the belt was never taken from the body, not to sleep, not to defecate. Crane no longer wore his belt. Crane had his back to Holt. He gazed up high onto the hillside as if his eyeline was a half a mile higher than the rock overhang, as if his eyeline was far to the south.

Holt heard Crane's shout. Crane's hands were at his mouth, cupped to amplify his shout. Crane bellowed toward a place on the hillside. Holt thought that Crane shouted in Hebrew, that he called a warning.

Crane started to run at an angle on the hillside.

More understanding, but then a child could have understood.

They were young, the pursuers. They were fast on the hillside. They were swarming among the rock outcrops, over the broken ground. He was taking them away. His warning was a deception, he was leading them away from Holt.

There was the first ranging burst from the machine gun. Three, four rounds. There was the first red light of a sighting tracer bullet.

Holt could not take his vision, his magnified gaze, away from Crane. The pursuers, teenagers, half the age of Crane, must gain, would gain, on the quarry. A second burst, a second flailing flight of tracer. Holt could no longer see Crane's face, could see only the heaving shake of his back as he ran, away from Holt, ran for his life. Holt saw the puff pecks of the bullets striking rock and scree and stone.

Crane sagged. He stumbled, he fell. He rose again.

Out aloud, Abu Hamid shouted his triumph.

Three 4-round bursts of 12.7mm ammunition. Aimed bursts from a tripod. Muzzle velocity 900 yards a second. He had seen his target go down, rise again, collapse, rise again. He had his hit.

Holt saw Crane go forward.

He seemed to hobble. He was ducking and weaving as he went, but slower, each step deeper into pain. He understood. The vixen's loyalty to her cub. A scarred, world-weary, bitchy old vixen giving life to a wet-behind-the-ears cub. The gunfire had stopped. No more shooting. Holt could see that the pursuers were now too close to Crane to make it either safe or necessary to fire again. The pursuers bounded over the diminishing ground, hunted down their man. He heard Crane shout again, make another pretense at a warning to phantom men in a position ahead of him.

Holt saw the cave mouth.

Holt saw the first head, shoulders, appear at the mouth of the cave. The mouth of the cave was a hundred yards ahead of Crane's line. It was the edge of Holt's vision. It was the place that was half masked from him. Four men came out of the cave's mouth. One man wore only the gray-whiteness of underpants upon the pink-whiteness of his body. Chaos on the hillside, chaos for Crane who was wounded, chaos for three men of the Hezbollah who were discovered and flushed out, chaos for a hostage prisoner. The three men ran. The hostage prisoner stood alone. The gap between Crane and his pursuers narrowed.

Holt watched. Crane was engulfed.

He let the binoculars fall from his eyes.

His head drooped, down into the dirt floor of the rock overhang.

The tears misted his eyes, ran bitter to his lips.

Crane was dragged down the hillside. The hostage prisoner was escorted after him.

A moment when the lights seemed to go out, when hope was lost.

The argument was ferocious.

"I wounded him, my shooting. My boys captured him. I should take him."

"You've work here."

Abu Hamid and Lieutenant Fawzi face to face.

"It was us who caught him . . ."

"Me who will take the Jew . . ."

"You want to take the credit from us."

"You have men to choose, you have a mission to perform. You will stay."

"So that you will take the credit."

"So that you can prepare your mission."

In the hand of Fawzi was the dog tag ripped from the neck of the prisoner, kept safe in Fawzi's hand just as the prisoner would be safe in Fawzi's possession.

"I should take him to Damascus."

"I order you to stay here. You will perform your duty."

Fawzi walked away. He went to the knot of recruits that had gathered round the prisoner. He shouldered aside the man kicking the prisoner. He thought that by now they would all have had their turn with the boot. He saw the blood seeping from the knee of the prisoner. He saw the mouth twisted to stifle an agony. He told the recruits that the prisoner should not again be kicked.

He went to his tent. He knew enough of the English language that was common between them to receive the garbled thanks of the hostage prisoner.

He sat at the table that was set between his bed and the bed used by Abu Hamid. He switched on the battery power for the radio. He waited. When the lights glowed, when he had transmission power, he broadcast his success to Damascus.

Holt watched.

The body of the cook was carried down the hillside on a stretcher made of rifle slings and the wood he had been collecting, and along with the body was the Armalite rifle that Crane had carried. A second search party had scoured the cave and brought down to the camp boxes of food and weapons and bedding.

Holt saw all that. He was undisturbed. The recruits of the

Popular Front had no interest in that part of the hillside where Holt lay under the rock overhang and the screen of scrim netting.

Holt watched the camp. He could see Crane lying prone on the earth, he could see the blood on his legs. He could see the rifles that covered Crane's every pain spasm.

They had not found Crane's belt. The belt lay among the rocks, deep among them, at the place where Crane had begun his decoy flight. Holt tried to memorize the place, tried to recall each detail of Crane's movement so that he could remember that exact place where Crane had crouched to conceal his belt.

Major Said Hazan swiveled his chair so that his back was to the traveler, so that he faced the wall map. He studied the two red-headed pins that he had set into his map. It was Major Said Hazan's style to repeat each piece of information given him so that there should be no possible error, no missed inflection, no false interpretation.

"And the information came from an Englishman?"

"An Englishman of middle years, staying at the guesthouse of the Kibbutz Kfar Giladi, and he said, 'How did you know about the infiltration last night?' That is what he said."

"And that 'last night,' that was the night that Olaffson said the Israelis had fired flares to blind the night equipment?"

"That is correct, Major."

He spoke to himself, he ignored the traveler. He stared at the red-headed pin that marked the unsubstantiated interception.

"Why are the British going into the Bekaa?"

The traveler shrugged. Fragments of walnut tumbled from his clothes to the white pile of the carpet.

"A wretch such as I, Major, how could I know?"

He needed to think. He required moments of contemplation. Major Said Hazan was denied the moments.

A sharp tap at the door. A bustling entrance from his clerk, a sheet of paper handed to him. He studied it. He seemed no longer to see the traveler. He reached for a telephone. He demanded that the Jew prisoner be brought to Damascus by Air Force helicopter. To win his demands he invoked the authority, and the fear of that authority, of that building in which he worked.

Major Zvi Dan rocked on his feet. He stood in the middle of the communications center. He held loose in his hand the report of the intercepted traffic. For the third time he read the message, as if in the frequency of the reading he might find a straw. No comfort, nothing to cling to.

INTERCEPT.

TRANSMISSION TIME:	10:47 HOURS LOCAL.
TRAFFIC ORIGINATED:	PFLP TRAINING CAMP, NR KHIRBET QANAFAR, BEKAA.
TRAFFIC DESTINATION:	AFI HQ, DAMASCUS.
CODE:	2ND SERIES, AFI.
MESSAGE:	ISRAELI SERVICEMAN CARRYING IDENTIFICATION OF NOAH CRANE, REL: JEW, ID NO: 478391, CAPTURED WHILE ON SURVEILLANCE OF CAMP, WOUNDED. IN SAME OPERATION, LINK UNCERTAIN, FRG NATIONAL HEINRICH GUNTER, HOSTAGE, FREED, UNHURT. SEARCH OF AREA INTO WHICH CRANE FLEEING FAILED TO FIND REMAINDER OF INFILTRATION PARTY. REQUEST EYE BRING TO DAMASCUS. SIGNED, FAWZI (LT).

No comfort, no straw, each reading worse than the last. The communications officer came quietly to his side. He asked, "The frequency we are to monitor—we are still to monitor it?"

"Yes," Major Zvi Dan said.

He went outside. He went into the bright sunlight. Midday and the sun swirling off the dust of the parade area, and off the tin roofing of the huts, and off the armor plate of the personnel carriers. From the troops' quarters he heard the cheerful playing of music from the Forces' station. He passed beside the veranda outside the canteen. He knew that Rebecca watched him, but he could not bring himself to speak to her. His face would have told her.

He was familiar with disaster. His work often traveled in tandem with catastrophe. Many times he had known the pain and the catastrophe of losing a field agent. The hurt was never more manageable for being familiar.

He went into the building block. He walked to the sentry who lolled in his chair outside the door. He gestured for the door to be opened. Percy Martins sat on the bed. Major Zvi Dan saw the dulled scowl of Martins's welcome. He passed the sheet of paper to the Englishman. He let the Englishman hold the sheet of paper, as if for authenticity, then he translated line by line from the Hebrew.

"God . . ."

"You had the right to know."

"Holt, what about Holt?"

"He is alone."

"What can we do for him?"

"He is beyond our reach."

"He's just a boy."

"Then he should never have been sent."

"Can he not be helped?"

"If it were Crane who were free, if it were Holt who was taken, then there is perhaps something we could do for Crane, something; but he would have to do much for himself. I doubt if it works on the other side of the coin."

Percy Martins's hands covered his face. His voice was muffled through the thickness of his fingers.

"Is it because of what I did?"

"I have no means of knowing."

"What will they do to Crane?"

"Torture him."

"Will he talk?"

"How would you respond to torture, skilled torture, Mr. Martins? Put on your shoes, please."

"Where are you taking me?"

There was a cold, rueful smile on Major Zvi Dan's face. "London will want to know what has happened. They will want to set in train whatever machinery they can to minimize the damage."

He took Martins to an office with a secure telephone. He dialed for him the number of the station officer at the embassy in Tel Aviv.

In a dust storm the helicopter of the Syrian Air Force took off from beside the camp. The power of the rotors, thrashing for lift, buffeted the tents, scattered the refuse that clung to the coiled wire on the perimeter.

Heinrich Gunter now wore the tunic and trousers of a recruit of the Popular Front. Clothes he had been given, explanations none. He could not comprehend how his escape from his captors had come about. He thought his freedom had been gained by the man who lay on the floor of the helicopter. The man was dressed in military clothes that were indented with camouflage tabs, and his leg was badly wounded and no one had attempted to dress the wound, and he was handcuffed to the bulkhead and he was covered by the handgun of the Syrian officer who had boarded the helicopter at the camp. He saw that the man he believed had brought about his freedom bit hard at his bottom lip as though he were suffused in pain, as if he would not show his captor his pain, as if he refused to cry out, gasp.

Through the portholes of the Gazelle helicopter, Gunter saw laid out beneath him the bright and tranquil breadth of the Bekaa Valley.

They clapped, the men and the boys, and the women from behind their face scarves trilled their appreciation. There was the drone of the working generator, there was the splash of water lifted from great depths and now free to run in the dug channels.

The merchant grinned and bowed to receive the congratulations.

The merchant was asked by the headman of Khirbet Qanafar to take food at his table, to share the midday meal. He was pleased to accept. He fancied he could smell the cooking of partridge. He was pleased to accept because it suited him to stay at the village town of Khirbet Qanafar until last light.

The merchant had heard the shooting perhaps two miles north up the valley. News came that a Jew had been captured, that a hostage prisoner had been freed. Only one man captured . . . In his long years in Lebanon he was practised in deceit, he could guard his emotions.

He would be honored to take food with the headman, and with the headman's sons.

He had done it as he thought Crane would have done it.

When the sun was behind him at last Holt crawled out of the fragile cover of the net and down the hillside. He thought that he had been moving for a little more than an hour. Flat on his stomach, stomach ground against the earth and sun-scorched rock, he had gone the four hundred yards from the lying-up position to the place where Crane had killed the cook.

The blood was there. The blood reinforced the truth. The truth was the capture and the throwing of Noah Crane through the hatch door of the military helicopter.

He could hear the shouting and the triumph from the camp. Singing and the yelling of slogans, voices competing one with another. Then he found Crane's belt. It was wedged down between two small rocks and half buried by a trailing network of undergrowth.

Crane had left his belt on purpose. Crane's bible, do nothing without a reason.

Slowly, with great care, each movement weighed and considered, young Holt began the stomach crawl back toward the lying-up position, and the heat shimmered over him, and the sun burned through the cotton of his tunic top.

As Crane himself would have done it.

19

It was two o'clock in the afternoon.

It was that part of the daytime during which the valley slept. Low on the Bekaa, where the Litani River and the irrigation channels made the shades of green, only the butterflies moved, hovering between flowers. That part of the day when the men had slid off to their homes, and their women to the coolness of their houses, and the children had gathered under the shade-spreading trees. The soldiers in their nearby temporary barracks had taken to their sleeping cots. The shepherd boys dozed, their flocks had tucked in their legs and knelt and panted. A great sloth blanketed the valley.

At two o'clock in the afternoon Holt managed to reach his lying-up position again.

He lay under the scrim net and he gasped down the warm air. He heaved to draw the strength down into his lungs. He felt the sweat running on his body. He drank water until his belly, his bladder, could take no more. He had no shortage of water. He had the water from Crane's pack. He had no shortage of food because he had Crane's food. As he dragged the air down into his chest, as he poured the water down his throat, he could lie outstretched under the rock overhang because he had also Crane's place. He had Crane's water, food and his place. He was alone.

When he had rested a little, when he had drunk heavily, he turned to Crane's belt. He opened each pouch in turn.

Two pouches holding liter water bottles.

One pouch holding a single day's emergency dehydrated rations.

One pouch holding two of the spare magazines for the Armalite rifle.

One pouch holding the survival kit. Matches, candle, flint, magnifying glass, needles and thread, fish hooks and line, compass, Beta light, flexi saw, capsules of sedative and antibiotic and antihistamine, surgical blades, plasters and butterfly sutures, and a condom.

One scabbard pouch. The knife was in the cook.

One small pouch holding five rounds for the Model PM. He took the pouch from the belt, clipped it to his own belt.

He anticipated that there was only one pouch that mattered to him. It was days ago, nights before, that he had identified the one pouch on Crane's belt that was not duplicated on his own. Perhaps he was nervous of intruding into a secrecy that was particular to Noah Crane. He did not doubt that it was this last pouch, the largest on Crane's belt, that Crane had meant for him. Holt opened the flap and drew out the rectangular green-painted metal-cased box. He saw the switches and the dials. There were signs, directions, printed on the box, in English.

He read. His lips moved. The words croaked in his throat.

"Property of the Armed Forces of the United States of America."

His eyes flitted.

"Search Air Rescue Beacon, Mark V."

He strained to read, in the dappled shadow of the scrim netting, the smaller printed information.

"Three-second bleep pattern . . . Can guide to 100 meters . . . To last 14 days . . . Extend aerial for maximum effect . . . Power switch . . . Red Spot, Green Spot . . ."

Holt shivered. In the heat he trembled. He understood. The beacon device was the last-ditch defense. It was for a cock-up, and because Crane didn't talk about cock-ups, then he didn't talk about it. The beacon had been left to him by

Crane. He saw that the switch could go to the green spot or to the red spot, and he didn't know to which frequency they would be locked, and he didn't know what the range was, and he didn't know how the bleep transmission would be affected by the mountain and valley terrain, but it had been left for him by his mentor . . . Wait on, wait on, Holt. No bloody stupid ideas about crying in the sand and switching to green spot, or to red spot, and sitting on your backside offering up prayers. He was stuck between the training camp in the valley and the commando camp further up the valley and the armed men of the village town of Khirbet Qanafar, all that below him, and above him there were the troops guarding the surveillance installations on the Jabal al Barouk . . . Wait on, Holt . . . He wondered whether the leaving of the beacon was meant as a means of escape or whether it was meant as an encouragement.

He repacked the pouch. He found a space for it, just, on his own belt.

An encouragement.

He turned, heaved his body round. He lifted his binoculars. He had seen that Abu Hamid had not boarded the helicopter. He had watched Abu Hamid into his tent. The camp was now in siesta. Just the sentry at the entrance on the move and that rarely.

"He awaits you, Major."

"You are to be congratulated, Fawzi."

"For which, Major, I thank you."

"Tell me what happened."

Fawzi sat forward in the chair. He had the attention of Major Said Hazan, of the once-burned eyes and the once-scorched ears.

"I was taking a class through the detail of the assembly and stripping of a DShKM machine gun. The camp cook was on the hill above the camp collecting wood for the fire on which he cooks. I think he must have stumbled on this Crane. He shouted. He had a chance to shout before he was stabbed to death by the Jew. His shout alerted us. Immediately I took over the machine gun, and when the Jew started to flee I began firing. I have to confess, Major, that at first I was not successful, but in moments I had the range. I achieved a disabling hit. The moment I had done that, and seen that the Jew no longer had the capacity to run, I organized the capture party. I led a group of the Popular Front recruits onto the hillside, and we captured the Jew. He was not in a condition to resist."

"It was well done, Fawzi."

"I was carrying out my duty, Major."

"And the hostage, Heinrich Gunter?"

Fawzi shrugged. "I can only give you what is an opinion, Major. I think that our finding him was chance. I cannot see a connection between the Jew and a hostage. And the hostage has given no sign of any link between them. I believe that the flight of the Jew happened to take him toward a cave where the hostage was held. I believe that in fear the Hezbollah or the Islamic Jihad simply abandoned their hostage and much equipment besides. But it is good for us, regaining the hostage?"

"It is very good indeed. In the power play of diplomacy at the moment when our nation is confronted with the lies of the West European nations that we are a state which sponsors terrorism it is a beautiful thing that we are able to deliver this Heinrich Gunter to his ambassador, quite excellent. But it is the Jew that matters."

Fawzi warmed. "To me, in the direction of his flight, from his actions, he tried to warn the others in his infiltration group of danger . . ."

Major Said Hazan clapped together his mutilated hands. "Closer to the security zone we block them. The orders have been given. So, he awaits me."

So much to concern Major Said Hazan. He had the evidence of an infiltration. He had an unconfirmed interception. He had the report of the conversation of an Englishman at Kiryat Shmona. He had the detail of the capture of the Jew named Crane, on the hillside above the tent camp occupied by the recruits of the Popular Front.

Major Said Hazan stood in front of his mirror. He tugged down the jacket of his uniform, he straightened his tie, he smoothed back the few hairs left on his scalp.

"I have bad news, Prime Minister."

The Director General stood in the center of the room. His pipe was in his pocket. The Prime Minister had been in a full meeting of the Cabinet. A note had been carried in, the discussion on the plight of the inner cities had been shelved, the Prime Minister had come out.

The Prime Minister was at the window, staring down at the spring-bursting garden.

"Lebanon?" The voice was a murmur.

"You will remember that we sent two men in. We sent an expert in covert infiltration who was also an accomplished marksman, and we sent the young diplomat who was the eyewitness . . ."

"Of course I remember."

"We have lost the marksman. The marksman has been captured alive by the Syrians, and taken by helicopter to Damascus." It was the voice of a bell tolling.

"This is neither more nor less than I expected."

"The diplomat has not been held."

"And I wanted it called off."

"You said, Prime Minister, that the diplomat was fortunate to have the chance of real adventure. He has that chance now."

"Where did it happen?"

"In the target area."

"Holt, that's his name isn't it, the diplomat? Can he get out?"

"Frankly, no," the Director General said curtly.

"They were at the target and they had not fired?"

"If they had succeeded at the target we would have known of it. There is no information."

The Prime Minister twisted, venom in the eyes, a spit in the words. "You have made a fool of me. I will be ridiculed in the chancelleries of Europe, in Washington. This government will be badly damaged. You don't concern yourself, of course, with such matters."

"Prime Minister, my concern at present is for the safety of young Holt, and it is for the life of Noah Crane."

"And if your Mr. Holt is captured or killed, as seems most probable, will you still blather to me about vengeance? Will you send another clandestine team to Lebanon? . . . It was utterly preposterous, indeed it was criminally stupid."

"Recriminations, Prime Minister, regrettably do not help them."

"And what does help them, pray?"

"Sadly, nothing that I know of. I will keep you informed, Prime Minister."

When he had gone, the room was silent. The Prime Minister paced. Beyond the closed window the wind whipped the dust on Horse Guards and bent the trees in the walled garden. The clouds scurried low, the lights were dull in the room, and the face of Holt was unknown. The Prime Minister's lips pursed in angry concentration, but no effort could conjure up the face of the boy in such danger, nor of the assassin Abu Hamid, nor of the faraway terrain of the Bekaa.

The Prime Minister lifted a telephone, asked for the Cabinet Secretary in his Downing Street office.

The Prime Minister said briskly, "A covert mission in Lebanon has failed. I want the Foreign Secretary here at two, I want his principal Middle East people with him . . ." The Prime Minister paused. "And I would like you to draw up a list of names, three, four if you prefer, for us to consider as replacements for the Director General . . . Casualties? What do you mean, are there casualties? My dear man, we are dealing with a diplomatic catastrophe, not a train derailment."

The Prime Minister went to lunch—soup and whole-meal bread and a glass of fresh orange juice. A working lunch with close advisers, and the agenda involved future government initiatives to encourage industrial investment in Scotland.

He ate his food cold. Holt did not dare light the hexamine tablets to heat the water. The packet told him that the dehydrated flakes were intended as a beef goulash. He poured cold water into the packet and stirred it to a dark porridge with his finger. He ate as much as he could, as much as he could without vomiting. He drank a pint of water. He checked his watch, he measured the passing of the afternoon. He tried not to think of Noah Crane.

When he had eaten and when he had drunk, when he had stifled the hunger pain, and the pain of isolation, Holt took the condom from the barrel of the Model PM. Meticulously, stage by stage, he started to clean the rifle with the graphite grease.

From his vantage point, as he wiped the working parts of the rifle, he gazed down onto the tent camp. He reckoned the siesta would soon be finished, he reckoned they would emerge soon.

As Crane would have done it . . .

Holt couldn't help himself, couldn't wipe away the thoughts of Crane, tried and failed. In a dungeon, in a basement, in a cell. The interrogators howling at him, the blows raining on him.

He wondered if he would have the time, the time to wait until he was ready, until the sun started to slide in the late afternoon.

He said, "My name is Noah Crane. My IDF serial is 478391."

The kick heaved him across the tiled floor.

"My name is Noah Crane . . ."

The army boot again, into the kidney area at the small of his back.

"My IDF serial is 478391."

The army boot stamped onto the knuckle of his hand.

His eyes were closed. They had gone with their gloved fists for his eyes first. His eyes were puffed shut. His leg, where the 12.7mm round had taken away the flesh tissue and the bone at the knee, no longer hurt him. Too much hurt from the fresher wounds. He was not handcuffed and his legs were not tied, yet he was too weak, too exhausted, to protect himself. He lay on his side, he tried to curl himself forward into his sleeping position, but that was no protection because they could then kick the back of his head, the back of his neck, the small of his back, the base of his spine. He knew that there were four of them in the room. He knew they were high in the building because strong light filtered through the dropped venetian blinds. He knew that in the room were two men who wore the uniforms and arm markings of sergeants in the air force. He knew that also in the room was the lieutenant who had brought him from the Bekaa. He knew that these three men were not the ones that mattered. The one who did matter wore the uniform of a major. The man sat on a hard wooden chair against the wall and ground his spent cigarettes on the tiles. The face of the man had been rebuilt. Before his eyes had closed he had seen the smooth baby skin of the major who asked the questions in quiet and cultured English.

"Mr. Crane, you are being your own enemy."

"My name is Noah Crane."

"You need attention for your leg, the doctors and the nurses and the surgeons are waiting . . ."

"My IDF serial is 478391."

"You have to tell me what was the tasking of your mission into the Bekaa . . ."

"My name is Noah Crane."

"You have to tell me what was the object of your mission."

"My IDF serial is 478391."

"Mr. Crane, by your own hand, with your own knife, you murdered a poor cook boy. You are not a prisoner of war, Mr. Crane. To us you are a common criminal. Do you know, Mr. Crane, what is the fate of common criminals convicted of the murder of innocents . . . ?"

"My name is Noah Crane."

"We have in our criminal code, Mr. Crane, an instrument of execution. In our native tongue we call that instrument the *khazuk*, sadly I do not have present with me such an instrument to show you. It is, Mr. Crane, a sharp pointed staff that is driven down into the body of the condemned. To our judges the *khazuk* is a deterrent. It is the decision of the executioner into which part of the body he drives the *khazuk*. The result is the same, it is simply the timing of death that is at variance . . ."

"My IDF serial is 478391."

He heard the rustle of the cigarette packet. He heard the click of the lighter. He stiffened his muscles. He could not protect himself. It was the signal. When the major lit a cigarette and leaned back and inhaled, then the boots flew. The lieutenant kicked hardest. Crane gasped. The lieutenant kicked as if his promotion depended on it. He wanted to cry. Heavy toe caps belting at his shoulders and his back and his spine.

"Mr. Crane, I think you are a racist. I think you believe that because you are a Jew and I am an Arab you are superior to me. I think you believe that I am foolish . . ."

"My name is Noah Crane."

"Would you like me to demonstrate to you, Mr. Crane, that I am not foolish?"

"My IDF serial is 478391."

The boots in again, the kicking and the stamping, and the hands going for his short-cut hair and dragging up his head so that his face could be kicked. He thought he was falling, falling in a pit, dark sides, black bottom. He thought of Holt, white light on a hillside, white light of a bullet path over a hillside. Falling, tumbling, helpless. And he thought of the face of Holt, the face of the youngster. A thousand yards, and getting into five inches . . . God, the pain . . . God, the pain in the bone at the end of his spine. And the pain was blackness, darkness, the pain riddled through him, and he was falling, backward, down.

He felt a calmness. He felt a peace through the battery of the boots. A hillside. Rose flowers and oleander bushes and watered cyclamen. He heard the singing of the rabbi's prayers. He heard the rattle crash of the volley. He heard the beauty of the bugle playing. He walked on the slope of Mount Herzl. He was a stranger among the men from Kiryat Shmona who had come south to the cemetery, and the rabbi in army fatigues, and the chief of staff in starched uniform. It was the bottom of the pit, it was the end of the darkness, the blackness. It was sunlight on the slopes of Mount Herzl.

"Mr. Crane, because I have to demonstrate to you that I am not foolish, answer me . . . When you were infiltrated through the NORBAT sector there was an Englishman staying at the guesthouse of the Kibbutz Kfar Giladi. Why was the infiltration the concern of the Englishman?"

He forced open his eyes. His vision was narrowed by the swelling at his cheeks, his eyebrows.

He hesitated. "My name is Noah Crane."

"When you were infiltrated you traveled with an Englishman. Mr. Crane, who is the Englishman? Why is an Englishman involved in the infiltration?"

He stared at the constructed face, at the pink underskin. There was no challenge in his voice. "My IDF serial is 478391."

He pushed himself up, the pain flooded inside him. He knelt in front of the major. He gazed into the face. He was losing, he had reacted. He thought of Holt, the clean young face of Holt. He thought he loved the boy. He thought he should have been the father of the boy. And he asked the boy for a thousand yards, and he asked the boy to shoot into five inches diameter. He felt the wash of despair.

"Mr. Crane, in me rests a decision; the decision that is mine is whether you go from here to a military prison to await some exchange, or whether you go from here to the El Masr prison to await the convenience of the executioner and the *khazuk* . . . Mr. Crane, why is an Englishman concerned in an infiltration? Why were you on surveillance on the hillside above the camp of the Popular Front recruits?"

He whispered hoarsely, "My name is Noah Crane."

As if they were the only men in the room. As though the tormentors had evaporated. The major with his surgeon's face, the marksman with his slashed, puffed, bleeding face.

"Why are the English concerned with this camp? Help me,

Mr. Crane, because I am trying to understand. What is particular, what is important about this camp?"

The major shook his head. His laugh tinkled. He used his hands—how could he have been so blind? The major beamed his pleasure at Crane. A low voice, as if he confided in the wretch who knelt in front of him.

"Abu Hamid?"

"My IDF serial is 478391."

He saw the pleasure in the peculiar wide-apart eyes of Major Said Hazan. He saw the satisfaction curl the mouth that was lipless.

"You know the name of Abu Hamid, Mr. Crane?"

"My name is Noah Crane."

"Abu Hamid is the commander of the camp where the Popular Front recruits are undergoing training . . . Abu Hamid is the slayer of a British official . . . Abu Hamid is like a toy to me . . ."

Again the major laughed.

"You thought me a fool. You mistook me, Mr. Crane."

"My IDF serial is 478391."

"You are boring me, Mr. Crane. I have what I require. I have the target for your infiltration. You may take it, Mr. Crane, that from this moment the target is taken out of the reach of your English plan."

He seemed to see Holt. He seemed to see the jutting barrel of a Model PM.

Noah Crane lurched to his feet. The weight gave at his wounded knee. He fell forward. He cannoned down onto the sitting major. He saw the throat, he saw the grafted skin above the knotted tie, below the stubbed smooth chin. His hands found the throat. His hands locked on the throat.

He seemed to see the corridor aperture of the telescopic sight, and the wavering of the crosshairs on the chest of a sallow-skinned, dark-haired man who was marked by a crow's foot scar on his left upper cheek.

He clung to the throat. He felt the blows of the lieutenant. He felt the scrabbling fingers of the sergeants. He heard the shortening gasps of breath.

He seemed to know the gentle two-stage squeeze on the trigger of the Model PM. There was the sunlight shafting between the water-green trees on Mount Herzl. There was the ripple of the singing, there was the floating of the flowers, there was the love of his people, and there was Holt's love.

He squeezed. They could not pull him back. He could hear their shouts, he could feel their hammered blows. He clung to the throat. The man no longer fought him. He saw the pinkness of the face dissolve, washed to pale gray-blue. He saw the pistol in the hand of the lieutenant.

Noah Crane seemed to hear the youngster, Holt, fire.

The Foreign Secretary slammed down his hand onto the mahogany polished table top.

It was a theatrical gesture, but he was not ashamed of it. One of his aides took a shorthand note, for posterity. His two senior advisers on the Middle East Desk at FCO shuffled their hands. He knew they were having an affair . . . An affair, albeit adulterous, between an Assistant Secretary and a Deputy Assistant Secretary, between two 70-hour-a-week aides, was a regrettable but supportable nuisance.

Lebanon, the Bekaa, was totally insupportable. It was the end of the world.

"I do not understand how this could have happened."

The Prime Minister drew doodle faces on a pad and kept silent.

The Foreign Secretary warmed, "Only at this moment of failure am I for the first time informed of a clandestine adventure into Lebanon. At no stage was I consulted, but for the record I'll tell you what my advice would have been: Forget it, that's what you'd have been told. My opinion was not asked for, and where do we find ourselves? We sent in two operatives. One is now captured and presumably pouring his heart out in Damascus. The other, untrained, will be blundering around in the Bekaa, a headless chicken with capture inevitable. Prime Minister, have you any remote idea of the damage that will be done to British interests in the

Middle East and in the Gulf when Crane and Holt are paraded in open court in Damascus? Years of hard economic endeavor, years of patient diplomacy, will have been undone by this folly. It goes without saying that I shall be forced to consider my position as a member of Her Majesty's Government."

"It stood a good chance of success," the Prime Minister said bleakly.

"Ah, success . . . success is different, success is all important, but we do not have success. We have instead a mission so ill prepared that even the basement of the White House would have blinked at it."

"If the brute had been killed . . ."

"If, Prime Minister, *if* . . . but one is captured and the other is certain of capture. It is a disaster, and a perfectly avoidable disaster, had you chosen to confide in your colleagues."

"We had to show our strength, the strength of the Free World against terrorism."

"Your concept of strength is different to mine. I cannot see that I can be of further help to you."

The Foreign Secretary pushed back his chair. He swept his papers, and his map of Lebanon, into the mouth of his attaché case. He stood.

"Then get out," the Prime Minister said. "If all you can offer is the threat of your resignation, just go."

The aide who took the record wrote furiously then slapped shut his notepad, buried it in an inner pocket. The Foreign Secretary led out his team.

For a long time the Prime Minister sat bent at the table, digesting the loneliness of the room.

And no comforting face. Only the prayer that the young man, Holt, was running, running hard, from that godforsaken place that was the Bekaa.

As Crane would have done it . . .

Everything that Holt could remember.

The light was going down. Below him the shadows of the

tents lengthened. He saw the first figures emerging from the tents, as if in the coming coolness their rest time was complete.

He shared the rock overhang with a small lizard. The reptile showed no fear of him. He thought there was a cheerfulness about the lizard, as he would have said there was a cheerfulness about the chaffinches and the robins that came to the lichen-covered bird table on the lawn of his parents' home.

He had cleaned the rifle. He had pulled the four-by-two-inch cloth through the barrel, pulling from the bolt end, according to Crane's bible, because to pull from the muzzle end was to risk damaging to a fractional extent the precision of the rifling. He had pulled back the bipod legs and adjusted them so that each was calibrated to the same length. He edged the antiflash extension to the barrel out through the scrim netting. He took from Crane's Bergen a plastic water bottle and pushed the bottle out under the netting, and then tipped its mouth so that the water ran onto the rock and dirt that was below the muzzle. He saw the dribble of the water, and the coloring of the ground. According to Crane's bible, wet ground under a muzzle reduced the chance of a dust puff at the moment of firing when the bullet and the gases burst from the barrel. A dust puff, youngster, can give away the firing position.

As Crane would have done it . . .

He had a degree in Modern History, and his special subject was 1653–58, when Oliver Cromwell was Lord Protector of the Commonwealth. He was an entry into the Foreign and Commonwealth Office through the diplomatic service "fast stream." He was a Third Secretary with particular interest in the political development and sociological movements inside the Union of Soviet Socialist Republics. He was on his belly and watched by a lizard and under a rock overhang on the other side of the hill. He was considering whether he could put a 7mm Remington Mag bullet into a 5-inch-diameter target at 1,000 yards.

Holt saw the tent flap move. He reached for his binoculars.

Holt saw Abu Hamid step clear of the dark opening of the tent. He watched Abu Hamid yawn and stretch and spit.

He looked for the length of the shadows. He tugged his watch up from under his shirt. Holt thought that the sun was still too high, that he must wait for a minimum of another half an hour.

Zvi Dan said, "From what we've picked up on the monitoring they've lifted Crane to Damascus."

Martins asked, "Will you get him back? In an exchange?"

"Alive? If he is alive? Not for months, years, and then only if we have a jewel to trade. We don't have such a jewel. Dead? If they have killed him? They extract a high price. The last time we sent them back a swarm of prisoners, we had in return three coffins, in one was the wrong body, the other two were filled with stones. Does that answer your question?"

From the bed Martins looked up at Major Zvi Dan. "Nothing on Holt?"

"They haven't caught him, we would have heard. They know Crane was not alone, they have set blocks further south, nearer to the border."

"Thank you, I appreciate your telling me."

"It is too late to be angry," Major Zvi Dan said.

Abu Hamid had not slept. He had lain on the camp bed and had watched the radio. The radio would tell him what fate awaited him.

He thought that the radio would have told if they had found the body of Margarethe Schultz. He could see her in his mind, and he could see on her breast the crimson flash of the flower that he had laid there. He felt no guilt. He thought that what he had done was justified. He thought that what they would do to him would also be justified. Of course, he would not be arrested. Of course, he would not go to the El Masr prison. Of course, he would not be driven to a small square at dawn and be dropped from a gallows beam. What they would do to him, what would be justified, was that they would send him ashore on the beaches of Israel.

In his spider handwriting on a food carton he had written the names of the ten. He walked through the camp. He sought out each of the ten. They were those who would stand at his side. They were those who would protect him.

He would never be taken.

He heard the first bickering argument flare behind him. One had not been chosen, one had been chosen. The imbeciles did not even know for what they were or were not chosen. But already the argument. When he had spoken to the ten men, he drifted toward the cooking area, and gave encouragement to the pressed volunteer who would prepare their food, and he kicked more wood onto the fire and spluttered in the surge of smoke.

It was a bargain.

Jane was no part of the bargain. Nor was his country, the United Kingdom of Great Britain and Northern Ireland. The bargain was with Crane, for his being taken and for the freeing of the hostage prisoner. That he would fire a sniper rifle for the first time in his life, try to get into five inches' diameter at 1,000 yards, no longer had anything to do with vengeance or patriotism. He would fire for Noah Crane, miserable old goat. He would use the rifle for Crane who had a disease in the retina of his shooting eye. He would not walk away from Noah Crane.

He saw the smoke surge up from the fire. He watched the smoke climb and then curve where the wind took it. With the compass from his belt he could estimate that he would be firing on a line east southeast. He followed the smoke trail, he matched the trail to his compass. This was the crucial calculation. If he made the wrong calculation then he would betray the memory of Noah Crane. He reckoned that the trail of the smoke was moving east northeast. Burrowing down into his recollection of figures that he had once been told, he dragged out the figures showing a bullet's deviation with wind blowing at 10 miles an hour at a deflection of 45 degrees. At 1,000 yards the wind deflection would push the bullet a matter of 5 feet and 2½ inches off course. But at 900 yards the wind deflection would be 4 feet and a quarter of an inch. And at 1,100 yards the wind deflection would be 6 feet and 7 inches.

Crane had said that the lying-up position was 1,000 yards from the center of the camp. If Crane had it wrong, was 100 yards too long, then Holt would shoot 14¼ inches wide. If Crane had it wrong, was 100 yards too short, then Holt would shoot 16 inches wide. It was the difference between a killing shot and a wounding shot, and a shot that missed altogether.

The target had to be still, and not about to move. To cover 1,000 yards the bullet would need two seconds of time. If the target took one step in that two seconds . . . God . . . miss.

The distance of 1,000 yards had to be exact, because that was what the sights would be set to. If in reality the distance was 900 yards then the bullet would reach its target 18 inches too high. If in reality it was 1,100 yards then the bullet would drop to a target point 20 inches too low.

All of these minute calculations had to be correct. If any were wrong, he would be breaking his bargain.

Holt grinned at the lizard. The lizard was his only friend.

He checked that his safety was on. He eased back the greased bolt. He gazed for a moment at the bullet that lay in the palm of his hand. He thrust the bullet into the breach of the Model PM, then drove the bolt handle forward.

He had seen two of the recruits fighting, teeth and boots and fists. He could remember the queues that he used to see outside the GUM store in Simferopol. Men and women queued outside the GUM in Simferopol without knowing what they were queuing for. Two of his recruits were fighting, and more were arguing, and they could not know for what the ten had been chosen.

They sidled around him, those ten that he had selected. Inside the ten were four to whom he had assigned responsibility as squad leaders at the camp. Two of the other six were considered to be proficient soldiers on an all-round evaluation. There was one who had scored five consecutive hits in training with the RPG-7. There was one who played with wires and the forces of electricity and who understood the workings of a radio. There was one whose twin brother had been killed by the Israelis in 1982, he would fight hard. There was one who would make Abu Hamid laugh, and who could write in Hebrew and in English, and speak the Jewish tongue.

Perhaps they thought they were going to be sent to Simferopol . . . He waved for them to sit.

It was the center of the camp. It was between the cooking area and the first line of the bell tents. He had prepared what he was going to say. In Simferopol the Russian instructors had always said that a commander should prepare his statement of orders and tactics.

The low sun was warm on his shoulders, on the back of his neck, the sun that was soon to dip into dusk behind the great escarpment of the Jabal al Barouk.

He was a changeling.

No longer the graduate and the diplomat, Holt was the technician.

He had no love in his heart, he had no hate in his mind.

The fine crosshairs of the Schmidt and Bender PM 12 × 42 telescopic sight did not flicker over the back of a sitting, living, breathing human being. The crosshairs lay upon a target.

He had no thought of his girl, no thought of his dead ambassador. His thoughts were on the time of a bullet in flight, and the angle of wind deflection, and the distance between the lying-up position and the center of the tent camp as measured by Crane from his aerial photographs.

With his thumb, Holt drew back the safety.

None who had known him before would have recognized the changeling at that moment. Not his parents, not the men and women at FCO, not the staffers who had been his colleagues in Moscow . . . not Jane, certainly not Jane Canning.

He held the stock forward, just behind the bipod, with his left hand. The butt was pulled hard into his shoulder. His right eye was locked against the circle of the sight. His index finger searched for the trigger guard, and inside the guard to the trigger.

He took a long singing breath, forced the air into his lungs.

As Noah Crane would have done it . . .

"It will be a mission that will bring anguish to our enemy. It will bring pride to our people. Each one of you, of us, has known the cruelty of our enemy. We are honored to have the chance to strike a blow at that enemy . . ."

He saw the glow in their eyes, he saw the fervor in their faces. He felt the swelling pleasure that he was their leader.

Half the breath heaved out.

Trigger squeeze to first stage.

Wish me luck, as you wave me goodbye,
Cheerio, here I go, on my way,
Wish me luck as you wave me goodbye . . .

He hummed. The breath was pressing for release in his throat. The crosshairs were steady.

He squeezed.

Holt fired.

The path of a bullet in the Bekaa.

"Our target is Tel Aviv . . ."

He seemed to rise up. He seemed to be lifted from his haunches and then punched forward. There was a force that drove him.

Abu Hamid fell, bursting blood, against the body of the recruit who had scored five consecutive hits with the RPG-7 and against the recruit who understood the workings of a radio.

Abu Hamid fell and he did not move.

20

The economic subcommittee of the Cabinet had ended. It was a full fifteen minutes since the secretary had slipped silently into the room and laid the message form beside the Prime Minister's papers.

The chairman of the subcommittee, the Chancellor, was neatly packing away his papers at the far end of the table.

"You'll forgive the presumption, Prime Minister, but you are displaying a certain cheerfulness that I can hardly put down to our business of the last two hours."

"That obvious, Harry?"

"Very obvious, Prime Minister."

The Prime Minister leaned back, there was a comfortable smile. The meeting hushed.

The Prime Minister said, "One of the hardest features of my office is to exercise real power, to exercise real influence. I try often enough, and I rarely succeed."

"But this time you have succeeded?" The Chancellor was adept at the unsubtle prompt. "Can you say?"

The Prime Minister glanced down at the cryptic handwritten message. "Not yours, not mine, but Abu Hamid's, on the salver."

"You'll keep this to yourselves of course. . . . When Ben Armitage was shot dead in Yalta, and an aide also died, we let a lie be known, that the murderer was a local criminal. We knew in fact that the killer was a member of the Palestinian Popular Front. I put in hand an intelligence operation that located the killer in the Bekaa Valley of east Lebanon. I took the decision, not lightly, to send a covert team into the Bekaa Valley so that a precisely calculated vengeance should be wrought upon this murderer. It would be the clearest indication to his Syrian masters that we will never be attacked with impunity. . . . Last night, gentlemen, at dusk, that vengeance was exacted."

"That's first class, Prime Minister."

"I'll not deny that I agonized over the decision, over the consequences of failure, for which of course I would have taken the blame, but if you venture nothing then you win nothing. This government, our government, has shown that we are in the forefront of the war against international terrorism."

"You are to be most warmly congratulated, Prime Minister."

"Thank you, I accept your congratulations with pleasure, and later, when I telephone him I anticipate receiving the congratulations of the President of the United States. We are not a nation of boasters, gentlemen, I like to think we are a nation of quiet achievers . . . It's been a good meeting. Thank you, Harry."

Major Said Hazan was buried with full military honors in that section of the military cemetery reserved for air force officers who had died in the service of the Syrian Arab Republic. There was a large turnout of dignitaries and senior-ranking officers. The cause of death, as announced in the Damascus morning newspapers, was given as heart failure brought on by the ravages of an old war wound, bravely borne. Amongst those who carried the coffin to the deep-cut grave was Fawzi. He wore a new uniform for the occasion, and the uniform carried the insignia of a captain, and the brigadier who headed Air Force Intelligence, and who was the pallbearer immediately ahead of Fawzi, had told the young man that in the circumstances he was right to have shot the

Jew. And no doubt the brave major had been so severely injured in his throat that the Jew's very first assault was fatal.

After the service, after the mourners had dispersed, after the band and the honor guard had been bussed away, the brigadier walked with Captain Fawzi to a distant part of the cemetery where the cypress trees shaded the closely mown lawns. The brigadier offered Fawzi a job in his department, and offered him also the task of finding a replacement leader for a seaborne mission against the Defense Ministry on Kaplan. When they had finished, they walked back toward the cars, and the brigadier linked his arm to Fawzi's elbow.

"Tell me, who shot Hazan's boy?"

"In shame I do not know."

The name of Holt was not known. The secret of Holt had died with the locking of Crane's fingers on the windpipe of Major Said Hazan, with the blasting away of Crane's life by the Makharov pistol fired at point blank range.

"Come in, Percy. . . . For God's sake, man, you look dead beat."

"Didn't get to bed last night, sir, and had to be at the airport at five."

"It's been a first-class show." The Director General beamed, and waved Martins to a chair, and he shouted through to his outer office for coffee, and he lifted a half bottle of cognac from his desk leg drawer.

"Thank you, sir."

"I tell you this, when I heard that the sniper chap had been caught, I thought it was all over for us."

Martins eased back in the chair. The personal assistant handed him coffee, in cup and saucer, and the Director General topped up the coffee with cognac. He seemed not to feel his age, nor his tiredness.

"Well, a fair amount of work had gone into preparing young Holt. I thought from the start, from the time I had him down in the country, that this couldn't be a man and boy operation, that they had to go in as equals. I put Holt through a pretty tough induction, toned him up so that he would be just about as able to operate on his own as in tandem, and it paid off."

"And you had damn all help at the far end—more cognac?"

Martins reached forward with his cup. He was a good deal surprised: there was no shake in his hand. He drank. He felt the glow beneath his stubble-covered cheeks. It had been a conscious decision not to shave. He was straight in from the front line.

"Couldn't put it better, sir, damn all help. I had to insist, lay down the law, that we should have a hot extraction program after the snipe. Didn't win me any friends, but I had my way. I arranged for them to carry in a Sarbie beacon, and I cudgeled the locals into putting a receiver into the transport of an agent they had operating in the Bekaa. That was the first thing I made them do, when they got windy about the chopper backup in the first place. So, Holt fired, knew enough to have avoided detection, then he laid up until darkness, then he moved off. I had predicted that such a long-range shooting would create total confusion in Hamid's camp, not much of an idea where the shot had come from. Holt moved off after dark and when he was well clear he activated the bleep. The car driven by this Mossad fellow, their agent, picked him up. I'm the last one not to give credit where credit is due, the agent did his part well, used his lights and his horn to attract Holt, took him on board and drove like hell for the border . . ."

The cognac was coursing. He felt the dampness in the socks he should have changed on the aircraft. The Director General sat on his desk, hunched forward, an eager audience.

". . . So far so good, but of course the Syrians had picked up the bleep and were reacting, and they had roadblocks between Holt and the safety of the UNIFIL sector and the security zone. I really lost my rag, sir. I was in their communications area, and I just demanded that a helicopter be sent. Made the air quite blue, sir. They were jabbering about missile umbrellas, all that sort of rubbish, but I won the day. Well, in the end they sent up a helicopter, they located the car about three miles short of the roadblocks, quite a short run thing, they lifted out Holt and the agent. I've no complaints about the way they managed that. That's the short of it, sir."

"Remarkable, Percy."

"Thank you, sir."

From the leather box on the table, the Director General passed Martins a cigar, and lit one himself. The smoke fogged the room.

"You'll take the weekend off. Go and get yourself an ugly big pike. You'll be back here on Monday morning. Your ears only, for the time being. For your information, Mr. Anstruther informs me he is seeking fame and fortune in the commodities market in the City. Mr. Fenner is returning to Cambridge, an academic future. As from Monday morning, Percy, you will head the Middle East Desk."

"That's very good of you, sir."

The Director General swung his legs down to the carpet.

"And Holt, Percy?"

"Peculiar young man, sir. Not the easiest to handle. Of course, he's been under strain, haven't we all? He was pretty insistent that I drop him at Paddington Station on my way in from the airport. I've got the number where he'll be for the next few days. He's gone home . . . I've got something for you, sir, something of a souvenir."

Martins led the Director General through to the outer office. Behind the coat stand, in the corner next to the door, was the Model PM Long Range. "He wanted the sling. That would be enough to remind him of Crane, he said. That was the sniper, sir." Martins laid the gun, immaculately clean, on the table in the corner of the Director General's office.

"Good of you, Percy. The Department will be proud of the trophy."

After Percy Martins had gone, probably in search of bait from a fishmonger, the Director General stood at the window of his high office and he traversed the skyline, and his eye was hard against the sight circle, and he aimed at the flags that flew from the corporation tower blocks across the river, and he followed the flight of a gull. He thought the boy was, as the Prime Minister had said, lucky to have had the opportunity. He thought he would have given an eye tooth to have had the opportunity to fire that rifle in the service of his country. He would take it to Downing Street in the early evening, just the thing to cap a damn good show. He asked his personal assistant to warn the Cabinet Secretary to alert security that he would be coming over at six o'clock and would have a rifle with him.

Together, Major Zvi Dan and Rebecca cleared the barracks room at Kiryat Shmona that had been the home of Noah Crane.

They needed only one black plastic dustbin bag. Into the bag went the second pair of boots, the two sets of old uniforms, the underwear and the socks and the pajamas, the few items of civilian clothing. There was a letter from a clinic in Houston, there were a few old newspapers. All went into the bag until it bulged. The intercepts from Hermon had told Major Zvi Dan that Crane would never again use the contents of the bag.

He knotted the top of the bag.

Rebecca said, "Did we win anything?"

Major Zvi Dan muttered, "We lost a man who was without price."

"Not anything?"

"We lost an agent. Menny can never go back. Perhaps he, also, was beyond price."

"The British won."

"They won only vanity. Only conceit."

"Didn't Holt, at least, win?"

"If you had asked him I doubt he would have told you that he had won anything that was of value to him."

Rebecca carried the bag and Major Zvi Dan hobbled behind her. She took the bag to the corner of the camp where the rubbish of the troops was burned. With his finger Major Zvi Dan made a hole in the bag, exposed the paper, and with his lighter set fire to the bag.

A team of army engineers was set to work to dismantle the bell tents. They worked, stripped to the waist, in the midday heat. The recruits were not there to help them, they had in the morning been taken by bus to the Yarmuk camp outside Damascus.

High on the hillside above the work party was a small and unnoticed rock overhang. Under the overhang, hidden in shadow, undiscovered, lay two Bergens, and on top of one pack was a carefully folded square of scrim netting, and on top of the other pack was a single, used cartridge case.

Beyond the camp perimeter wire was a cairn of sun-bleached stones. The cairn marked the grave of a young man who had given himself the name of Abu Hamid, who had been a fighter for a refugee people, who had been a foreign cadet at the military academy at Simferopol, who had once been frightened of death, who had a crow's foot scar on his cheek.

The depth of the grave, the weight of the stones, were reckoned to be proof against the hyenas who would come to scavenge the camp site once the army engineers had lifted the tents onto their lorries and driven away.

21

In the darkness he walked on the moor.

Away below him, distant and separated from him by the black void, were the lights of cars moving on the roads between Dulverton and Exford, and Hawkridge and Withypool, and Liscombe and Winsford.

The moor was his, as the Bekaa had been his and Crane's. He walked silently in this wilderness, each footfall tested, and for company he had the deer herds, and the hunting foxes, and the rooting badgers, and the sheep that had been freed from the pens in the valley and allowed to wander in search of the new summer grass of the higher ground.

He walked until the dawn light seeped onto the royal-purple expanse of the moor, and when it was time for him to settle into his lying-up position then he came down from the moor and took the road to the stone house that was the home of his mother and father.

In the early morning he packed a bag, and he told his mother that he was going back to work, and he asked his father to drive him to the railway station at Tiverton Junction.

His father gazed into the secret and unexplaining eyes of his son.

"Are you all right, Holt?"

"I'm all right, it's the others who have been hurt."

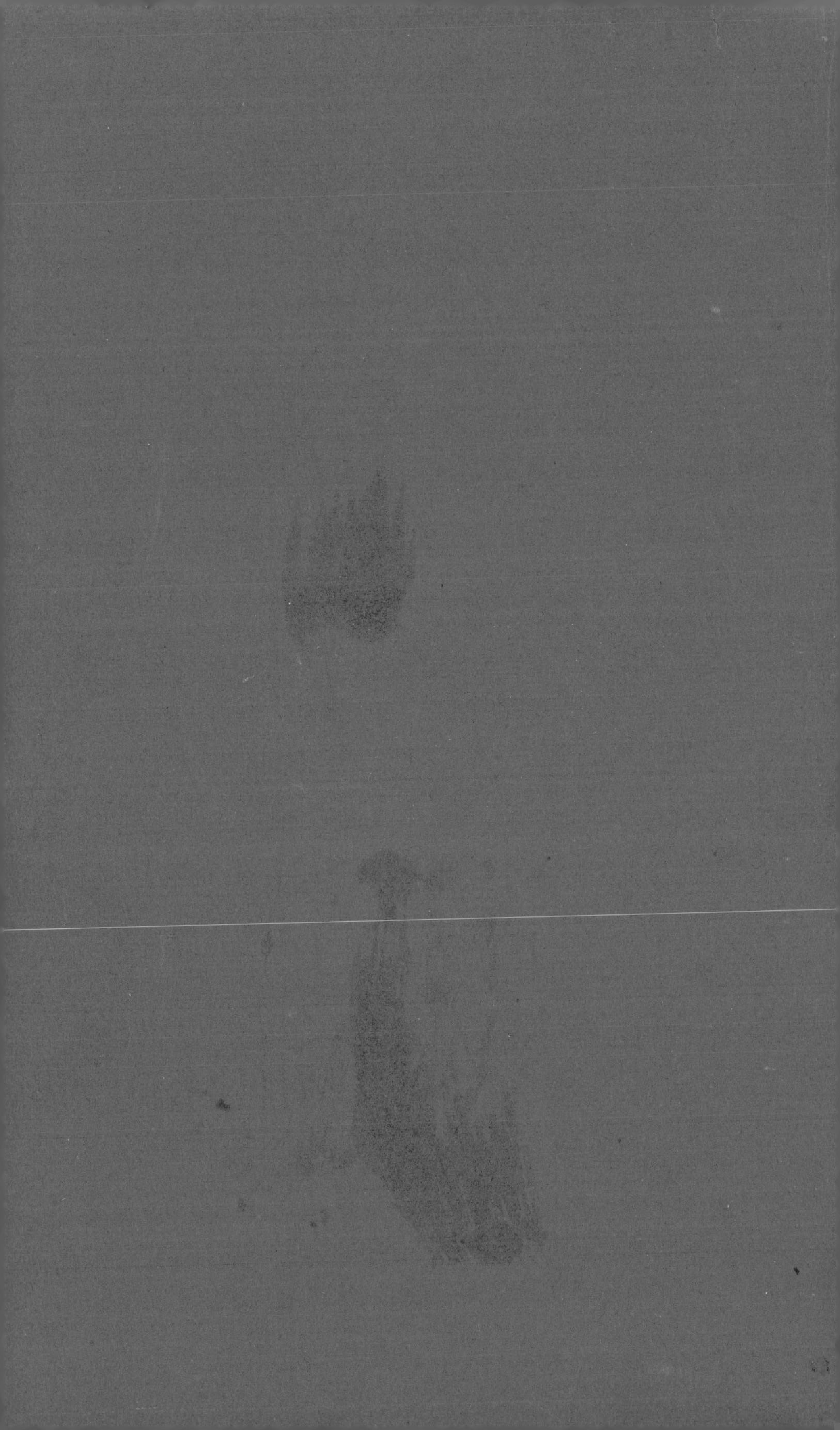